Same As It
Never Was

Claire Scovell LaZebnik

Same As It
Never Was

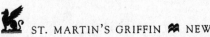 ST. MARTIN'S GRIFFIN 🐾 NEW YORK

www.stmartins.com

Design by Sarah Maya Gubkin

Library of Congress Cataloging-in-Publication Data

LaZebnik, Claire Scovell.
    Same as it never was / Claire Scovell LaZebnik.
        p. cm.
    ISBN 0-312-31249-0 (hc)
    ISBN 0-312-31250-4 (pbk)
    EAN 978-0312-31250-3
    I. Title.

PS3612.A98S26 2003
813'.6—dc21   2003041358

First St. Martin's Griffin Edition: July 2004

10 9 8 7 6 5 4 3 2 1

For Max, who writes rock songs.
For Johnny, who thinks every spider is a beauty.
For Annie, who climbs way up high.
For Will, who laughs when he sneezes.
And for Rob, who takes care of us all.

Acknowledgments

Thanks go to my editor, Diane Reverand, who is kind and brilliant in equal measure, and to her wonderful assistant, Melissa Contreras. Also to the amazing Kim Witherspoon and Alexis Hurley, who magically turned me from a depressed maniac (ask my husband) into a very happy soon-to-be-published author. Thanks, too, to Matthew Snyder, who helped me out enormously.

Rob LaZebnik was the first person I showed the rough draft to, and his notes improved it beyond recognition. And not once did he write "Could be funnier" in the margin. I owe a big debt to Alice Scovell, who years ago told me the true story that inspired this novel, and who was an early and very supportive reader of it. Thanks, too, to Colin Summers, whose enthusiasm never wavered, even when mine did. A huge thank-you to Mel and Cynthia Scovell, Julie Kaufman, and Ted Scovell, for their love, support, and patience. Thanks also to Anjalé Armand and Stephanie Burt, who kept my kids so happy that I was able to escape to the computer whenever they were here. This novel would not have gotten finished without them.

I owe any writing career I have to Nell Scovell, who never stops promoting me, and who cheers me on every step of the way.

Same As It
Never Was

one

"Do you think *she'll* be there?" was my mother's first question when she got in the car. I hadn't bothered getting out, just honked and waited. I endured her kiss on my cheek, then shifted into first and roared out into the street. She didn't even have her seat belt on yet.

"Yes, Barbara, I think she'll be there because she lives there, it's her home, and he's her husband. Any other questions?"

She pulled down the shade to look at herself in the mirror. "He's her husband for the *moment*. It won't last. It never does with him."

"Two sweet young things like Richard and Alicia? Of course it will last."

"I don't know why I'm going. I really don't. How do I look?"

"Beautiful. He'll fall in love with you all over again and leave her for you. And then I'll move back in with my mommy and daddy and we'll all live happily ever after."

"I wouldn't take him back even if he begged me."

"Don't worry," I said. "He ain't begging you."

"I don't know why I'm going," she said again.

Neither did I. Know why she was going or why I was, except that we had this insane family thing of getting together every Thanksgiving even though we weren't anything like a family, my mother, my father, and I.

So here I was, on break from my third year of college, taking my mother to have Thanksgiving dinner with my father who couldn't stand her but saw enough of himself in me—of course, he did, we were like *twins* the two of us, dark-haired, dark-eyed, thin, short, and restless, the opposite, in every way, of the woman who gave birth to me—to put up with her once a year. And a lovely time we always had of it, too. As you can imagine.

Once, when I was fourteen, my father took me out for my birthday. He brought along his current girlfriend, who either had a cocaine habit or a bladder the size of a corn kernel, because she kept going off to the ladies' room. It was her only personality trait as far as I could tell—her eyes were as vacant as her attempts to join in the conversation.

At any rate, it was one of the only times in my life I found myself alone at a table with my father. Encouraged by the half glass of wine he had let me drink, I got up the courage to say to him, "Why did you marry my mother? Why you? Why her? It doesn't make sense."

"You didn't see her when she was twenty-three," he said.

"I've seen photos."

"You didn't see *her*."

"So it was just about looks."

"It sure as hell wasn't for her brains," he said.

"But didn't you realize—I mean, you had a *kid* with her. Why?"

"It wasn't like I planned it," he said. "Your mother could have found a way to screw up contraceptive implants."

So there you go. My family. And I was going to spend Thanksgiving with these people.

We sat around Richard and Alicia's enormous dining room table in their enormous dining room in their enormous Little Holmby house, a jolly crew of seven at a table that could easily seat twice that many.

I was sitting next to some cousin of Alicia's named Marcus, who was around my age and who looked like her—they were both olive-skinned, black-haired, tall, and handsome. He seemed mostly interested in his food, although his head did swivel in my direction when I peeled off my sweater—there was a fire in the dining room fireplace, even though it was in the eighties that day. The sweater must have held a promise the T-shirt underneath just couldn't deliver, because he immediately lost interest and went back to his plate of food.

On my other side was some business associate of my father's named Dennis Klein, who made the mistake of trying to be polite by complimenting Alicia on her cooking.

She smiled in that regal way of hers, the queen gracefully accepting the peasant's tribute, but Richard ruined the effect by snorting and saying, "She didn't cook the meal, the help did. Alicia's hands have never touched a frying pan in her life."

"Alicia has beautiful hands," said my mother.

"You're too kind," Alicia said.

"No, really, they're lovely," my mother said. Too loudly.

At which point I asked my father if I could have "one of those," indicating the martini he was pouring down his throat.

Dennis Klein said, "Are you old enough to drink?"

I said, "I'm eleven, but I'll be twelve next month, and Mommy lets me ride the bus all by myself."

My father said, "Keep it up, kid, and you won't live to see thirteen." But he got me the drink I wanted.

It tasted like medicine, but at least it was cold medicine with a kick. And I needed something to get me through that meal.

It wasn't that anyone was uncivil—actually, I would have enjoyed that. It was just so boring, really, with my mother fawning on Alicia, just to show that she really was okay with the fact that this gorgeous Latina princess was now married to the man whose child she had once borne. And there was Alicia, who hated my mother—probably hated me, too—narrowing her eyes and smiling with her lips at every compliment, taking out her own tension by snapping at the quiet women who were serving us. She spoke a Spanish that was way too fast for me to follow, but there was no mistaking her tone—Cleopatra raking her slaves over the coals. And my father, not particularly civil to anyone, maybe slightly less rude to his ex-wife than his current one, and that guy Marcus on one side of me, shoveling food into his mouth, that guy Dennis on the other, barely saying anything, and little Celia—Richard and Alicia's kid—running around the table in a pink dress with pink bows in her hair, the kind of girly little girl who paints her fingernails and thinks she's just adorable. No one paid her much attention except for a nanny who followed her around, whispering to her and working very hard to keep her away from Alicia, who glowered every time the child came too close.

Almost made me appreciate my own dear old mom, who was matching my father martini for martini and who was casting curious looks at Dennis Klein, I noticed. He was a little on the young side for her, but she was still pretty beautiful thanks to her great WASP bone structure. Something I had stupidly neglected to inherit. Strange that more men hadn't found their way into her life. Maybe they were turned off by the despair and incompetence that came with all the beauty.

The martini was working. My head felt kind of buzzy, and the conversation had faded into an ignorable white noise. I picked at my food, not being a fan of turkey and stuffing, and waited for it all to be over. After an eternity or so, the turkey made its way back into the kitchen, and Alicia said we would have dessert later, in the living room. Why she wanted to prolong the meal was beyond me. And what were we supposed to do in the meantime?

My mother solved that problem by cornering Alicia in the hallway. She immediately started going on about how beautiful the house looked, how magnificent the new pool was, how adorable Celia was, and—get this one—"how wonderful Richard looks these days. I've never seen him happier or healthier."

It was fun for a second or two to watch Alicia writhe under the relentless praise, but not fun enough to make me want to stick around longer. I went into the family room where Richard and Marcus were watching football on the giant flat-panel TV.

I didn't care one way or another about football, but I appreciated the fact that television made conversation unnecessary, so I leaned against the arm of the leather sectional and watched. Marcus was sitting nearby. He didn't say anything during the game, but when there was a commercial, he said to me, "Lot of partying going on at your school?"

"I wouldn't know," I said.

He was silent a minute, but then Richard got up to refill his martini glass over at the bar, and Marcus said quickly and quietly, "I can get you some Ecstasy, no problem. Just call me. Any time. I can get it to you in twenty minutes, guaranteed. I'll give you my phone number."

"Thanks," I said, "but my pimp gets real mad if I buy from anyone else." I got up and walked out. Then I walked back in and poured what was left over in the martini shaker into a glass and took it with me as I left again.

Richard, back on the sectional, said, "Go easy on those, kid."

"I will if you will," I said over my shoulder.

I swear he growled.

Now where to? Alicia's vast army of servants swarmed over the kitchen and dining room, Richard's two wives were still doing their little politeness dance down the hallway, and I felt a need to put some distance between myself and the charming drug dealer Alicia called her cousin.

I took a left, went down another hallway, and was accosted by a small child who said, "Come here. You need to be on my team." Celia, of course. She had changed her clothes. She was now wearing a different pink dress from the one she had been wearing earlier, and her cheeks had spots of pink on them that looked like badly applied makeup and were probably badly applied makeup. She took my hand and dragged me into her bedroom. Some of my martini slopped over the edges of the glass and spilled. I wanted it back.

Inside Celia's room, Dennis Klein was sitting cross-legged on the floor. His socks showed above his expensive shoes, and a thin band of skin showed above the socks. Not a good look.

"Hello," he said. "We're playing Connect Four."

"Have fun," I said. I backed away.

"No," said Celia, pulling on me again, "you have to play with us."

"Don't you have a nanny somewhere?"

"She went home already," Celia said. "It's Thanksgiving. She only worked a half day."

"It looks like you two are having a lot of fun in here," I said. "I don't want to interrupt."

"Celia was looking for someone else to come play," Dennis said. "She wants to be part of a team."

"I don't even know how to play this." I drained what was left of the martini and wished I had taken a different turn down that hallway. Then again, maybe there was just no escaping being miserable in the House of Torture, where every room obviously just offered a different hell. "I'm not very good at games. And I think we're eating dessert soon."

"She's just afraid she'll lose," Dennis Klein said to Celia.

At least this particular hell didn't involve any close family members. I sighed and put my martini glass down on Celia's night table, then joined them on the floor. "All right. One game. How do you do this?"

It turned out just to be a version of tic-tac-toe. Easy enough. Pretty soon, though, I discovered that being on a team with Celia meant she'd let me set us up for a potential win, which she would then blow by dropping a checker into the wrong slot. Not a rocket scientist, that kid. Dennis annoyed me by deliberately playing badly. I didn't get why adults always let kids win at games. Seems to me you should teach them early the way life works, that big, smart people can pummel you, and the only solution is to get big and smart yourself.

Anyway, with Celia and Dennis both incapable of making four in a row, the game went on much longer than it should have, and I was so bored I could have screamed. Finally, I just shoved aside Celia's hand and finished off a row of four.

"We're done," I said. "And we won."

"I want to play again," said Celia.

"Not on your fucking life."

"Hey," Dennis Klein said, "watch your language."

"If I know my father, it's nothing she hasn't heard before," I said. "A lot."

He just pressed his lips together.

"Want to play Barbies?" Celia asked.

"Not really."

"I'll get them." She jumped to her feet and crossed her room, which was large, stuffed with toys, and—big surprise—pink as to walls, quilt, and curtains. She started rummaging through some shelves that were crammed with boxes of toys. She had an insane amount of stuff for a little kid.

Dennis Klein got up and wedged himself into a child-sized armchair. His knees came up around his chin. "Having a good Thanksgiving?" he asked stiffly. I had clearly pissed him off with the swearing. Oh, and let's not forget the drinking.

I stayed on the floor, leaned back on my elbows, and stretched out my legs. "Oh, yeah, it's great," I said. "Nothing like spending the holidays with your parents. And their spouses." I yawned. "I *have* to be here. But you don't. I can't figure out why anyone would actually come to this if he didn't have to. What's your story?"

"Your father invited me."

"Bet you're regretting saying yes."

"Maybe a little bit," he said. "But it was nice of him, just the same."

"Nice?" I repeated. "That's the first time anyone's used that word to describe Richard. The man who once screamed, 'Stupid isn't helpful!' at a waitress because she brought him Coke instead of Diet Coke."

"He's a brilliant man, your father," Dennis Klein said.

"Now *that's* how people usually describe him," I said.

"And with good reason."

I shrugged. Richard wasn't brilliant enough to marry well or be happy. He was just a good lawyer. But I didn't bother saying that, so there was silence.

Then Dennis Klein said, "I can't remember—what year are you at school?"

So now it was going to be *that* kind of conversation. I closed my eyes. My body felt like it was floating. "Third."

"And you're majoring in—?"

"Wasting time."

"With a minor in sarcasm?"

I opened my eyes. "No, I already have a degree in that."

"Yes, you probably do."

"I'm an English major," I said.

"Do you know what you want to do after college?"

"No."

"Any interest in law school?"

"Yeah, right," I said. "I could become a lawyer like you and Daddy. Wouldn't that be fun."

"Hey, watch it. Some of us like what we do."

"Sorry, I didn't mean to—" Then again, maybe I did. "I just don't think it would be right for *me*. I don't know what would. I'm in no hurry to find out."

"Do you like being in school?"

"Not particularly. But I don't dislike it, either."

"I don't want to play Barbies. I want to play mommy and baby." This from Celia, of course. I had forgotten about her. I should have made my escape while I could.

Dennis said to her, "How do you play that?"

"I'm the mommy and this is my baby." She was clutching a naked doll with tangled hair. "You can be the daddy and she"—at me—"can be the nanny."

"Excellent," I said, not moving. "It's my day off. Thanksgiving, you know."

"No!" she said. "You can't have a day off. You're always asking for days off and what am I supposed to do with the *child*?" She drew her eyebrows together and hurled the doll at me. Since I was leaning back on my arms, I didn't have a chance to block it, and it hit me in the chin. "Here, take her! I have to get my nails done!" She turned her back on us and marched away to the other side of the room.

I sat up, rubbed my chin, and tossed the doll aside.

"You okay?" Dennis Klein asked.

"Yeah. Except for the pain part."

He sat there, looking at me, then over at Celia. "You see your sister often?" he asked after a moment.

"My 'sister'?" For a moment, I was confused. Then I realized. "Oh, you mean Celia. I don't think anyone's ever called her that before. I see her a couple of times a year."

"Maybe you should come more often."

"I'm not the baby-sitting type."

"I just think she could use a big sister."

"A lot of people don't have big sisters and survive," I said. "Me, for example."

"Yes, well, there you go," he said.

"There's an insult in there somewhere—"

"What's in where?" said my mother, coming into the room. "Oh, hello, Dennis. I didn't realize there was a party going on in here. And there's that beautiful Celia. Such a gorgeous child. And so lively. I wish Livvy had been more like that as a child."

"Gee, thanks," I said.

"Well, you were so sullen all the time."

"Hard to believe, isn't it?" I said to Dennis Klein.

"I think I can manage it." He had stood up when my mother entered the room. A gentleman, no less.

"Manage what? Huh? Oh, well, never mind. Are you two having fun? Oops, I mean you three." She was ducking and cooing in his direction. I glanced sideways at him, kind of hoping he'd show some interest in her. It had been a few years since her last boyfriend, and she was getting a layer of desperation on top of her base coat of . . . well, desperation.

Dennis had a pleasant enough expression on his face as he regarded her, but not much more than that. At least he didn't look repulsed or anything.

"That Celia, so cute!" my mother said. The girl in question was standing with her back to us, picking her nose. "Do you have any children, Dennis?"

"No," he said. "Not yet."

"I was very young when I had Livvy," she said. "Too young, really. But Richard—you know how he is—when he makes a decision, that's it, isn't it?" A far cry from his more believable explanation of failed contraception. "I could never say no to him. I still can't. Alicia is a much better match for him, much more his equal. She's so intelligent. English isn't even her first language. At least, I don't think it is. And she's so stunning . . ." She trailed off and there was a moment of silence. Then, remembering, "Oh, my God, Alicia! She sent me to find you all

and tell you it's time for dessert. Livvy, I'm begging you not to let me
eat too much."

I got up and said, "I don't give a shit how much you eat."

"Really, Olivia!" She forced a laugh and we all moved into the
hallway.

We sat on overstuffed chairs in the living room, eating dessert off
of plates we were balancing on our knees, trying not to spill the hot
coffee we had to put on the carpet because there was no other place
to put it.

And I'd thought *dinner* was agonizing.

I noticed Marcus looking at me. Guess my pimp comment had made
me more interesting to him. Maybe he hadn't realized I was joking. Or
just wasn't sure. The drugs had probably scrambled his brains.

Celia went running by and knocked over my mother's cup of coffee.
It spilled all over the blue and crimson carpet. My mother apologized
and knelt down to dab at it with her linen napkin.

Alicia said, "Don't do that. I'll get one of the girls." She called out
and a middle-aged woman came. Alicia said something rapid in Spanish
and the woman took Celia away, and then someone else—a different
middle-aged woman—scurried in with a rag and wiped at the stain, not
looking at any of us.

My father said, "This is why dining room tables were invented."

Alicia glared at him. "It's the child. She's wild." She said it like it had
nothing to do with her.

"It's my fault, really," my mother said. She was back on her chair. "I
shouldn't have put my coffee there."

"And where should you have put it?" my father asked. "On your
nose?"

"Silly!" she said to him, as if his comment had been flirtatious and
not contemptuous. "I could have put it on the coffee table. A little far,
but I certainly could have—"

Richard shifted impatiently and his eyes fell on me. "Finals coming
up, Olivia?"

"Yeah."

"You going to do well on them?"

"Haven't decided yet."

"Very funny," he said. "It's your future you're talking about."

"You're talking about it, not me."

He took a swig of his drink. At some point, he had switched from martinis to some amber liquid. Port? "I'm not paying for college so you can sit around on your ass and make jokes. I expect you to work hard and do well."

I didn't answer. He was looking for a fight. Too much alcohol had done nothing to improve a mood that had been sour to begin with — sour by nature, and sour from being forced to spend a day away from the office and with his family.

My mother said, "Olivia does very well in school, Richard. You know that." She looked back and forth between us, nervous.

"She could do better."

"She works hard—"

"Maybe I should stop paying," he said to me. "Maybe it's time you learned the value of an education. Maybe scrubbing toilets to pay your tuition would make you appreciate how lucky you've been."

"Not to mention make my hands smell all minty-fresh," I said.

"You think I'm joking?"

"No," I said. "I think you're threatening me. And I'm fighting a very strong urge to tell you to fuck off."

"Livvy!" A moan of distress from my mother.

"But it just wouldn't be polite," I said.

"Go ahead," Richard said, a little smile on his lips, his eyes hard. Years of terrifying assistants, associates, and other people's clients had perfected that look. "Tell me to fuck off, Olivia. And see what happens then."

"Oh, for Christ's sake," I said and met his glare full on. "Fuck off or don't fuck off. Pay for my college or don't pay for my college. But stop trying to scare me, because it's annoying."

A pause. He made some kind of decision. "You're lucky it's Thanksgiving, Olivia."

Like I would have been there if it hadn't been.

My mother said to me in a stage whisper, "Apologize to your father. He's very good to you."

I ignored her. So then—her idea of defusing the situation—she turned to Alicia and started to rave about the desserts.

Richard snorted, got up, and left the room.

Dennis Klein was sitting near me. He hitched his chair a little closer and said in a low voice, "Still shaking?"

I was startled. I thought I'd hidden it.

two

My father actually had a perfect right to question my attitude toward school. I had what you might call a rocky academic history. My mother, who had dropped out of high school to become a model and yet managed to give birth to a child whose father was a graduate of Columbia Law School, had always looked to him to instill some of the respect for education that I obviously lacked.

In my defense, I didn't torment *all* my teachers. Not the ones I liked. But the others, the ones who I felt were tormenting *me* with their stupid jokes and boring classes, their nervous tics and badly chosen favorites, their endless lectures and little vanities . . . they were fair game.

The principal of the high school already knew me pretty well by the time we were a couple of months into my freshman year. He was a saggy, tired kind of man, who looked like he was about sixty and was probably closer to forty-five. A lifetime of soothing the hurt feelings of easily offended female teachers had made him prematurely old. We saw each other often, but our conversations were usually brief.

Once, when I was in eleventh grade, I came into his office with a note, and he read it, then handed it back to me with a sigh. "Well?" he said. We had developed a sort of shorthand, he and I.

"She spelled *authority* wrong."

"Is she right? Are you always late for class?"

"Sometimes. Not *always*."

"Why?" he asked. "Olivia, you're a bright kid. Every one of your teachers says so. Why can't you show a little respect for our rules?"

"I don't know."

He shook his head. "If you continue to be late to Mrs. Elkins's class, I'll have no choice but to give you detention. You know that, don't you?"

"I'll get there on time," I said, and I did, only then I sat in the back and read a novel until Mrs. Elkins lost patience with that, too.

"Lacks respect for authority"—or, occasionally, "athority"—was what you might call the theme of my school transcript.

The thing I liked best about college was that when a teacher bored you, you could just stop going to class so long as you showed up for the final. Which explained the uneven report cards I kept getting.

"Your average is a B," said my sophomore adviser. She was a nice middle-aged woman who genuinely seemed to want to help me, although she probably felt a little less friendly after I missed our first two scheduled appointments. "Normally, I would congratulate someone with a B average, but you come to it in an unusual way, never actually having received a B of any kind. I find it difficult to believe that a bright young woman like yourself, who gets so many As, should also receive more than her share of Ds."

"I believe in balance," I said. "It's an Eastern philosophy sort of a thing."

"And you've chosen a major?"

"I'm working on it."

"What interests you?"

"Haven't found anything yet," I said and picked up my backpack.

But eventually I had to declare a major. Since I liked to read, I chose

English literature, which is how I ended up that fall—my third year—in English 34, "The Eighteenth-Century Novel." A lecture course, taught by a famous lesbian professor who began each lecture by reading out loud a pornographic passage from *Fanny Hill* and then stopping suddenly at the filthiest moment and saying, "Now that I have your attention—"

Actually, she did. I liked Professor Greene and went to all her lectures.

The class was large, and we were divided into sections that met weekly, each one run by a graduate student. The second week of class I made my way to a small room in the basement of Rolfe Hall where a group of about ten other students had already taken seats around the table. I was late, but apparently the TA was later, because people were just kicking back, lazily chatting about the book we were reading. One guy had his feet propped up on the table. He was chewing on an apple, nodding as one of the girls explained why she found Defoe "just so incredibly *modern*, you know what I mean?" She giggled and flung her hair back. Maybe she thought she had made a good point.

I sat down and dropped my backpack on the table in front of me. Ten heads swiveled in my direction. The apple guy sat up and tossed the core into a nearby trash can. "You're late," he said.

Got it. Just because he looked and acted like an undergrad didn't mean he *was* one. But did he really think it was cool to act like he was one of the kids?

"At least I'm here," I said. I had missed the previous week's class. I think I was napping.

"I prefer my students to arrive on time," he said.

"I don't blame you one bit," I said.

He opened up an attendance notebook. "Olivia Martin, yes?"

"Yes."

"Well, Miss Martin, how about you buy a watch between this week and next?"

"I own a watch," I said, showing him. "It has Mickey and everything."

"Then use it."

I just looked at him. He expected me to say something—apologize for being late, say it wouldn't happen again. I didn't say anything. After a moment, he turned back to the girl who had been talking and asked her to go on.

It was pretty clear she would have done anything he said. What with his blue eyes and all. He was handsome beyond anything even vaguely appropriate for a room full of undergraduate girls. Apparently, every female English major had heard of Joe Lowden by reputation, except for me. "You're in *his* section?" a former roommate of mine said when I ran into her later that week. "In Joe Lowden's section? Oh, my God!"

It wasn't just that he was handsome. Which he very much was with his thick hair and blue eyes and good body. It was his manner, too, familiar and edgy and funny and relaxed, but he wasn't stupid and he kept things interesting.

It didn't take me long to figure out why all the girls were wearing skimpy tops even though the room was over air conditioned and I was freezing with a sweatshirt on. Every one of them had a crush on him. So did Jacob, who had large brown eyes and thick lips and looked like he wanted to cry every time Joe called on him. I ran into Jacob one day soon after that first class, and he told me he'd heard that Joe was gay. He was obviously wrong, but I just nodded and wished him luck.

I was glad I had missed the first week of class. It was more fun coming to the whole scene when everything was in play already, when the girls were already dressed to please and so anxious to attract his notice that they had—hold onto your hats here, folks—actually *done the reading*. Not that they had anything interesting to say about it. Most of their comments were along the lines of, "Like, if I were Clarissa? I would have slept with Lovelace *right away*. I mean, her family's so mean anyway, and he's so . . . you know . . . well . . . *sexy*."

These girls killed me. They lingered when class had ended, hoping to get a moment or two alone with *him*, and you just knew they showed up during office hours, with a question about the paper we were supposed to write, or maybe just wanting to talk about Samuel Richardson's brilliance, because when you read something as exciting as *Pamela*, well, you know, you just want to talk and talk and talk about it with someone who understands. Right.

I had been late that day by accident, not knowing where the class was and not having allowed enough time to look for it. But the following week, that time, it was on purpose. I didn't like the way he'd told me to wear a watch.

Once again, I was the center of attention as I took my seat.

Joe pushed a half-empty box of Krispy Kremes in my direction. "I brought doughnuts today," he said. Of course he had. He was that kind of teacher.

"Thanks." I took a chocolate.

He watched me. They all did.

"Don't suppose there's any coffee," I said.

"Sorry," Joe said.

"My fault. I went right by a Starbucks." I yawned. "I could really use a cup, though."

"I'm beginning to wonder whether this class is at an inconvenient time for you, Miss Martin." He was on a first-name basis with everyone else.

"Don't worry about it," I said.

"I do, though," he said. "I mean, you didn't even have time to stop at Starbucks. That's just wrong." The class laughed. He smiled. "Maybe we could all switch our schedules to suit you. What about it, guys? Shall we start class fifteen minutes later next week for Miss Martin's sake?"

A couple of the girls giggled. Someone said, "No!"

Joe said, "Oh, come on, guys, I think we should. Let's help Miss Martin out. Next week, we'll all come fifteen minutes later, which should make Miss Martin right on time." They all looked at me.

I said, "Great. I'm all for that."

Discussion of Richardson resumed. I ate my doughnut.

At the end of class that day, Joe said, "Remember, everyone—we start at two-fifteen next week. For Miss Martin's sake."

"Are we really going to come later?" asked Joanne Woo, looking slightly panicked. She was the type of girl who put everything into her Palm Pilot. Those fifteen minutes would probably throw her whole week off.

"Absolutely," Joe said. "Miss Martin needs our help."

"Oh, okay," she said, trying to look like she was game because Joe would want her to be.

I got up and slung my backpack over my shoulder. "See you at two-fifteen," I said.

I got there at two forty-five. As I walked in the room, Joe threw the attendance notebook at my head. I ducked and cursed. The rest of the class cheered.

Joe turned to the girl sitting next to him—that day it was Luisa Conchas who had the memorable habit of wearing baby T-shirts without a bra—and said, "Now look what you've done. You knocked that right out of my hand. You should be more careful." More delighted laughter from his fans.

I picked up the notebook and tossed it back to him. "At least it's not *War and Peace*."

He caught it. "Next time it might be."

"Remind me to wear a helmet."

"Right," he said. "How about you see me after class?" Someone made an "Eww, you're in trouble" kind of a noise. But a couple of the girls looked pissed off—I think they figured that getting a few minutes alone with Joe Lowden was more reward than punishment, no matter what the reason.

When class ended, I waited in my seat, watching the girls as they clustered around Joe, fighting for his attention. After a few minutes, he told them all to go. They'd have to wait until office hours for their next fix. One of them scowled at me as she went by and whispered "what a bitch" to another one.

"What's so funny?" Joe asked. He had come over. He leaned against the table.

I pushed my chair back so I could look at him. "Nothing. What did you want to see me about?"

"I bet you could figure it out."

"Let me think . . . Lacks respect for authority?"

"Thumbs nose at authority. Drives authority up a wall."

"Sorry," I said. "Don't take it personally."

"Look," he said. "I don't ask a lot of my students. Just that you show up on time and do your work."

"The blondes show up on time," I said. "Isn't that enough?"

"The blondes? Oh, right. I bet if you tried real hard you could be on time, too, Miss Martin."

"And I should try real hard because—?"

"You might miss something that's worth learning. Or if you don't give a shit about learning anything—and you seem like the type who doesn't give a shit about anything—then maybe because I'll be grading you."

"And if I don't give a shit about grades?"

"Then don't waste my time or yours by bothering to show up at all."

"You're the boss." I stood up.

"Hold on a second." He raised his hand in a sort of time-out gesture. "Let's try this again. I'm willing to meet you halfway. Like, say, I'll stop throwing books at you if you come to class on time and join the discussion. Deal?"

"I don't mind having the occasional book thrown at me," I said.

"Help me out here," he said. "I'm trying to be a good guy."

"You're a prince among men," I said. "But you don't need me to tell you that. You've got the blondes to do that."

"Enough with the blondes already," he said. "So what's the story here? Do you actually have a problem with my teaching? Or do you just enjoy being a little shit?"

"What's the matter?" I said. "Charm not working? Must be a shock when that happens."

He walked away, pissed off. Then he turned around and came back. "You know, this attitude you've got going . . . Not that I don't get it. I get it. In fact, I was a lot like you when I was your age—"

"I bet you think that's a compliment," I said.

"Go to hell," he said and started to walk away. Then he stopped. "But just to remind you: I'm the one who'll be grading you. So you should know that I'll be marking you down for every class you're late and for every class you don't contribute to. And if you do badly on either the papers or the exams . . . I'm usually an easy grader, but it would be a privilege and a joy for me to fail you."

"It wouldn't be my first time," I said.

"Yeah, and I bet it won't be your last, either."

"Probably not. Are we done yet?"

"I don't know," he said. "Are we?"

"I hope so," I said. "I'd hate to be late to my next class."

He shoved aside a chair and walked away.

My father once told me I was consistent only in being perverse. I came to the next few classes on time and sat quietly, doodling in the margins of whatever book we were reading. Joe didn't seem to notice or care that I was punctual. His attention seemed to be mostly focused those days on Sarah Figueroa, a senior with thick, dark hair and thick, dark eyelashes, who actually occasionally had something interesting to say. Joe certainly seemed to find her contributions fascinating, and what started as a class discussion often turned into an intense dialogue between just the two of them.

It finally reached a point where it felt like the rest of the class was eavesdropping on something private. Then one day Joe stopped calling on Sarah in class—or even looking in her direction—and a few days later a broken-hearted Jacob told me over a couple of beers he'd heard that Sarah and Joe were secretly dating.

Mid-November, we handed in our first big papers. When I tossed mine on top of the pile in front of him, Joe said, "I can't tell you how much I'm looking forward to grading this." It was the first thing he had said to me directly since our little conference.

I said, "Have a ball," and left.

We got our papers back at the end of the following class. I didn't even glance at mine, just stuffed it in my backpack and left.

Back at my apartment, I pulled it out. Nothing written throughout the body of the paper and then at the end, in red: A.

And five short words: "Fuck you, you little shit."

I smiled. I had worked hard on that paper.

So when Richard was grilling me about school on Thanksgiving, I guess I could have told him that I had just gotten an A on a paper. It might even have kept us from fighting.

But for some reason I kept it to myself.

three

The Sunday after Thanksgiving, I ran into Joe Lowden at one of the campus cafeterias.

He was drinking coffee and grading papers. We saw each other at the same time and nodded uncomfortably. We had never spoken outside class. And not so much inside class, not recently.

The room was crowded, and I had to look for a table, and then he said my name and pointed to an empty chair at his. I hesitated.

"Go ahead," he said. "If there's one student I can be reasonably certain won't waste my time by actually *talking* to me . . ."

I nodded my thanks and took the seat. I had a book to read—for his class, actually—and a coffee and chocolate chip cookie. My usual lunch.

I curled up in my chair and started to read. When I stopped to take a sip of coffee, I stole a look at Joe, who was frowning down at a paper. Then I went back to reading. The next time I looked at him, he was watching me.

"How's the book?" he said.

"It's okay."

He didn't say anything else, just went back to work.

After a while, a student came up, a young woman who apparently had Joe for another class. She looked my way after she had greeted him, but when I kept my nose in my book and didn't pay attention to either of them, she seemed satisfied I wasn't actually *with* him. Joe meanwhile leaned back in his chair, and, after a few lazy comments about class, proceeded to compliment her on how she looked that day, then asked her why she never wore her hair down when she had such beautiful hair, and said he'd heard she was dating a drummer. She laughingly denied all rumors and said something about being very much available for the right guy. Joe then made some comment about how lucky that right guy was going to be and—

Well, you get the idea. Flirting for him was like breathing to the rest of us—natural, instinctive, necessary. Both of them glowed from the buzz of it all, laughed a bit too much, darted looks at each other.

Talk about learning things at college. I was getting a crash course—Flirtation 101. Maybe when I got to be a senior, I'd graduate to Foreplay 200. But probably only as an ungraded auditor.

She didn't seem to be in any hurry to leave, but after a while Joe sat up and pulled his papers back toward him. End of class.

After she had walked away, he picked up his pencil and said, "She's pretty, isn't she?"

"Beautiful," I said. I took another sip of coffee.

"Yes." There was a pause. Then he said, "Nice and friendly, too. The kind of girl you want to talk to."

"And more."

"Absolutely. But that kind of thing isn't allowed."

That had never stopped him before. Not with Sarah Figueroa or dozens of others. At least not according to rumor. I thought he was about to say something else, but then he stopped, shrugged, and went back to work.

It was hard not to steal looks at him. His hair was slightly overgrown and falling into his eyes. He would impatiently push it back every now and then. He shifted around a lot, restless in his seat. He caught me peeking at him.

"Wish they could all write like you," he said. Gesturing in front of him. "Most of these papers are so boring I want to slit my wrist."

"Don't do that," I said. "Think of the broken hearts you'd leave behind."

"You think there'd be a few, huh?"

"They'd get over it."

"Ouch. Build me up and knock me down."

"We're a full-service establishment," I said. "We aim to please."

"Oh, no, I'd say that's exactly what you don't do." Then he said, "But you do, anyway." Flirting because that's what he did, and I happened to be sitting there.

That's when I remembered I had to be somewhere and got up with an abrupt good-bye. Hating myself because I was just as bad as the rest of them. Worse, because I knew enough to fight it, and I still tumbled like every goddamned blonde one of them.

No college teacher should ever be allowed to have blue eyes and thick hair. What girl can defend herself against all that?

With Thanksgiving out of the way, the quarter was almost over— just two more weeks of classes, and then finals. At one of the last meetings of our English 34 section, Joe asked whether we were interested in having an end-of-the-quarter party the following week. He offered his apartment, said he could provide pizza and beer, maybe show an old movie based on one of the books we'd read.

You can imagine the response this got. While the others wet their pants with excitement, I drew a picture of a small box on the cover of *Robinson Crusoe*, then made it look three-dimensional. Never tired of that one. A classic.

The next week was our last class, and Joe took questions about the final. He didn't know exactly what would be on it—that was up to the professor—but he did know it would consist of a series of quotations to be identified, three short essays, and one long one. The professor expected us to use examples from all the literature we had read that quarter. Joe would be the one grading it.

"How much does the final count for?" asked William, who was straight and actually cared about the coursework.

"Final's fifty percent of your grade," Joe said. "The two papers you wrote count for twenty-five percent. Participation and attendance—uh, Miss Martin, you might want to pay attention to this—make up the last twenty-five percent."

"Guess I'm screwed then," I said, looking up from my doodling.

"Do well on the final," he said, "and you'll be okay."

He told us the party would be at eight that night and gave us his address. I drew a couple more boxes, while everyone else wrote it down. Then class was officially over.

There was no way I'd be at that party, but I left without saying anything. I would take the final, and I would get my grade, and then I would be done with Joe Lowden and his fan club for good.

I met a friend for dinner that night. She was in town for her Christmas break. In high school we had hung together, wearing black clothes and fierce expressions, but college had softened Charlotte more than it had me, and now she wore pastels and a gentle smile. She had always been pretty; now she was beautiful. While we ate our dinner, men kept glancing over at her from the bar. She was oblivious the way only someone who was an outcast in high school can be oblivious to the world's approval.

Anyway, Charlotte was in no mood to smile at strangers. Her heart had been broken. She started telling me about it while we sipped our first glass of wine, continued on through our salads, teared up a bit during the pasta, and by the time dessert rolled around was too emotionally weary for anything but coffee. I had a brownie sundae.

He was her first love. Like me, she hadn't dated in high school. He had said he loved her, even said it when he was telling her he wanted to see other people. "It's a guy thing," he had said at the end. "You may be the right woman for me. I may regret this for the rest of my life. But I have to see what else is out there."

"He said he could see us married one day," Charlotte said. "He said he's not ready to be with one woman yet, but when he is, he said he would come looking for me, and he hoped I'd still be there."

"Don't be."

"You're so lucky, Livvy. You've never had your heart broken."

"It's not luck. I've actively avoided it."

"There really hasn't been *anyone*? In two and a half years of college?

"Nope."

"How about now?" she said. "Right now? Isn't there anyone you like to watch or think about?"

"Not really." I was telling the truth. I didn't like thinking about Joe.

"Well," she said, "the right one will come along, and then you'll have no choice but to fall in love."

"I never knew you were such a romantic, Lottie."

"I'm not," she said with a bit of her old fierceness. "It's not romanticism. I think it's lousy that it happens. I wish it didn't. But it does." She pushed at her coffee cup, then looked up. "Did I tell you yet about running into Henry Cardoza?" Henry had gone to high school with us. "He's going to school near me and I ran into him one day on the bus. It's funny, I was never friends with him in school, but just because he was from back home, I was so glad to see him. Anyway, we went out for coffee. You won't believe what he said to me."

"What?"

"He said half the guys at school were madly in love with us—you and me. They called us 'The Untouchables' because we wouldn't go out with any of them."

" 'Wouldn't'? Don't remember ever being asked."

"Well, would you have dated any of the guys in high school?"

"Probably not."

"Me, neither. But you're right—no one ever asked. Isn't that funny? 'The Untouchables.' "

"I kind of like it," I said.

"Yeah, I figured you would. He also said they all wondered if we were gay. What with the black clothing and hanging around together all the time."

"We weren't, were we?"

"Not that I can remember." A sigh. "Right now, I kind of wish I were. Gay. Spare myself some pain."

"Yeah, right," I said. "*Women* never break hearts."

"No, I know," Charlotte said. "It's not that. But if a woman broke your heart, it would be for a reason. Because you shouldn't be together. Not because she was wondering what else was out there. It's just guys who are terrified of missing out on something."

"I don't think women are any more loyal than men."

"Are you defending the male sex? I wouldn't have expected that of you."

"Not at all," I said. "I'm just including women in my hatred of all humanity. I think people suck in general."

"Well, anyway, I can't believe that lesbian sex is as good as the real thing. Which is very good. Almost worth all the shit you have to go through to get some."

"I wouldn't know."

"No, you wouldn't. What's it like being a twenty-one-year-old virgin? Oh, and happy belated birthday."

"Could you say that virgin thing a little louder? There's a guy way over there who didn't hear you. Oh, wait, no, my mistake, he did—he's grinning at me."

"He's been grinning at you all night because he thinks you're cute, not because he thinks you're a virgin. Definitely *not* because he thinks you're a virgin."

"She's a mind reader, too, folks. Is there no limit to this girl's talents?"

Lottie said, "The only other girl I know who's still a virgin is named Mary Elizabeth McCarthy, and she took a vow of abstinence back in high school. I kid you not, wrote it herself and read it in front of her family and friends at a little ceremony. She told me all about it. The only one I know other than you . . . And from what I've heard, Mary Elizabeth defines abstinence as abstaining solely from actual inter-course. Anything else is fair game, up to and including sodomy. From what I've heard."

"Your point being?"

"You're even more pathetic than she is."

"Go to hell," I said. "And I'd like to point out that I'm not the one sitting here crying about my broken heart."

"No, your heart is as intact as your hymen."

I moved her wineglass away from her. "I think you've had enough of this."

She dropped her head onto her hands. "Oh, Christ, Livvy, I'm so fucking depressed." And we were back on topic.

I invited Charlotte to spend the night at my apartment, but her parents were expecting her back that evening.

I lived with two other girls off campus. Housing was so expensive in Westwood that the three of us could just manage to split the rent for a shabby two-bedroom apartment. No one wanted to share a bedroom, so Betsy—the token extrovert of the group—had agreed to put her bed in the living room. It was undeniably good-hearted of her, but it meant I couldn't make it to my room without enduring her cheerful greetings. Sort of like living at Wal-Mart.

My other roommate, Ruth-Anne, lived in the larger of the two bedrooms and kept the door shut. Friends visited occasionally, but they just vanished inside her room and never made a sound. She was the perfect roommate, really—unseen, unheard, unknown, and she paid her bills on time.

My own bedroom was pretty cozy, all ten by eleven feet of it. And for this I got to pay $600 a month, plus utilities. I had a bed, a desk, a TV set with a VCR, and a phone. Oh, and a window, which I did appreciate, especially on cool December nights like that one, when whoever controlled the building's thermostat always cranked the heat up way too high. First thing I did when I got home from dinner was throw open the window. Then I brushed my teeth, put on a pair of sweatpants and a T-shirt, and curled up on my bed. I was pretty sure Ruth-Anne was in her room, but Betsy was still out. The apartment was quiet. I listened for a while to the cars driving by, and then I dozed off.

I woke up because someone was knocking on the door. I got out of bed, cursing Betsy for not being home yet, since it was always her friends who came by after midnight.

I stumbled out of my room and across the living room and opened the door.

"Pizza anyone?" said Joe Lowden, holding out a box.

I opened my mouth, and nothing came out.

He said, "Well, now I can die happy. I've seen Olivia Martin speechless."

"Just give me a second," I said.

"So do you want pizza or not?"

"If I had wanted pizza—"

"You would have come to the party," he finished. He dropped the pizza box on the floor of the hallway. "Or would you have? There was some discussion about why you weren't there. No one was surprised, incidentally. Apparently you're stuck-up and don't get along with anyone."

"I could have told you that," I said.

"May I come in?"

I stood aside and he entered. "You had one champion in the group. Jacob said you have beautiful eyes, and you're very interesting." Then he said, imitating me, "I could have told you that."

"I knew I liked Jacob."

He leaned against the wall, shoving his hands in his pockets. He wore black jeans and a dark V-neck sweater over a white T-shirt. "He also said that your rudeness masks insecurity and that you're really very shy."

"On the other hand, I never really liked him at all. So he was the only one who stood up for me, huh?"

"I might have," Joe said, studying me, taking in the sweatpants, the messed-up hair, the T-shirt that was slipping off my shoulder. "But I was too pissed off. Why the hell weren't you there?"

"Why the hell do you care?"

"You throw a party, you want people to come."

"People came," I said. "Your apartment was swarming with blondes, I bet."

"I invited the *whole* class."

"Well, ten out of eleven's not bad."

"It is when you were looking forward to seeing the eleventh."

"Don't," I said.

"What?"

"Don't flirt with me. It's not something I do. And given the fact that there are plenty who do . . ."

"What?" he said.

"Go find one of them. You already have, from what I've heard. Found a lot of them. And that's great, I'm very happy for you, and for them, too. Just leave me out of it."

A pause. He still leaned against the wall, next to the open door. Neither of us had moved much. Then he stood up straight and jerked his head toward the door. "Come have a drink with me."

"Good night," I said and turned around.

"What are you afraid of?"

"Did it ever occur to you that someone might just not be interested?"

"No," he said, coming around from behind me. "And you do know how to flirt, Olivia. You do it a little differently from most people, but it's still flirting."

"Fuck you."

"See?" he said. "Right there, that's flirtatious." I was silent, and he said, "And that was a smile. You were trying to hide it, but it was."

"I thought you were leaving."

"All right, all right, I'll go. But next week's the final. I'll wait until I've graded yours. And then . . ." He didn't finish his sentence, just left.

And I went back into my room and didn't know whether I hated myself for not getting a drink with him or for wanting to in the first place.

No, wait. Actually, I did know.

The night before the final, I went to bed early, figuring I'd studied as much as I could and should get a good night's sleep.

My phone rang at eleven P.M. Normally not late for me, but that night it woke me up. Pissed me off, too, since I knew I'd have trouble going back to sleep.

"Yeah?" I said.

"Darling, how are you?" It was Alicia, her accent curling the edges of each word.

"I'm fine. In the middle of finals. What's up?" She never called just to find out how I was. In fact, she pretty much never called. I hadn't spoken to her or Richard since Thanksgiving.

"I have a very exciting invitation for you. We're going on vacation, your father and I. Up north, to Big Sur. There is a beautiful inn there that looks over the ocean. The coast there is breathtaking. And we had the most wonderful idea: You should come with us. You *must* come with us. You would love it."

"Thanks, but like I said, I'm in the middle of finals."

"It's not until the end of the week. You should be on vacation then, no? Did you have plans?"

"Sort of."

"You must come with us. The view is intoxicating."

I had no objection to beautiful views, and I knew Alicia and Richard traveled first class in every way. I was a fan of luxury. But I was also suspicious. "It sounds . . . amazing. And it would be just the three of us?"

"The four of us, yes. We will bring Celia, of course. She loves going to hotels. But you know our wonderful Rosivel? She will not come. She won't fly, not even for such a short flight as this one. An hour in the air at the most." A snort of disgust. "And of course she doesn't drive." Then, "You know, darling, Richard and I . . . we need time to be alone together. You'll understand when you're married. Or in love. So then we realized. The perfect solution. You come with us, and you and Celia can sleep in the same room. She adores you so much, and you know she is such a sweet child. . . . We would be together during the days, of course, going to the beach, eating lunch, playing together . . . but you two girls would have your own room to sleep in, and we would have ours."

So that was the catch, and it was a big one. I wasn't going to be spending my vacation lounging on my private balcony, gawking at some fantastic view of the Pacific. Nope, I'd be stuck inside playing Connect Four for hours on end in my own little version of *No Exit*.

No wonder Alicia was eager for my company—she was picturing unlimited free baby-sitting.

"Thanks, Alicia," I said. "It sounds great. But I promised Barbara I'd be around for the holiday break. She gets a little depressed then." Not a lie.

"We'll be back by Christmas Eve."

"Even so . . . I just couldn't do that to my mother. She's already having trouble dealing with the season. If I left town, she'd be all alone."

A short silence. Then, "I hope you reconsider, Olivia. I know your father will be very disappointed, as will I. And your mother . . . well, she's a big girl, you know. You can be back to spend Christmas with her, and I think that would be fine, don't you?"

"Man, I'm so sorry, Alicia. Maybe you can give me a rain check."

"I don't think so," she said, icicles dripping from her voice. "These opportunities don't come so often."

"My bad luck, then," I said. "Have a great trip. Bring me back a souvenir."

She didn't even bother to respond, just muttered a quick good-bye and hung up. I had not been useful to her. I was no longer worth her time.

I kicked ass on the final. I identified every one of those goddamn quotes, and I filled up two and a half exam books with an essay on why Pamela succeeded where Clarissa failed. With specific examples from at least six other novels. I was on fire.

During the exam, Joe hung out at the front of the room with the other teaching assistants and the professor. When I came down to drop off my blue books, he turned and said, "How'd you do?"

And I said, "I'll wait for you to tell me."

But it was shameful of me, really. To try so hard. Knowing he'd be grading it. Like writing a love poem to someone in sixth grade and then actually giving it to him to read. I wished I'd had the guts to do badly on the final or to skip it altogether. The right kind of pride would have taken me there. Instead, there I was, writing like a maniac, exposing myself in all the worst ways.

Christ, I was a disappointment to myself.

four

Jacob called on Friday and asked me if I wanted to come with him to Joe's office to find out our final exam grades. I told him I wasn't in any hurry to find out.

"You're joking, right?" he said.

"Call me when you get yours."

Later that afternoon, he called me back. "B-plus," he said. "Thank God. I thought I blew it. I always think I blew it."

"I never do," I said. "Except when I know I did."

"Aren't you going to check? He's still there, you know. Half the girls in the class were there when I left. All crowded around him like in class."

"I think I'll pass," I said.

"But you won't know how you did."

"I'll get my grades in a month. I can wait."

"Doesn't not knowing drive you crazy?"

"Not really."

"It does me."

"You need to relax," I said. "Come meet me for a drink. We can celebrate your B-plus and the beginning of break."

"I like that idea," he said, "but it would be more fun if you'd find out your grade first, so we could celebrate that, too."

"Not gonna happen," I said.

We met a couple of hours later in front of a bar in Westwood Village.

"I so need this drink," Jacob said as he came up to me. "I'm flying home tomorrow. I want to get drunk tonight and stay drunk for the next twenty-four hours, until my plane touches down in beautiful downtown Newark. Then I plan to throw up."

"You don't like to fly?" I said.

"That's one way to put it. Scared senseless is another. Being drunk is the only way I can deal with it."

"Come on, then," I said. "Let's go get totally wrecked and tell all our most embarrassing secrets."

He linked arms with me. "You don't have to get me drunk to hear my secrets," he said. "And I bet it takes more than a few beers to get you to tell yours."

"I don't have any secrets," I said.

"Oh, sweetie, we all have secrets."

We did get drunk, and Jacob did tell me quite a bit about his life, his loves, his past, present, and future . . . He had been thrown over at the end of the summer by his boyfriend, and, halfway through our second pitcher, I realized with a wave of boredom that his breakup story was identical to Charlotte's—guy loved him but wanted his freedom . . . maybe sometime in the future they would find each other again . . . needed to see what else was out there . . . blah, blah, blah. Clearly the breakup line of the moment. And, to judge by my two examples—both bright, both attractive, both reasonably sane—a very successful one, too. Like Lottie, Jacob was willing to wait for his love to come to his senses and return to him.

Man, what crap people were willing to take in the name of love.

It was a good thing Jacob and I lived close enough to the restaurant to walk home, because we were both too drunk to drive. When we reached his place, Jacob gave me a hug. "I'll call you when I'm back from break," he said and staggered off.

I wasn't walking all that straight myself.

Back at my apartment, I had some trouble getting my key to go in the lock, and it took me a minute to get the door open. By the time I did, Betsy was already smiling expectantly in my direction. She was sitting on her bed entertaining some guy.

"There you are, Livvy!" She looked at her friend with satisfaction. "See, I *told* you she never stays out past eleven. Wasn't it good you waited?"

"Yes, it was." He stood up. "Hello, Olivia."

I raised my hand in silent greeting.

"I missed you at my office hours today," he said. "I left you a phone message, too."

"Haven't been back to my room till now." Boy, I was wishing I wasn't drunk. I could barely hold my head up, let alone my guard.

"Can we talk somewhere?"

Betsy said, "Livvy's room is right back there. She got the smaller bedroom, but it has a window. I took the living room. It's not that private, but I don't mind. It's got the best view."

"Uh-huh," he said and turned to me. "Come on." He led the way, like it was his apartment.

I just stood there, blinking.

Betsy said, "Come on, Livvy! Go!" Adding, in a stage whisper, "He's so cute!"

It was funny, really. Betsy was so excited I had a guy coming to my room. Then again, she got excited about scented candles.

Joe had already flicked on my light. I came in, but stayed near the doorway. He sat on the bed.

"Close the door," he said.

"No way."

"What are you afraid of?"

"Closing the door," I said, and he had to laugh. "So what about my final was so important that you had to come to my room at ten o'clock at night?"

"It was very useful coming here," he said. "I learned all sorts of things about you from your roommate. Like you've never stayed out overnight. Or had a boyfriend that she knows of. But she's certain you're not a lesbian, because she has a radar for that kind of thing."

"She's wrong, I'm a dyke," I said. "Tell me about the final."

"Oh, and she doesn't understand why you don't go out more because you're, well, just so *cute.*" His voice went up high. Since the door was still open, I was pretty sure Betsy would be listening in on us. I hoped she appreciated the imitation.

"About the final—" I said.

"Oh, yeah. I didn't grade yours."

"Glad I didn't bother going to your office, then." My knees felt all slidey. I really wanted to sit down, but he was on the bed and I didn't have any chairs. My eyelids were slidey, too. The best I could do was get them to stick at the halfway point. Which meant I had to tilt my head back just to see straight. "Why didn't you? Grade it?"

"Because Professor Greene did."

Nothing was making sense. "You said you were doing the grading."

"I was. Most of it. But she wanted to grade a couple of exams from each section. She let us choose which ones to give her. I gave her yours."

"Why?"

"Because I didn't want to be in the position of grading you."

"Oh." I took that in. Everything was taking me a while to process. "Who else's did you give her? Whose else's. Who else's."

"Sarah's. Not that it's any of your business."

I laughed.

"What's so funny?"

"No boys made the list, huh?"

"Aren't you curious about your grade?"

"No," I said. I let my knees go free and they slid me down until I was squatting on the floor, my back still against the wall. "Can I go now? I mean, can you?"

"I'm in no hurry," he said and leaned back on his elbows to prove it. He looked around. "This room's a mess."

It was, actually. It wasn't food or anything piggy like that, but papers and books were everywhere. In my defense, I had just gone through finals week. "So how'd Sarah do?" I said, closing my eyes.

"None of your business. Don't you want to know how *you* did?"

"Why do you keep asking me that?"

"You did well. I thought you'd be pleased." A pause. "I wanted to see what you look like when you're pleased. I can only imagine."

I hugged my knees to my chest and rested my forehead against them. "Christ, I'm tired. Are you still here?"

Actually, he wasn't just in the room—he was suddenly next to me, and I heard the door swing shut very gently. Betsy would be disappointed. No more eavesdropping for her. Then he was kneeling down at my side. I pressed my face harder against my legs. I could feel his breath near my cheek.

He said, "I smell alcohol."

"Beer," I said, not moving. "Lots of it."

"That explains the limpness. Were you drinking alone?"

"No."

"With whom, then?"

"A guy."

I could feel him settling down next to me, his warmth right up against my body, making me tremble. "Anyone I know?"

"Yeah. Jacob Reiser."

"Good," he said. "You could have lied, you know. Made me jealous."

"I don't lie, and I don't have any reason to want to make you jealous."

I felt his arm go around my shoulders. My body went tight. "Relax," he said, pulling me toward him. "I'm not going to hurt you. There. Not so bad, is it?"

I stayed curled up like a roly-poly but leaning against him now. I turned my head a little and looked at him sideways. Saw part of a chin, part of a cheek. I had never seen a guy's cheek that close. I swallowed and said, "Right now I'm so drunk I'd let any piece of shit put his arm around me."

He dropped his arm, and I righted myself. "Man, you always know what to say, don't you? It's like verbal warfare with you."

"I have a strong instinct toward self-preser—presver—pres—" I took a deep breath and said carefully, "Self-preservation."

He stretched out his legs, crossed his arms, made himself comfortable against the wall. "I'm getting the feeling you don't trust me."

"And here I thought I was doing such a good job of hiding it."

"You can, though. Trust me."

"Trust you to do what?"

"You tell me."

"What were we talking about again?" I asked. "Oh, never mind. I'm going to lie down. I've got to lie down."

"Be my guest."

"Stop being mine," I said. "Go talk to Betsy. She's a very nice girl. She has lots of friends and smiles all the time."

"She smiles too much," Joe said. "I like a girl who scowls. If I go now, can I come back when you're sober? Take you out? For a drink, for coffee . . . you name it. Or are you going away for break?"

"I'll be here," I said. "For most of it, anyway."

"Is that a yes?"

I hugged my knees even closer, rocked a little, and then nodded.

He got up on his knees and bent toward me. He whispered, "I'm going to woo you, Olivia. You're not going to be able to resist me."

"I know," I said with a moan. "And then what?"

He patted my shoulder, laughing at me. "It won't be so bad as you think."

"Should I ask Sarah Figueroa about that?"

He stopped laughing. "She's irrelevant. You don't even know what you're talking about."

"Relevancy," I said. "I'm talking about relevancy. Or the lack thereof."

"When did you become incoherent?"

"She's a lot prettier than I am."

"Yes, she is," he said. "A lot of girls are. That's what confused me at first. I could pass you ten times in the street and not even notice you. And I notice pretty girls. But then, the eleventh time . . . it would be hard to *stop* looking."

I looked up, my mouth suddenly dry. Because it had fallen open. I closed it. "Oh," I said. And then, "How many times have you used that one?"

He reached down, grabbed my arm, hauled me to my feet, and

pushed me against the wall. "Only on you, you little shit," he said and kissed me, the length of his body pressing against mine.

And that was it, really. Eventually, he stepped back and left.

I had enough to think about as it was. Enough to keep me awake most of the night.

five

Since I was up most of the night, I slept late the next morning. By the time I stumbled out of my bedroom at eleven, Betsy was on me. "I think he's adorable, Livvy, really adorable. I mean, those *eyes* . . . I just want to make sure you know what they say about him. About how he dates *everyone*."

"Uh-huh," I said heading past her into the kitchen. "You want some coffee?"

"I don't drink coffee," she said. "I thought you knew. . . . Anyway, I called like three different friends who are English majors, and they all said the same thing—he loves them and leaves them."

"Them, personally?" I ran some water into the coffee-pot.

"No, it's an expression. But one of my friends has a friend who, you know, hooked up with him. And everyone knew *someone* . . . I just don't want to see you get hurt, Livvy." She was practically bursting with concern. Not to mention self-importance.

I switched on the coffeemaker and said, "I had half a

scone from Starbucks somewhere around here. You haven't seen it, have
you?"

"No. Sorry." She crossed her arms in front of her chest and tilted her
head to let her hair bounce on her left shoulder. Betsy had very bouncy
hair. "I want you to have fun, Livvy, honestly I do. And I know it's
exciting to be with someone like that. Just promise me you'll be careful."

"I promise I'll be careful," I said. Like I had it in me to be anything
else.

When Joe came to pick me up that night, I told him that Betsy was
worried about how he might end up hurting me. Since she was sitting
right there in the living room when I said it, I think she was a little
annoyed with me. After all, she had just given him one of her big
greetings, so it did make her look slightly hypocritical.

"Livvy!" Betsy said. "That was told to you in confidence! I have nothing against you," she said to Joe. "You seem really great. It's just I care
about Livvy and, well, you know, she hasn't had much experience with
men. Not much at all."

"We're going now," I said.

Betsy smiled.

"I thought you were going to woo me," I said to Joe as we left the
apartment.

"What makes you think I'm not?"

"No chocolates? No flowers? I'm disappointed."

Joe shook his head. He was walking at my side, but he made no attempt to take my arm or touch me in any way. "No. Not for you.
You'd stamp on the flowers and flush the chocolates down the toilet.
I'm making a study of you, Olivia. I'm figuring you out. And one
thing I'm pretty sure about is that if I start treating you for a second
the way I might treat anyone else, you're going to slip through my
fingers."

"Where are we going?"

"To my car," he said and wouldn't tell me anything else.

He drove a classic convertible, of course. What else would Joe Lowden drive? And he drove it fast, and he drove it hard.

"Do you like it?" he asked when we were tearing along the PCH, dodging around the other cars since there was a fair amount of traffic and he didn't seem to think he should have to wait his turn like everyone else.

"What? The car? I would have liked you better if you were driving a station wagon. It would have surprised me."

"And you like to be surprised."

"Yes. It doesn't happen often."

"I'll do my best to surprise you, then," he said.

I doubted he ever would. There was too much that was clichéd about him, from his car to his leather jacket to his blue eyes. Not that he could help the eyes. But he could have worn a windbreaker or something.

We drove forever, but it was a nice forever. Because the top was down and the convertible was noisy, we didn't talk much, just enjoyed the wind and the rush. We ended up near Santa Barbara, at a small shack of a restaurant on the beach, where you ordered your fish tacos at a counter, and they were brought to you in plastic baskets with fresh salsa on the side. We drank beer. Since it was December, the beach was cold and dark, but the restaurant had heat lamps.

After I'd had a beer, Joe told me not to get another one. "I don't want you to go all floppy, the way you were last night," he said. I didn't argue with him. Sobriety seemed like a good idea.

When we were done eating, he sat back in his chair and said, "Tell me about yourself."

"Divorced parents, only child."

He waited. Then he said, "Wow. You really opened up right there. I'm starting to feel like I really know you."

"Watch it, or I'll shut back down."

"What about boyfriends? How many? When? Who?"

"No boyfriends," I said. "None, ever."

"With those eyes, that body? I find it hard to believe."

"Maybe it's the 'No Boys Allowed' tattoo on my forehead," I said.

"Yes, that could be off-putting. Any other tattoos I should know about, maybe go looking for?"

I shook my head and there was a longish pause. He said, "No questions for me?"

"About what?"

"My childhood? My parents? Former girlfriends?"

"I could ask questions," I said, "but then you'd answer them, and then you'd ask *me* more questions. And so on and so on. What's the point?"

Joe stretched out his legs and took a swig from his beer bottle. "Okay. We've established that there are many things in life that Olivia Martin doesn't give a shit about, including grades, family, and making polite conversation. Which begs the question: Is there anything you do give a shit about?"

"Oh, lots of things." I looked at him sideways. "Like walking on the beach. At sunset. Naked, with just a flower in my hair—"

"You're starting to piss me off."

"Why? Wasn't that what you wanted?"

"Okay, fine. Don't talk to me. But could you at least stop fidgeting? I mean, it's beautiful here, you can see the ocean, and there's a breeze, and the moon is full—and I don't think any of it's made the slightest impression on you. You just keep turning around like something's going to pounce on you if you're not careful."

"You never know what might crawl out of the ocean," I said.

"Oh, forget it," he said. "Let's go back."

We stopped for ice cream at a Baskin-Robbins on the way. Joe asked me what I wanted. I said, "Seems like I should just order the flavor of the month, don't you think?"

It took him a second, and then he shook his head, disgusted. "Fuck you," he said, and walked out of the ice cream store. I didn't really want any, anyway.

We drove back to my apartment. He pulled over in front, where the curb was red, and said, "I can't figure out why I want to see you again. I must be a glutton for punishment."

"Who said I wanted to see *you* again?"

"I don't give a shit what you want."

There was something about the way he was looking at me. Made me shrink back against my seat without meaning to.

"So tomorrow night?" he said. "Same time?"

"What will we do?"

"Gee, I don't know . . . I'm guessing I'll make desperate conversation, and you'll look bored and not say much."

"It's a date, then," I said and started to reach for the door.

"Wait," he said. "*This* date isn't over until I've gotten a good-night kiss."

A jolt went through my body, but I just said, "Not if you're not even going to walk me to my door."

"You don't deserve that," he said. "You deserve—"

"What?"

He got that smile on his face again and pulled me over to him. And then he kissed me. Our second kiss, but I was drunk the first time.

It was absurd, really, like using a bazooka to knock down a house of cards. There I was, never having been kissed by anyone before him. And there he was, a black belt in the romantic arts. He knew where everything should go and which parts should rub against which and all sorts of things like that. And we're only talking *faces* here.

Because it was my first time, I hadn't known. What it was like to give in to an invasion like that, to the warmth and the pressure and the taste of someone else. Or how there was this . . . *wire* that ran from your mouth down into the center of your body so that just kissing made you want to push your body hard against the other person, made you want more kissing, more touching, more pushing . . .

Finally, he sat back. "Okay," he said, "you can go."

An embarrassing admission—I was out of breath. So I didn't say anything, just slipped out the door, even though I didn't really want to leave anymore.

"I'll see you tomorrow," he said as I turned to close the door. "Good night, you little shit."

Not the loveliest of endearments, but I had to admit it suited me.

So I'm walking upstairs, feeling pretty cloud nine-y, and even forgiving myself for feeling that way, finally thinking that I'm getting what all the fuss is about—why people act like idiots about each other—really almost feeling like a normal human being . . . but this being my life, I pull open the door to my apartment to find Betsy with her arm around—

Who else? My mother. And she's sobbing, of course, and Betsy's patting her on the shoulder. And I'm wondering what's triggered it this time—did I forget it was their anniversary? No, that's in the summer. Must just be the Christmastime thing, maybe she heard some song that got to her, that would be like her.

The two look up at me. Betsy's got tears in her eyes, too. The sympathetic type.

My mother stands up, holds her hand toward me, says, "Where were you, Livvy? I was calling you and calling you and then I came and you weren't here, oh, Livvy, oh, Livvy, oh . . ."

"I'm here now," I say, with a little roll of my eyes in Betsy's direction, to let her know this isn't serious, it's never serious. "Why? What's wrong?"

She keeps saying, "Oh, Livvy," and she's putting her arms around me and my body is stiffening with annoyance, and then she says, "He's dead, Livvy. He's dead. I don't know how else to tell you."

"Who's dead?"

"Richard. Richard's dead, Livvy. Your father."

And I say, "Does this mean you're finally over him?"

And it isn't until I see the look of horror on Betsy's face that it sinks in that my mother actually means it, and Richard really is dead.

six

"I'm sorry," my mother sobbed out. My shoulder was getting damp. "I should have found a better way to tell you. My poor Livvy."

"What happened?" I led her to one of Betsy's chairs and gently forced her down into it. "When did he die?"

"Today," she said, moaning and clutching at my arm. "This morning. I got a call a few hours ago from someone in his office. It was quick, Livvy, they don't think he could have suffered much."

"A heart attack?"

"No, no," she said, like I was being stupid, like I should have known already. "He was in good shape. He exercised every day. He had the heart of a kid. It was the car, Livvy. It crashed."

"Holy shit."

"They were up north," she said. Getting into the telling of the story a little bit now. "Way up near Big Sur. The freeway twists so much up there. No one knows exactly what happened—he was going too fast, though, I'm sure. Richard always drives too fast. And it was at night. He always drives too fast at night."

"I grew up in Carmel," said a voice from the other side of the apartment. It took death to get Ruth-Anne out of her room. She stood near the doorway, eyes blinking behind thick glasses, hair rumpled. "People crash on the PCH all the time."

"Yes, that's right," my mother said. "And it was a rental car, too, so who knows? Maybe it had something wrong with it that they hid. Maybe the brakes weren't working right. You can't trust anyone."

"What about Alicia?" I said. "And Celia?"

My mother said, "Alicia also . . . passed away. Beautiful Alicia. She was so . . . so . . ." Groping. "So beautiful. I never blamed him for marrying her, Livvy. You know that. And even if she wasn't always . . . she never deserved this. Not this. But the little girl, she wasn't with them, thank God."

"Are you sure?" I said. "I talked to Alicia last week. She—" She had wanted me to go with them. If I had gone . . . Forget it. No way I was going down that path—I'd end up one of those insane people who believe in angels. "She said they were taking Celia."

"I don't think they could have," my mother said. "The person I talked to—from Richard's firm—he said Celia was safe at home."

It was possible. Maybe Alicia had decided that without the free babysitting she didn't want to bring Celia. It would be like her to take a vacation without her own kid.

"I hope that's right," I said.

"I don't know. To lose both your parents at such a young age. Maybe she'd be better off dead. Oh, Livvy, I can't believe Richard's gone. I can't believe it." Her shoulders started shaking again.

I saw her purse over by Betsy's bed and got it. I opened it and pushed around the stuff inside, until I found a bottle of Xanax. I knew she'd have something like that. She always did. "You had any of these yet?" I asked her, holding it up.

"Just one," she said.

"I'll get you another one." I went to get her a glass of water in the kitchen, and while the water was running leaned my head against the cabinet door and closed my eyes.

So what was this? A morality tale for Olivia? I mean, Jesus, the first

time a guy kisses me, my father *dies*. Must be a lesson in there somewhere.

Then I almost laughed, because I suddenly thought of how Alicia
would feel to find out that her death was just part of *my* life lesson.

How—what was the word?—solipsistic. How solipsistic of me. Ego-
centric. Thinking it was about me, when it was Richard and Alicia who
went through the crash, who felt—what? A sudden jolt that turned into
a huge smoosh of metal and flesh and blood and heat and God knows
what else? Was there pain—huge, blinding, searing, tearing pain, like
nothing I'd ever felt with my visits to the dentist and my one broken
leg and the occasional stubbed toe? Like nothing anyone who's lived
to talk again has ever felt?

I put the cup of water on the counter and spilled out a Xanax. For
me.

I brought my mother two pills and asked her who I could call to hear
the whole story. I didn't trust her to get it right.

"That man we met at Thanksgiving," my mother said. "The one with
the noble chin. Rodney something."

"You mean Dennis Klein?" I didn't remember anything unusual
about his chin.

"That's right," she said. "Dennis. He gave me his cell phone number
and said if you were okay and felt like it, you should call him. But he
thought I should tell you first." She looked at me. "Are you okay,
Livvy?"

"Yeah. I'm fine. Do you have that number?"

"In my purse," she said, so I went and rustled through the makeup
and perfume again and found a slip of paper with a 310 phone number
neatly written on it. My mother had beautiful, rounded handwriting. I
scrawled, could barely read my own writing.

"Can you keep an eye on her for a moment?" I asked Betsy, who was,
admittedly, a good kind of roommate to have in a crisis, since she liked
being involved. Ruth-Anne, on the other hand, had already disappeared
back into her room.

Betsy immediately pulled up a chair next to my mother and took her hand and made soothing noises, which was all my mother, getting mellower by the second thanks to the miracle of pharmaceuticals, wanted or needed at the moment.

I went into my room, shut the door, and called the number. It rang a couple of times, and then a weary voice said, "Yeah. Dennis Klein."

"Hi," I said. "This is Olivia Martin. Richard's daughter."

There was a short pause, and then he said, "Olivia. You've spoken to your mother?"

"Yes."

"I'm so sorry for your loss."

"Thank you," I said. "I'm sorry to call so late."

"Don't be silly."

"I need—my mother wasn't sure—about the little girl. Celia. Remember, Connect Four and all that? Was she in the car with them?"

"No," he said. The phone went out for a moment, and then I heard him saying, "—with the nanny. She's with her now, in fact."

"So she's okay," I said.

"She's fine. You could go visit her at home if you felt like it. But your father and his wife . . ."

"What happened?"

"I don't know. No one does. The car was found the next morning."

"Listen, I'm sure it's not your concern, but do you know anything about funeral arrangements, that kind of thing? My father didn't have any immediate family. Except for me, I guess."

"It is my concern," he said. "I'm the executor of your father's will."

"Really? I didn't know that."

"Yes, well, he and Alicia just made new wills. Which was fortunate." Yeah, nothing luckier than having your wills come in handy. He was going on. "—a lot we need to talk about, Olivia. But I'm still up north—"

"Up north? You mean you went up there?"

"Someone had to . . . make arrangements. I didn't want it to fall on you or your mother and there was no one else. Anyway, I'll be back in town in the morning, and we can talk about the funeral then, if you're up to it. I do know it will be as soon as possible."

"Was it hard?" I said. "Identifying the bodies?"

A long pause. "I'm glad you didn't have to do it," he said finally. "Good-bye, Olivia. Take care of your mother. She took the news hard."

"Yes, she did," I said. "Thank you for your help. If you need me for anything, call me at my mother's. I'll be there for the next day or so."

"Good-bye," he said again, and I hung up.

I packed a few days' worth of clothes, including a decent dark dress that I figured I'd be needing, and drove my mother back to her apartment in her car. I wasn't sure when or how I would get back to my own car, which made me edgy, but I couldn't let her drive all doped up.

The next twenty-four hours were pretty agonizing. Stuck in that small apartment in the Valley, nothing to do except listen to my mother moan and cry about what a wonderful man Richard had been and how he was too good for the world, and try to distract her with her corny soaps and dramas, and answer the phone as various friends of hers called in to see how she was doing, most of them obviously rooting for some nasty downswing, and wonder what kind of unnatural daughter I was that I didn't feel particularly sad my father had died. I felt strange, disoriented, not quite myself . . . but not sad. How can you miss some-one you barely knew?

Dennis Klein called late the following day to let us know about the funeral plans. He had already arranged everything but said we were welcome to make changes.

The plans were fine. It would be a double funeral, take place at a funeral home, and anyone who wanted to could speak. From Dennis's reluctance to say much about the bodies, other than the fact they were on their way back to LA, I got the sense that it was a good thing Jews don't have open-casket funerals. Alicia wasn't Jewish, of course, but I doubted her face would be showing, either. Apparently the car had turned into an incinerator at some point during or after its tumble down the side of the cliff.

The funeral was set for the next day. To get them in the ground as soon as possible. That left me with one more day stuck in my mother's apartment, pacing around and watching her watch TV.

Before he hung up, Dennis Klein said that if I were feeling up to it, maybe I could drop by my father's house and check in on Celia. He said he'd be over there later. I told him I'd see. I floated the idea out to my mother, but she said she wasn't up to going over to Richard's house yet and told me I couldn't even think of leaving her alone. Besides, she needed a dress for the funeral and we had only that evening to go buy one.

I could have insisted, but I didn't really want to go over there, either. What the hell did I have to say to Celia other than, "Hey, our father died"?

Joe called late that night. He had shown up for our date, and Betsy had filled him in and given him my mother's phone number. Like everyone else, he offered condolences and asked if I was okay. And like everyone else, he didn't seem to believe me when I said I was.

"Will you call me when you're back at your place?" he said after we'd talked awkwardly for a few minutes.

"Yeah, I'll call you then."

"Is there anything I can do for you now? Bring you anything? Drive you anywhere?"

"Thank you," I said, "but I'm all right." I couldn't believe how polite death made everyone. Maybe that was why I felt so strange. Politeness wasn't something I normally did.

The next day we went to the funeral. And it was after that that I found out how my father had really screwed me.

seven

"You know," my mother said on the way to the funeral, "it's not wrong to think about the fact that Richard may have left you some money."

"Not wrong?" I repeated. I was having trouble finding the street the synagogue was on and was slightly distracted.

"You're not materialistic, Livvy. It's a wonderful thing in you. And I would give every cent I've ever had to give you back your father. But we have to be realistic. Your father is gone now. And you said Dennis Klein wanted to talk to you about something. Since he's the executor of the will—"

"Oh, I see," I said, because I did now. "You think I'm about to inherit a fortune."

"Not a fortune," she said primly, smoothing her new black dress over her knees. At Nordstrom's the night before, she had explained to the saleswoman that she was "newly widowed." That's how she put it, "newly widowed." After having been divorced from Richard for more than fifteen years. The saleswoman had hugged my mother and cried with her. "But Richard did well for himself, especially recently. And when he married Alicia, well, you know she was *extremely* wealthy. I think her family was some kind of South American aristocracy. Lord knows how they made the money in the first place, but her parents are dead, and she has no brothers or sisters that I know about, so she must have gotten everything there was to get. And half of that would be Richard's now."

"You've been thinking about this," I said.

"Don't make it sound like I'm mercenary, Olivia. I'm only thinking of you."

"Think about it all you want," I said. "Just keep it to yourself."

A pause. Then, "Of course, there's Celia—"

"Oh, for Christ's sake—"

"What? I'm only saying she would also get her fair share. As she should. Do you think I'd begrudge a small orphaned child her inheritance?" My mother's voice broke. "Just how badly do you think of me, Livvy?"

"You don't want to know," I muttered. Two days of living with her had driven me near insanity. How I'd survived eighteen years of it was beyond me.

She was still pitying herself, little laments escaping from around the edges of the tissue that was now pressed up against her nose and mouth. "On this day, of all days . . . need your support . . . all we've got . . . have to face everyone . . . look terrible, feel worse . . . the great love of my life . . ." and so on.

At least the subject of Richard and Alicia's money had been laid to rest.

Unlike their bodies.

That was the next activity.

"Are you sure you're up for this?" Dennis Klein asked once my mother and I were seated in his office. He had taken her hand and led her to a chair and brought her some water.

"I am," I said. "And she's . . . she'll be fine."

"The service was so draining," my mother said in a small voice. For her, it probably *had* been exhausting, since she had sobbed and moaned through the whole thing. It had actually gone pretty quickly for me. Some rabbi no one knew made a few general comments about life or death—I zoned out during that—then Dennis said a few words about how much everyone who knew Richard respected him. Two other men I'd never met also got up and told a couple of stories about how admirable he was. Alicia was mentioned only in passing. She may have had some friends in the audience, but apparently no one who wanted to speak.

If my mother hadn't embarrassed me by sobbing so loudly everyone kept looking at us, it would have been a pretty easy thing to get through.

"So exhausting," my mother said now, shaking her head. "But still . . . I think we should take care of business. Richard would want us to."

"All right," said Dennis Klein. "Olivia, you can sit there, next to your mother. We have a lot to go over. Your father's will was somewhat complicated. Lawyers' wills often are. But I'll try to simplify it as much as possible. Anything you don't understand, feel free to ask about."

"Thank you," I said and waited.

He explained that Celia and I were cobeneficiaries of some kind of trust that Richard had previously set up. We would share equally in whatever was left in Richard's estate after taxes.

"I should mention that the house is in Alicia's name alone. She owned it before their marriage. It belonged to her late father before it belonged to her, and she owned it outright—no mortgage. She left it to Celia, so it belongs entirely to her, and its upkeep will come out of her portion of the trust, not yours."

"See?" my mother said in a stage whisper to me. "I told you Alicia's family had money."

Dennis Klein pretended not to hear that. He was sitting behind his desk, documents in front of him, but he wasn't looking at them. He was looking mostly at me, curious, I think, to see my response. He wasn't going to see anything interesting—I didn't care much one way or another about all this. It would be nice to have some money of my own, but Richard had taken care of all the big financial items in my life, anyway, like school and cars, so as long as he had left me enough money to live on, his death wouldn't change things very much.

Dennis said, "Now, I have to explain the terms of this trust to you,

Olivia. Your father felt—" He hesitated. "You know I'm executor of the will, so we discussed this quite a bit and . . . well, he wanted to keep a certain amount of control. He didn't think—" He took a quick breath. "Okay. Let me put it bluntly. You won't inherit anything until you're twenty-five. Then you'll inherit a third of your share of his estate. Another third will become available to you when you're thirty. And the last third when you're thirty-five."

It sank in. "He didn't trust me at all, did he?"

"He just wanted to wait until you were older," Dennis said. "I know he felt he had seen other people's kids lose a sort of . . . of hunger to succeed when they had trust funds that were too large. I think he wanted to protect you from that. And Celia, too—the terms are the same for her."

"Only she has to wait a lot longer. I guess I'm relatively lucky."

"What will she live on?" my mother asked. "Olivia, I mean. We both . . . Richard always took care of Olivia financially, you know." And her, too, which was what she was trying to say without saying.

"Well, that's where I come in." He cleared his throat. "I'm not only the executor of the will, but I'm also the administrator of the trust. Which means I essentially hold the strings to the moneybags until you come into your inheritance, Olivia. I have the jurisdiction to dole out whatever amounts you need to live on until you're twenty-five—which will be in, what, about four, five years?"

"And if I decide I really need a Porsche before then?"

He smiled. "You ask me, and I use my judgment."

"Which, I'm sure, is totally brilliant."

"Are you flattering me, Olivia?"

"I just want to make sure I'm on your good side," I said. "What with you being the banker, and all. Richard must have trusted you a lot."

"I guess he did."

My mother said, "I don't want to intrude into Livvy's affairs. But she hasn't . . . I mean, you haven't—" Appealing to me. "Don't you want to know how much is in Richard's estate?"

"You do," I said. "And I guess I do, too."

Dennis said, "After estate taxes, it comes to roughly three million dollars. I hope it will be more than that when you and Celia come of age. Most of it is currently invested in various mutual funds. Whenever you like, I can show you the portfolio."

I glanced at my mother. She was pink with excitement. It sounded like a lot to her. It sounded like a lot to me, too. But once you divided it in half and doled it out in thirds, and allowed for expenses . . . not so much I could dream about a life of leisure.

Well, maybe a *careful* life of leisure.

I considered. I wasn't ecstatic. I wasn't disappointed. It was pretty much what I'd expected.

"When I need money," I said, "what do I do? Just call you on the telephone and beg? Or do I need to fill out a formal application, like for a grant?"

"You can call me on the phone," Dennis said, "but we'll also work out a regular allowance that should cover most of your needs — school, food, car insurance — "

"Can I use it to help out my mother?"

"My understanding is that Richard wanted you to." Quick glance at my mother. "Within reason, of course."

"He was the best, the most wonderful of husbands!" my mother said.

"Yeah, right," I said. "So we'll work out an allowance. Do we do that now?"

"I'd rather wait a bit," Dennis said. "If you don't mind. I'm still playing catch up from all that's happened the last few days." He did look tired. I hadn't really thought much about the fact that he'd taken care of everything connected to the deaths. No wonder he had rings under his eyes. "I'll set up the bank accounts as soon as I can. If you need any immediate cash — "

"I'm okay for now," I said.

"Let me know if that changes."

There was a pause. "We should let you get back to work," I said.

"Hold on," he said. "I haven't yet gotten to the most important — " He stopped, got to his feet, walked to the front of the desk and put his hands in his pockets. "Olivia — "

"What?" I didn't like the way he was looking at me so seriously.

"When you called me the night your father died, I was pleased that the first thing you did was ask me about Celia, whether she had been in the car or not."

"I didn't know," I said. "Alicia had told me they were taking her but my mother said they hadn't. I was confused."

"It spoke well of you."

I shrugged. "I just didn't know. Why are you bringing this up?"

"Olivia," he said. "Your father, and Alicia, too . . . they named you guardian. Of Celia. You're now your sister's legal guardian."

"What?" I said. "Excuse me?"

"You're Celia's legal guardian."

"You've got to be kidding."

"You know I'm not."

"There's no way," I said. Almost laughing. "That's crazy. I hardly know her. I've seen her a couple of times a year. I don't know her at all. I can't be her guardian."

My mother said, "Olivia is awfully young for that kind of responsibility."

"She's twenty-one," Dennis said, looking at me, not her. "She's young, but she's old enough."

"Let me get this right," I said. "Richard decided I was old enough to take care of his kid for the rest of my life—but not old enough to handle his *money?* Now that's just fucked up."

A slight tightening around his mouth, but all he said was, "He must have felt this was the best possible choice for Celia."

"There have got to be other people," I said. "There's got to be someone else out there who's closer to her, who would want to take her."

"I don't think so. There are no living grandparents or siblings on either side. It's possible Alicia has some extended family in South America, but that would mean uprooting Celia dramatically. With you as her guardian, she could stay in her own home, and go to the same school, see the same friends—"

"Sounds great," I said. "Only I'm not doing this. I can't do this. I'm sure she's a nice little girl, but I don't know anything about—I've never even baby-sat, for Christ's sake. For her or *anybody.*"

"You'll learn. And she *is* a nice little girl."

"Stop acting like this is going to happen," I said. My head felt like it was going to explode. "It's not going to happen. I'm not moving in with a four-year-old girl. Jesus, if I wanted to be saddled with a kid I'd be living in Oklahoma."

"The poor little girl," my mother said suddenly. "Oh, Livvy, think about poor little Celia. She's an orphan, with no one."

"It's very sad," I said. "I know, it's very sad. It's heartbreaking. She lost both her parents. That's why she deserves someone *nice* to take care of her." A sudden image of her at Thanksgiving, right after she spilled the coffee on the rug, her eyes big with terror as she backed away from Alicia. I hadn't gone to see her since her parents died. I hadn't even spoken to her. I hadn't seen any reason to. "This is unbelievable. Don't they have a backup? Don't I have the right to say no? What happens if I just say no?"

Dennis Klein said, "Richard and Alicia named only you. If you say no, Celia gets thrown into the court system. Someone could come forward to claim her. Alicia does have a relative or two in the area—I think you met one of them at Thanksgiving. I suppose he or his family could make a claim on her. If they wanted to."

Oh, God, Marcus the drug dealer.

Dennis said, "It's also possible that more than one person would claim her, in which case it could be a legal battle, and she'd have to spend time in foster care. Or if no one comes forward, she could end up there permanently."

"Shit," I said, pounding my forehead with my fist. "Shit, shit, shit. Why didn't they think of this when they had her? Why did they have her in the first place? It's not like Alicia liked being a mother."

No one said anything for a moment.

Then my mother said, "Oh, Livvy, I've got it! I'll help you! We'll move in with Celia *together*. I'll help you take care of her! After all, I know how to be a mom. And that will free you up to go to school and have fun. She's such a cute little girl! And you know I love kids." She leaned toward me. Her body was trembling with excitement. "Isn't that a wonderful idea, Livvy?"

I stared at her in disbelief. Then I looked at Dennis Klein. "Help," I said.

eight

Dennis Klein asked my mother if she would mind excusing us for a moment. She looked slightly stricken at the request but let him lead her out with the promise of a magazine and cold drink. He got her settled with his assistant, then came back inside the office and closed the door. He looked at me.

I said, "You're wasting your time. I don't have a warm and fuzzy side."

"She's a little girl, Olivia."

"I know. It's just . . . it's nothing against Celia. And I don't want her thrown into some foster home. I just don't think I can do it. Honestly. I'd be lousy at taking care of someone else. I'm not so good at taking care of myself."

"You seem to be doing okay." He came closer and leaned against the desk. "Olivia, I know you're being handed a rotten deal. You're twenty-one years old, a college student, someone who likes to go to parties and have fun." Not what you'd call an accurate description, but I let it pass. "And now you're being asked to become a full-time caretaker to a little girl you barely know. I don't blame you for being reluctant. In fact, I would have been nervous if you had accepted the responsibility too quickly, without realizing what you were getting into."

"But—?"

"But you should do it."

I waited. He was silent.

"That's it? Aren't you going to tell me what a good thing it will be for me, too? How it will strengthen my character and add meaning to my life?"

"I don't know if it will do any of those things," he said. "I just know that Celia's parents wanted you to take care of her if they died, and they died, and you should take care of her."

"I don't want to."

"I know. But you should, anyway."

"Remember at Thanksgiving?" I said. "I swore in front of her. I do things like that. I'm not sweet and motherly."

"You should take care of Celia, anyway."

"Stop saying that."

"What else can I say?" he asked. I swear the lines under his eyes had darkened since we'd gotten there. "I have to get you to see this, Livvy. That this may not be what you wanted, but it's the right thing to do."

"I don't do things because they're the right thing to do."

"You should. You can start now."

"You're not going to let me out of this office until I say yes, are you?"

"I can't force you to do anything," he said. "If I could, I probably would, though. Look, Olivia, you're not going to have to do this alone, you know. Your mother wants to help. I'll help as much as I can. And I know Celia has a nanny she's very attached to. It's not like you'll have to watch her twenty-four hours a day."

"The nanny," I said. "I forgot about her. What about letting her take Celia? I know Celia loves her—I've seen them together. She probably took better care of Celia than Alicia ever did. Give her to the nanny! It's the perfect solution."

"I can't 'give' Celia to anyone," Dennis said. "I told you, if you won't accept legal guardianship, she'll end up in the court system and the outcome is uncertain. Nannies don't 'get' their charges. It doesn't work that way. And as much as Rosivel may love Celia, and as lovely a person as Rosivel seems to be, she takes care of Celia because it's her job, not because of any deep-seated ties."

"Shit. I thought I was on to something."

"But she will be there to help you take care of Celia," he said. "She's there right now."

"Does she live there?" That would help.

"No. But I think there are other baby-sitters who fill in on the weekends and evenings. As you know, Olivia, your father and his wife weren't the most . . . involved parents. Which works out to your advantage now. It's not like you're being sentenced to full-time child care."

"What is my sentence, exactly? To live with her until she's eighteen?"

"That's part of it. Look out for her. Pick her schools, her clothes, her activities. Help plan her future. Steer her in the right direction. Make sure each and every baby-sitter is kind and trustworthy. Listen to her. Comfort her at night if she has bad dreams."

"That's mom stuff," I said. "That's being a mom."

"You'll be the only one she'll have. Possibly even the only one she'll remember."

"No," I said. "I'll take on this legal guardian thing, because I don't seem to have a choice. Because I *should*, since you say so. But I'm not going to be her mother. I'll be her legal guardian and her half sister, and I'll try not to screw her up. That's the best I can do. Take it or leave it."

Dennis Klein held out his hand. "I have faith in you," he said as we shook.

"You said you'd help. You better mean that. I'll need all the help I can get."

"Yes you will," he said.

I told him I needed the rest of the day and the night to myself, that I wasn't ready to face Celia yet. He said he'd arrange for the nanny to stay with her one more night. In the morning, I would take as much clothing and stuff as I could over to the house and pretty much move in. I had to finish out my apartment lease with my roommates—

couldn't leave them in the lurch—so I'd either find someone to take over my rent, or just use the apartment as a place to crash between classes. There was no reason for me *not* to continue with classes as planned, Dennis said. The next quarter was still two weeks away, plenty of time to get settled.

"At least this all happened during your break," he said.

"Yeah," I said. "Richard really came through for me on that one."

I drove my mother's car back to my place. My mother spent the entire ten-minute ride from Century City to Westwood raving excitedly about what life would be like when we "three girls" were all living together. "We'll play games and buy clothes and at night we'll make s'mores and eat ice cream! Oh, Livvy, it will be so much fun. I always felt awful that I wasn't able to give you the gift of a little sister or brother, and now it will be as though you have one."

"Celia *is* my sister," I said.

"Half sister. Anyway, I can't wait. And that beautiful house! We'll have a swimming pool, Livvy! And a big kitchen! I'll cook dinner every night. And when you have a date—I know you're going to meet someone wonderful soon, my darling—especially if you would wear makeup now and then, you know, it wouldn't kill you—when you have a date, Celia and I will just curl up on the sofa and watch TV together." She laughed and then sighed. "It's so funny how things work out, Livvy. I never wanted Richard to marry Alicia, but he did, and they had Celia. I thought it was such a mistake . . . And now, it's all come full circle!"

I had no idea what she meant by that, but there was no way in hell I was going to ask her. I wondered which would be worse—living with both Celia and my mother or living alone with Celia and being completely, totally, *solely* responsible for her.

My mother drove me nuts, but the thought of caring for a small child by myself terrified me. Terror was winning out, for the moment at least, so I let my mother rave on, unchecked.

When we reached my apartment building, I got out and said goodbye.

"You'll be back later tonight, won't you, Livvy?" she asked, sliding over into the driver's seat.

"No. I need one last night to myself. I'll call you in the morning."

"But you left your things at my place. And we have so much to talk about."

"I'll call you in the morning," I said again and slammed the door shut. I had something like fifteen hours of freedom left, and I sure as hell wasn't going to spend them with her.

My apartment was empty—no Betsy to greet me, which meant I didn't have to tell anyone what was going on. Which was good, because I was having trouble wrapping my brain around the fact I was about to move into my dead father's house to take care of my four-year-old half sister. Or was she three? Jesus, I didn't even know how old she was.

The whole thing seemed unreal, like I could just shrug it all off, forget about it, get on with my normal college life. It seemed especially possible here, in my apartment, without Dennis Klein or my mother bugging me.

I could actually make it go away, couldn't I? One phone call, to tell Dennis I wasn't going to do it.

And then he'd just tell me I *should*, and I'd be right back where I started.

I found a note on my desk. "Livvy—Ruth-Anne and I both took off for home today." Oh, right. Christmas break. I forgot I was on vacation. "Call me and let me know how you're doing. Lots of love, Betsy."

Four messages on my machine. Charlotte, calling to make plans to get together—I'd spoken to her since she left that message, so she knew about the accident. Jacob, saying good-bye for the holidays, wondering if I'd found out anything about my English 34 grade. Another friend who wanted to know if she could borrow my car for the holiday week if I wasn't planning on using it. Some school counselor or adviser or something like that, whom I'd never heard of, wanting to know how she could help me and to let *me* know that she was there for me to talk to and that the school could accommodate any special needs I might have "during this difficult time." I wondered how they knew about Richard's death. Betsy, probably. Be like her to start making calls on my behalf without asking me.

No messages from Joe. I hadn't expected any. Had I? He had said to call when I could and given me his number.

We didn't do well on the phone, though, Joe and I. If I called him, he'd ask about the funeral, and I'd have to be polite, and the awkwardness would set in. Better to see him in person than to go through all that again.

Anyway, I felt like taking a walk.

Hadn't he dropped in on me unannounced, not once, but twice? Time to turn the tables, throw *him* off his guard.

I knew where he lived. He had given out the address when he invited us to the party, and even though I hadn't written it down, it had seared itself on my brain. Mostly, I think, because I so much didn't want to remember it. Like trying not to think of an elephant in a pink tutu.

He lived on the other side of Westwood Village from me, a fifteen-minute walk away. I showered, changed, and looked through my mail, then headed out. It was early evening, and lots of people were on the streets, standing in line at the movie theaters, meeting in front of restaurants, getting out of cars and greeting each other, being normal in a way I never had been and now never would be.

On the way there, I thought about what I'd find when I reached Joe's apartment. There was a good chance he wouldn't be there at all or would be there with another girl. I was kind of rooting for that second possibility. It would give me the chance to show him I really didn't care what he did or who he did it with. With whom he did it.

It was colder than I realized, and even though I was walking fast, I wished I'd worn more than just a sweater. My cheeks and nose were stinging by the time I got to his apartment. There was a phone next to the entrance gate with a little screen that allowed you to scroll through the tenants' names and find a code that you dialed to reach them. While I was doing that, someone came out, so I hung up the phone and just walked in through the gate, into a courtyard. His apartment number I had also remembered because it was 2B. Like in *Hamlet*. Dumb, but it had stuck in my mind.

I went up a flight of stairs and knocked on the door that said 2B. The apartments ranged around the open courtyard, which meant I was out of the wind but still cold. I hugged my arms to my chest and waited.

Joe opened the door. He had on his leather jacket. "Wow," he said. "Olivia."

"I'm sorry," I said. "You're on your way out. I'll go—"

"Are you crazy?" he said, grabbing me by the arm and hauling me inside. There was no one else there. "I haven't heard from you in days. I didn't know what had happened to you." He put both hands on my shoulders and looked at me. "Are you okay?"

"I'm fine. A little cold."

He touched the tip of my nose, the way you would a dog. "You're freezing. Come on, I'll get you a blanket, something hot to drink."

"You were going out. I don't want to—"

"I'll cancel it."

"Won't she be disappointed?"

"Probably." I had forgotten how good-looking he was. No, I hadn't. "She'll get over it."

I said, "If you're being nice to me because you think I'm grief-stricken or something, don't. I'm fine. If you'd rather—"

"I'd rather be with you," he said. "I just need to make a phone call."

He went into another room but left the door slightly open. I could hear him dialing and then talking to someone. Telling her that a good friend's father had died suddenly, and he needed to be there, to help out. That he would call later . . .

I looked around. A small apartment kept painfully neat. Books were organized alphabetically by author in a cheap painted bookcase, except for the nonfiction, which was arranged by subject. There were no dirty dishes or scattered papers in sight, and even the remote control was placed at right angles on the television set. No wonder Joe had thought my place was messy.

I could see into a small, tidy kitchen. Another door opened to a tiny bathroom. Joe was in the bedroom—I could see the corner of his bed through the open door.

He hung up the phone and came back in. "All set."

"She okay?"

"Yeah, she'll survive." He sat down on the sofa. "So how about you? Other than not being grief-stricken? Are you sure you're not, by the way? Maybe it hasn't sunk in yet."

"I saw my father a couple of times a year," I said. "He wrote me checks and told me I should work harder. It wasn't the kind of relationship you grieve over."

"Still, a father . . ."

"Still a father," I agreed, changing the punctuation. There was a short pause. I said, "Has anyone ever told you you should do something because it's the right thing to do?"

"Sure," Joe said.

"Like what?"

"Oh, you know. The obvious ones. Like my parents think I should finish my goddamned thesis and get the hell out of graduate school."

"Because it's the right thing to do, or because they want to stop paying for it?"

"The latter, I guess."

"That's not what I meant."

"Then what do you mean?"

"I don't know. . . . How often do you think about whether or not you're doing the right thing at any given moment? The morally correct thing?"

"I don't like where this is going," he said with a little laugh.

"No, you wouldn't," I said. "Forget it. It's just that . . . Never mind."

"What?" he said. "Tell me."

"Never mind," I said again.

"I think," he said, "that you should come sit with me on the sofa. It would be the right thing to do."

"Morally speaking?"

"Morally, ethically, and any which way you like."

I thought about it. He watched me, his hand resting lightly on the sofa, inviting me over. I stood up, but I didn't join him. Instead, I went past him, into the bedroom.

Another neat room, clothes probably all put away in either the cheap wooden dresser or behind the closed closet door. Nothing to see except the furniture and a couple of English lit books on the night table. I studied the bed. Full-sized. It took up most of the floor space.

I heard him come in behind me. I didn't turn around.

"What are you looking at?" he asked.

"I'm looking for the notches. I figured I should know what number I'd be."

"You can't notch an iron bed," he said. "Anyway, I prefer to keep that information on a spreadsheet. It helps with all the cross-referencing—you know, cost comparisons of money spent, how quickly they put out, things like that."

"Funny," I said.

He sat down on the edge of the bed. "Yeah, it was. What do you want, Olivia?"

"I'm cold," I said, because I suddenly was again.

"Then come here," he said, a little impatiently now. He reached forward and pulled me down onto the bed next to him.

He did warm me up. I'll say that. And, in return, I surprised him. He hadn't expected a virgin.

A new category for the spreadsheet.

Or—more likely—a new entry in an old one.

nine

Afterward, I wanted to run away. How can people look at each other after *that*? Not that it had been unpleasant or anything. The opposite, actually. Even the pain I felt was exciting. But Joe seemed to think we should just lie there all wrapped around each other, and I felt like I needed to move around, think about what had happened, think about what was going to happen.

I wriggled away from him, slid out of the bed, and grabbed my clothes.

"What are you doing?" he said, holding out his hand. "Come back."

"I need to . . ." To what? "I'm just going to get a drink of water. I'm thirsty."

"You don't need to get dressed to do that."

"Too late, I am." It didn't take long to pull on the kind of clothes I wore—jeans and a T-shirt, with good girl cotton underwear. The sweater could wait. I was nice and warm now.

Joe pushed himself up onto his elbows. He did have a beautiful body, slender but muscular. I especially liked his shoulders, which were pretty broad for someone so thin. "Bring me some, too."

"Okay. Tap water drinkable here?"

"I have bottled water in the fridge."

"Of course you do," I said and padded to the kitchen in my bare feet. I found two glasses in the cabinet—from a matching set of eight—and filled them from the bottle. I gulped down a glass—I guess I really *was* thirsty—and then carried the other one into the bedroom. Joe was sitting up, a blanket now draped over the lower half of his body, his chest and shoulders still naked. I handed him his glass.

"Thanks." He drank, looking at me over the rim.

I perched on the edge of the bed, hugging my knees to my chest, thinking. About how I'd be packing up my stuff in just a few more hours and moving to Little Holmby.

"Well?" Joe said after a moment.

I looked up. "What?"

"Aren't you going to say something? Anything?"

"About what?"

"Jesus, Olivia. About what just happened. About . . . Wasn't it your first time? It seemed like—I mean, I don't know that much about it, but—"

"Yeah," I said, "it was."

"Well? What did you think?"

"Are you looking for a compliment, Joe? Don't tell me you're insecure."

"I'd like to think you enjoyed yourself."

"I did, thank you."

He shook his head. "I don't know why I expected anything else from you . . ."

"I thought I was being very polite."

He reached over, grabbed a pillow, threw it at my head.

"Hey," I said, batting it away, "I thought we were past the throwing things at each other stage of our relationship."

"I think where you're concerned, throwing things should always be an option."

I noticed the condom wrapper was lying on the floor near my shoes

and wondered how many others had lain there for a while, waiting to
be picked up and neatly disposed of. I closed my eyes briefly and then
said, "I'm hungry."

"Yeah? Want to go get something to eat? Or order in? Or just stay
busy and keep our minds off of food?" He patted the empty space next
to him.

"I want to go out," I said. "It's the last night of my life."

"Meaning?"

"Nothing. Come on."

"That wasn't a suicidal kind of thing, was it?" Joe asked. He slid out
of bed and stood up, naked and comfortable with it. And why not? He
looked good. I watched him reach for his clothes, and it was like looking
at a nice piece of sculpture. "Should I be concerned? Call university
health services for you? Honestly, Olivia, all joking aside, you've been
through a lot lately—"

"No. Oh, God, no. Nothing like that. Sorry. It's—" I kept thinking
I'd tell him and then backing away from it. What would he say? Sorry
you're turning instantly from a cute college girl into a middle-aged
suburban mom and don't call me, I'll call you? Anyway, I didn't want
to spend my last night of not having to deal with a kid talking about
how I was going to have to deal with a kid.

On the other hand, I didn't want to lie. So I said, "It's a lot of things
coming down at once. One of which is having to deal with my mother,
who decided at some point to be grief-stricken over my father's death,
even though they basically had no relationship. Now she thinks she
even wants to move in with me."

Joe pulled on a pair of boxers and said, "Hey, I've definitely made an
impact on you tonight. You actually told me something personal."

Yeah, but only to avoid telling him something even more personal.

I said, "Hunger must be making me light-headed. Hurry up."

"Yes, ma'am," he said. "It's a little distracting, though, the way you're
watching me."

"I like looking at you."

"You're a strange little girl," he said and was dressed a minute later.

In the restaurant, over bowls of noodles and glasses of sake, Joe
squinted at me. "You sure you're okay?"

"Okay? I'm great."

"No, really, Olivia. I mean, I don't want to be missing any signs here—"

"Signs?"

"You know . . . If you're feeling overwhelmed by everything—"

"Oh, we're back to that. I'm sorry I made that last night of my life crack. I don't even know why I said it."

"You sure? Because I'm here for you—"

"Will you cut that out?" I said.

He put his hands up. "Sorry. Don't mean to overreact . . ." He dropped them. "It's just . . . I had this weird thing happen with a girl a couple of years ago. She was a student in one of my classes and kind of nuts. She locked herself in my bathroom and threatened to commit suicide."

"Holy shit," I said.

"Yeah, no kidding."

"And you think I fit a similar profile?"

"No, of course not. It just struck a chord."

"What happened? Who was she?"

"I told you, just some nutty girl in my class a couple of years ago. She was always hanging around, trying to get me to talk to her after class. But I wasn't interested. So one day, I'm at home, and I answer the doorbell, and it's her. She runs straight into my bathroom and shuts and locks the door. Then she starts saying stuff through the door about how she's going to slit her wrists with one of my razor blades if I don't promise to screw her then and there. Which wasn't quite the turn-on she must have been hoping it would be. So I start begging her just to come out and be a good girl and I promise I'll talk to her and get someone nice over at health services to talk to her and so on and so forth. I mean, I'm saying all the things you're supposed to say. And meanwhile, I'm sweating like you wouldn't believe. I was scared shitless she might actually do it, slit her wrists in my bathroom."

"I'm assuming she didn't," I said, "since it's become a cute story to tell on dates."

"We're not on a date," he said. "We're on a break from being in bed together."

"A break?"

"We're going right back to my place after this," he said, "and you're spending the night."

"That depends," I said.

"On what?"

"On what happened to the girl."

"You're right, she was fine, didn't commit suicide. I got her out of there safe and sound."

"How?"

He hesitated, playing with a chopstick, then said, "Never mind. It's a stupid story. I only thought of it because you said that thing about how it was the last night of your life."

"But now I want to know what happened," I said.

He sighed. "She said she would come out only if I swore by everything I held sacred that I would screw her when she came out. So I finally said I would. I didn't know what else to do at that point."

"And did you?"

"What do you think?"

I studied him for a moment. "I honestly don't know."

"What would have been the right thing for me to do in this situation? Should I have kept my word and fucked a mentally unstable girl? Or broken a promise? You were the one who was questioning my morality earlier this evening."

"Yeah, I was."

"So what would have been the moral thing to do? The right thing?"

"I don't know. How does someone even get to a place where you have to make a decision like that?"

"Don't blame me," he said. "I was the victim."

"Sure you were."

There was a pause. "So," he said, an edge to his voice now, "still want to know what happened?"

"No. I changed my mind."

"Really?"

"Yeah. There are too many lousy ways for this story to end."

After a moment he said, "I'm not as bad as you think I am."

"God, I hope not," I said seriously.

He ran his fingers through his hair. Rumpled like that, it made him look like a kid. Innocent. He said, "Olivia . . ."

"What?"

"I'm going to get the check. And then you're coming back with me to my apartment and you're spending the night there. I'm not done with you yet. But I think it's very important for our relationship that we spend as much time together as possible not talking to each other."

I did go back to his place, but I knew I wouldn't spend the night there. Not that there was anything waiting for me back home. Actually, there was no "home" to speak of. There was the apartment I would be leaving tomorrow, there was my mother's apartment, which I never entered without counting the minutes until I could leave, and there was the house in Little Holmby that I'd be moving into, where I'd only ever been an uncomfortable guest. I was a—what did they call homeless people?—a transient. In every sense of the word. The idea of coming *home*, of being somewhere that meant more to me than a bed to sleep in and clothes to change into . . . I couldn't even imagine it.

Dinner had given Joe what you might call a second wind. He moved me quickly from his front door into the bedroom, his hand on the small of my back, steering me like a kid pushing a toy truck. He treated me differently this time. Before, he had been gentle, careful, anxious to please. This time, it was like some anger remained from our dinner conversation. Or maybe he had just exhausted his patience. There was an edge of . . . not violence, exactly, but a sort of wanting to crush me— his lips were hard, like he wanted to bruise mine, he pulled hard at my hair to make my head turn the way he wanted it to, he let me feel the weight of his body on mine, he pinned my arms down . . .

I'm not saying I didn't like it. I'm not saying that at all.

"It'll keep getting better," he said to me afterward. Also, "I like being the first guy to fuck you. First and only."

"Up till now," I said.

"You've waited twenty-one years. Somehow I don't think you're going to rush out and start sleeping with every guy you meet."

"Probably not."

We were lying in bed together, still breathing hard, still tangled up. "So what *have* you done with a guy before? Am I the first one you've seen naked?"

"Yes."

"The first one you've touched below the belt?"

"Aren't you supposed to be doing this in baseball terms? First base, second base . . . ?"

"Only thirteen-year-olds do that," he said. "You're revealing your ignorance. How many guys have you kissed before me?"

"None," I said. "Not one. Should I start asking you how many girls you've—no, forget it, we neither of us have enough time for that."

"Funny," he said.

I closed my eyes. I was tired, but there was no way I could go to sleep in a strange bed with a man lying next to me.

"You saved yourself for me," he said. Gloating.

"Not for you specifically."

"Well, maybe you didn't know it was for me. But in the end it was."

I got up on one elbow to look at him. He grinned up at me, pleased with himself. "The timing just worked out," I said. "That's all. You were in the right place at the right time."

"I don't believe you," he said. "Admit it, Olivia, you like me."

"You?" I said. "You're the enemy. The minute I forget that, I'm screwed."

"So to speak."

"Yeah. So to speak."

"You have the most beautiful shoulders," he said. He pushed back my hair and stroked me like you would a pet, along the side of my neck, across my shoulder blades, down my arm. "Man, I wish I didn't have to head home tomorrow. I could stay here with you for the rest of break, not leave this bed. Wish I could."

I shifted away from him. "I'd go nuts shut up in here."

He let his arm fall on the bed with a thud. "Did anyone ever tell you you're a true romantic?"

"Did anyone tell you *you* were?"

"Lots of times."

"I can't think of anything more cynical than someone who's romantic on cue," I said.

"How about someone who deliberately sees the worst in other people?"

"That's not being cynical—that's being realistic."

"What do I have to do to convince you that I'm capable of being sincere?"

"Be sincere."

"I have been with you." He boosted himself up on a pillow and crossed his arms behind his head. "Olivia, what have I ever done or said to you that hasn't been open and honest?"

"Or said and done with a hundred other women?"

"It seems to bother you that I've slept with other women. But I've never lied to you about that. I think I've been pretty open about it all."

"It doesn't bother me," I said quickly. "I didn't mean it that way. I don't care what you've done before. I just don't want to forget what you are, Joe. Because if I forget it for a second, if I start believing—" I stopped myself.

"What? Believing what?"

"Nothing. Forget it."

"That I'm capable of honest affection? Because I am, Olivia." He uncrossed his arms, leaned forward. "What I'm feeling for you, it's all new to me. No one's ever . . . I can't . . . Look, you're making me incoherent. And the thought that I won't see you for the next week or so is already driving me crazy."

I opened my mouth to speak and he cut me off. "And if you say, 'I bet you say that to all the girls,' I swear to God Olivia, I'll—" He stopped.

"What?"

"I don't know. Make you pay somehow. I can, you know. Because now I know you like me, no matter what you say."

"Because I slept with you? I told you, somebody had to be the first. It could have been—"

He cut me off. "Say whatever you want. I know the truth—you chose *me*. And you can't take it back now."

ten

"So," I said. "Now what?"

Celia stared at me, eyes big and dark from under surprisingly thick eyebrows for a little girl. "I don't know. I
forget . . ."

"What did you forget?"

"I forget who you are," she said.

This was going well.

I'll admit, I got there later than I'd said. More like early
afternoon than morning. If you're going to be picky
about it.

By the time Joe dropped me back at the apartment it
was pretty late, but I wasn't sleepy, so I stayed up a while
longer packing my things. I went to bed at three, didn't
fall asleep until four, then slept past ten. I got up and
took a long shower, then finished packing. I loaded up
my car, stopped at Starbucks for breakfast, and didn't
arrive at my father's house — which I probably shouldn't
call my father's house anymore — until one o'clock or

maybe it was closer to two, if you want to be really precise, which I don't when it comes to time.

I had to ring the bell, since I didn't have a key. Rosivel and Celia opened the door so quickly I guessed they'd been waiting and watching for me.

The house seemed even larger than I remembered. Empty of any holiday fuss and crowd, it was the goddamned Sistine Chapel. Celia and Rosivel looked lost in the two-story foyer with the inlaid marble floor.

Rosivel said, "Hello, Missus Olivia." Up close, she was younger than I'd ever noticed before, probably not more than twenty-five. She had long thick black hair that she was wearing in a ponytail and a pretty face made less pretty by a mouthful of bad teeth.

I wasn't crazy about being called missus but didn't want to get into the whole "don't call me that" thing right then, so I just said hello back and hi to Celia, too. She was clinging to Rosivel's leg. She wore her usual pink, but the dress was too tight and short, and the sash was torn.

"Remember?" Rosivel said to Celia, taking her arm and trying to move her forward. "Remember your big sister? Remember what I told you? She's going to take care of you."

"No," said Celia, shrinking back against her. "I want you."

"I love you, *mi vida*," Rosivel said and bent down to kiss her on the top of her head. "And your big sister loves you, too."

I kind of bobbed my head like I was agreeing with her. "We'll have fun," I said to Celia. She didn't even look at me.

"I want you," she said again to Rosivel.

Rosivel sighed and stroked Celia's hair and shoulder. "Her dress is old," she said to me. "It doesn't fit her anymore, but she said it was the only one she would wear. I didn't want to fight with her today."

"Yeah," I said. "She looks fine to me. You look nice, Celia."

"No," she said and turned her back on me, her arm still twined around Rosivel.

"She's shy," Rosivel said.

"Yeah," I said again. Then, "I better get my stuff. It's in the car."

"I'll help you," Rosivel said, but when she tried to follow me, Celia wouldn't let go of her leg. She tried to take a step or two with Celia clinging on, but eventually gave up, and they both just waited for me. It took me three trips to move everything into the house.

I dropped the last couple of bags on the floor and closed the front door. "Okay," I said, "next activity?"

"Excuse me, missus?" Rosivel said. "You know, I have to go home now."

My stomach twisted. "Now? But aren't you . . . I mean, isn't it kind of early?"

She said, "I have been here since Celia's mother and father first went away on their trip. I have seen my own son only once since then, when his father came here with him. He is only five. He misses me. And today is Christmas Eve."

"Christmas Eve?" I said. "Today is Christmas Eve?"

"I'd like to buy some presents," she said, "and be with my family."

Jesus, I'd had no idea. Since my father's death, time had sort of collapsed in for a while, and I'd forgotten about the whole holiday thing. Shouldn't I be doing something about Christmas? Celebrating it with Celia? Having us a grand old time of it? Break out the eggnog and fruitcake, and let's go hang some stockings with cheer! Santa Claus is comin' to town, but you're not going to catch mama kissing him *this* year. Mama's dead.

I was losing it. Fear of being alone with Celia was making me lose it.

Rosivel was still talking. "I would not leave Celia, of course, when no one was here. I stayed as long as Mr. Klein asked me to, but now—"

"But now I'm here," I said. "Of course, you should go. I'm so sorry. I had no idea. I didn't realize you'd been here so long. Of course, you should go. Thank you for staying so long, taking such good care of Celia . . . Go, be with your family." I was babbling. Terror was setting in. I had thought I'd have a few hours at least before going one-on-one with Celia. But fucking human decency required that I let Rosivel go home.

Fucking human decency probably also dictated a Christmas bonus for someone like Rosivel, but I had no idea how much to give her. A week's salary? Which would be—what? I didn't have a clue. But maybe Dennis Klein had taken care of it. He said he'd be in charge of money, and that household expenses came out of Celia's account. Wasn't Rosivel a household expense? Even if not, she'd have to cut me a little slack, wouldn't she? What with the family tragedy and all?

Anyway, I didn't have much cash on me — just a few bucks. Enough to tip a cab driver, not a nanny.

Rosivel didn't seem to be waiting for me to produce my wallet or anything. In fact, she was already backing away. "I'm going now, okay? I will be back the day after tomorrow." Yeah, she was backing away, but since Celia was still attached to her leg, she wasn't going very fast.

"We'll see you then," I said and put my hand out in Celia's general direction. "We'll be fine. Right, Celia?"

She burst into tears and tightened her grip on Rosivel's thigh. "Don't go!" she screamed. "You can't go! I want you!"

It was all kind of horrible for a while. Celia was screaming and sobbing and wouldn't let go of Rosivel who obviously wanted out of there but was still managing to stay patient with Celia, squatting down to explain how she needed to go and see her own little boy.

"Take me with you!" Celia said. "Take me with you! I'll be good, I promise."

"I can't, *mi vida*," Rosivel said. "Your sister, she will take care of you now. She loves you, too, Celia. She loves you." And then she pulled Celia's arms off her leg — not cruelly, but pretty firmly — and thrust her at me, with a look. As if to say, "For Christ's sake, step in here, lady."

And, man, if I've ever wanted to run away from anywhere in my life, it was that place at that moment. I was measuring the distance to the door, thinking, "If I leave before she does, she'll have to stay."

But there was this screaming kid already being pushed against me and I had no choice except to grab on to her and try to keep her from reattaching herself to Rosivel, which she was desperately trying to do. Fortunately, she was a pretty small kid — couldn't have weighed more than a medium-sized dog — and I was a lot stronger than she was.

As the nanny stood up and walked away, Celia twisted around in my arms. I still had her around the waist — I was on my knees, holding her — but she stretched her arms out in Rosivel's direction and gave the loudest shriek I'd ever heard in my life. You'd have thought she was being left to be tortured and killed.

Rosivel said one last, "I have to go. I love you, Celia," over her shoulder, and then she really was gone, not through the front door, but down the hallway to the kitchen, and presumably out the back door there, on her way home—by bus, I was guessing, since she didn't have a car out front—abandoning Celia, abandoning me.

So there I was on my knees, holding this screaming kid. At least she stopped struggling with me once Rosivel disappeared, just went limp in my arms, sobbing and calling for her nanny.

I sat there, listening to her screaming and crying, and tried to will myself into feeling sympathetic. Her parents just died, I thought. Her parents just died and her nanny left. She doesn't know me, but here I am taking care of her. She's scared and sad and alone. She has every right to cry.

It worked a little. I did feel kind of sorry for her. But I still wished she'd stop making so much noise. My head ached.

After she'd been sobbing against me for a while, my legs cramped up and I had to move, so I carried her into the kitchen and found a cookie in the pantry, which, to my huge relief, she accepted as a bribe to calm down. We sat down, and she gulped and sighed for a while and then started to eat the cookie. And that was when she said she had no idea who I was.

"I'm your half sister," I said. "Your daddy and my daddy are the same guy. Were the same guy." Oh, shit. Quick, change the subject. "Remember I was here on Thanksgiving?"

She chewed on her cookie. Crumbs collected in the corners of her mouth and stuck to the strands of snot all over her face. "I think so. Why did you bring suitcases today?"

"I'm going to live with you."

"Why?"

I didn't even try to answer that one, just said, "It'll be fun, don't you think?"

"Where will you sleep?"

"I don't know. I guess I'll look around. You want to help me find a good place?"

"You can't sleep in my room. I only have one bed, and I sleep in there."

"You're right. I need my own room."

"I wish Rosivel could sleep here again," Celia said. "She was sleeping here before, but she said not tonight. She slept in my room with me. On the floor. I was scared sometimes at night, so she said she'd sleep on my floor."

"Why were you scared?"

"There were monsters." She said it very matter-of-factly.

"Are you sure about that? Because I've always been pretty sure that monsters aren't real."

"That's what my mommy says. She won't sleep in my room with me. She says only babies think there are monsters. She gets mad if I wake her up. She's in heaven now, Rosivel said."

"Yeah?" I said. Not being a "they're in heaven now" kind of person.

"Yes. She said I'll see them there. It's up in the sky. Can I have another cookie?"

"Why not?" I said and gave it to her. Now there were also smears of chocolate around her mouth. Someone would have to wipe her face off soon.

Someone? Me. Christ.

Not yet. I couldn't deal with that yet. A messy face wouldn't kill her.

"I have a couple of phone calls to make," I said. "Where's your phone?"

"I'll get it," Celia said. She got down from the chair and ran over to the built-in desk in the corner of the kitchen. She grabbed the cordless phone out of its cradle and came running back. She held it out to me but let go too soon. The phone fell on the floor, and the back came off, and the battery fell out. "Sorry," Celia said with a shrug and walked away.

The problem, I realized as I watched cookie crumbs trail off of her dress and settle all over the Spanish tiled floor, was that I didn't really like little kids.

I called my mother first and then Dennis Klein. I told my mother she could come over whenever she wanted. She had phoned me three times that morning at my apartment to ask if she should pack her clothes and come stay "for at least a while and then we'll see from there." My few minutes alone with Celia had already convinced me that having another person in the house could only be a good thing. Even if it was my mother.

When Dennis answered his cell phone, I didn't even say hello, just, "You said you'd help," and he didn't have to ask who it was. He said he'd come as soon as he could.

"It's Christmas Eve," I said. "I had no idea. Did you know it was Christmas Eve?"

He said he did, because people were already leaving the office and he'd be able to take off early.

"Is there someplace you're supposed to be tonight?" I asked, wondering, if he said yes, if I would let him off the hook or not. He had ruined my life, so I was in favor of at least ruining his evening. On the other hand, it wasn't really his fault that my father had left such a shitty excuse for a will. "Is someone expecting you for eggnog in front of a cozy fire?"

"No," he said. "I don't normally do Christmas. I'm free, except for work. And I won't be able to do much of that once holiday fever sets in, and everyone else is out of his office."

"Rosivel left," I said. "She won't be back until after Christmas. You didn't tell me she had a kid of her own."

"I didn't know," he said. "She never told me. I've got to go, Olivia. I'll get there sometime early evening, and I'll do what I can to help with Celia. How's it going so far?"

"I'm okay so long as the cookies hold out. Am I allowed to give her as many cookies as she wants?"

"I wouldn't worry about overindulging her at this point. Just don't make her sick. Are you two connecting?"

"Yeah," I said. "Every time I give her a cookie she acknowledges my existence."

"Go easy on her. Think of how confused she must be right now."

"She's not the only one. Why am I here, again?"

"I'll be over as soon as I can," he said and hung up.

Celia didn't even finish the second cookie. Her stomach wasn't all that big, I guess. She not only had chocolate smeared around her mouth now but also up by her right eye and across the front of her dress. I handed her a wet paper towel and suggested she clean her mouth, hoping maybe it was something she could do herself. She swiped briefly at her cheek and handed the paper towel back to me. I suggested she try again, and she turned her back on me and walked off.

I sat down at the kitchen table and put my head down on my arms. There was something about being in that big empty house on Christmas Eve with the sun already going down, knowing it was only the beginning of days and days of trying to make this thing work . . . I wanted to get back in my car and drive far away, but I couldn't leave. I was responsible now for a small child. I couldn't leave the house without her.

I couldn't leave.

I wondered if this was what a prisoner felt on the first night of a long sentence. Just this heavy weight of the time that would have to be dealt with before being free again. Also a sense of unfairness—what the hell did I do to deserve this? Which would make me an unjustly convicted prisoner in the land of metaphor, I guess.

Even the hour or so until my mother arrived seemed like it would stretch on forever. Unbelievable—I was counting the minutes until my mother would show up. *My mother.*

What did you do with a four-year-old kid? Or a three-year-old kid? How old *was* Celia, anyway?

"How old are you?" I asked her. She was drawing on a piece of paper on the telephone desk, the top of which was a slab of bluish granite, which matched the counters in the rest of the kitchen. Up close, the piece of paper turned out to be some phone list. Alicia might need that, I thought, wondering if I should rescue it. Then realized what a stupid thought that was.

Celia was drawing a person with circle eyes and a circle nose and circle ears. It looked just like something an adult would draw, if she were trying to draw like a little kid.

Celia said without looking up, "I'm three and a half. I'll be four soon."

"When?"

"On my birthday."

"When is your birthday?"

"I don't know."

How could she not know her own birthday? Was she an exceptionally stupid kid or did most three-year-olds not know their birthdays? I'd have to ask Rosivel when it was. Or Dennis Klein—he probably had it on all the official documents.

At least I knew Celia was three. Unless she was wrong about that.

"How old are *you?*" she asked, pushing her piece of paper aside.

"Twenty-one."

"My mother is twenty."

"You sure about that?"

"Yeah. Can I watch TV?"

TV. Why hadn't I thought of that? She could watch TV!

Celia led the way to the family room. She walked on tiptoe, but it didn't seem to be on purpose or to be quiet or anything. She just walked that way.

We passed the living room as we went down the hallway, and I noticed a huge decorated Christmas tree in there, the kind where all the ornaments are made out of crystal and big white ribbons hang in perfect loops. So Alicia must have trimmed the tree, or, more likely, paid someone to do it for her, before she left on her vacation.

There were some wrapped presents underneath, all in white and silver paper. It gave me the creeps—gifts put there by someone who was dead now. I looked at Celia but she was heading straight toward the family room and television set and seemed oblivious to everything else.

In the family room, she climbed onto the enormous leather sectional and said, "Try Disney or Nickelodeon. Those are good." So she knew the names of cable stations but not the date of her own birthday. The sofa was so deep that her feet only just reached the edge when she put her legs straight out in front of her.

I found the remote on the coffee table and turned on the TV. Pretty soon Celia was absorbed in some cartoon, her mouth open, her eyes wide and staring. I said her name once, just to see if it would register, and she didn't even turn her head. I thanked God and the United States of America for providing us with children's programming and threw myself into another corner of the sofa.

I hadn't bitten my fingernails in ten years, but I found myself gnawing away at my thumb as I sat there, watching Celia more than I did the cartoon, wondering what was going to happen to the two of us, how we were going to survive this.

I wanted to explore the house a little, figure out where to stow my stuff and spend the night, but I didn't know if it was okay to leave Celia alone. She seemed all right, and it wasn't like she was a baby or anything, but I just didn't know enough about small children — could they be left in a room by themselves in a big house for a few minutes? Was it safe?

I had no idea, so I stayed.

I ran to let my mother in when she rang the doorbell. I can honestly say I was never so happy to see her in my life.

"Where is our sweet girl?" she asked. "I have a lot of bags. Livvy, will you bring them in? I'll go talk to Celia. Where is she?"

I directed her to the family room, then went out to her car and discovered that she wasn't exaggerating when she said she had a lot of bags. Her Cadillac was filled with them. Boxes, too, including an open one filled with framed photos of her, me, and my father. I was still carting it all into the foyer when I heard shrieking.

I ran to the family room, where I found Celia in tears, desperately fighting to break free from my mother who was trying to keep her in her lap. "Let me go! Let me go!" Celia was screaming. "I want my mommy! I want my daddy! Let me go!" She saw me and wriggled even harder. "Help me!" she cried, reaching out to me.

My mother released her suddenly, and Celia toppled off the sofa headfirst. She hit the coffee table and screamed even louder. I ran and picked her up, and she yelled, "I hurt myself! I want Rosivel! I want my mommy!" She had a red welt on her forehead.

I patted her on the back and tried to calm her down. Her face was all wet and slimy. "What the hell happened?" I said to my mother over Celia's screams.

"Nothing happened. We were just talking. I was explaining about how her parents had died, and how you and I would be like her parents now, and then she started to cry, so I was trying to hold her and make her feel better."

"Jesus Christ. You couldn't have just said hello?"

Celia said, sobbing, "I want Rosivel."

"I know you do," I said. "She'll be back soon. Look—isn't that duck funny? He's eating ice cream. I've never seen a duck eat ice cream before, have you?" I went on for a while like that, describing what was on TV. Not the most exciting conversation, but it distracted her and pretty soon she was back in glazed-over-TV-watching mode, now with tear streaks on her cheeks and fresh snot running out of her nose.

Once she was back in her trance, I dumped her on the sofa and went over to my mother. "I wouldn't rush to unpack those boxes of yours," I said.

"I was just trying—"

"From now on, you don't say anything to her unless it's about food, TV, or the weather. That's it. You talk about anything personal, and you're leaving."

My mother pouted. "I was just trying to get through to the poor little thing. Look at her. She's so alone over there. I know she was crying, Livvy, but it's cathartic, really, she needs to cry—"

"Did you hear what I said? The weather. Food. Television. That's it. You break the rule, you leave."

"Why are you so angry?" she asked. "It's not my fault she got hurt."

I shook my head. Why had I wanted her to come? What was I thinking? When had she *ever* helped me out? "Look," I said, "I mean it. This whole situation is tough enough. You're a stranger to her. So am I. So let's start out nice and slow. If you can't do that, Barbara, then you can leave right now. You understand?"

"You know nothing about children," she said.

"And you're such an expert?"

"I raised you."

"Yeah," I said. "And look at what a fine, healthy specimen I am."

"I loved you," she said, her eyes filling with tears. "I always loved you. You don't know how lucky you are to have a mother who can say that to you. Mine never, not once did she ever—"

"Fine," I said, "whatever. Just do me a favor and don't get too comfortable here."

She settled back against the cushions with a sigh. "We're all on edge," she said, "because of the tragedy. It will all work itself out."

I didn't say anything.

We both watched TV for a minute, and then she said, "So, Livvy?"

"What?"

"What are we girls doing for dinner?"

eleven

My mother was disappointed with the selection of
food in the walk-in pantry.

"You'd think, with all that money to spend, Alicia
would have something *good* in here," she said, poking
through some boxes. "Macaroni and cheese, spaghetti,
linguine—you'd think she'd buy something other than
pasta once in a while, wouldn't you? Of course, they
probably never ate at home. Alicia was no cook. You
could tell from looking at her, couldn't you? That she
was the type who expected to be waited on hand and
foot? I think she had servants growing up, and women
who have that as a child just never learn to take care of
themselves or anyone else. That must have been hard
on Richard, never coming home to a hot dinner, always
having to go out."

"He probably cared more about a cold drink than a
hot dinner," I said. I was perched on the edge of the
huge granite kitchen island and could hear every word
my mother said, even though she was hidden inside the
pantry. Celia was still watching TV in the family room—

she seemed okay with being left in there by herself, just nodded absently when we said we were going to make some dinner.

"What did you say?" My mother poked her head out of the pantry.

"Nothing. Let's have macaroni and cheese."

"Well, I'm sure Celia would like it . . . but it's Christmas Eve, Livvy. Surely we could do better than that. We should have something special tonight. We could order in! Someplace expensive and fun."

"I'd be okay with macaroni and cheese," I said.

She made a face. "That's no fun. It's Christmas Eve, Livvy."

"Oh, for Christ's sake. We're not going to start getting into the holiday spirit, are we? Because I don't think I could take that."

"Why not, Livvy? What's wrong with celebrating the holidays a little bit? Why do you have to be so glum about everything? Just because . . . well, anyway, you have to admit we could all use some cheering up. Did you see the beautiful tree? We could order some dinner, eat it around the tree, in the dark, with just the lights on. And maybe have some champagne or eggnog—something right for the holidays, to get us in the mood. And put on music." She came out of the pantry and clasped her hands, excited now. "It will be magical. Celia will love it. And I have presents for you both for tomorrow morning. Did you know that? You used to love Christmas when you were little, Livvy. You would tear open your presents with such *passion*—"

"I was hoping I'd find keys to my own apartment inside."

"Very funny. Don't pretend you don't love Christmas."

"Why would I love it? I always spend it with *you*."

"What's that supposed to mean?"

"Just that for all your talk of magic and lights, midnight has never come on Christmas Eve without your falling apart and sobbing on my shoulder about how miserable your life is."

"You're exaggerating."

"I'm not. And this year, with death paying us a visit—"

"What about Celia? Would you deny a small child the joys of Christmas?"

"How joyful do you really think this Christmas is going to be for her?"

"Not very if Scrooge here has her way."

I jumped down. "Look, if you want to order in something to eat, be my guest. I'll pay. But let's stay away from the holiday cheer, okay?"

"Scrooge, Scrooge, Scrooge," she said, hands on her hips.

"I'm going to check on Celia," I said and left the room.

She was asleep. Right there on the sofa in front of some loud, colorful cartoon about two animals whose species I couldn't identify. I hadn't expected that. Was it okay that she was asleep? I looked at my watch. It was six-thirty. That seemed early for anyone to go to sleep for the night, but maybe it was her bedtime. Or was it her naptime? I had no idea. Should I move her to her bed? Or leave her? If I moved her, she might wake up. On the other hand, how comfortable could it be sleeping on leather? Drooling on leather, too, from the looks of it. Did leather stain? Alicia would flip out if—no, she wouldn't, and I had to stop thinking like that.

Celia hadn't brushed her teeth, of course. And she was still in that tight dress except now it had chocolate stains all over it. And she had chocolate on her face, which was probably going to rub off all over the sofa.

Also . . . did kids her age wear diapers to bed? Was she old enough to know to wake up and go to the bathroom in the middle of the night if she needed to? What kind of stain would *urine* leave on leather? Urine and chocolate and drool all mixed together?

"I hate this," I said out loud. "I really hate this."

There was a fancy cashmere throw folded up in a woven basket in the corner of the room. I threw that over Celia. I turned off the TV and left the room. I thought about turning off the light, too, but I was worried she might get scared if it was dark when she woke up. She sounded like the kind of kid who got scared a lot, what with all that talk of monsters.

God, I hoped she would sleep all night long. How many hours did a kid her age sleep, anyway? I had a vague memory of Alicia's complaining that Celia never slept as a baby, but that was a long time ago, and maybe now Celia slept twelve hours every night. That would use up 50 percent of every day. Which left only twelve hours that I would be accountable for, right? And if she watched TV for a couple of hours and Rosivel came most days for eight—

I was pathetic.

"A glass of wine will make everything better." The creed my mother lived by. I wasn't surprised to walk into the kitchen and find her holding out a glass to me.

"Oh, goody," I said, looking at it. "Now it's really a party."

"I know," my mother said, pushing it against my chest so I had to take it. She picked up her own glass and took a sip. "It's just what we needed. A little bit of cheer. I found some cheese in the fridge, and a tiny bit of pâté that's still good. Oh, and I had the cutest idea: We'll pour some juice in a wineglass so Celia can feel like she has her own!"

"Great," I said. "Let's encourage her to drink."

"It's just for pretend. When I was little, I loved drinking out of adult glasses. It made me feel so grown-up. I'd pretend I had wine or scotch, just like my mommy and daddy."

"And when you were fifteen, you started drinking for real and you haven't stopped since then."

"I don't drink much at all," my mother said, fondling the glass in her hand. "If I'm out with people, I'll have what they're having, of course. And, at home, a little glass of wine now and then to quiet my nerves and to help me sleep. I never overdo it. Oh, maybe when I was your age, I had my little binges . . ." She laughed. "Well, what's the point of being young if you don't go a little wild now and then?" Then she raised her perfectly tweezed eyebrows and cocked her head with a sideways smile in my direction. "Or maybe you could enlighten me about that, Livvy?"

"Was that a slam, Barbara? I'm impressed."

"It wasn't a 'slam,' " she said, leaning back against the counter. She played with her wineglass, tilting it slightly so the wine caught the light. "It's just . . . I wonder sometimes why you don't go out more. I'd understand it if you were ugly or, you know, *handicapped* in some way, but you're pretty, Livvy. I mean, you're short, of course, and not exactly curvaceous, but . . . I think there are boys out there who would enjoy your sense of humor. You just need to smile more. It makes your whole face *work* when you smile. Even that jaw of yours." She looked up. "Why aren't you drinking? Take a sip, for me, Livvy. It will make you feel better. Here, we'll make a toast—" She raised her glass. "Merry Christmas, darling!"

I took a small sip to shut her up, then put the glass down on the counter. I wasn't in the mood.

My mother took another long pull, eyes shut in enjoyment. "It's good wine," she said. "I love Italian reds, don't you? Richard always knew his wines." A sigh. Then, "There's something about a good wine that makes me have to have a cigarette. If only I hadn't sworn off of them. Don't you think, maybe just this once, since we've all been through so much . . . ?" My mother was always quitting smoking. "Livvy, would you mind if I ran out for some cigarettes? Just one little pack. It would only take a second."

"Be my guest," I said. "Just so long as you go now, before you have any more to drink. You wrap your car around a tree, and I'm an orphan. How could I ever survive?"

She wagged her finger at me. "You think you're joking, but you'd miss me more than you realize. It's not easy being alone in this world, Livvy. Believe me, I know."

"Cigarettes?" I said and pointed toward the door.

It's a terrible thing, encouraging your own mother in a deadly habit just to buy yourself a few minutes of privacy. But I forgave myself. I was having a tough day.

And if I could just get her hooked on cocaine, maybe she'd spend most of her time in the bathroom. One quick call to Marcus the drug dealer . . .

I could have sent her home, I guess. Or never allowed her to come in the first place. But the thought of days and days alone with Celia scared the hell out of me. Anyway, I was used to my mother—she could irritate me, but she couldn't shock or overwhelm me. Celia, on the other hand . . . I didn't know what to expect from her. Or what she needed from me.

I'd keep my mother here, for a little while at least. If things started to get easier with Celia, if I started to feel like I could handle this job on my own, I'd find a reason to make my mother move back to her apartment. If things *didn't* go well with Celia . . .

Well, then, we were all screwed, weren't we?

I wandered through the house, flicking lights on as I went, glancing in rooms. Did anyone really need a house this big? Three families could have lived in it and never even crossed paths. I was finding rooms I never even knew *existed*, like a two-story library with a circular stairway that went up to a balcony filled with more books. A door out of that area led into what must have been an office for Alicia. I knew my father had his own office downstairs, since I had been "called in" there on a couple of occasions to discuss college plans, receive checks, explain the odd D grade, be told I was a disappointment to him . . . Anyway, Alicia's office had a huge modern desk—no drawers—with an endless bank of file cabinets on the opposite wall. I saw a stack of mail waiting neatly by the computer and wondered if I would now be responsible for paying the household bills.

It felt wrong to look through any of their papers, or even to be in that room at all without permission, so I went out through another doorway and found myself in an upstairs hallway that led to the master suite. I knew they had built this part of the house just a couple of years ago, adding on to the original outline. It had been a one-story monstrosity, and they turned it into a two-story monstrosity, much to the annoyance of their backyard neighbors, who lost either a view or their privacy, I couldn't remember which. They had threatened Richard with a lawsuit, and he had written them a single calm letter on his office letterhead, and they never complained again.

The master suite was unbelievably large. Unbelievably. Like something out of the Hearst Castle. A king-sized bed that was almost as high as I was tall. A stone fireplace that a person could stand upright in. A chaise longue, upholstered in velvet, that could fit at least two people side by side. Two walk-in closets the size of most people's bedrooms. Two—count 'em, folks—*two* bathrooms. One in a very masculine-looking black marble, the other in pink. There was a dressing room area off of that one, with a vanity table covered with makeup, perfume, hair sprays, and gels. Alicia probably sat there the morning of their vacation, brushed rouge on her cheeks, lined her already enormous black eyes, blown her hair dry and styled it carefully . . .

The doorbell rang and I jumped. My mother, back sooner than I expected, but I was actually kind of glad. The house had turned creepy on me.

It wasn't my mother. It was Dennis Klein carrying a white bag. I had forgotten about him.

We greeted each other, and I let him in.

"How's it going?" he asked. He still wore a suit and tie, but the tie was loosened and the top button of his white cotton shirt was undone. Lawyer Man at the end of a long day. "How's Celia?"

"Asleep, actually," I said. "She fell asleep on the sofa about half an hour ago. Do you think that's okay?"

He looked at his watch. "I don't know. Will she stay asleep all night?"

"I was hoping you'd know. God, it's really the blind leading the blind around here, isn't it?"

He raised the bag he was holding. "I didn't have dinner yet. It's Chinese food. I brought extra in case you were hungry."

"Thanks," I said. "I am, actually." I hadn't noticed it until I smelled the food. For all her talk of dinner, my mother hadn't gotten further than the wine.

We checked on Celia on our way to the kitchen. She was still out.

"This house is even more impressive than I remembered," Dennis said, putting the bag on the table and looking around. He spotted the filled wineglasses. "Do you have company or are you a two-fisted drinker?" He looked slightly wary. He probably remembered how I'd been slinging down martinis on Thanksgiving.

"My mother poured those," I said. "She just ran out to buy cigarettes. She wants to stay with me and Celia for a while."

"Yeah, I remember her saying that," he said. "Are you okay with that?"

"I don't know. I'm not exactly okay with any of this, you know? You and your 'you should do it.' It's all your fault."

He took a deep breath, then blew it out slowly. Then he said, "I need silverware."

We both started pulling open drawers, looking for it. I found serving pieces, dish towels, monogrammed napkins, steak knives . . .

"Found it," he said, holding up some forks. "Now plates."

I found those on my second cabinet and put out three. Then thought again and put out one more. In case Celia woke up.

Dennis sat down at the kitchen table and said, "By the way, I don't think your mother should smoke in front of Celia."

"Another should," I said. "Or should not, at least. Did anyone ever tell you you're a regular Jiminy Cricket?"

"Olivia—"

"No, it's good," I said, sitting down at the table with him. "Everyone needs a little angel on her shoulder. Or at least a talking bug."

"Do you want noodles?" he asked. "Or mu shu? Or do you think we should wait for your mother?"

"You tell me, should we?"

He sighed and put down the spoon he was holding. "Olivia, I'm tired. I've had what you might call a bad week. One of my friends died, and I had to drive hundreds of miles to identify his body. I'm trying to sort through his estate and take over all the work he was doing. His clients—and mine—are jumping down my back, because I'm so behind. Meanwhile, everyone else in the world is filled with holiday cheer. Do you think maybe you could try not to show how much you resent me for the next, oh, ten minutes or so? Long enough for me to eat? After I've eaten, I'm sure I'll be able to deal with your resentment in a much more positive way."

There was a pause. Then I said, "I'm sorry. I don't resent you. I just resent . . . you know. Everything." Then, "It was nice of you to come help out tonight. Thank you."

"You're welcome," he said and spooned some food on his plate. I watched him eat for a moment, studying him. My mother had said he had a noble chin. I didn't see that, although there was nothing wrong with his chin, either. He still had those terrible rings under his eyes, and his shoulders sagged with exhaustion.

He looked up, caught me watching him, chewed, and swallowed. "Aren't you going to eat?"

"I don't know. I thought I was hungry, but it keeps going away. Something about being in this house without them."

"I know," he said. "It feels strange to me, too."

"I don't even have a key," I said. "I need a key to the house and the alarm code. And there are bills in the office. And there's this huge pile of mail in Alicia's office that probably needs to be dealt with. It'll keep coming in, too. I don't know where anything is or what needs to happen or anything. I'm like a guest here, only I'm supposed to be—Christ, I don't know. Head of the household, I guess. I never even *liked* being a guest here. And then there's the whole Celia thing . . ."

He reached out and patted me on the shoulder. "I know it's hard. I'm sorry I snapped at you before."

"Don't be," I said. "You were right. Anyway, I don't mind when people snap at me. What I can't stand is being patted on the shoulder."

"So I should probably stop?"

"Yeah, probably."

He stopped. I put some food on my plate and ate a little bit, then felt hungry and ate some more.

Dennis looked around again. "What about your wine? You want it?"

"Not really. You want a glass?"

"I do," said a little voice, and we both turned around. Celia was standing at the doorway, blinking sleepily, her hair mussed, her face dingy from the chocolate, snot, and tears that had stained it before her nap. Because nap it was, clearly, all hope gone of her being asleep for the entire night. My heart sank at the sight of her, and then I felt bad about that.

"I'm thirsty," she said. "Can I have some wine?"

"Sorry," I said, "adults only." Dennis and I had both risen to our feet the second we heard her. I'm not sure why, probably with some thought of rushing to her side, only neither of us actually did that.

"Daddy lets me taste when he has wine," Celia said.

I wasn't surprised. He used to give me tastes of his wine, too. As did my mother. Amazing I didn't stagger around drunk all the time as a kid. I didn't actually like the taste of alcohol back then, though. "I'll get you some water," I said. I found a glass and took it to the sink.

While I was doing that, Dennis said, "Hi, Celia. Do you remember me?"

She shrugged. Not particularly interested. Something else had caught her eye. "What are you eating?"

"Chinese food. Do you want some?"

"Is it from Chin-Chin's? I only like Chinese food from Chin-Chin's."

"No, it's not," Dennis said. "But it's very good. Why don't you try it? Maybe you'll like it."

"No, I won't," she said. "I'm very picky." I handed Celia her water. "This is the wrong kind of cup," she said, holding it back out to me. "This is the kind adults use. My mommy says I can't use this kind because I'll break it. I need the other kind. And this is the wrong water. I only drink water from a bottle. Mommy says I'll get sick if I drink water from the sink. And it has to have ice in it. I don't like it unless it has ice."

I looked at Dennis. "She's very picky," I said.

"Just knows what she likes," he said, smiling at her. "An excellent thing in a woman. Come sit with me, Celia, while I eat. Maybe you'll change your mind about the food. You could always try it and—"

"Where's Rosivel?" she said, looking around.

"She went home," I said. "Remember?" I was looking in the refrigerator for a bottle of water. As I found it and turned around, I saw her eyes were filling with tears. Dennis and I looked at each other, alarmed.

Celia opened her mouth. For a moment, there was no sound, and I thought maybe she would just shut it again quietly, but then suddenly there was a huge, piercing scream that ended in the words, "I want Rosivel!" Followed by sobs.

I put down the water and went over to her. I squatted and put an arm around her shoulder. "Rosivel went home for just a little while," I said. "Remember, we said good-bye? She'll be back soon. I'm staying with you now. And Dennis is here, too."

She just kept going on and on about how much she wanted Rosivel. I just kept repeating that Rosivel would be back soon. I didn't know what else to do.

"Where's my mommy and daddy?" she said after a few minutes of this. "Why aren't *they* here?"

Man, I thought she'd understood about them. She had seemed so aware before. "They're . . ." I stopped. I had no idea what to say. I wasn't about to tell her they were in heaven, like Rosivel had, but telling her they were dead seemed kind of harsh, even for me. "They're not here."

Before she could ask where they were, I picked her up and carried her over to the kitchen table. She didn't fight me, but she didn't exactly put her arms around me either. She kept her body rigid. I sat down, positioning her on my lap. "Look at all this food. Dennis brought it. Wasn't it nice of him to bring us some dinner? Try the noodles. They're really good."

"I don't want any," she said. At least she had stopped crying. "When will my mommy and daddy be back?"

"They won't," I said. "They can't come back, Celia. Remember what Rosivel said? About how they were in the sky?"

She looked at me like I was crazy. "They can't be in the sky," she said. "They'd fall down."

Good point. "You were the one who told *me* that," I said.

She suddenly reached forward and grabbed some rice with her hand and shoved it in her mouth. Rice rained all over both of us. "Where's my water?" she said through a mouthful of half-chewed rice.

"I'll get it," Dennis said.

And then, "I'm baaaaack!" sang out my mother, who was standing in the doorway, holding a couple of bags. She must have left a door unlocked, since she got back in without ringing. "Merry Christmas, everyone! It's time to sit around the tree and sing songs! And I've got candy!"

Celia jumped down from my lap. "Candy!" she said. "I want some!"

My mother shot me a smug look. "Follow me to the tree!"

And we did.

twelve

"So far today, Celia's been silenced with cookies, TV, and candy," I said, curling my legs up under me. "Child rearing's not hard so long as you don't have any rules."

"I think for the moment we're in do-whatever-it-takes mode," said Dennis. He and I had chosen to sit on the sofa, ignoring my mother's invitation to sit on the floor and "drink in the tree's beauty." She and Celia were down there, though. My mother's legs were decorously tucked up under her skirt, Celia's were sprawled apart showing the white underpants under her pink dress. I could hear them discussing the lights and decorations on the tree and greedily devouring their treats—wine for my mother, candy for Celia.

My mother had turned off the living room lights, all except the ones on the Christmas tree, which were set on some sort of dimmer/brightener so they'd get soft and go out briefly, giving us a moment of total darkness, before building up again to a pretty good glow. They were all white, of course. Color would have ruined the silver and crystal purity of the decorations. This was a tree for adults—fragile, cold, and colorless. But I had to admit it looked pretty cool in the dark.

"Would anyone mind if I smoked a cigarette?" my mother called over to us, reaching into one of the bags.

"You're not allowed to," Celia said before either Dennis or I could object. "Not in the house. Mommy doesn't like the way it smells."

"Yes, but since she's not here, maybe I could just—"

"Go outside, Barbara," I said.

"It's cold. And it's so nice and cozy in here. Just one little teeny tiny cigarette?" She looked back and forth hopefully among the three of us. "I could open a window."

"Outside," I said.

She sighed and took her hand out of the bag. "I'll wait."

"Why do you smoke?" Celia asked. "It makes people die. And it smells bad."

My mother smiled at her. "Why do you eat candy, darling? It's bad for your tummy and can make you sick."

"I like candy," said Celia.

"Well, I like cigarettes," my mother said. "But only once in a while, because I know they're not good for me. And *you* shouldn't ever smoke because it's much better not to start than to spend your whole life trying to stop. Livvy, darling—" Raising her voice. "Remember how angry you used to get at me when I'd smoke?" She turned toward Dennis. "When Livvy was only five, she took a pack of my cigarettes and flushed them down the toilet. She said she hated the way they smelled."

"I still do."

"Livvy doesn't have any vices of her own," she said to Dennis. "She's perfect. That's why she's always so hard on me and my little . . . idiosyncrasies. She can be so mean about them."

"Wouldn't that be a vice, in itself?" I said. "Being mean?"

"Are you as perfect as your mother says?" asked Dennis.

"Perfecter," I said. "I don't drink, smoke, or use heavy machinery, I brush my teeth after every meal, and I say my prayers before I go to bed at night."

"You're being silly," my mother said. "All I'm saying is that you have

no interesting vices. You act like a saint. Which is an annoying way to
be, you know."

That made me laugh. Dennis, too. Which pleased my mother, who
felt she had made a successful, if unintentional, joke. She ducked her
head, smiling over at Dennis, who nodded pleasantly at her. Maybe
there *was* hope there. I had a sudden vision of her marrying Dennis
and of the four of us—my mother, Dennis, Celia, and I—all becoming
one nuclear family. I could be the rebellious older daughter again and
forget about being anyone's guardian. Dennis would take care of us all.
From what I'd seen of him, he was likely to be an improvement in the
father department over what I'd had before. Of course, fatherhood
might not be a role he was eager for. Or marriage, either. For all I
knew, he was gay. A single guy his age, decent-looking, with no apparent
girlfriend . . . He could definitely be gay.

Which made me realize how little I knew about him. Celia was
diving back into the bag of candy, and my mother was reading the
names on the gifts under the tree, so I said to Dennis, "I never even
asked you if you had any kids of your own."

"I don't."

"Ever think about it? Were you ever married?"

"I was married," he said. So he probably wasn't gay. "And I was interested in having kids. She wasn't."

"Are you still in touch?"

"No," he said. "She's dead."

"Oh." I didn't know why I always assumed people were divorced. Oh,
yes, I did. "Sorry."

"It's okay. If it makes you feel better, we were well on our way to
getting divorced when she got sick. Then we ran out of time." He
grimaced. "I'm starting to feel like the Angel of Death is looking over
my shoulder. You might not want to hang around with me for too long."

"We saints don't fear the Angel of Death," I said.

"Really? I always heard the good died young."

"Richard and Alicia pretty much disproved that theory."

He hushed me then, glancing over at Celia, who was busy sorting
through a bag of M&M's. Probably picking out her favorite colors.

I laughed. "What, we can't say bad things about them now that they're dead?"

"You can, just not in front of their offspring."

"Hey, I'm one of their offspring. His, at least. And you can say whatever you want about Richard in front of me. Doesn't bother me a bit."

"You're twenty-one," he said. "She's three. Leave her a few illusions."

"Why? It only makes things worse when you realize they're not true."

"Are you guessing? Or speaking from experience?"

"I don't know. Both, I guess. When your parents get divorced, you kind of come to grips with the fact you don't have the perfect family. But I'm all in favor of finding out the truth at any age. It's better than standing around with your thumb up your ass."

"Eloquently put," he said. He was watching Celia. I watched him watching her. The tree lights did their dimming thing, and the hollows in his face got darker and bigger until his whole face was dark, and then the lights glowed again and the hollows separated and got smaller. He said, "Celia's got enough to deal with. Let's save the whole 'your parents had feet of clay' discovery for later. Let her resent them when she's fifteen, like the rest of us."

"Yeah, but maybe if she knew the truth now, she wouldn't waste any time mourning them."

"You think mourning's a waste of time?"

"It is if you're mourning people whose death wasn't much of a loss to begin with."

"You can't tell a kid she shouldn't be sad her parents have died because they weren't all that great to begin with."

"Why not? It's better than her spending the rest of her life sobbing over how much better her life would have been if her darling mother had survived the car crash. When we all know that Alicia was a shitty mother who basically ignored her, and they would probably have ended up hating each other."

He turned back to me. "You think she'd be better off knowing *that?*"

"Maybe. Wouldn't it make Alicia's death more bearable for her?"

"How bearable would it be to spend your life wondering why your own mother didn't want to spend time with you?"

"Alicia wouldn't have been a good mother to any kid," I said.

"Yes, but how could Celia know that?"

"Any good therapist would tell her," I said. "Hell, I'll tell her."

"Speaking of therapists—"

"What?"

"I think we better find one. For her. And for you."

"You think I'm losing it?"

"No, of course not. I meant specifically for this situation. Celia needs help with the adjustment and you . . . need help with Celia."

"Oh, well . . . if you know any therapists who are available for *baby-sitting*—"

"Not that kind of help, Olivia."

"It's what I need." I wiggled myself deep into the sofa cushions. "No, I know you're right. Every time Celia says anything about her parents, we all freeze. That can't be good for her. And I could definitely use some advice. It's just . . . I don't like shrinks."

"Why not?"

I glanced over at my mother. She was singing "Jingle Bells" with Celia. The soft tree lights were kind to her, and she looked very pretty and younger than she was. She saw me looking at her and smiled proudly, pointing down at Celia who was curled against her now. It may have been the candy that had done the trick, but the two seemed to have bonded. I said, "My mother saw this creepy therapist once. She dragged me in to see him, too. He was a total lech, I swear. Kept telling me what a pretty girl I was, then invited us both to go to his cottage for the weekend."

"Please tell me you didn't go."

"My mother wanted to, but I talked her out of it and said I wouldn't go back to see him again."

"Did she? Keep seeing him?"

"For a little while, but then she had some kind of spiritual awakening and left him for a psychic tarot card reader."

"How did that go?"

"Pretty well, actually. The psychic keep telling her she was going to find the love of her life any day. Cheered her up a lot more than therapy, even if it wasn't true."

"Does she still see him?"

"Her. Paula the Psychic. Nah. She lost interest when that love thing didn't come through."

"Too bad," Dennis said. "I wouldn't mind a glimpse into the future right about now."

My mother saw him looking at them. "Come sing with us, Dennis. You, too, Livvy."

"I don't sing," I said. "Ever."

She sighed and stood up. Gracefully. "Forget it, then. You're no fun. I've got to have a cigarette. Outside, since you all insist on it. Anyone want to come keep me company?"

"I'm beat," Dennis said, glancing at his watch. "I should really go home and go to sleep. I haven't had a good night's sleep since—" He stopped, looking at Celia who had also gotten to her feet. "Not for a long time."

"Why don't you stretch out on the sofa?" my mother suggested, coming over and patting it. "Or in one of the extra beds? This house is so big. You could take a nap and then we could stay up late, all together. After all, it's Christmas Eve!"

"Sounds like fun," he said, "but I think I'm too tired to do anything other than crawl into my own bed for the night."

"Oh, but not yet. The evening's just begun. You wouldn't leave three young women all alone in a strange house, would you?"

"Don't worry, Barbara," I said. "If we get in trouble, and we don't know right from wrong, we'll give a little whistle. And always let our conscience be our guide."

"What are you talking about?" my mother said. "Livvy can be so strange sometimes," she told Dennis, who just shot me a look without saying anything. My mother turned to Celia, who had followed her over. "Sweetheart, don't you think it would be nice if Mr. Klein stayed a little while longer?"

"Who's Mr. Klein?" Celia's face was one big mess now, candy-coated drool having mixed with all the crud already there. She needed a bath. Which meant I would have to give her a bath. I had never given a child a bath. Maybe my mother or Dennis could give her a bath. I didn't know how to give a fucking bath.

"I'm Mr. Klein," said Dennis. "Sometimes. Mostly, though, I'm Dennis."

"You can remember that because it's like Dennis the Menace," my mother said to Celia.

"Who's that?" she said.

"You know, the kid in the comics. Dennis the Menace."

Celia just stared at her.

"Dennis the Menace," my mother said again.

"She's never heard of him, Barbara," I said.

"I have to pee," Celia said. "I think some came out already."

Both Dennis and my mother turned to me. Like I knew how to deal with that. "Come on," I said to Celia. "Fast. Where's the closest bathroom?"

"The pink one, but mommy won't let me use that because it's only for guests. It's all coming out!"

I swore, grabbed her hand and ran with her down the hallway—we were close enough to her room to use her bathroom. By the time I got her in there and she was on the toilet, her underpants were soaked and her dress was pretty damp, too. We pulled them off, and she perched on the edge of the toilet, naked and surprisingly skinny. You could count the ribs on her. She looked like she could fall right through the hole in the toilet seat. I assumed she usually didn't, but I held on to her arm just to be safe.

"I don't have to go anymore," she said after a moment of nothing happening.

Of course not. It had all gone in her underpants.

She pulled about ten feet of toilet paper off the roll, wadded it up, kind of patted at the top of her leg, then stuffed it all in the toilet, between her legs. She hopped down, her thighs still shining with moisture. A snake of toilet paper trailed out of the seat, down the side of the toilet.

I said, "How about we throw you in the bath since your clothes are off, anyway?"

"I don't want to take a bath."

"You need one. You're a mess."

"No!" she screamed and ran out of the room. She kept running, and by the time I made it back into the hallway she was halfway down it. I chased after her. She ran into the living room. I heard her telling the two adults there that she didn't want a bath.

She screamed again as she spotted me. "I don't want to take a bath! I hate baths! I want Rosivell!" She hid behind my mother and peeked around her legs. Her little body glowed white in the lights from the Christmas tree.

"She doesn't want to take a bath," my mother told me.

"I thought she seemed really into the idea." I turned to Dennis. "See this? I don't know what to do about this. And this isn't even a *big* problem."

"Take it one step at a time," he said.

"Oh, now that's helpful."

"You used to run around naked like that," my mother said. "You hated wearing clothes. You would have spent your whole childhood naked, if I'd let you. And I was tempted to—you had the cutest little tushie—"

"Okay, remember those rules I talked about before?" I said. "The things you can't do in this house while I'm in charge? Include among them telling stories about me when I was a kid."

"I can't help it if Celia makes me think of you," my mother said. "She even looks a little like you."

"Help it," I said.

"I like hearing those stories," Dennis said.

"No one asked you."

"Livvy!" My mother. "I don't like that tone. Dennis has been very kind to us. I think you should apologize."

"She doesn't have to," Dennis said. "No offense was taken."

"She can be so rude," my mother said. "I remember when she was fourteen, she got sent to the principal's office—"

"That's it!" I said. "One of us has to leave."

There was a moment of silence. My mother smiled and said, "I'm going to go smoke that cigarette now, darling."

Dennis said, "I'm going to go home, but I promise I'll come back tomorrow morning."

"And Celia is taking a bath," I said. "Whether she wants to or not."

We all turned to look at Celia who was squatting on the floor, diving back into my mother's bag of candy, shoving fistfuls of m&m's into her mouth, ignoring the pieces that were missing her mouth and bouncing off her naked chest onto the carpet.

"Good luck," Dennis said.

I couldn't get her in the bath. I gave up after fifteen minutes of begging, insisting, coaxing, and wrestling. I did wipe her off with a soapy washcloth, a compromise she finally sobbed out an agreement to. The whole time she screamed that I was getting soap in her eyes and the washcloth hurt her and the water was too hot. She kept pushing my hand away and shaking her head wildly.

It was impossible to do a good job, but at least her face, hands, and chest were a little bit cleaner than they had been before. It wasn't what you'd call a victory for my side, but at least I hadn't surrendered completely, either.

We fell asleep on the living room sofas that night, all three of us. We were watching the tree lights and waiting for midnight to come, because my mother said it wasn't right to go to bed before then on Christmas Eve, and we all just kind of drifted off.

Celia and I were sharing a sofa. She crawled on top of me before falling asleep, and all night long I felt like I was being suffocated.

thirteen

When I opened the door for Dennis the next morning, he was carrying a big brown bag that sagged with something heavy inside.

"What's that?" I said.

"A ham."

"A ham?"

"Yeah. Isn't that what people eat on Christmas morning? I'm Jewish, so I'm only guessing."

"I thought Jews weren't supposed to eat ham."

"I didn't say I was a *good* Jew."

"See, it helps to be half Jewish and half WASP like me," I said. "That way, one half of me feels virtuous no matter what I do."

"But then doesn't one half of you always feel guilty, too?"

"Never."

My mother said the ham was cooked but we should put it in the oven to warm up, and it would be ready right around noon, which was perfect, she said, for a

Christmas brunch. She wasn't much of a cook—as a kid I mostly ate peanut butter on crackers—but precooked hams seemed to be a species of food she was acquainted with.

Celia sat at the kitchen table, yawning. She had fallen off the sofa twice the night before. I tried to move her back to her bed, but she woke up just enough to protest, and I had to bring her back to the sofa where neither of us slept well.

I gave up trying to sleep around seven that morning and turned on the TV. For hours, we just switched back and forth between PBS and Nickelodeon. Celia knew every show on both channels. I kept thinking I should be checking things out, getting to know the layout of the house and looking for things I needed—like the extra keys—but I was tired, and it was easy to stay on the sofa and stare mindlessly at the set with her.

Dennis, on the other hand, had definitely gotten a decent night's sleep. The circles under his eyes were almost gone. For once he wasn't wearing an old-man-lawyer suit, just khakis and a dark blue sweater.

My mother closed the oven door on the ham and was ready for the next activity.

"Since we're all together again," she said, lowering her voice and beckoning to me and Dennis. "Don't you think we should do the p-r-e-s-e-n-t-s? I know a little girl who's been waiting very patiently to see what Santa brought." I don't know how she knew whether or not Celia had been patient, since she had slept through most of our morning, but, in fact, Celia *hadn't* asked about presents. Probably because she was too tired and disoriented to know what day it was.

"Hold on," I said. "Can I talk to you both in the hallway a second? Celia, wait there—we'll be right back."

She nodded and blinked and went back to staring off into space. I kind of liked her sleepy. She was very mellow, and her curly dark hair frizzed out wildly about her face. Under the throw blanket we'd shared that morning while we watched TV, she'd been soft and warm, my own little space heater.

In the hallway, I said, "The presents under the tree—Alicia put them there."

"Not all of them!" my mother said. "I may have sneaked one or two little things into the living room when no one was looking."

I turned to Dennis. "Can we open someone else's presents like that?"

"Oh, why not?" my mother said. "We can at least give Celia hers, and the ones for—well, any others we can put aside, look through later. We can't just leave them there forever."

"I'm just wondering what effect it might have on Celia," I said, still looking at Dennis. "Opening presents from parents who aren't here. Who won't ever be here again."

"We could tell her they're from us," my mother said. "Cut off the tags first, of course. Although she probably can't read yet, anyway."

There was a pause. Dennis realized I was waiting for him, and said, "I don't think we should pass their gifts off as our own, but other than that, I have no idea what the right thing to do is. I'm sorry, Olivia."

"Couldn't you have been a child psychologist instead of a lawyer?" I said. "Some grief-counseling kind of training would have come in handy right about now."

"Yes, well if you had majored in psychology, that would have been something, too," he said. "I don't see English literature coming to the rescue here."

"There are tons of orphans in English literature," I said. "Like in every Dickens novel. If the workhouse were just an option, we'd be set."

"What are you talking about?" my mother said. "Sometimes I really think you're not all here, Livvy."

"I dream of not being all here," I said. "But I still am. Okay, here's a plan—we give Celia whatever presents you brought with you, Barbara, and hide the other ones until we've had a chance to talk to someone who knows something—*anything*—about small orphaned children."

"I only bought her two tiny little things," my mother said. "Two veɪ small presents and I don't even know if they're right for her. I figured she'd have so many others . . . Didn't you even think about bringing her something, Livvy? I mean, it is Christmas. Only the biggest holiday of the whole year."

"Yeah, well, I guess it just slipped my mind."

"Mine, too," said Dennis.

"No," my mother said. "*You* remembered. You brought ham."

"No gifts, though. But I could run out and get something right now."

"Me, too," I said.

"Nothing's open now," my mother said.

"The supermarkets are," I said. "Dennis got the ham, right? And some other stores may still be. We can go out and drive around till we find something."

"And what about me and Celia?" my mother said. "What are we supposed to do until then? I was so excited about opening presents. And the ham will be done soon."

"Watch TV," I said. "That always seems to keep her happy."

"It can't be good for her," my mother said. "I never let you watch this much TV when you were a child."

"That's because we only had one TV, and you were always watching your soaps."

"And what about the ham?"

"Keep it warm till we get back," I said. "Let's go, Dennis."

Truth was, I liked the idea of getting out of the house for a little while. I'd been there for less than a day, but it felt like a lot longer. I needed some fresh air.

We took Dennis's car, one of those well-built Japanese sedans that all look the same and do well in crash tests. He had sprung for a leather interior and a decent sound system, but it really was the perfect boring lawyer's car.

I was still curious about the guy. He had devoted Christmas Eve and Christmas to us, and those were major holidays, the ones most people traveled hundreds of miles to spend with their families.

"Wasn't there anyone else you wanted to see today?" I asked him as he drove us toward Wilshire.

"What do you mean?"

"I mean, you must have had other plans for today at some point. It's Christmas."

"Yeah, well, I guess there were places I could have gone. Nothing special. I told you, it's not a holiday that means a lot to me." He drove carefully, periodically checking his side and rearview mirrors. A textbook driver. He signaled before he switched lanes and raised his hand in thanks to the driver behind him.

"You were with us at Thanksgiving, too," I said. "That's a major holiday, no matter what your religion."

"If you're asking me whether I have any friends or family I like to spend the holidays with, the answer is not really. My parents live in Florida. I visit them once a year, and it's moderately excruciating—"

"But you do it because you *should*," I said.

He hesitated. I think he was trying to decide whether to be annoyed at me or not. Then he shrugged. "Yes, actually. Which isn't the worst reason to visit family. It's not that I don't love them—"

"It's just the kind of thing where you say 'It's not that I don't love them.' "

"Right."

"I get it. It's not that I don't love my mother, either. Or maybe it is. You have any brothers or sisters?"

"An older sister who lives in New York. We talk about twice a year. It's not a close relationship."

"Any good friends?"

"A few, but mostly back east. I only moved here about a year ago, and I've been pretty busy at work. I haven't had much time to make new friends."

"I didn't know that. That you just moved."

"Richard was responsible for bringing me to the firm, you know. He recruited me from my old one."

"Did you like him?"

A pause. "He was what you'd call my mentor. I admired him, and he was very supportive of me. I'm grateful to him for all he did for me. I was honored when he asked me to be the executor of his will, although I certainly didn't expect it to be relevant so soon."

"Was he nice to you?"

Another pause. "We got along."

"Do you miss him?"

"Yes, I do. More than I would have expected, actually."

"Do you mind my asking so many questions?"

"Not at all. So long as you'll answer mine when it's my turn."

I shook my head. "I didn't agree to that."

"It's a basic rule, isn't it? You ask me personal questions, I get to ask you some."

"If you want to live by *rules*—"

"You make it sound like a bad thing."

"No, rules are great if you don't want to think for yourself."

He shook his head, smiling a little. "I almost forget what it's like to be your age and think you're the first person who ever questioned the status quo."

"Maybe I should just be a good little girl and go play outside."

"You took the words right out of my mouth. There's the Ralphs. It looks open. Should we stop or try to find something better?"

"Let's see what they have."

"I can tell you from personal experience—they have hams."

We weren't the only people roaming the aisles looking for a last-minute gift. I saw one man pick up a box of Rugrats fruit snacks and say out loud to himself, "She likes Rugrats. Good."

Not that we were any better. I found a stack of plastic Barbie plates and actually got excited. "She'll like this. I know she will."

"Maybe," Dennis said, "but I think we should move on, try to find a better store. There's not much here for kids."

"What if we can't find anything else that's open?"

"Let's get the Barbie plates and . . . I don't know, oranges or something. And then if we can't find another store, at least we'll have *something* to give her."

"Oranges?"

"Don't kids like oranges?"

"If my parents had tried to give me oranges for Christmas . . ."

"Well, what would you have wanted from a supermarket?"

"Not these." Indicating the Barbie plates. "But I wasn't like Celia. I didn't like playing with dolls or wearing pink."

"So maybe she'd like oranges."

"Stop with the oranges," I said. "We'll get her a little cake or something."

"She's already had a lot of candy in the last twenty-four hours . . ."

"It's Christmas, Jiminy," I said. "Give it a rest."

He made an annoyed sound, but he followed me to the bakery section where I picked out a cookie that was shaped like a flower and painted with glossy frosting that had dried to a hard finish. I had a feeling Celia would like that.

In Brentwood we found a toy store that had a couple of cars parked in front of it. "Open until noon on Christmas Day," said a handwritten sign in its window, and I looked at my watch. It was eleven-fifty.

The store was surprisingly empty. I would have expected even more traffic there than at the supermarket, but there was only one other customer. She was pawing frantically through a bin of dolls. "Don't you have a Garden Baby?" she called out to the salesman behind the counter as we walked in.

"There should be one in there somewhere," he said, without making any move to help her. He was a gray-haired guy with a gruff voice and a sour expression. He noticed us and said, "We're closing in five minutes."

"More like ten by my watch," I said.

"Five." He turned away. End of argument.

I looked at Dennis. "We have five minutes," I said. "Grab anything."

He picked up a box of Legos.

I shook my head. "Not for Celia."

He put it back on the shelf. "You find something, then. You're the expert."

"Hardly."

"Well, relative to me you are. At least you're a girl."

I ran through the store and found an Eloise doll you could dress up in different outfits. I always liked Eloise. She had a great life—no parents, an indulgent nanny, tons and tons of money . . . All of which, come to think of it, Celia had. Some things read better than they live, I guess.

Anyway, it was a cool doll and came with a miniature copy of the first Eloise book.

I also found a necklace with a dozen gold ballerinas dangling from it, a feathery stole-type thing for dressing up, and a Barbie whose hair you could style. Your basic nauseating girl toys. Which meant Celia would probably like them.

Dennis was waiting at the cash register. He pointed to an enormous stuffed Minnie Mouse that was propped up on the counter in front of him. It was easily twice Celia's size. "I'm going to get her this," he said.

"It's big."

"That's good, right? Big is good?"

"Spoken like a true male," I said.

"Very funny. What did *you* find?"

I slid it all onto the counter, and he said, "You did well."

The salesman said, "This all together?"

Dennis said, "Uh, yeah."

I said at the same time, "No, separate."

"Well?" said the salesman, annoyed, looking between us.

"It's easier to just keep it together," Dennis said. "It'll speed things up. And I already have my card out." He handed it to the man.

I said, "You don't have to—"

"I want to," he said and pushed the toys across the counter.

I shrugged. If he wanted to pay, it was fine with me. Besides, if anyone in the world knew how much money I had or didn't have, it was the guy holding the credit card next to me. And if he felt like it made more sense for him to pay than for me to, who was I to argue?

I asked if we could have the gifts wrapped, and the salesman said, "It's too late. As soon as I ring you up, I'm closing the store."

"Could we at least get some wrapping paper from you?" Dennis asked, just as the woman who had been looking through the dolls came up behind us and said, "Oh, you have to ring me up, too. Please."

The salesman, who was slowly punching some numbers into a keypad in front of him—something to do with our credit card—looked up and said, "It's past noon."

"Give her a break," Dennis said, in a friendly way. "It's Christmas. And according to my watch, it's not twelve yet."

The man narrowed his eyes, but he held out his hand and the lady handed him the doll she had chosen. He checked the price tag and hit some buttons on the cash register. "Should have done your shopping earlier," he muttered, to no one in particular.

Like he was doing her a favor taking her money.

"Thank you," the woman said to Dennis. "I'm desperate."

"We know the feeling," he said.

"If he hadn't rung me up, I think I would have grabbed the doll and made a run for it." She laughed and then noticed the toys still on the counter in front of us. "Oh, how cute—I love Eloise. How old is your daughter?"

We both hesitated. The idea of explaining who Celia was and her relationship to both of us . . . well, *I* wasn't going to do it. So I just said, "She's almost four."

"Mine's seven," she said. "She wanted one of these Garden Babies—have you seen them? They're different vegetables, only they're babies? Anyway, I promised her, but then I forgot, and then when I was cleaning up last night, I found this note she'd written to Santa about how much she wanted this doll and how she'd tried to be a good girl all year . . . Well, you know how it is. They break your heart with stuff like that, don't they?"

We must have looked totally blank, because she said, "Maybe that's not the right way to put it, but anyway . . . well, I had to get her one. Her father's trying to hold her off from opening presents until I get back. It took me forever just to find a store that was open."

The salesman said, "Forty-two eighty-five," to her and she handed him her credit card. He ripped our slip out of his keypad machine and ran her card through. He shoved a pen and the slip toward Dennis and pointed at them.

"Wow," I said, "Garden Babies don't come cheap."

"Neither do big Minnie Mouses," Dennis said. He leaned over to sign the slip.

"Minnie Mice," I said.

The woman said, "I know. I'll have to lie to my husband about how much it was. He'd kill me if he knew I spent that much on a single doll." She smiled at Dennis as he stood back up. "Not all fathers understand that some prices are worth paying. You're very lucky," she added, to me.

The salesman had crammed all the gifts except for Minnie into a too-small bag. He handed me the bag and said to Dennis, "The mouse won't fit in a bag."

"That's okay, I'll carry it. But you were going to give us some wrapping paper."

He rolled his eyes but went over to a big roll of green and red paper that was mounted on the wall behind him and pulled a fair amount down, rolling it up as he went. He ripped it off and handed Dennis the wad he'd made.

"Merry Christmas," Dennis said and gave me the paper to hold. He scooped up Minnie in both arms.

The guy didn't answer, just went back to punching at his keypad. Dennis turned to the Garden Baby woman and repeated his Merry Christmas.

She said, "Thank you again. Have a wonderful holiday. I hope your daughter likes her presents."

"Thank you," Dennis said. "Yours, too."

"Merry Christmas," she said, and we took our stuff and left.

Dennis was carrying Minnie Mouse facing him, with his arms around her in a big hug. I said, "Hey, get any more intimate, and you'll have to marry her."

"I wouldn't do that to Mickey. It would break his heart."

"It would never work, anyway. You being different species and all. Speaking of which, for a Jew, you work the Christmas angle pretty well." We reached the car.

He rested Minnie on the sidewalk, and reached into his pocket for his keys. "Yes, well, I've been living in America for thirty-nine years, and I've picked up a few of the native customs."

"Where'd you live before then?"

He stopped, keys in hand, and looked at me. "My mother's stomach." I felt my face turn hot. "Oh, right."

"How old do I look to you?"

"I don't know. I just thought—you know, because you were my father's friend . . . I mean, I assumed—lawyers just always seem—" I hit my head with my hand. "Oh, fuck. Listen, now that I think about it—you look like you're eighteen. A young eighteen. Can I go now?"

He pressed the car remote, the locks sprang up, and he opened the trunk. He picked up Minnie again. "I feel old these days," he said. "Especially after this week." He stuffed Minnie in the trunk and I tossed in the bag of toys and the wrapping paper. He started to close the trunk and stopped. Minnie was lying on her back, smiling up at him. "I feel like a Mafioso," he said. "There's got to be a law against this."

"You could put her in the front seat, and *I* could roll around in the trunk."

"Don't tempt me. Especially after that age thing." He slammed the trunk shut, went around to the passenger door, and opened it for me. I followed him and slid inside. He shut the door and got in the driver's side.

"Seriously, I only said that because you were Richard's friend, so I thought—"

He cut me off. "It's okay. I don't have a lot of ego invested in having people think I'm younger than I am. Or in this case, as young as I actually am. Anyway, when I was your age, I thought anyone over twenty-five was ancient."

"I'm not like that, though. At least, I didn't think I was."

"It's okay," he said again. "Although, after I turn forty—which is only a couple of months away—you might want to avoid the topic of age. Unless you want to see a grown man cry."

"Forty's not that old," I said. "Now sixty . . ."

"Blink your eyes and I'll be sixty," he said. "At least, I'm guessing, since I feel that way about turning forty. You'll see what I mean. You can't help but get old faster than you think you will."

"Not Richard and Alicia," I said.

"No," he said. "They found the one way out."

fourteen

We opened presents soon after Dennis and I got back
with our loot. First I sneaked off and hid Alicia's presents
in a closet before bringing Celia into the living room.
She noticed they were missing, but we were able to distract her with the ones we had just put there.

She actually seemed pretty jazzed by the gifts we'd
just bought her, although my mother's gifts — sparkly
pink nail polish and a rhinestone-studded hairbrush —
were equally well received.

My mother gave me a makeup palette from Chanel.
I opened it, registered what it was, and put it aside without comment.

"It cost a lot," she said, picking it back up. "You could
at least say thank you."

"Thank you," I said. "But you know I don't wear
makeup."

"You could start," she said. "It wouldn't kill you."

"Can I see it?" Celia asked and ended up playing with
it for the next hour. She trashed the makeup and stained
her clothes and the sofa, but at least she was having fun.

Then we ate ham on some water crackers that we

found in the pantry, and Celia got her pink cookie for dessert. After that, we all took turns keeping her busy. Dennis played some board games with her, and then my mother turned on the radio and danced with her. When it was my turn, I took her outside. I wanted to wear her out so that maybe she and I would both sleep well that night. I found a playground ball on the grass, and we kicked it back and forth for a long time. She was surprisingly good at connecting with the ball and liked it when I shouted "score" after every solid kick.

The phone rang while I was outside, and my mother called me to come in. It was Charlotte. She had gotten the machine in my apartment which now had a message telling people to call me at my new number. I told her to come over as soon as she could get away.

By the time Charlotte arrived, we had already ordered in some pizza for dinner. I tried to get Celia to eat a few bites, but by then she was so exhausted that all she could do was whimper about how she didn't want to go to sleep and where was Rosivel anyway? I shoehorned her into her pajamas—no bath again, didn't even try, just wondered when she'd start to smell—and my mother offered to read her books in bed while Charlotte and I talked. Dennis stayed a few more minutes, chatting with us, asking Charlotte about school and stuff like that, and then he took off.

Leaving us alone in the kitchen with a pizza, a couple of glasses of wine, and a sense that everything had changed since we'd last had dinner together.

"I can't believe all this," Charlotte said. "I saw you a *week* ago, and now look."

"You have no idea," I said.

"It's like you're a mom now."

"Don't say that. Please don't say that."

"Well, it is, and you know it. She's cute, though, Livvy. I like her."

"She whined the entire time you were here," I said. "What's to like?"

"She's *cute* with those big eyes and curly hair and all. Don't you think so?"

"I guess. I never paid much attention to little kids before. You think she's cuter than the average kid?"

"She's cuter than my cousin's daughter, who's around the same age. Then again, my cousin's kid is kind of ugly—God, that's a terrible thing to say."

"No, it's not. Why do people think they can't say bad things about small children or dead people?"

"I don't know. Maybe because they can't defend themselves." She ran her finger along the rim of the plate in front of her. "Are you okay, Livvy? I know your father wasn't the most involved dad in the world, but are you okay?"

"I think so. I feel okay. How are *you*? Last time I saw you, you were sobbing into your wineglass."

"That's an exaggeration," she said, pushing the plate away from her. "I was mildly depressed, that's all. He called me, you know."

"You're kidding. When?"

"This morning. Said he wanted to wish me a Merry Christmas. Also wanted to know what I'm doing New Year's Eve."

"Please tell me you told him you're busy."

Charlotte studied the back of her hands as if they were suddenly fascinating. "I told him I wasn't sure what I was doing yet, and I'd call him when I got to town."

I shook my head. "Lottie—"

"Don't get all holier than thou on me, Livvy. Not about this. You don't know what you're talking about."

"That's what you think."

"It's what I know. Unless things have changed a lot since just last week—"

"They have, actually."

She sat up straight. "Are you serious, Livvy? Did you meet someone?"

"I met him a while ago."

"You told me you had nothing going on! You liar!"

"I didn't. It all happened after that night we had dinner."

"How did you have time with all the rest that's been going on?"

"I don't know. Squeezed it in somehow."

"Man, your life is exciting these days. Tell me all about it. Every detail."

"I'm thirsty. You want some water?"

She leaned across the table. "Livvy, I will kill you if you don't tell me exactly what happened this week."

"Did I mention my father died?"

She let out a strangled scream.

I shushed her. "You'll wake up my mother and Celia. Okay, okay, I'm sorry. I'll tell you everything, but I swear, Lottie, if the word *hymen* crosses your lips—"

"Just tell me!"

I told her, as briefly as I could—graduate student, had a section with him, didn't know how things got to where they were, but they did, and now he was away for the break. Slightly longer than that, but not much.

She said, "So you slept with him."

"Yes."

She pointed her chin up in the air and hooted. Her ponytail bobbed behind her. "Welcome to the twenty-first century, my friend. You've left Mary Elizabeth McCarthy eating your dust."

"I don't know about that," I said. "She's a sodomist. Sodomite? Sodomizer?"

"At the rate you're going, give it another week, and you'll have tried that, too."

"Shut up."

"So . . . what does he look like? Is he cute? Of course he is. How did he win you over to our side? I can't believe anyone got past your defenses, Livvy. He must be a *god*."

"He thinks so."

"Come on, lady, give it up. He's cute, isn't he?"

"He thinks so."

"Livvy! I want details! What color are his eyes?"

"Blue. Very blue."

"Okay, now you're gushing. For you, I mean. Hair?"

"Curly brown."

"Body?"

I couldn't help it, I grinned. "Not bad. Not bad at all."

"Do you get it now?" Charlotte asked. "Do you get why it's good in spite of all the bad stuff?"

"I'm starting to."

"Is it—excuse the expression—a *relationship?*"

"I don't think I know what that is exactly."

"Let me see . . . Do you assume you'll see each other every weekend night?"

"I don't know. It hasn't been long enough. Plus he's been out of town."

"Well . . ." She thought for a moment. "Are you going to do something with him on New Year's Eve? Will he be back then?"

"I don't even know. Anyway, I hate New Year's Eve." I thought of something. "Oh, and let's not forget, it's the toughest night of the year to get a baby-sitter. And I'll need one. Can you believe it? I'll need a baby-sitter if I want to go out."

"I'll baby-sit! Of course I'll baby-sit!"

I whipped my head around. My mother was standing in the doorway, her hair rumpled up on one side of her head—poster girl for when good hairspray goes bad—her clothing slightly askew, her mascara-smudged eyes bright with delight. She held out her hands and came toward us. "Oh, Livvy, you have a man in your life! It's so exciting! I'm so incredibly excited!"

I stared at her for a moment, then looked wildly at Charlotte. She saw the desperation on my face and said casually, "Oh, hi, Barbara. We thought you were asleep."

"Asleep? Oh, no, I was just putting Celia to bed. As soon as she fell asleep, I came to find you, and couldn't help overhearing your wonderful news."

"There is no news," I said. "No news at all. I met a guy, but it doesn't mean anything. It's nothing."

She wagged her finger playfully at me. "Say whatever you want now, Livvy, I heard what you were saying to Charlotte." Oh, God, please don't let her have heard *everything.* "And he's cute! I heard you say so. When do I get to meet him?"

"I think he's dead."

"Oh, stop that." She turned to Charlotte. "Are you this bad to your mother, darling? Do you refuse to tell her anything? I have to eavesdrop if I want to know anything about Livvy. She forces me to, never tells me anything. And it's not like I'm judgmental in the least, am I, Livvy? Be fair—aren't I a very accepting mother? I mean, I heard you tell Charlotte you had sex with him, and I'm thrilled! Most girls would kill to have a mother who's that hip."

I stood up. "If anyone needs me, I'll be in the bathroom slitting my wrists."

"Let me help you," said Charlotte, jumping to her feet.

"You can't fool me!" my mother said. "You girls just want to tell secrets."

"No," I said. "I really want to slit my wrists."

We went into Richard's office, and I closed the door. "Fuck," I said. "Fuck, fuck, fuck."

"Oh, come on, it's not such a big deal. You're overreacting."

"Easy for you to say. You don't have to live with . . . you know . . . what you just saw."

"She's happy," said Charlotte. She plumped down into a big leather chair. "Nothing wrong with that."

"It's all wrong," I said, pacing in front of my father's desk. "And this thing with this guy, it's not even going to last."

"Why do you say that?"

"It never does, does it?"

"Well, if you're talking over a lifetime . . . Are you worried he's not going to *marry* you?"

"No, of course not. I don't mean it that way." I stopped, fingered a shapeless blob of painted clay on top of some papers. "It's just . . . this particular guy is known for moving on. Quickly."

"Maybe it'll be different with you. You're not the average girl."

"You say that like it's a good thing. What the hell is this, anyway?" I picked up the thing I was playing with. It looked sort of like a bowl, sort of like an ashtray, sort of like a paperweight, but not really like much of anything. It was painted unevenly in different colors that had run together and turned a muddy brown on the lower half. "It looks like something a kid would make."

"Yeah? Celia probably made it, don't you think?"

"Oh, right. I was thinking he bought it. God, I wouldn't have expected Richard to keep something ugly around just because—" I stopped and shrugged. "Whatever."

Lottie said, "Anyway, if he does break up with you—or you with him—then you just tell your mother and that's that. With the added advantage of totally disappointing her, which you know you'd enjoy. Being a heartless bitch and all."

I put the pottery blob back on the desk. "I just think some things should remain private. Like, for example . . . everything."

"That's what makes being with you such fun, Livvy. The fact that you don't tell anyone anything."

"Yeah, well, look what happened when I told you stuff tonight. My mother heard everything—the one person I wouldn't want to know about it."

"Your problem is that your mother has no life, so she's overinvolved in yours. Did you hear how fast she offered to baby-sit on New Year's Eve? That's a woman with no life." Charlotte tapped her finger on her chin. "You need to find her a boyfriend. Or a career." She paused. "No, definitely a boyfriend."

"Believe me, I would if I could a thousand times over."

"What about that guy who was here? The lawyer. He was cute."

"Cute?"

"I mean for someone that age. He has nice eyes. And all his hair. Any interest there?"

"I think she'd be interested. I'm not so sure about *him*. He's younger than she is, for one thing. He's not even forty yet."

"How old's your mom?"

I had to think about it. "God, she lies about it every time someone asks her. The last time I did the math, she was like ten when she had me. But I think she's actually somewhere around forty-five or forty-six."

"That's not too old for a forty-year-old guy. Plenty of couples these days have bigger age differences. My boyfriend's father, for example—"

"Ex-boyfriend," I said.

She shrugged and went on. "He's twenty years older than his new wife. She's closer in age to Evan than she is to his dad."

"Now there's a savory thought."

Charlotte grinned. "Yeah, and apparently she's not uninterested. In Evan, I mean. Dropped her towel in front of him once. You know, like, 'Oops, am I naked?' He said he was incredibly embarrassed. But not interested."

"That proves my point—men don't like older women. An age difference only works the other way around."

"Think outside the box, Livvy. Just because our society is sexist doesn't mean you have to be. And there's no yuck factor with your mom—she's still beautiful, has a great figure, and since she lies about her age, he doesn't even have to know she's a little bit older."

"All right, you've convinced me," I said. "They should get married and live happily ever after. Do you tell them or do I?"

"There's no reason you can't help it along," she said. "Leave them alone the next time he comes over. Make sure your mom is looking her best—offer to do her hair or makeup or something."

"I'll have to buy a trowel."

"Gee, Livvy," Charlotte said, "I'm getting the feeling you're not taking me seriously."

"No, I am, I am," I said, leaning back on the edge of the desk. "It's not a bad idea in some ways. It's just . . . He's actually a good guy, and he doesn't have a bad sense of humor."

"Sounds like stepdad material to me."

"Yeah, but . . . my mother? Isn't that cruel and unusual punishment? What has the poor guy ever done to us?"

She shook her head. "You feel that way because she's your mom. I say again: she's beautiful, she has a great figure, and I think she's very sweet. In her own way."

"Her own insanely stupid way."

"She may not be a rocket scientist, but in my experience, men aren't looking for brains."

"What are they looking for? In your experience?"

"Hey, you've had your own little fling now. You tell me—what is it about you that made your graduate student go nuts?"

"Actually, I think it *was* my brains. He hated me until I got an A on a paper. It's more complicated than that, but still . . ."

Charlotte threw up her hands. "Well, there goes my theory. Maybe I should go home and read some Plato or something."

"Don't strain your pretty little head," I said. "I'm sure you have a lot to offer some undiscriminating young man."

"Watch it," she said, "or I'll tell your mom you told me you're really, really in love. Are you, by the way?"

"If I ever say anything like 'I'm really, really in love,' will you shoot me? Please?"

"Still the same old Livvy. Except for the broken hymen."

I ran across the room and threw open the door. "That's it. You're out of here."

"I have to go anyway," she said and got up. "Do you know my parents actually wait up for me when I'm home for the holidays? And ream me out if I'm later than I said I'd be? It's unbelievable. Like I'm not entirely on my own the other three hundred and sixty days of the year."

I leaned against the doorway. "Aw, it's sweet. You're still their ickle baby girl."

"Yeah, and your mother loves you, too. She's probably on the phone right now to all her friends bragging about how you finally had sex with a boy."

I groaned. "Maybe Celia's lucky. Growing up without parents."

She shook her head. "No, that sucks, too. There's no good solution. . . . Anyway, what are your plans for the next few days? I haven't decided when I'm heading back up north yet."

"Bet you anything it'll be before New Year's Eve."

She smiled. A cozy little smile. "Maybe."

"For a smart girl, Lottie, you can be an idiot."

After I'd closed the door on Charlotte, who promised to come again the next day and take a ride with me in the Lexus convertible I'd discovered in the garage, I went looking for my mother. I couldn't find her anywhere. I glanced in all the rooms. Celia was still sound asleep, her legs hanging off the side of the bed.

I checked out the kitchen and even the inside of the pantry. No mother. So I headed up the stairs—in addition to the ones in the library, there was a spiral stairway behind the kitchen—and called for her. She called back, telling me she was in the bedroom up there.

When I walked into the master suite, I found my mother lying on the bed, under the covers, watching TV.

"You look comfortable," I said.

"I thought I should just go ahead and get settled in this room," she said. "Is that okay? It makes sense, doesn't it? You need to be downstairs, close to Celia, and, anyway, this room isn't right for you. It has all of Richard and Alicia's things, and I know that would make you uncomfortable."

"But not you."

"I'm used to living with Richard's things," she said. "I did it for years."

"I guess that's true."

"He slept on the left side when we were married, too. I guess he liked it there." She looked around the room. "Sometime soon, we'll have to go through all of their things, you know. Alicia had some beautiful clothing. We should save the good pieces for Celia, like the dress Alicia wore to their wedding. Remember that? It was an Armani, very beautiful, although I wouldn't have chosen it to get married in—it was so dark. Well, maybe she knew what she was getting herself into." She smoothed the cover on the bed. "Isn't this quilt gorgeous? I don't always agree with Alicia's taste, but I love the way she did this room, especially the colors. Oh, and I love the two bathrooms. Brilliant. If Richard and I had had two bathrooms, we might still be married."

"Then you would have died in the car crash," I said.

She thought briefly then shook her head. "No, life doesn't work that way. Oh, Livvy, I hope it's okay—I already emptied out a few drawers in one of the dressers so I could put some of my things away. I had to take Alicia's underthings out and put them in a paper bag. Her lingerie is gorgeous. What do you think we should do with it all? Do you want it? Or we could donate it somewhere, I guess."

"We'll figure that out later," I said.

"Poor baby, you sound tired. Where will you sleep tonight?"

"I don't know."

"I'm tired, too. It was sleeping on the sofas last night. It wore us all out. You could set up a bed in one of the guest rooms. Just make sure you're close enough to Celia to hear her if she calls out. Poor little thing. Every time I think about her, my heart breaks. You know what? Maybe you should think about sleeping in her room for the next night or two. You could put some blankets on the floor. I'm sure you'll be comfortable—there's a nice thick carpet." She suddenly sat up and reached over to the night table. "Oh, and Livvy, I didn't even tell you the best part!"

"The best part?"

She picked up a book and showed it to me. "I've been reading this wonderful Grisham thriller, and I forgot and left my copy at home. I was so mad at myself—I was halfway through it and I was dying to know how it ended, but I didn't want to drive all the way back to my apartment to get it. And look, Alicia was reading it, too, and left it right here! It's like she left it just for me! Of course, she had read a little more than I had—it's not like we were on the same page or anything weird like that—but still . . . There's something very right about all of this, Livvy. I can feel it."

"Can you?"

"Oh, yes. Don't you think it's almost as if Alicia was welcoming me into her house, telling me it's okay for me to be here, that she wants me to be here?" She put the book down and lay back against the pillows. "You know I've always been very interested in matters of the spirit. I don't want to be too New Agey or anything about this, but . . . You would have expected her to take that book with her on vacation, wouldn't you? But here it is, waiting for me."

"Great," I said. "That's all just great."

"It is, isn't it?" she said. "And, no matter what, it's just so nice to be able to finish the book I was reading."

I nodded and went back downstairs.

I was exhausted after two nights of not enough sleep and didn't really want to camp out on Celia's floor. I looked for, and found, a better place.

The house had originally had three large bedrooms off of the back hallway downstairs. One was now Celia's, one had been converted to Richard's office, and the third was a guest room/sitting room kind of thing that no one seemed to use much. There had also been an original master bedroom at the end of the hallway. That had been rebuilt into the library, which led upstairs, which led to the new master bedroom where my mother was happily reading a dead woman's book.

There was a daybed in the spare room. I pulled off the velvet covers and tufted cushions and discovered the bed had no real sheets or blankets underneath. I found those in the closet and made the bed. By the time I did that, it was eleven o'clock, and I was so tired I was stumbling over my own feet. The bathroom off the room didn't have Alicia's usual luxurious touch—it was plain white with simple fixtures and no bath, just a shower—but it was still a lot nicer than the one in my apartment that I'd had to share with two other girls and a few hundred ants.

I got ready for bed and fell asleep within minutes of closing my eyes.

A few hours later, I woke up, my heart pounding. I wasn't sure why I had woken up until I heard the second shriek. I went running into Celia's room. She was sitting up in bed, her face screwed up, tears on her cheeks. She kept screaming, and I came over to her and held her and tried to get her to calm down. She kept sobbing out something I couldn't understand, something about a "ginch" or a "kinch" or something like that.

When I finally got her calm enough to talk, I asked her if she'd had a bad dream.

"Yes! The Ginch. He was looking at me. He was green!" She rubbed her snotty face against my shoulder.

"Who was? Who was green?"

"The Ginch, the Ginch! In the movie!"

It suddenly hit me: green face, movie, ginch. Of course. "You mean the Grinch?"

"Yes!" she sobbed. "The Ginch! He's green, and he was looking at me."

"Oh, but the Grinch isn't bad, Celia. He's nice deep down. He only looks mean."

"He's scary!"

"Yes, he is." Who the hell had let her watch that movie, anyway?

Although, come to think of it, the book was kind of scary, too, and it was a kid's book. "But he's not here now, Celia. It was just a dream. See? Everything's fine."

"Where's Rosivel? Where's my mommy?"

"They're not here. But I am. Do you want me to stay here with you for a little while?"

"Not a little while. A long time."

"Okay. A long time. Now lie down." I helped her lie down and tucked her in. Her arms went around my neck and squeezed so hard I thought I was going to choke. She pulled my head down against her shoulder. I was choking and my back was breaking.

"Hold on," I said. "Just let go for a second." I managed to pry her arms off of me. I lay down next to her. She immediately moved her head to be right against mine but misjudged the distance and knocked my forehead with hers so hard it hurt. I moved my head away but then she moved hers, knocking into me again, so I sighed and just let her stay like that, her head hard against mine.

So then there was no way I could sleep, balancing on the edge of her bed, my head flattened by hers, her breath loud and uneven in my ear . . .

I stared at the ceiling, which was dark and green in the dim glow of the night-light, and wondered what I was doing there.

Celia's breathing grew regular after a while, and I figured she had fallen asleep. I started to get up, but she immediately stirred, cried out, "No!", grabbed at me, and pulled me back down. This happened two more times over the next half hour, until I just gave up on escaping and tried to make myself comfortable on her bed. At some point, what felt like hours later, I guess I did actually fall asleep. I woke up again, squashed and sore, and slid slowly and quietly off of the bed. This time she didn't wake up, but I didn't think I should leave her all alone again.

So in the end, I slept on the floor of her room, just like my mother had said I should.

fifteen

My mother answered the phone when Joe called, a few days later, to say he was back in town. Like Charlotte, he had gotten my new number off the answering machine in my apartment.

Rosivel had left for the day, and I was sitting at the kitchen table, eating dinner with Celia. My mother winked wildly at me while she asked Joe his name and told him she'd "check to see if Olivia can come to the phone."

Mildly alarmed by the faces my mother was making, Celia said, "What's wrong with Barbara?" and I said, "Oh, so many things, Celia. So many things."

My mother put her hand over the receiver—she had never learned to use either the hold button or the mute—and in a loud stage whisper said, "Livvy, it's Joe. He's the *one*, isn't he?" I stood up, but she put her other hand out, holding me off. "Not yet! Make him wait—you don't want to seem too eager."

"What cave did you crawl out of?" I said and grabbed the phone.

Then I talked to Joe. It was strange, hearing his voice again. It felt wrong, in that house, with Celia behind me complaining that the only vegetables she liked were carrots and potatoes, and peas weren't either carrots or potatoes so she wouldn't eat them.

"Where are you?" Joe asked, after we'd said hello. "Who's the kid?"

"No one," I said and walked with the phone out of the kitchen and into the hallway. "How was your Christmas?"

"You really want to know?"

"Sure. Why not?"

"Well, Christmas Eve, my mother took a few too many of her quote unquote pain pills and decided it was time 'we all told the truth for once, goddamn it.' At which point, my father left the house and didn't come back for hours, at which point my mother convinced herself that he had crashed the car and killed himself, at which point she sobbed until he showed up again, at which point she threw a fruitcake at him. Meanwhile, my brother and his girlfriend couldn't keep their hands off of each other and I'm talking X-rated in front of the parents, and my little sister kept screaming that we'd all ruined her life, and she would never be able to have a normal relationship thanks to us."

"Oh," I said.

"All in all, I'd say it was one of our happier family get-togethers. No blood spilled. How was yours?"

"Comparatively uneventful."

A pause. "And that's all I'm going to get, isn't it? So when do I get to see you?"

"Tonight, if you like."

"Eager little girl, aren't you? Should I come pick you up? Where are you?"

"I'll come get you," I said. "I want you to see this car I've been driving."

"Why? Is it new?"

"Sort of. Hold on a second." At least *I* knew how to use the hold button. I walked back into the kitchen. "Hey, Barbara, can you stay with Celia tonight while I go out?"

"Can I? Of course I can. Of course I will. But be sure to make him come get you. The man should always pick up the woman. Anyway, I want to meet him." She turned to Celia. "We want to meet Livvy's boyfriend, don't we, darling?"

"And that's why you're not meeting him," I said. "Because you'd call him my boyfriend." I got back on with Joe. "What time should I pick you up?"

"I like this. You're taking charge. I like a woman who takes charge."

"You'll like me even better when you see this car," I said.

As the garage door opened, I could see Dennis walking up the circular driveway. He had made it a habit to stop by every evening on his way home from work. I couldn't tell whether he was just being a nice guy, or whether he didn't trust me to take care of Celia. Fine with me either way—I liked having someone around who could play with Celia after Rosivel left. My mother was always asking Dennis to fix things, like lightbulbs that needed replacing or phones that weren't working, but he didn't know any more about that stuff than I did, and already I'd made a couple of calls to the plumber and electrician to take care of things neither of us could fix.

Dennis saw me now and changed direction, coming toward the garage. I waited for him, car keys in my hand, and when he was in earshot said, "Hi."

"You coming in or going out?"

"Going out. I figure Celia's old enough to take care of herself for an evening."

"I assume your mother's with her."

"Can't fool you for a second, can I?"

"You driving the convertible?" He frowned.

"I was planning to. Is that a problem?"

"Only from a safety standpoint."

I laughed. "It's a well-built car, Dennis. State of the art. With airbags and everything."

"A car's only as safe as its driver. A twenty-one-year-old driving a convertible doesn't sound like a good idea. I also don't think you should have the top down after dark."

"I'm driving from here to Westwood. It's not exactly east LA."

"Just keep to the speed limit, will you? And wear a seat belt."

"No problem," I said. "Any other requests, Jiminy? Shall I call home every hour? Brake for children? Be home by ten?"

"Yes," he said, "all those things. And while you're mouthing off to me, I might point out it's within my jurisdiction as executor of Richard's estate to sell this car."

"Yes, sir," I said, saluting. "Sir, you're the boss, sir."

"That's better. Where are you going, anyway?"

"Out with a friend," I said.

"Charlotte?"

"No."

He waited for a moment, but I didn't say anything else. Then he said, "I'll go see if I can help out. How's Celia?"

"She's good. She spent the whole day with Rosivel, actually. Made my life easy."

"Why? What were you doing?"

"I don't know. I read a little, I guess. Napped. Looked through some of that paperwork you keep throwing at me. Went for a walk. My vacation's almost over, you know. Just a few more days."

"At least you had one."

"Yeah." The only day he'd taken off had been Christmas.

Dennis said, "I know it's easy to just let Rosivel take Celia when she's around, but you might want to still . . . you know, pay some attention."

"I'm around," I said. "It's not like I'm taking off for Hawaii. Anyway, Rosivel's much better at taking care of Celia than I am."

"Maybe. But she needs to feel connected to you. And since you're not in school now, it seems like a good time to get to know each other."

"We have plenty of time together." I rattled the keys in my hand. "And Rosivel is wonderful with Celia, really wonderful. They have a great time together. Compared to her, there's not much I can offer."

"True," he said. "You're not intelligent, interesting, or capable of affection."

"Yeah, well, we're in agreement there."

He sighed and stepped back. "Go, have fun with your friend, Olivia.

Just think about what I said. I'm not begrudging you your free time. I just want you to realize this is an important commitment you've made."

"An important commitment you forced me into, you mean." I threw myself into the car and slammed the door, then roared out of the garage before he'd even made it inside. I deliberately sped down the street, knowing he was watching me.

I was pissed off. There I was, on my way out of the House of Horrors for the first time in what felt like forever, ready for a quick visit to my former life, and Dennis had to go and perform his usual guilt trip on me. Hadn't I been good all week? Hadn't I slept on the floor of Celia's room and comforted her when she woke in the night? Yes, I was enormously relieved whenever Rosivel walked through the front door, but I bet no more than any mother who was lucky enough to have a babysitter. I hadn't been irresponsible or negligent. Dennis should have been congratulating me, not making more demands.

I pulled over so I could put the top down—it was a thing of beauty the way the mechanism worked—and chewed on my fingernails while it settled into place. Fuck responsibility. And to hell with Dennis Klein.

I drove to Joe's.

I buzzed up for him, and when he picked up the phone, I told him to come down and see my car, which was illegally parked in the red zone in front of his building.

"I was hoping you'd come up," he said. "It's been a long time since—"

"I'll be waiting in front," I said and hung up.

I was leaning against the car when he came down. He gave a low whistle.

"Was that for the car or me?" I said.

"The two of you together," he said. "You make a purty picture." He approached me, then stopped and folded his arms across his chest. "I get it. We're not the hugging type, are we?"

"No, we're not," I said.

"Am I allowed to say it's good to see you?"

"Sure."

"It's good to see you."

"Thanks. Want to go for a ride?"

"Yes," he said. "But only in a manner of speaking. Come upstairs with me."

"After I show off the car."

"I like the car," he said, "but I want to be alone with you in my bedroom. Is that so much to ask?"

I turned and opened the passenger door. "Get in," I said and went around to the driver's side. He probably thought I was making him wait just to torture him, or make him want it more or something. But it had nothing to do with him, really, I just wanted to prove to myself that I could wait. And it wasn't easy.

"This is a very cool car," he said after we'd been driving for a few minutes. "Is it yours?"

"Kind of."

"Meaning?"

"I get to use it, but I didn't buy it."

"Whose is it?"

"It was my father's. Or his wife's. I'm actually not sure which."

"It smells brand-new," he said.

"Yeah. I think maybe it was a Christmas present for one of them or something. I don't know. It doesn't have plates yet."

"So this dead father thing . . . it's not all bad?"

"I like the car," I said. "But it comes with—" I stopped.

"What?"

"I like the car," I said again.

We were silent a moment. Have I mentioned I loved driving that car? I was on Sunset now, going pretty fast, and it handled all the curves beautifully. It felt great, like there was something alive under my hands, only I was controlling it. My shitty old Toyota never felt like that.

I looked over and Joe was watching me.

He said, "You miss me?"

"Not really. I was busy."

"You keep lying like that, your nose will grow."

Funny, his making a Pinocchio reference. I said, "That's okay. Jiminy Cricket's watching out for me."

"I know you missed me," he said. "You couldn't wait to see me to-night. Come on, let's go back to my place. Or to your place. Or to a hotel. Hell, one of these bucket seats will do—they're leather and I'm not picky."

"So I've heard."

He put his hand on my knee. "Come on, Olivia. You're making me crazy. It's been too long."

"Five days," I said. "That's not so long."

"Five days can be an eternity," he said. "Like if you're at home with my parents, and you're spending the whole time wishing you were with this girl you've only just fucked for the first time."

"First two times," I said, "if I remember correctly."

"Yeah, you remember correctly."

"Okay," I said. "We're near my old place. My roommates should still be gone. Let's go there." It would give me a chance to check my mail and messages, anyway. And it would be my turf, not his.

"Fine," he said. "And if they are there . . . the more the merrier. That Betsy's a cute girl."

"But she doesn't trust you," I said.

"So? What does trust have to do with getting down and dirty?"

"Nothing, I guess."

"Damn right."

"I just love these intellectual debates," I said, "don't you?"

He squeezed my knee. "It's good to see you, Olivia."

I had forgotten what a mess I'd left my room in. Trying to pack and figure out what to take to my father's . . . It looked like the wreck from some natural disaster, with clothes hanging from half-emptied drawers and boxes, some shampoo spilled on the corner of the rug, the bed torn apart, the sheets halfway off . . .

We stood side by side in the doorway between the living room and my bedroom, our shoulders touching. We had both stopped when we'd gotten a load of the chaos. I remembered how Joe's apartment had been neat as a pin. I looked at him and he had a funny sort of disgusted look on his face, his nose squinching up. The room didn't smell bad or anything—actually, with the spilled shampoo, it smelled kind of flowery and nice—but he looked like it did.

"Forget it," I said, turning. "Bad idea. Let's go back to your place."

"Too late," he said, taking my upper arm in a strong grip that hurt and pushing me into the room. "We're here, and I'm not waiting any longer. Make the bed."

"You've got to be kidding."

"Make it, Olivia."

I jerked my arm away from him. "Make it yourself."

He went over to the bed and dragged all of the covers right off of it, so they landed in a heap on the floor, and the bottom sheet was laid bare. "Come here."

"You keep giving me orders, like I'm going to obey them."

"Come here, like I know you want to."

"I feel like a cup of coffee," I said and turned to leave the room.

He was on me in a second, spinning me around, bending me back, his mouth searching for mine, hot and eager. It didn't take long for me to give in. He knew as well as I did that I didn't want any coffee.

But, still, he had come to me, not me to him. It was only a distance of a few feet, but it was something. Wasn't it?

Yeah, cling to that, Livvy. You little moron.

We were lying in bed afterward, and my heart was still racing when the phone rang. I was so startled to hear my line ring that I actually answered it without thinking.

"Livvy? Thank goodness you're there! I was worried you wouldn't be, but then I thought, how could it hurt to try? So I did, but I really think you need to get a cell phone. Although they're now saying that cell phones should be illegal when you're driving, but what do you do if it rings while you're on the road? I mean, it could be an emergency, and then you'd answer it and then, what? You get arrested?"

"Barbara. Barbara. Stop talking for a second. Concentrate. Why are you calling me? It better be important."

"I'm sorry to bother you, Livvy, I really am. Are you with your boy-friend? Tell him I'm sorry, too. I wouldn't if it weren't kind of an emer-gency."

"What is it? Is Celia okay?"

"Well, she's crying. A lot. She says she won't go to sleep until you're here. She's very upset that you went out without saying good-bye to her."

Hadn't I said good-bye to her? She had been watching TV, and I had been rushing from the shower to the door . . . Well, anyway, I thought she knew I was going out. And what difference did it make? My mother and Dennis were there. "Tell her I'll be back soon."

"I did. I've told her and told her. She said she's scared to go to sleep without you."

"Can't you lie down next to her until she falls asleep?"

"I tried. She said I smelled like cigarettes."

"Do you?"

"She has to have the strongest sense of smell in the world. One little cigarette two hours ago, Livvy. Honestly."

"She's let you put her to bed before."

"Yes, but the last few nights, you did it. Maybe it's become a habit."

"Great. That'll teach me to be nice. Where is she now?"

"She's right here. She wants to talk to you."

"All right. Put her on."

Celia's voice, then. Thick with mucus and self-pity. "Livvy? I want you to come home. Now."

"I'll be back soon," I said. I was aware of Joe watching me, eyes narrowed as he tried to figure out what was going on. I sat up and turned my back on him. "What are you getting all worked up about?"

"I want you," she said, her voice breaking. "The Ginch is going to come back, I know it. You have to come sleep here. And you didn't say good-bye. I thought you were here and I called for you and Barbara said you weren't here. You didn't say good-bye."

"I'm sorry," I said. "I forgot. I'll be back soon and then I'll come sleep in your room. Just wait for me. Is Dennis still there?"

"Yes," she said. "He's right here."

"Well, you know Dennis is the best Grinch-fighter in all the world. He's won awards for it, and everything."

"Really?"

"Yeah, really. He's the number one guy. People call him all the time to come fight the Grinch, or they would if the Grinch existed, which we know he doesn't. Right?" Nice save, Olivia.

"I don't know," Celia said, with some justification.

"Yeah, well, anyway, tell him to sit and watch for the Grinch while you go to sleep — even though there's no Grinch to watch for — and he'll stay until I get there. He'll be my deputy."

"What's a deputy?"

"Someone who does your job for you when you can't do it. Can Dennis be my deputy tonight?"

"When will you be back?"

"I don't know. Not much longer. And as soon as I get back, I'll come check on you and go to sleep in your room. Until then, Dennis can watch out for the Grinch."

She took a deep, quivering breath. "Well, okay, but *you* have to tell him."

"No, you."

"No, you."

"All right."

Dennis came on the phone. "What's this about the Grinch?"

"Celia's scared of him. I told her you'd watch out for him while she goes to sleep. Do you mind? Just sit by her bed until she falls asleep."

"I tried that before, and she just wanted you."

"I think she'll let you now. If not, call me back here."

"All right. I'm sorry we had to interrupt your date."

"It's okay," I said. "Don't worry about it. I'll be back soon."

"Don't rush. I didn't even want to call you, but your mother was worried."

"It's all right," I said. "Call me if she falls apart. Celia, that is. If my mother falls apart, leave me out of it."

I hung up the phone and leaned back against the pillows.

"Well?" Joe said. "Are you going to explain that conversation, or should I just assume that you have a child somewhere you've never told me about?"

"Yes and yes," I said. I leaned over to the side and dragged my blanket back up on the bed and covered myself with it. "She's my father's daughter by his second wife. When they both died, I inherited her, along with the Lexus convertible. Actually, I'm not sure the Lexus is really mine. Celia is, though."

Joe sat up. "Are you serious? What do you mean she's yours?"

"I'm her legal guardian."

"Holy shit."

"Yep."

"What's she like? Do you like her?"

"I don't know her that well," I said. "I barely said two words to her before this week. She's okay. She's kind of cute, and nice and warm when you cuddle with her."

"You make her sound like a stuffed animal. Or a dog."

"No, a dog would be less work."

"Are you living with her? Is that why the new phone number?"

I explained the living arrangement.

"And who's Dennis?" Joe asked. He leaned back against the pillows and folded his arms behind his head. You could see the muscles working in his shoulders. "I heard you say something about a Dennis."

"He's a lawyer. Friend of my father's. Also the executor of the will." I hugged my legs to my chest and rested my chin on my knees.

"So you're a mom now," Joe said, idly reaching to pull at a strand of my hair. "Here I was thinking you were just a carefree kid, years to go before you got the urge to procreate."

"Yeah, me, too," I said. I shifted away from his hand. "What time is it, anyway?"

He looked at his watch. "Nine-thirty. Do you need to go?"

"Soon."

"It sounded like you were needed back at the ranch."

"Soon," I said again.

There was a pause. He said, "How does this affect school and everything?"

"It doesn't," I said. "I'll be back."

"What about your social life? Such as it is."

"Such as it is," I repeated. "What about it?"

"You going to be stuck at home a lot? With the kid?"

"I'm here, aren't I?"

"Yes." He ran his finger along my shoulder. "How about New Year's Eve? I was going to see if you wanted to go with me to a friend's place. He's having a party. But if you want to ring in the New Year with the little one . . ."

What had Charlotte said about New Year's Eve? That assuming we'd be together meant we had a relationship of some sort? Something like that. I said, "I can go, but I don't know if I want to. What kind of party? Will people be drunk and throwing up at the stroke of midnight?"

"If you don't like it, we can always sneak out," he said. "There are better things to be doing at the stroke of midnight, anyway. I wonder if anyone's ever had an orgasm that spanned two different years . . ."

"I've never liked New Year's Eve much," I said. "I just don't get why people care about it."

"That's because you've never had a date on New Year's Eve," he said. I was silent. He was right about the never having a date part.

"Give it a try," he said. "You can always zoom home in your convertible."

"All right."

He pulled at my shoulder until I fell back against him. "Little Olivia is a mommy," he said. "Who'd have figured?" His hand moved under the sheet and curled around my breast. "Such a cute little mommy she is, too." His fingers tightened.

I should have told him to shut the fuck up, but I liked what he was doing with his hand, so I didn't say anything.

sixteen

When I got back to the house, I found my mother asleep on the sofa in the family room, flat on her back, with the TV still on. I was always finding her asleep in random places around the house, at all times of the day and night, which probably explained the insomnia she liked to complain about. She slept so well *out* of her bed, she just didn't need all that much sleep once she was in it.

I went to check on Celia. She was also sound asleep in her bed, and Dennis was sacked out beside her. He was still in his suit pants and dress shirt, and his black shoes were neatly lined up on the floor next to the bed. Celia had thrown out her arms and legs, starlike, which left Dennis crammed against the wall with barely a third of the narrow twin bed to call his own. Still, he had managed to fall asleep, so I guess it couldn't have been too uncomfortable. Or maybe he was just that tired.

I tried to leave quietly, but the room was dark and my foot struck an electronic toy that said, "Hello! Let's play!"

I swore out loud, and Dennis sat up.

"Sorry," I whispered. At least Celia hadn't woken up. "Go back to sleep."

"No, no," he said, hoarsely, looking around, confused. "I didn't mean to . . . I've got to get home."

Celia had a bed rail on the open side of the bed, to keep her from falling out, and it turned her bed into a sort of cage. Dennis had to move to a crouching position and scuttle, crablike, toward the foot of the bed, where he was able to roll over the footboard and onto his feet with a thud. It wasn't graceful but it got him out. And Celia didn't wake up.

"Don't forget your shoes," I said. As he reached down to grab them, he almost lost his balance. He caught himself against the bed and followed me out of the room.

I left the door partly open, having learned the hard way that Celia flipped out if she woke up and the door was closed.

In the hallway, I said, "Did you enjoy your nap?"

He yawned. "Actually, I did. Any sleep is good sleep, as far as I'm concerned."

We went into the kitchen. Dennis sat down and started to pull on his shoes. He said, "I have no idea when I fell asleep. I was just keeping her company and then . . . What time is it, anyway?"

"Ten-thirty."

"Jesus, it's been over an hour. . . . I've got to get home." He looked around, rubbing his neck. "I think I twisted something. . . . Where's your mother? Did she go to bed?"

"Sort of. She fell asleep on the sofa."

"Her, too, huh?" He finished and sat back, blinking.

I was getting myself a glass of water. I held up the glass and said, "You want some?"

"Sure." I brought over the glass I'd already poured and handed it to him. He thanked me and drank. While I was filling another glass for myself, he said, "You smell good. In an oddly masculine sort of way."

I stiffened and didn't say anything. I wasn't crazy about the fact that Joe wore cologne, but I didn't consider it a topic of conversation.

Apparently, he did. "Your mother tells me you have a boyfriend."

"My mother overstates things," I said. Something about that word—

boyfriend—rubbed me the wrong way. Maybe because it didn't fit with whatever it was that Joe was. Maybe because I knew how much Joe would hate to hear himself referred to that way.

At least, I assumed he would.

Dennis wasn't giving up. "So . . . who is he? Does he go to school with you?"

"With me? No. But the prison lets you take courses on-line, so I'm sure he'll get his high school diploma before he comes up for parole."

"Funny," Dennis said. "Do I get the real story?"

I leaned back against the counter. "He's just some guy I've gone out with a couple of times. Barbara gets a little overexcited about these kinds of things."

"Does it ever occur to you, Olivia, that people might have a right to take an interest in your personal life?"

"People?" I repeated. "Like you and my mom, for example?"

"Yes."

I shook my head. "Nope. No one has that right."

"Not even your own mother?"

"She's not the one sitting here asking questions right now, is she?"

Now it was his turn to stiffen. "Good point." He took another sip of water and put down his glass. "I should go."

I said, "But if it were—my mother, I mean—I still wouldn't want to talk about this stuff. It's a waste of time. It's not . . . meaningful."

He started to say something, then he stopped. Then, after a moment, he said, "Celia was pretty distraught tonight. She really missed you."

"I'm sorry about that," I said, "but it wasn't like I left her here with some stranger or something. She knows you and my mother almost as well as she knows me. And it's the first time I've gone out at night since moving in—"

"Whoa," he said, raising his hand. "Don't get defensive. I wasn't criticizing."

"That's a first."

"I was going to say that I'm impressed that she's so attached to you already. I think that's a good thing, even if it makes your life a little more difficult from time to time."

"I don't think it's that she's attached to me so much as she's terrified of the Grinch."

"She wasn't asking for Rosivel tonight," Dennis said, "or for her mother. She was asking for you. I was glad."

"Except I wasn't here."

"You're allowed to have a personal life."

"Which was exactly my point at the beginning of this conversation."

"I guess that's true. Anyway, I'm sorry if I seem overly critical to you. I just worry about Celia. And you. About both of you."

"Yeah, well, you probably should."

"This is the hardest part you're going through right now, Olivia. It's going to get better." He sat up suddenly. "Oh, and I am getting together some names of child psychologists for you. I haven't forgotten—I've been asking around. You'd be amazed how many people in my office have used one. I don't know if we have an unusually high percentage of kids with problems, or just of overanxious parents. Either way, I'm guessing it has something to do with all the hours lawyers spend working instead of being at home with their loved ones."

"Who *are* your loved ones, Dennis?"

He looked startled. "Mine? I told you before, I don't really have any. I mean, my parents and my sister, but—"

"You don't really like them."

"I didn't say that."

"Did you work too much when you were married?"

"Olivia, why is it okay for you to ask me personal questions but not for me to ask you any?"

"Do you *mind* my asking?"

"Not really. I'm not like you—I think it's nice for people to take an interest."

"Well, that's the difference then, isn't it? You don't mind, and I do."

"And you mind because—?"

I shrugged. "I don't know. I guess I've just gotten used to keeping my thoughts to myself."

"Habits can be broken. And usually should be."

I put my water glass down hard on the counter. "Jesus Christ," I said.

"Look where I'm living, look who I'm living with. Aren't I sharing enough here? Can't I even keep my fucking thoughts to myself?"

He put his hands up. "Calm down," he said. "I'm sorry. You're right. You keep your privacy and I'll keep mine. If we get bored we can always talk about the weather."

"And Celia," I said. "We can talk about her."

"She's in the public domain?"

"Something like that."

"All right," Dennis said, "we'll talk about Celia and the weather." A pause. "It's been unusually cold out, don't you think?"

"That's none of your fucking business," I said.

He laughed, but pretty soon after that he got up to leave.

I was brushing my teeth when my mother appeared in the bathroom doorway.

"You're back!" she said. "I thought I heard you in here. When did you get back? You must have sneaked right past me."

I ran some water into my hand, took a sip, then leaned forward to rinse and spit. I lifted my head and looked at her in the mirror. "You were sound asleep."

"I wasn't asleep. I was watching TV in the family room."

"With your eyes closed and your mouth snoring."

"I wasn't asleep," she said. "Did Dennis leave?"

"A few minutes ago."

"He waited up for you! How sweet. Although he might have said good-bye to me—"

"Probably didn't want to wake you up."

"I wasn't asleep. You know, I really think Dennis feels in some ways like a father toward you and Celia. He really seems to care a lot about both of you."

"He's just worried I'm going to screw up."

"I think he's a very nice man."

"Yeah, he's nice," I said. I pushed past her and went back into the sitting room.

"The way he comes here all the time . . . very nice. He does come a lot, doesn't he?" I didn't say anything. She was looking at herself in the bathroom mirror. She reached up and smoothed out her hair. "You know, Livvy, I may be an old witch now, but in my day, I wasn't bad."

I sighed, then gave her what she wanted. "Your day isn't over yet, Barbara. You're around the same age as a lot of really sexy movie stars. Like Sharon Stone. You look a lot like Sharon Stone. Only better."

"I would never cut my hair that short. I don't like short hair on women. You know whose hair is too short now?"

"I'm guessing Sharon Stone's."

"Well, yes, but that's not who I meant. Lindsey Patrick's. Remember her? My friend from my modeling days?"

"Do I remember her? I talked to her less than a week ago, Barbara. She called after Richard died, and you were in the room with me when I got the phone. You told me to tell her you were too upset to talk to anyone."

"Oh, right. Anyway, she went and cut all her hair off. I'm sure *she* thinks it's chic . . ." She rolled her eyes. "You can decide for yourself. When she comes by to pick me up."

"To pick you up for what?"

"Oh, you know, that New Year's Eve thing we always go to together. That Sarah Territo throws each year. You probably remember her as Sarah Blackwell—that was her maiden name. She married that gorgeous Italian photographer, Gianni Territo—Lord, it must be fifteen years ago now. Amazing that they stayed together, since everyone knows he sleeps around with young boys. But then, Sarah has her own, shall we say, weaknesses—nothing that's fit for your ears. Their New Year's Eve parties are always fabulous."

I pressed my hands against my eyes. "Wait, stop. Stop talking. Back up. You're going out New Year's Eve?"

"Yes, of course. I always do. You know that. Why?"

"You told me you'd baby-sit Celia."

"Not on New Year's Eve. I always go to this party. You must have gotten your dates confused."

"Yes," I said. "There's that New-Year's-Eve-or-did-she-mean-New-Year's-Eve confusion. It happens all the time."

"Maybe you said New Year's Day. By accident. But of course you're going to think it's my fault, you always do. I go to this party every year, you know that. I've been going since you were little."

"Back when you still needed a baby-sitter for me?"

She nodded.

"Great. You have her number?"

"Whose?"

"My old baby-sitter's. Maybe she's available."

I was joking, but she said, "Oh, I used a high school girl who lived downstairs. Very sweet but not very attractive. She never had a date, which is why she could always sit. Poor thing. You're lucky you're attractive, Livvy. Or would be if you made an effort. Did you want to go somewhere with your boyfriend?"

"I don't have a boyfriend," I said. "But I did make plans. It's no big deal. I'll just cancel them." I shouldn't have minded. Why did I mind?

"Just ask Rosivel," she said. "I'm sure she'll stay."

"Maybe. There is a chance she might want to be with her husband and son on New Year's Eve."

"You think so?" My mother considered for a moment, then shrugged. "You can offer her extra money, you know, since it's a holiday."

"It's possible she values special times with her family more than money."

"Well, it can't hurt to ask." Which was one of the few things my mother had ever said that I couldn't argue with.

I asked Rosivel the next morning, even though I hated doing it. The whole idea of enjoying yourself at someone else's expense bothered me.

Or maybe that was just an excuse for not wanting to approach her, since the truth was I always felt uncomfortable talking to Rosivel. I was supposed to be the one in charge, but she knew a lot more about both the household and Celia than I did. It seemed wrong that I was her boss. That I could be anyone's boss. But I was the one who wrote out a check for her every week, from the account Dennis had set up for me, so I guess that made me her employer. We didn't talk much. She came every morning to take over with Celia, and then she left late in the afternoon, and I'd take over with Celia. That was pretty much it. We worked our shifts.

Anyway, I asked her if she could stay late on New Year's Eve and she said no, that she always spent it with her husband. I didn't have the guts to try to sweeten the deal with more money. I wouldn't have liked her if she'd been mercenary enough to give up a special time with her family for a few more bucks, and I certainly wouldn't have liked myself for trying to get her to.

I knew I should phone Joe and tell him I couldn't make it, but I kept putting off making the call. I was sure he could find another date with a single phone call and probably never even notice the difference. The best thing for me would be to cancel on him and see just how quickly he could move on.

But still, I didn't make the call.

Charlotte dropped by to say good-bye that afternoon. She was leaving first thing the next morning, and her parents wanted her home for a farewell dinner that night.

She was going back up north to spend New Year's Eve with her ex, who, I guess, wasn't exactly her ex anymore, but I was betting would be again once New Year's Day rolled around, and the frenzied goodwill of the holiday season—and the need for a date—had worn off.

"Don't do it," I said, as I walked her out to her car.

"I know what I'm doing."

"No, you don't. Don't be an idiot, Lottie. It'll feel all romantic for one lousy night, and then he'll just break your heart again."

"So what's the alternative? Stay home with my parents on New Year's Eve? Thank you, no. I want to have fun, Livvy."

"Will you at least promise me you'll be mean to him and make him pay for what he did?"

"I promise," she said and that was the best I could do.

That evening my mother and I took Celia out to Burger King. It was my mother's idea—she loved places like that, used to take me all the time when I was a kid. I think something about fast-food joints made her feel like a real all-American mom. She wouldn't order anything for herself there, but she liked to nibble a few of my fries and have a bite or two of my hamburger.

Celia said she didn't want a hamburger. "Mommy tells Rosivel to get me the chicken salad because it's healthy. I want the chicken salad."

"Really?" I said. "Because there's nothing wrong with a hamburger. I'm getting one."

"I want the chicken salad."

At the table, my mother said to Celia, "You're a very good girl, you know. Eating so healthfully. You'll be nice and skinny, and all the fat girls who eat french fries will be jealous."

"Hey, Barbara," I said.

"What?"

"Shut the fuck up."

"You said the f-word," Celia said.

"Yeah, I know. Sorry."

"You owe me a dollar."

"Okay." It was an arrangement we'd worked out a few days earlier. I was having trouble controlling my language around her and felt bad about it. We talked about how it was something I needed to learn not to do and agreed on this punishment.

"And you shouldn't tell people to shut up, either," Celia said.

"No, you shouldn't. Does that mean I owe you another dollar?"

"Yes." Celia liked money, although she never actually spent any of her own. She put every dollar I gave her into her toy cash register and used it for playing games. I could have sneaked a few bills back out and she would never have noticed. But I didn't.

In the end, she ate only the croutons and cheese out of her salad, which pretty much busted my mother's "health food" assumption about it, and then she tasted my chocolate milkshake and liked it a lot. She'd never had one before. I liked watching her try to drink it—the shake was so thick that she had to suck hard to get it up the straw, which made her cheeks cave in and her eyes bulge out comically.

An old couple was walking by our table. The wife stopped and said to me, "Your daughter's very cute."

"Thanks," I said.

She smiled at Celia and patted her on the head before moving on.
Celia said, "Who was that?"

"I don't know," I said. "Just some nice lady." I pulled the shake back toward me so I could have some.

"You shouldn't talk to strangers."

"No, *you* shouldn't talk to strangers. I'm allowed to because I'm over eighteen."

"Why is it okay for you and not for me?"

"Because I'm old enough to know when it's okay and when it's not."

"Olivia was once my little girl," my mother said to her. "Can you believe it? She was once as little as you, and I took care of her."

Celia turned her large dark eyes on me for a moment, studying me seriously. "How old were you?"

"How old was I when?"

"When you were as little as me."

"Oh, probably around your age."

"I'm going to be four soon."

"I know."

"Can I have a mermaid party for my birthday?"

"Sure. Why not?"

"Mommy said I should have a party at Bright Child but I don't want to. Kelsey had a party at Bright Child and she cried because she hurt her leg. I don't want to hurt my leg."

"How'd she hurt it?"

"She went the wrong way down the slide."

"Maybe she shouldn't have done that," I said.

"Why not?" Celia asked.

"Why not what?"

"Why shouldn't she go down the slide?"

"Because she hurt her leg."

"She didn't hurt her leg going down the *slide*," Celia said, as if I were a moron. "She hurt it . . . I don't know why she hurt it. Not because she went down the *slide*."

"You said that was why."

Celia shook her head. "No."

I gave up. "Are you done yet? Can we clean up here?"

"I want some more of that." She pointed to the shake.

"That was supposed to be mine. You've already drunk most of it."

"I want more."

"All right." I pushed it over to her. "Finish it."

She got up onto her knees on the chair and leaned over the drink. Her hair fell forward around her face, baring the small, white nape of her neck. I reached out my hand and touched it lightly.

She turned her head to look at me a second, the straw moving to the corner of her mouth. Then she wiggled her body a little closer to mine, nestled against my side, and went back to work on the shake.

seventeen

It was all my mother's fault, the misunderstanding, but of course I was the one who felt bad about it.

Dennis showed up a little while after we'd put Celia to bed that night. He had his own key at this point, but he always knocked before using it. My mother and I were watching TV and didn't hear his knock, but when he called to us from the foyer, I yelled back that we were in the family room. He came in and handed me a cell phone.

"I went ahead and got you one," he said. "It seemed like it would come in handy."

"Great," I said, looking at it. It was an ugly wild purple color—was that the kind of thing he thought I'd like? "Now there's really no way for me to escape for a few hours, is there?"

"You could go underwater," he said. "I already set it up for you. You want to write down your number?"

"I'm not the one who's going to be calling it," I said. "Give it to Barbara. I have a feeling she'll be dialing it every time I think I'll have a minute to myself." I tossed it onto the coffee table.

"Write it down next to the phone in the kitchen," my mother said to Dennis. "Make sure you put it somewhere safe — the maid is forever misplacing things."

My mother loved talking about the "maid." The cleaning woman who had worked for Alicia still came three days a week. I was shocked to discover she charged a hundred dollars a day, but since the money came out of the estate, I figured I'd just go on paying it with the checks Dennis had set up for me for household costs. I certainly wasn't going to scrub any toilets I didn't have to. Still, whenever I came across Elena quietly working away in some part of the house to keep it clean for us, I ducked and ran. And the fact that she collected all the dirty clothes I left lying around, then washed, dried, and pressed them, only increased my guilt and embarrassment. Also my desire to keep her around.

My mother was asking Dennis if he was hungry or wanted something to drink.

"No, I'm fine," he said, looking at me. "I could have used a thank you for taking time out of work to get that phone set up, but otherwise, I'm fine."

"Oh, did I forget to say thanks?" I said, yawning. "Man, that was rude of me."

"I'm used to it."

"Did you hear that, Livvy? He said he's used to your being rude. I wish *I* could get used to it. Dennis, if you'd heard the way she spoke to me at dinner tonight, and in front of Celia, too — "

"How much do you owe her?" asked Dennis, who knew about our little arrangement.

"Two bucks," I said. "But only because I gave her 'shut up,' which I'm still not convinced counts as a bad word." I shot a glance at my mother. "Given the circumstances, I think I should have been given 'shut up' as a freebie."

"I'm glad Celia knew it wasn't a good thing to say," Dennis said. "She may grow up to be civil in spite of you, Livvy."

"If she grows up to be anything decent, it will be in spite of me."

———

Later, after Dennis had gone, my mother scolded me for not having been more grateful about the phone. "Here he went and did something nice for you, and you don't even appreciate it."

"First of all," I said, "the cell phone isn't for me, it's for everyone else *but* me, since it's a way of making me come home whenever I think I've escaped. Second, Dennis doesn't mind when I'm rude. He knows it's just the way I am."

"Yes, well, *I* know that and you still hurt my feelings all the time."

"A 'Don't Walk' sign hurts your feelings."

"You see? Like that. You get sarcastic and try to make me feel bad. All the time."

"Not all the time," I said. "Sometimes I sleep."

"What kind of example do you think you're setting for Celia?"

"A bad one. But I didn't ask to be an example for anyone."

"I don't know why you're the way you are," my mother said. "Well, yes, I do—you're like your father. You certainly don't get it from me."

I didn't say anything.

"A lot of people have told me I'm very nice," she said.

Again I was silent. I picked up my book—science fiction, which is what I liked to read when I was on vacation. My mother turned back to the TV, but then, during a commercial, she said, "Well, at least we're set for tomorrow night."

"What do you mean?"

"Oh, you know. Since Dennis is coming."

"Dennis is coming?"

"Well, yes, of course, you were sitting right here—oh, wait, no, we had that conversation when you were with Celia." Celia had woken up earlier that evening, screaming as usual, and I'd had to calm her down, bring her water, lie with her for a while, and so on. Actually, I was kind of glad she'd had her nighttime freak-out at nine instead of the usual two in the morning. I was hoping it meant I'd get to sleep through the night for once. "Dennis said he could baby-sit for Celia."

"Really? He didn't have any other plans?"

She shook her head. "He seemed happy to be asked."

I should have been suspicious about that, but instead I just felt relieved that I hadn't called Joe yet to cancel.

It wasn't until I spotted Dennis coming up the walk with a bottle of champagne in his hand that it occurred to me to wonder whether my mother had made it clear he was coming to baby-sit.

She and I were in the kitchen, where I'd been trying to get Celia to eat a hot dog before we went out. She didn't like it, because it was a different brand from the one she was used to. "It's brown," she said. "I like the red ones."

"They taste the same," I said.

"I like the red ones," she said.

"Hot dogs are too salty," my mother said. "I can't eat them. I don't know how anyone can." She was wearing a purple silk skirt with a tight flowered top that showed how fine her figure still was. She could have gone a little lighter on the makeup, but, then, I always thought that about my mother.

She felt the opposite way about me, and already I had had to block several of her attempts to powder and mascara me, "so you don't look so washed out." Even now, as I gave up on the hot dog and went to toss it in the disposal, I was suddenly attacked from the side by one of her brushes.

"Jesus," I said, knocking her hand away and wiping at my cheek with the back of my hand. "Don't you ever give up?"

"Now you have to let me do the other cheek or you'll look uneven."

"All right," I said, "even it out. But that's it." As soon as the brush went over once, I jerked away.

"Just a little bit more, Livvy. Please. Girls like you who don't have cheekbones need to create them. Just a touch more and you'll look so much better."

"Stay away from me," I said.

"Do me, do me!" shouted Celia, jumping up from the table. "I want cheekpones!"

"Good for you, my love." My mother turned her attention to Celia, who happily submitted to the brush, shifting excitedly from foot to foot until she was told to go look at herself. She went running to a mirror and came back, ecstatic. "I look beautiful," she said.

"I liked you better without the gook," I said.

"Now do me a favor and tell Livvy she has to put on some mascara," my mother stage-whispered to her. "She *cannot* go to a New Year's Eve party without mascara. It would be a crime."

Celia said, "I like your dress, Livvy." She stroked it.

I was wearing a black sleeveless dress. Unusual for me, but every once in a while I liked to admit that I was, in fact, a girl.

"It is a nice dress," my mother said, tilting her head to look at it. "It's a good length for you, Livvy. You have decent legs for someone so short."

That's when Dennis came walking in with the bottle of champagne. He saw how dressed up my mother and I both were and did what you might call a double take. And that's when I knew for sure that my mother hadn't been clear about why he'd been invited over that night.

"Champagne!" she said the moment he walked in. "Perfect! We can have a toast before Livvy and I go out."

"Where are you going?" Celia asked. She had already asked us a dozen times that evening. She did that a lot—asked the same questions over and over again. It drove me a little nuts, but I was beginning to get the idea that that was just the way a three-year-old makes conversation.

"You know, darling," my mother said, crouching down, "I told you. Livvy and I have parties we have to go to. It's New Year's Eve!" Making it sound like anyone with a social life would have a party to go to. Ignoring the fact that Dennis was facing an evening of baby-sitting.

"I don't want you to go out," Celia said, grabbing at me. "Don't go, Livvy. Stay home."

"Dennis will be here," I said. "You'll have fun with him."

"I don't want you to go." Her face crumpled.

"Whoa, there, little girl, you're going to hurt my feelings," Dennis said. He picked her up. "We're going to have so much fun, you won't believe it. We're going to watch the ball drop in New York City and celebrate the New Year at nine o'clock just like the old folks do."

"What ball?"

"Oh, it's just a really big ball that falls and when it reaches the bottom, it's the New Year."

"What does that mean?"

"Not a lot," Dennis said. "Not a lot."

"Oh, don't listen to him—New Year's Eve is exciting!" my mother said. "It's the most exciting night of the year."

"That's what you said about Christmas." I wished she'd shut up.

"I just love holidays, I guess. Dennis, could you pop the top on the champagne? It's a man's job."

"Like baby-sitting?" he said, and took the champagne bottle. "Keep Celia out of range, will you? I don't want to take out one of her eyes."

"We have eyes, too," I said.

"You, I don't care about." He went to the far end of the kitchen and started fiddling with the foil.

My mother was looking for champagne glasses in one of the cabinets. I went over to her and said in a whisper, "You didn't tell him he was baby-sitting, did you? You made him think we were going to be home, that he was being invited to a family party or something."

"What are you talking about?" she said. "Of course, I told him. I can't remember my exact words—"

"Why do you always have to—" I was about to swear at her, but stopped myself. Guess I was making progress in that area, after all. I left her and went over to Dennis.

"You offering yourself as a target?" he asked, but he had already wrapped a kitchen towel around the champagne cork so it wasn't likely to hit anyone.

"Look," I said, "if there was something you wanted to do tonight—"

"Don't be silly." He seemed overly intent on wrapping the kitchen towel perfectly around the bottle. He kept undoing it and doing it again, not looking at me. "Go. Have fun. I'm looking forward to spending the evening with Celia. She's always good company."

"And a cheap date," I said. "A bag of m&m's and you've won her heart."

"Thanks for the tip." A pause. He pulled at a wrinkle in the towel, then glanced at me. Briefly. "You clean up nice, Olivia."

"You think? My mother looks great, doesn't she?"

"She does," he said. "Stand back, I'm going to pop the cork."

As he held it up, I saw the bottom of the label peeking out from under the towel. Even though I didn't know much about champagne or wine, I had heard of Dom Perignon, and I figured it had to be good. "Wait," I said. "Are you sure you don't want to save that for a more important occasion?"

"There are none in my life," he said and popped the cork.

Celia screamed and my mother whooped and came running with champagne glasses. Dennis was so careful with the bottle and the towel that none of the champagne spilled. It all just went right into the three glasses.

My mother held up her glass and said, "To a wonderful new year— may we all find love and happiness in the year ahead!"

I gulped my champagne down, not in support of the sentiment, just out of sheer discomfort.

Dennis barely tasted his, while my mother daintily sipped hers— daintily, but she was getting it down.

Celia was watching us intently. She begged me for a taste. "Daddy lets me."

"One sip," I said, refilling the glass and beckoning her over. "That's all." I didn't think she'd like it, and I was right. She made a face and pulled back before it even touched her lips.

"Ow," she said. "Something hurt my nose."

"The bubbles," I said. "They hurt my nose, too."

"So why do you like it?"

"Adults like a lot of yucky things," I said, raising it to my lips. "They're stupid that way."

"Stupid is a bad word," Celia said. "You owe me a dollar."

"Make sure she pays up," Dennis said.

"Stupid isn't such a bad word," I said. "I mean, if I'm going to pay a buck, it should be for something worthwhile like—"

"Olivia!" he said, cutting me off.

"What? I was just going to say dumbhead. Geez."

I slugged down my second glass of champagne and reached for the bottle again, and Dennis said, "That's three. You'd better not be driving."

"Only to Westwood," I said.

"Not after drinking three glasses of champagne."

"Two," I said. I put down my glass. "Besides, I'm just doing my part to keep up the great American tradition of driving drunk on New Year's Eve."

"You're not driving anywhere."

"That was a joke. Why are you being so serious tonight? I really am fine, you know. Don't feel a thing."

"You're not driving anywhere," he said again. "Unless you want to wait for the alcohol to wear off."

"Which would be when?"

"An hour a drink is the rule. In two hours you can drive anywhere you want."

"I don't even feel tipsy," I said. "And I'm only going ten minutes away. Not even."

"Ten minutes?" he said. "Good. Then Celia and I can take you where you need to go."

"No," I said. "It's almost her bedtime." I wasn't about to be dropped off, like a teenager going out with her dad's permission.

"It's New Year's Eve," Dennis said. "She can stay up a little later tonight."

"That's right," I said. "It's New Year's Eve, and people are out there driving drunk. Better to be one of them than to put an innocent victim like Celia out on the road. Anyway, you've been drinking, too."

He put his glass on the counter. "I've had two sips."

My mother said, "I'd ask Lindsey to drop you off, Livvy, but we're going to Malibu—wrong direction, you know."

"We'll drive you," Dennis said.

"Jesus Christ, Jiminy, don't you think you're overdoing it?" The champagne was hitting me, but if Dennis thought that would win his argument, he was wrong. I just felt shaky with righteous anger. "I promise I won't go above twenty miles an hour for the whole two miles it takes me to get there, and when I arrive safe and sound, I will call you on the cell phone you got to keep tabs on me." My keys were lying on the kitchen island. I grabbed them. "Good night, all." I picked up my purse and headed toward the garage.

Celia cried out, "Don't go, Livvy!"

I was almost to the door when she and Dennis both caught up with me. Celia grabbed my leg. Dennis grabbed my arm.

"You're acting like a teenager," he said.

"Why not?" I said. "That's basically what I am. Which is what I keep telling you but you won't believe me."

"I had more faith in your judgment than this."

"Yeah, well, stupid you." His fingers were digging into me and I jerked my arm free. "I probably shouldn't be responsible for any young children, either, should I?"

"Maybe not," he said. "Maybe I made a mistake in thinking you could be."

"Now you tell me. Get off my leg, Celia."

"No!" she said. "Don't go."

I limped through a couple of steps with her attached to me and reached the door to the garage. I opened it. "Leave me alone, will you? Both of you. Dennis, you're supposed to be the baby-sitter here. Will you get her off of me?"

"No," he said, from behind me now.

I grabbed Celia under her arms and pulled her hard up and off of my leg. She screamed. I thrust her at Dennis. "Take her or I drop her."

He took her and she let him, but she didn't stop yelling at me not to leave. Dennis had to raise his voice so he could be heard over her. "Olivia, if you get in that car and drive it, I swear I'll call the police and tell them you stole the car. It's not in your name. You'll spend New Year's Eve in jail."

If my mother had said something like that, I'd have laughed in her face. But Dennis probably meant it. I punched the garage door opener and the door started to creak upwards. "I'll take my own car, then."

"I'm not going to let you."

Celia sobbed out that I had hurt her arms and was being mean. I wouldn't even look at her. I was sick to death of both of them.

Dennis bent down and put Celia on the floor. "Go back to the kitchen for a second, Celia. We'll be right there."

She hesitated, whimpering. "I don't want Livvy to go."

"Don't worry. She's not going."

Celia ran back to the kitchen. Dennis stood up again and looked at me.
"She is too going," I said.

"Your father just died in a car accident," Dennis said. "Or didn't that
make any impression on you at all?"

It was hard to stand up straight, so I leaned against the doorway. "It's
not the same. I wouldn't drive if I didn't think it was safe."

"I don't care what you think," he said. "You're not driving."

"What right do you have to tell me what I can and can't do?"

"Certain rights don't have to be given to you, Olivia. They come with
the package of being a member of human society. Something you may
actually aspire to one day."

"I doubt it."

"You're not driving," he said again, taking a step toward me.

"Yes," I said, "I'm beginning to see that." I wasn't about to wrestle
my way down the driveway and out to my car, and it was looking like
Dennis wouldn't let me go any other way. I wanted to scream with
frustration—mostly anger at myself for drinking the goddamned champagne in the first place—but I bit my lip and tried to be rational, to
decide which was worse, being dropped off at Joe's apartment like a
fucking teenager, or calling him and asking him to pick me up. Like
a fucking teenager.

I wished I'd just decided to stay home that night. I was already
having a miserable New Year's Eve, and I hadn't even reached the
party yet.

"All right," I said finally, "you and Celia can drop me off." I would
make sure they had driven away before I rang up to Joe's apartment.
"We'd better go. I'm late."

"Give me the keys," he said, holding out his hand.

"Why? Afraid I'll take off when your back is turned?"

"Just give me the keys, Olivia."

I dropped them into his hand with a shrug.

My mother appeared in the hallway. She said, "Celia just ran upstairs."

"Oh, great," I said. "Now I'll be even later."

"I'll get her," Dennis said and moved off.

The doorbell rang. My mother said, "There's Lindsey. Hold on, both of you. I want you to say hi. Try to be polite, Livvy. It wouldn't kill you to smile and say something friendly."

"Still want me to be Shirley Temple for your friends, Barbara?"

"Oh, that reminds me," she said, as she walked away. "I want her to meet Celia, too."

Dennis had already gone upstairs. I followed him while my mother went to answer the door. I found him in the master bedroom. He was standing in front of the walk-in closet, looking in.

"What's going on?" I said.

He pointed. I looked. Celia was in there.

She had her face buried in a row of Alicia's dresses and she was crying.

eighteen

I brushed past Dennis and went to her.

I had seen Celia cry plenty of times before, but that was always the loud, theatrical kind of crying, the kind that demanded an audience. This was different. She was huddled into a tiny wreck of a little girl, her face smushed into an armful of Alicia's dresses.

"Hey," I said, "what's going on?"

She raised her face, aware of us for the first time.

She blinked, confused. Then she whispered, "I sorry. I'm not supposed to be in here." She always said "I sorry" instead of "I'm sorry."

"It's okay." I knelt down. I wished my head wasn't floating. It made it hard to focus and say the right thing. "Are you feeling sad?"

She nodded.

"Why are you sad?"

"I don't know," she said. Her mouth was trembling, and she kept swallowing. "I don't know," she said again. Then, "I don't want you to go out tonight."

"I know."

"I told you and told you but you wouldn't listen to me."

"I heard you, Celia. It's just . . . sometimes I have to go places. Is that what's making you sad?"

"Please, Livvy, don't go." She leaned her head against me, and I put my arms around her.

"Why did you come in here?" I said.

"The dresses smell like Mommy."

"Yeah? What does she smell like?" I couldn't say "did."

"I don't know. Like this. Smell." She pushed the dresses at me and I put my face in them and sniffed. There was some fragrance I recognized, and it was definitely something you'd associate with Alicia. I couldn't have told you the perfume's name, just that it was Alicia's. And maybe it wasn't perfume at all, just a mix of scents from deodorant, lotion, hairspray, and whatever else Alicia put on every morning.

"It smells nice," I said. "Kind of like flowers. And a little bit like spices, too. Do you know what spices are?"

"No," she said.

"Like cinnamon. Remember the cinnamon oatmeal you had? Cinnamon is a spice. My mother used to make me cinnamon toast when I was little."

"Your mother is Barbara," she said. She let go of the dresses and curled up against me.

"That's right."

"Who's your father again?"

"Richard," I said. "Remember, same daddy, just like you?"

"Right," she said. "Only he's dead, and so is my mommy, right? They're not going to be here anymore."

"That's right," I said. "They're not."

"Sometimes I forget that," she said. Whispering, like she didn't want anyone else to hear. Like she might get in trouble for it. "Sometimes I think they're going to come home."

"Would you like that?"

"Yes," she said. "I want them. But I don't want you to go away. Could you stay here, and Rosivel, too, *and* my mommy and daddy?"

"I'll always stay here," I said. "And Rosivel will keep coming for a long long time. But your mommy and daddy can't come back, Celia. I'm sorry. I'm really, really sorry."

"What if I keep forgetting that?"

"That's okay. That's fine. I forget things, too. And it's okay to come up here and smell your mommy's dresses whenever you want." I'd have to forbid my mother to touch them. Let alone get rid of them.

"My mommy always smelled nice like that," Celia said. "Sometimes she'd put stuff on me so I could smell like her."

"I bet you liked that."

"Yeah. You don't smell nice, Livvy."

"Hey, watch it," I said. "You don't want to go around telling people that."

"Why not?"

"I don't know. You know what? I'm wrong—you say whatever you want. Don't let other people edit you."

"What's 'edit'?"

I had to think about that one. It would have been hard to define even if I'd been sober. "Uh, correcting you, I guess. Don't let people tell you what's okay to say and what isn't."

"What about bad words?"

"Those you should probably stay away from, or you'll end up owing all sorts of money like me."

She rubbed her cheek against my upper arm like a cat. "Livvy?" she said. "Are you still mad at me?"

"I wasn't mad at you before," I said. "I was just . . . frustrated."

"You said you'd drop me."

"I'm sorry. That was a lousy thing to say."

"Would you really have dropped me?"

I tightened my arms around her. "I hope not. I wasn't thinking too clearly when I said that."

"Are you going to go out?"

"I don't know."

"Don't go out." She sighed and it turned into a yawn. "Can I watch *Powerpuff Girls* now?"

"If it's on. Should we go check?"

"Uh-huh."

I tried to stand up, but it was hard, my legs all cramped from kneeling, holding onto her, wearing a dress and shoes with heels, half drunk . . . I lurched, partway up, and we both fell sideways. I hit the dresses and then fell through them and hit the wall, still gripping Celia who only fell against me. Before I'd even registered what was happening, Dennis was hauling me back into a standing position. I'd forgotten he was in the room.

"Thanks," I said once I'd gotten balanced again. "Those dresses jumped me. They looked so innocent, too." My shoulder hurt where I'd bashed into the wall.

"And you wanted to drive." He let go of me and held his arms out to Celia.

"Hi," Celia said to him and let him take her. She seemed unfazed by the fall. She put her arms around his neck.

"Hey, there," he said. "Let's go downstairs. We have to take Livvy to her party." He carried her out of the closet and headed toward the bedroom door.

"I'll be right there," I said. "I'm just going to make a quick call."

"Okay," he said, and they left the room.

I called Joe, using the telephone on Alicia's night table, and told him I was running late and didn't know how much later I'd be and that, if he wanted, he could just go on to the party, and I'd either meet him there or not, depending on how things worked out at home.

"What's going on?" he said. "You inherit another small child without warning?"

"Just wrangling the one," I said. "I mean it, Joe, go on to the party if you want. I can meet you there later."

"I don't want to go without you," he said.

"Are you whining?"

"Olivia—"

"Because that sounded a lot like whining."

"Fuck you. When will you be free?"

"I don't know." I figured if I waited until Celia was asleep, I wouldn't worry so much about leaving her while she was feeling so sad. "Probably in an hour. But I can't drive for another hour after that."

"Why not?"

"I drank too much champagne."

"Champagne? You aren't supposed to be drinking champagne yet. That's for later. For when you're with me. Why were you drinking? Who were you drinking with?"

"There was champagne, and I drank some. My head's a little woozy now. It was stupid, I know. Give me an hour and a half and I'll be fine. I'll come then. It'll still be way before midnight."

"Are you really at home? You didn't go out with someone else, did you?"

"No. I'm at home."

"Then why don't I just come get you there right now?"

"I still have stuff I need to do."

"What stuff?"

"I've got to put Celia down."

"Put her down?" he repeated.

"Put her to sleep."

"I'll help you put her down," Joe said. "I'm great with kids."

"Yeah, right."

"Okay, that was a lie, but I'm curious. I want to see her. Give me the address. We'll put her down together and go to the party."

"Forget it," I said. "I'll call you later. Unless you want to meet me at the party."

"So those are my choices?" he said. "Wait around until you call me or go by myself to a party with no one to kiss at midnight? It's New Year's fucking Eve, Livvy."

"I know," I said. "That most holy of holy nights. New Year's fucking Eve. You want to just call it off?"

"What? The evening, or the relationship?"

"Either, I guess." I suddenly felt very tired, so I lay down on the floor, because the idea that my mother, my father, and Alicia had all slept on the bed made it way too loaded with baggage for me to fit on there. I lay on my back on the carpet and closed my eyes, propping the phone on the floor and leaning it against my ear.

He was saying something. "—ever tell you you were annoying?"

"Yeah. Should I call you later?"

"Fine," he said. "Call me later. But I may not be here." And he hung up.

I lay on the floor for a while and watched the ceiling rotate above my head. Cool how it did that. Who needed ceiling fans when you could make the whole ceiling turn around just by drinking a little alcohol?

What the hell had just happened?

If A was getting ready to go out and C was lying on the floor in my dead father's bedroom looking at the ceiling, what exactly had B been? And what kind of an idiot was I, anyway, for thinking I would actually get to go out on New Year's fucking Eve?

After a little while the phone started beeping because I hadn't hung it up, so I got up off the floor, put it back, and made my way downstairs. The kitchen was empty. I found everyone standing in the living room, where, I assumed, my mother had felt Lindsey would be most impressed by the hugeness of the house we'd landed in.

Lindsey Patrick. My mother's friend since the grand old days of modeling. Those two lovely creatures had been stabbing each other in the back since the late seventies. They started when they were rivals for the same jobs and apparently found it so much fun that neither of them wanted to stop, not even now, when their careers were pretty much over and backstabbing no longer served any useful purpose.

Lindsey wore her short blonde hair—silver-blonde, not honey-blonde like my mother's—gelled into dramatic spikes. She had on a loose, flowing dress in the same silvery shade as her hair, but her fingernails and lips were black-red. Like my mother, Lindsey was still beautiful, still had her figure, still had her bone structure. Only a slight leatheriness of the skin betrayed her age. In that, my mother had the advantage. Given how much she smoked and drank, her skin was in surprisingly good shape.

"Hello, Lindsey," I said, submitting to the obligatory air kiss. "When did you turn so artsy?" I gestured at the dress and the large pieces of silver jewelry.

"Oh, I've always been in touch with the aesthetic side of my nature," she said, tossing her head so the silver hoops in her ears could flash at us.

I had to give her credit—she had a look and it worked. Next to her, my mother looked matronly and conservative, even with the flowered top. Maybe it was the flight attendant hair.

"Well, it suits you," I said. "So, you're off to a party?"

"Oh, we have to make an appearance, you know," Lindsey said. Another toss. "They'll all want to see how decrepit the old girls have become."

"You know you don't mean that," my mother said, wagging her finger. "The years haven't done a thing to you. You're as beautiful as ever."

"I don't know about that," Lindsey said. "But thank you, love." Then there was an awkward silence while we all waited for her to return the compliment. She didn't. Just tilted her head, twisted a spike of hair at her temple, and kept smiling.

My mother gave a little cough into her hand and looked sideways at Lindsey. Still no comment. Then my mother said quickly, "Oh, you missed the funniest thing, Lindsey. Right before you came. Livvy started drinking champagne—Dennis here brought it—and she drank too much too quickly and Dennis said she couldn't drive and she said she was going to anyway, and then the two of them just went at it! I thought it would come to blows, they were so angry. But it didn't. Everything's all right now. I think."

Lindsey turned to Dennis. He was still holding Celia, who was staring at Lindsey, her mouth open in awe. Fascinated by her. Or at least by her jewelry.

Lindsey said, "It must be nice to have a man around to lay down the law. Especially such a gorgeous one."

"Dennis has been very helpful," my mother said.

We all looked at Dennis whose face turned bright red.

Lindsey extended a hand toward him. She had a silver ring on her thumb. "Poor man, have we embarrassed you? I have a bad habit of always saying what I'm thinking, and sometimes I say things I really shouldn't."

"It's okay," he said. "Uh, we should go, shouldn't we, Olivia?" Pleading.

I was enjoying this. "No, actually," I said. "Change of plans. That phone call I made . . . Hey, why don't we all sit down and have a glass of champagne together before you two girls take off?"

"I don't think you need any more champagne," Dennis said. "What do you mean by 'change of plans'?"

"Does Livvy drink too much?" Lindsey asked my mother. "It would be a shame if she inherited your . . . you know . . . little weakness in that area."

"I don't have a problem with drinking," my mother said. "I don't know what you mean, Lindsey."

"No," said Lindsey, "of course not. I must have been thinking of someone else." A careful smile and a quick eyebrow raise. "At any rate, we should be going now. I'd like to get there before all the caviar is gone. People can be such pigs."

"Drive carefully," I said. "You never know when some idiot will try to drink and drive on New Year's Eve."

"I'm a very careful driver," Lindsey said. "And I never drink. It's bad for the complexion."

"Yes," my mother said eagerly, "you need to be careful about that, don't you?"

"I guess I do," Lindsey said, touching her cheek. "My skin definitely isn't what it was. I guess I'm paying the price for all those trips to the south of France and Rio and God knows what other gorgeous beaches, but how could I have turned down so many invitations from so many wonderful men? You were lucky, Barbara, you always led such a quiet life. You could nurture that gorgeous skin of yours like a baby."

"I was looking after a real baby," my mother said. "*That's* why I stayed home. I had Livvy very young, remember." My mother draped an arm over my shoulders. The self-sacrificing maternal type. That was her.

Lindsey shook her head. "Oh, but even way before Livvy was born, you never were all that social, were you? There was Richard, of course, but not for very long. . . . Come now, darling, let's go while it's still the old year. Good-bye, Livvy." A kiss for me, inches away from my actual cheek, accompanied by the light tinkle of silver bracelets moving against one another. She turned and blew a kiss in Dennis's direction. "So nice to meet you. If you help out here as much as Barbara claims,

I'll have to come by more often, and when I'm not in such a rush. I wouldn't mind spending a bit more time with you. Quite a bit more."

"Yes," he said, looking at her shoes. "Nice to meet you, too."

She patted Celia on the head. Up till then, she hadn't even seemed to notice that there was a kid in the room. "Good-bye, little girl. Be good." She stopped patting her and moved toward the door.

My mother grabbed the opportunity to show how wonderful *she* was with small children and descended on Celia with open arms, a somewhat awkward thing to do at that moment, since Celia was clinging to Dennis. My mother managed to hug Celia without actually hugging Dennis, though, and smothered her cheek with kisses. "Good night, my darling little lamb. Take good care of Uncle Dennis now." Uncle Dennis? When had he become an uncle? "Thank you so much for your help tonight, Dennis, darling." Daringly, she pecked him on the cheek, something she'd never done before. I assumed it was for Lindsey's benefit.

Then it was my turn. She threw her arms around me. "Good-bye, my Livvy! Have a wonderful, romantic evening and make sure you kiss the man you love at midnight. That seals your love for good, you know."

I pulled back. "Oh, for Christ's sake! Will you just leave?"

She blinked, then recovered. "Good night, all! Good night, good night! Don't wait up for me!"

And, finally, they were gone.

"Well, that was fun," I said.

"What did you mean, 'The plans have changed'?"

I turned to them, and Celia held out her arms. I let her transfer over to me, the weight and shape of her already so familiar it was hard to believe I had started holding her only a week or so earlier. "I'm not going to the party right now. Maybe later. Maybe not even then."

"Why not?"

"I don't know. It just wasn't working out."

"Because I didn't want you to," Celia said, putting her cheek against mine. "That's why, isn't it, Livvy? Because I didn't want you to go."

"That's part of it," I said.

"You're not going out, right? For real?"

Dennis said, "I didn't mean to ruin your whole evening, Olivia. Can't you still go to your party?"

"Yeah, I can go later. If I want. Look, it's no big deal. It had nothing to do with you, anyway. It's—" I jerked my chin in Celia's direction. "I just didn't feel like it was a good time to leave. You know?"

"Yes," he said. "I know. But, still, Olivia . . . We'll be okay. Celia's my pal, right, Celia?"

She nestled against me. "I don't want Livvy to go."

"You're not helping," he said to her.

"I can go later," I said again. "After Celia's asleep."

"No, don't!" said Celia, and Dennis said, "If Celia's asleep, I won't be able to drive you."

"Yes, but I'll be sober by then. I'm already less wiggy than I was a few minutes ago. Barbara and Lindsey would scare anyone sober. By the time Celia's asleep, I'll be fine."

"I'll be the judge of that," he said, but he smiled.

"Bring it on," I said. "Breathalyzer, walking a straight line, touching my nose—whatever it is, I'm sure that in an hour's time, I'll pass it. Assuming it's something I can do when I'm sober. I've never been too good at that rubbing your stomach patting your head thing."

"Don't go out after I'm asleep," Celia said. "Don't, Livvy. Please?"

"We'll see. Hey, what time is it?"

Dennis said, "Eight forty-five."

"Don't you think we'd better turn on the TV? That ball is going to start falling pretty soon in New York. We don't want to miss it."

"Why not?" Celia said. "I don't understand about the ball."

"What's to understand?" I said, moving us toward the hallway. "The ball hits bottom, it's New Year's Eve on the East Coast. Everyone shouts and hollers and kisses each other. Then they go to bed."

"What happens to the ball?"

"I don't know," I said. "I think maybe it breaks on contact." We headed toward the family room. "Or maybe they save it till the next year."

"Why?"

"Why what?"

"Just why."

"In that case, because." We entered the family room. "Quick," I said to Dennis, "turn on the TV before she asks any more questions."

He turned it on, but Celia didn't want to watch the festivities in Times Square. "I want *Powerpuff Girls*," she said.

We changed the channel until we found something she liked—not *Powerpuff Girls*, which didn't seem to be on, but some other cartoon. She was definitely not picky when it came to cartoons—so long as they were brightly colored and loud, she'd watch them. I put her down in a corner of the sofa, and she curled up into a little ball. She was like me, that way, both of us truly comfortable only when our knees were near our noses.

"Are you hungry?" Dennis said to me.

"Starving." I was, too. I hadn't eaten dinner. And the buzz of the champagne was wearing off, leaving me with a headache.

"Chinese? Pizza? Thai?"

"Whatever's fastest."

"I want pizza," Celia said. "But nothing on top."

I waved my hand. "You heard the lady."

"I'll take care of it," he said and left the room. There were take-out menus in the kitchen.

I sat down and leaned back against the cushions. Here I was again, where I always was these days. Wearing a groove in the sofa the size of my ass.

No exciting New Year's Eve party for Livvy, no dancing in the moonlight, no kiss at midnight. Not that it couldn't all still happen, but it seemed less likely every minute. I had spent a lot of New Year's Eves eating pizza with friends while other people got dressed up and went out. Why not this one, too? I didn't even feel all that bad about it. There was actually some satisfaction in having canceled on Joe. I bet there hadn't been a New Year's Eve since he was a teenager when he hadn't kissed *someone* at midnight. I was guessing he'd find a way to make that happen this year with or without me. That was his inevitability—getting kissed and probably laid. Mine was pizza and TV.

Dennis came back. "Forty-five minutes to an hour," he said, as he sat down.

Dennis, on the other hand, was more like me. He'd probably eaten a lot of pizza on a lot of New Year's Eves. Although he did say he had been married, so maybe I was wrong, maybe he had a much more interesting social life than I was giving him credit for. Just because he was willing to spend his free time with us didn't mean he didn't have any other offers.

"Only a few more minutes till nine," Dennis said.

"Okay." I reached for the remote.

Celia reacted when I changed the channel. "I was watching that! Stop it, Livvy!"

"Sorry, kid, you're celebrating New Year's Eve whether you want to or not. See, that's the big ball I told you about." Richard had satellite, so it was easy to find a New York channel.

"It doesn't really look like a ball," she said. "I mean, not a real ball."

"It's round, isn't it?"

"Yes."

"What more do you want from a ball?"

"Why are all those people there?"

"I guess they like being cold and crowded and pushed and yelled at," I said.

"Why aren't *we* there?"

"It's in New York. It's far away."

"My daddy goes to New York all the time," Celia said. "On business."

I didn't say anything. After a moment, I was able to point out that the ball was starting to go down and the people were counting backward. Celia liked the counting backward and when they reached five, she joined in. When the ball hit and the band started playing "Auld Lang Syne," I leaned over and kissed her on the cheek.

"Why'd you do that?" she asked.

"Just something you do when it's the New Year."

"Kiss him," she said, pointing to Dennis.

"Sure," I said. "Why not?" I went over to him and bent down and gave him a peck on the cheek. Not unlike the one my mother had given him earlier. His cheek was warm and slightly rough.

"Happy New Year," I said. He wished me the same, then moved across the sofa to drop a kiss on the top of Celia's head. "Happy New Year," he said to her.

"It's almost bedtime," I said.

"No, it's not," she said. "I get to stay up late tonight."

"It *is* late," I said. "In New York, it's midnight."

"What time is it here?"

"Past nine. Way past your bedtime."

"I want some pizza," she said.

"All right. You can have some pizza when it comes, if you promise to go right to bed afterward—no books or anything. And you have to go put your pajamas on right now."

"Come with me," she said.

"No. You can do it by yourself."

"I want you to help."

"You don't need me to help. You put your pajamas on by yourself all the time."

"But I want you to come with me."

"Come on, Celia. Just do it yourself. Or no pizza."

She made a face, but left. I watched her go then sat down again.

Dennis said, "Any New Year's resolutions, Olivia?"

"Why? Think I need some?"

"Maybe one or two."

"Save your breath. I'm too far gone. A few resolutions won't fix me."

"They couldn't hurt."

"Yeah, well, maybe I should think about staying away from alcohol. It seems to get me in trouble."

"That's not a bad idea. All joking aside, you run a genuine risk of inheriting a taste for alcohol from both of your parents."

I had never thought about that before—Richard with his martinis, my mother with her "little" glasses of wine. "I actually drink less than most kids I know at school," I said.

"Good."

"I've just never been into the bar scene."

"I shouldn't have brought that champagne tonight," Dennis said. "I don't know what I was thinking."

Oh, why the hell not say it? I still had enough alcohol in me to go ahead. "You were thinking you were about to have a pleasant New Year's Eve with a couple of other adults. You didn't know you were going to be stuck baby-sitting while everyone else went out."

He flushed. "I . . . wasn't entirely clear on the plan. But it was fine, either way."

"I'm sorry," I said and it was a relief to say it. "I'm sorry my mother misled you. I didn't know she had, or I would have stopped the whole thing."

"It doesn't matter," he said. "I like being with Celia."

"Was there somewhere else you might have gone tonight?"

"Nowhere important."

"That means yes."

"Look, Olivia, I'm here," he said. "And I'm not unhappy to be here. Can we leave it at that?"

"Yeah," I said. I slipped off my shoes and tucked my legs underneath me. Normally I would have curled my knees up to my chin, but I couldn't in the dress I was wearing, unless I was going for an X rating.

We watched the people in Times Square, laughing, hugging, singing, drinking, doing all that New Year's Eve kind of stuff that I'd never done, would probably never do. They all looked really drunk. Maybe it was just that I was sobering up.

"Why do we do it?" I asked. "Why do we get all excited about the new year when everyone knows it's just a made-up date?"

"I don't know," Dennis said. "I think people like the idea of a fresh start."

"Only because we always fuck up whatever it was we had going."

"That's one way of putting it. A particularly Olivia-like way of putting it. You now owe Celia a dollar. Or do I get it?"

"You can split it fifty-fifty. Only I don't have a fucking cent on me. See, I gave you that one so you could each have a dollar, and no one would have to make change."

"You're capable of using perfectly decent language," Dennis said. "I've heard you. You swear for effect."

"No fucking way."

The doorbell rang. "That was fast," I said.

"They knew you were hungry." He got up and left the room.

I kept watching the Times Square scene on TV. Some band was playing and people were swaying to the music, too crowded together actually to dance but doing the best they could. I saw a couple freaking, the woman rubbing her ass all over the guy's groin, but as soon as the image registered, the picture changed—some producer probably panicked and switched to a different camera feed. Too bad—they looked like they were having fun.

I heard Dennis in the hallway. I called out, "Let's eat in here," as he entered the family room without a pizza and followed by Joe.

nineteen

"Yes," said Joe, "let's eat in here. It's so cozy."

I sat up straight. "I never gave you this address. How the hell did you find me?"

"It's nice to see you, too."

A pause while we looked at each other. Then I said, "Joe, Dennis. Dennis, Joe."

"We met at the door," Joe said.

"We thought you were the pizza delivery," I said.

"So you were planning on eating dinner here."

I shrugged. "Just taking things as they came."

He looked around. "I thought you said something about a little girl. Maybe I misunderstood."

"Celia's in her room," Dennis said. He was standing back by the doorway. "I'll go see how she's doing." And he fled.

I didn't blame him. Joe was . . . well, Joe always brought a lot of energy into a room. Usually it was a wild, cheerful kind of energy, but right now he wasn't seeming so cheerful. He stood over me, wearing his leather jacket, black T-shirt, black Levi's, looking angry, looking good. He said, "I felt bad after I hung up. I thought maybe you were just being responsible. So I figured I'd come help you out. No matter what, we'd spend New Year's Eve together. But you seem like you're doing okay. You've got pizza coming, a comfy spot by the TV, company—"

"That's Dennis," I said. "He's baby-sitting."

"He must not be very good at it," he said. "Since you're still home and all."

"What do you want from him? He's a lawyer, not a nanny."

"Oh, right, Dennis the lawyer. Why do I feel like I was set up?"

"Set up?"

"Yeah. You say you want to spend New Year's Eve with me, I make some plans for us, you keep stringing me along like you want to come, but you don't show up. I come here to be with you, and you're settled in for the night, eating pizza like you never really planned to be doing anything else—"

"I'm not eating pizza. It hasn't even come yet."

"Very hostile, Olivia. This whole thing. Not that I shouldn't have expected that from you."

"Probably not," I agreed.

A pause. He crossed his arms. "You could at least say you're sorry."

"For what? I was telling you the truth."

Another pause. "What kind of pizza did you order?"

"Plain."

"That's exciting."

"It's the only kind Celia likes."

"Oh, right. The mythical Celia. This is all some kind of *Who's Afraid of Virginia Woolf* kind of thing, isn't it? She doesn't really exist, does she?"

Celia answered the question herself, by running in wearing only a pair of underpants. Dennis followed her, a nightgown in his hand.

"Scratch *Virginia Woolf*," Joe said. "Now I'm thinking *Lolita*."

Celia threw herself onto my lap. "You can't go out," she said.

"Still think I was setting you up?" I asked Joe.

"You told her to say that." But he wasn't angry anymore. He sat down on the sofa next to me. "Hello," he said to Celia. "What's your name?"

"No!" she said and hid her face against my arm.

He said to me, "See how good I am with kids?"

"Celia, tell him your name," I said.

"No. You say it."

"Say what?"

"My name."

"What name?"

"Celia."

"Ha!" I said. "Got you to say it."

She made some sort of annoyed hmmphing noise. She turned and settled back against me. "I want to watch TV. But not this. Don't go out. Is the *Powerpuff Girls* on yet?"

"You're not watching anything until your pajamas are on," I said.

"Here." Dennis came over and handed me the nightgown. "I tried to get her in it, but she heard the doorbell and wanted to see who had come."

"I did," Joe said to her. "Do you want to know *my* name?"

"No," she said.

"See?" he said to me. "I'm great with kids."

"Yeah, I'm convinced." I pulled the nightgown over her head, and she pushed her hands up through the sleeves.

"Don't go out," Celia said as soon as her head emerged. "Stay here with me."

"But I want Olivia to go out with me," Joe said. "She promised."

Celia stared at him. She had a great stare. Very level, very intense, very intimidating, especially given the fact she was only three feet tall. She said, "Who are you? Are you Livvy's boyfriend?"

"If I say yes, will you let her go out with me now?"

"No," Celia said.

"I don't think she likes me," Joe said to me.

"A girl who doesn't like you?" I said. "Not possible. Maybe you haven't turned on the charm. Tell her the one about how you're going to woo her."

"Fuck you," Joe said, then, realizing, "Oh, sorry."

"He owes you a dollar," I said to Celia. "Give her a dollar, Joe."

"What for?"

"For using a swear word."

He reached into his pocket and pulled out his wallet. "Typical woman. I've barely known her five minutes, and already she's costing me money." He held it out to Celia. She reached for it. He suddenly pulled back so her hand closed on air. She reached again. He pulled back again. This time, she cracked a smile. The third time he did it, she giggled.

"Hey," he said, "why aren't you taking the dollar?"

She slid down to her feet and reached her hand out. He let her fingers touch the edges of the bill before pulling it away. Celia laughed out loud. She had a great bubbly laugh — made you realize how forced most adult laughs were.

"What's the matter with you?" Joe said. "Here I am, trying to give you this dollar that you wanted, and you keep laughing and not taking it."

"It's your fault," Celia said.

"My fault? I'm trying very hard to give it to you, but you don't seem to want it."

"I want it!" she shouted and tried grabbing at it. He pulled back so quickly she stumbled and fell against him, then righted herself against his leg. "Give it to me!" she said, reaching for it and trying to climb onto his knee to get higher.

He held it above his head, out of her reach. "I'm sorry," he said. "This dollar bill belongs to a little girl named Celia. I can't give it to you."

"But my name *is* Celia," she said, giggling.

"That's not what *she* said," Joe said, pointing to me. "She said your name was Ariel and that you live under the sea."

"That's the little mermaid! I'm *Celia*."

"Are you sure? You'll have to prove it."

"How?"

"Let's see . . . Can you spell 'Celia'?"

She shook her head. Her hands were on his knees and she was leaning against his legs. Totally comfortable with him already.

"Well, can you just tell me the first letter?"

"C," she said.

"Excellent. How about the second letter?"

"L?"

"Close enough. I'm convinced you're Celia." He handed her the dollar bill. She crawled into his lap and looked at it. "But no smiling," Joe said.

Celia immediately smiled.

"Hey, I said no smiling."

She laughed and leaned back against him. He grinned at me over her head. "Wish I could get you to smile that easily," he said. But I *was* smiling, and he knew it.

The doorbell rang. Dennis, who had been standing back by the doorway watching us, now said, "That's got to be the pizza this time. Celia, come help me get it."

"Okay," she said and slid down from Joe's lap. "Don't go out," she said over her shoulder to me as she joined Dennis, and they left the room.

"Go out," Joe said to me. Then he reached over and dragged me on top of him. He wrapped his fingers in my hair and pulled my head back, studying my face for a moment before kissing me. I thought about protesting, but Celia and Dennis were gone, and it was kind of a nice thing to be doing, especially after the evening I'd had. And after a few more seconds of feeling Joe inside my mouth, I got so lost in it that my dead grandmother could have walked in the door and I wouldn't have stopped.

He was the one to pull back suddenly. "I don't know whether to be pleased or annoyed that you look incredibly sexy tonight," he said.

I shrugged his hands off and moved away from him. "Why does everything you say sound like a line?"

"How about, 'Thanks for the compliment, Joe'?"

"Thanks for the compliment, Joe, and why does everything you say sound like a line?"

"Fuck you."

"Now you owe *me* a dollar."

"You're going to have to work harder than that for your money. Come with me to the party, Olivia."

"Why? Will I get a dollar?"

"Sure," he said.

"Well, for a dollar . . . Seriously, Joe, I've got to make sure Celia's all right with it."

"Are you talking about the cute little girl who was just in here laughing? She looked pretty all right to me."

"You didn't see her before."

"Before what?"

"No, I mean . . . she was having a tough time tonight."

"Not in any way that I saw. Do you just not want to go? Because if you don't, tell me."

"I want to go," I said. Which was true. Now that Joe was here, I didn't want him to leave without me. I didn't think I could stand another endless evening watching TV in that house.

"Good," he said. "Because, in case you didn't notice, I just spent half an hour on the Internet tracking down your father's address and another twenty minutes finding this place, just so I could be with you on New Year's Eve. I should have blown you off, after the way you treated me on the phone, but apparently the last few weeks of being with you have destroyed every last bit of self-respect I once had, so here I am, and the least you can do is want to go with me to the party."

"All right," I said. "Just let me go talk to Celia and Dennis."

"To tell them you're coming with me, right?"

"Yeah."

"And that you're madly in love with me and would follow me to the ends of the earth?"

"In your dreams. You want some pizza?"

"Yeah, okay, I'll have a slice." He followed me down the hallway, into the kitchen.

Dennis and Celia were sitting at the table eating. "Pizza's here," Dennis said unnecessarily.

"Are you going out?" Celia asked through a mouthful of food.

"I'm thinking about it."

Before she could protest, Dennis leaned over to her and said something in a low voice.

She listened, chewing. "All night?" she said when he finished whispering.

"All night," he said. "But only if you say good-bye nicely to Olivia."

"What did you just promise her?" I asked.

"She can stay up as late as she wants and watch as much TV as she wants, if she lets you go out with no more complaining. Is it a deal, Celia?"

"I guess."

"I think you just sold your soul to the devil," I said to him.

"She's got to fall asleep at some point . . . doesn't she?"

"Hey!" From Celia. "You just said I could stay up all night!"

"I know, I know," Dennis said. "And you can. I won't make you go to bed. I promise. Go on, Olivia, we'll be fine here."

"I don't know what time I'll be back, but my mother shouldn't be too late. I don't think."

"Don't worry about it," he said. "I can always sleep on the sofa if I have to."

"Thank you."

"You're welcome."

We were being very polite. No one would have guessed we'd been screaming at each other an hour earlier. "Come on," I said to Joe. "Sounds like I've got my freedom." I bent down and kissed Celia on the forehead. "Don't torture Dennis," I said.

"What's 'torture'?"

"Being mean to someone. Kind of. Not exactly."

"Look it up in the dictionary," Joe suggested. "You'll find Olivia's picture there."

"Joe's a funny guy," I said to Celia. "Real funny. Good night, Celia. Good night, Dennis."

"Good night," Dennis said, not looking at us, reaching for another slice of pizza.

Joe said, "Thanks for freeing Olivia up, Dennis. We owe you one."

"No problem."

"You know, I'm starving," Joe said. "Think I'll have some pizza." He reached down and took the piece that Celia was eating right out of her hand. "Mmmm. This one looks good." He pretended to take a bite out of it.

"Hey!" she said. "That's mine!"

"Really?" he said, examining it. "Are you sure? It doesn't say 'Celia' on it."

"I'm eating it!"

"No, I'm eating it."

"No, I am!" she said and chortled.

"All right," Joe said with a sigh, handing it back to her. "But I'm going to be very hungry without this pizza."

"There's more right there!" She pointed to the box.

"Oh," he said. "Don't mind if I do." He took a piece. "Good-bye, Ariel."

"I'm Celia!"

"Poor Ariel," he said to me. "She thinks she's Celia."

"I am!" she said and giggled.

"Good-bye, whoever you are," he said and winked at her. Then headed toward the door.

I followed him then stopped and turned around. I said, "Dennis? You were right. About my driving, I mean. I was too drunk to even realize how drunk I was. You were right to stop me."

"I know," he said.

The obvious next step for me would have been to get smashed at the party and spend the rest of New Year's Eve drunkenly making out with Joe. But I wasn't in the mood to drink anymore. I had meant it when I'd told Dennis I was thinking of giving up booze. Not that I was such a big drinker, but looking over the previous couple of months, I could think of several times I'd gotten wasted, and I wasn't particularly proud of my behavior on any of them.

Trust me to decide to give up alcohol, not on New Year's *Day* like any normal human being with a hangover, but on New Year's *Eve*, at a party where everyone else was already totally out of his gourd by the time we arrived.

There was a keg in the living room. A *keg*, for Christ's sake. Like these graduate students were still college kids. Most of them were pushing thirty and would have been considered adults in any other environment.

I kept getting more and more sober and everyone around me kept getting drunker and drunker. So many people spilled drinks on me that I smelled like I was having a much better time than I actually was.

Joe hung out with some pals near the keg, tossing back Styrofoam cups of warm beer. He introduced me to people, but the music was so loud I couldn't catch anyone's name. Joe didn't seem to mind the noise. He leaned over to his friends and shouted things in their ears and they'd shout back in his. I didn't even try to join in.

Joe kept a proprietary hand on me the whole time, sometimes rubbing my back, sometimes stroking my arm, sometimes nestling under the hair at the back of my neck. I didn't mind these fairly discreet signs of affection, but as Joe got drunker his attentions to me got less subtle, until, sometime shortly before midnight, his hand slipped under my dress. I pushed him away and walked off. He called after me but didn't follow, and I wandered into the kitchen in search of food. I still hadn't eaten and I was starving. I wished I'd had some pizza with Dennis and Celia. Hell, I wished I'd stayed with them and just gone to bed early.

There was food set out on a counter in the kitchen but unfortunately it was your basic cheap student food—chips, m&m's, little cubes of cheese and sausage, and some guacamole that was turning brown despite the pit someone had stuck hopefully in the middle of it. Ten unopened bottles of cheap sparkling wine were lined up on the counter waiting for midnight.

The kitchen was less crowded and a little bit cooler than the living room. The music wasn't so loud, either.

A large woman sat at the kitchen table, searching through a bowl of pretzels, carefully picking out the whole ones to eat. I went over and sat down next to her.

She glanced at me, then went back to sorting out the pretzels. "I know you," she said.

As soon as she spoke, I knew her, too. Professor Greene. Hard to recognize her away from her podium, especially since she was wearing a sweater and pants instead of a suit. But her voice was unmistakable— rich, deep, and stagey, like a bad actor going at Shakespeare with all his might. "I was in your class this fall," I said. "English 34."

"That's right," she said. "That's where I recognize you from. You sat in the back and never paid attention. Was I boring you?"

"No," I said. But she had the right person: I always sat in the back. "I liked your lectures."

"Maybe you always look bored," she said. "You look bored now. Is it something you cultivate?"

"No, I'm really bored right now."

"Who was your TA?"

"For English 34? Joe Lowden."

"Why are you here? You're an undergraduate."

"I am."

"Well? This isn't an undergraduate party."

"I came with someone."

She waited, looking at me with her eyebrows raised.

"Joe," I said.

She smiled and brushed a crystal of salt off of a pretzel before stuffing it in her mouth. "You know," she said, crunching, "that sort of thing is frowned upon. Though not by me. Two consenting adults and all."

I said, "Why are you here? You're not a graduate student, either."

"I was invited."

"By who? I don't even know whose house this is."

"No? That will making sending a thank-you note difficult." I couldn't tell if she was joking or not. "And it's 'by whom.'" Then, leaning back with an expectant smile, she said, "So tell me what you learned from my class. Obviously nothing about grammar, but . . . what *will* you take away from English 34, Miss Martin? What will remain with you for the rest of your life?"

She wanted me to stroke her. I wasn't in the mood. "In all honesty? Not much."

Her smile disappeared. "I was right. You weren't paying attention to my lectures."

"You asked what I'd remember," I said. "Not what I took notes on. I passed the class."

"Tell me, Miss Martin, do you think you'd be so quick to denigrate my teaching if you were still my student?"

"You mean would I be less rude if you were grading me? Probably not, but the odds of my sleeping with you would go up astronomically."

"Don't try to be funny. Not unless you're going to succeed."

"Hey," I said, "that hurt my feelings."

"I doubt that. It's almost midnight. Shouldn't you be looking for your date? Who was it again? Oh, yes, Joe Lowden. You're aware of his reputation, I assume?"

"Yes."

"Then you learned nothing at all from Richardson. I should have flunked you."

"I thought we were reading the books as literature, not as a girl's guide to dating."

"If you're incapable of learning from example, then you're going to have to learn everything for yourself," she said. "That's a hard road to take, Miss Martin. I wish you well on it."

"No, you don't," I said, standing up.

"I do. Arrogance in young people always brings out the pity in me. It gets beaten out of them so painfully."

"Oh," I said. "I'm the arrogant one here?"

"I've earned *my* arrogance," she said. "What have you ever accomplished?"

"Not a fucking thing," I said. "Happy New Year."

"Happy New Year," she said and went back to flicking through the pretzels.

I ran into Joe as I was leaving the kitchen. "I've been looking for you," he said. "Was that Professor Greene you were talking to?"

"Yes."

"What was she saying?"

"She thinks I'm arrogant."

"You're kidding. What the hell did you say to her?"

"Nothing."

"Fuck, Olivia, I hope she didn't know you were here with me."

"Why? What difference does it make?"

"I don't want her pissed off at *me*. She's probably going to be grading my thesis, you know. Bitch."

"Her or me?"

"You, of course. Someone should put a muzzle on you."

"I was bored," I said. "This is a boring party. Come on, let's go back to your place."

"What's in it for me?"

"You know what's in it for you."

"All right," he said. "You've convinced me."

Even though he was drunk, he wanted to drive. I couldn't convince him it was a bad idea.

Now I knew why Dennis had resorted to threats with me.

I went a different way. I pushed Joe up against the car and kissed him, wet and deep. When I slid my hand into his pocket, he writhed with pleasure, but I wasn't going for anything good. I hooked my finger around his keys and had them out before he figured out what I was doing.

I opened the car, jumped into the driver's seat, and told him either to get in the other side or get left behind. He got in.

The only problem was, the kiss had gotten him all worked up. He kept reaching between my legs even though I was driving. I had to keep pushing him away. I needed to focus on the road. I didn't trust the other drivers out that late on New Year's Eve.

"Jesus," I said when he made a grab for me and knocked into my arm. "Can't you zip it up for ten more minutes?"

Suddenly, all around us were popping noises and people shouting and screaming from houses and apartments. "Must be midnight," I said. The clock on Joe's car was slow. "Happy New Year, Joe."

"We should have stayed at the party," he said. "There was someone there I wanted to kiss. She had the most incredible blue eyes . . . I was just waiting for my chance at midnight."

"I can take you back, if you want."

"I'm joking," he said and his hand slipped between my legs again.

This time I didn't push him away, just slowed the car. "I don't even like blue eyes. Just green eyes. And only your shade of green."

"What the hell are you talking about? My eyes are brown."

"You're wrong. They're green. Maybe there's a touch of golden brown toward the center, but they're mostly a beautiful, mysterious green."

"You're drunk."

"Maybe so," he said. "I look at you and get lost in your eyes and they seem green to me."

"Drunk or insane."

"Can't you drive any faster? I want to have the first orgasm of the new year."

"I hear there's a contest for that," I said. "First baby born and first orgasm. You'll be in all the newspapers."

"You'll be right there alongside me," he said.

"Yeah? Hope you're right about that one."

I don't know if we qualified for first, but I'd say we were definitely in the running for best.

Later that night—actually, early in the morning—I nudged Joe and said, "I've got to get home. You want to drive or lend me your car?"

He didn't say anything for a moment, and I thought maybe he was asleep. Then he said, "I like that you made Professor Greene mad at you."

"Excuse me?"

He propped himself up on his elbows, just visible in the bits of light coming from the window. "I don't even know what you said to the old witch. I just like that you said what you wanted and didn't give a shit that she was a professor or head of the department or anything like that."

I sat up. "I thought you were mad at me for pissing her off."

"I've been thinking about it. Lying here with you next to me thinking about it. Thinking about how I've finally met someone who does what she wants and says to hell with the consequences, who doesn't give a rat's ass what other people think of her."

"You say it like it's a good thing."

"It's the best thing. I love that you're like that. I love you, Olivia."

Silence.

"Okay," he said, shifting. "That fell flat."

"Joe—"

"No, it's okay. I didn't expect anything from you—hoped, maybe, but didn't expect. Which is also, in a weird way, part of what I like about you." Another pause. He said, "Funny. There have been so many times people have wanted to hear me say that, and I just couldn't. And here it falls on deaf ears."

"Not deaf," I said. "I heard you."

"But you don't care."

"Yes, I do. Thank you for saying that."

"You believe me, don't you?"

"You had a lot of beer tonight."

"I feel very sober right now. I meant it, Olivia."

"Yeah, well, I guess it would explain why you think my eyes are green. Maybe that's a sign of true love." I lay back down and slid under the covers next to him. He put his leg over both of mine and I felt warm and pinned down in a nice way. "I should go," I said after a minute. "I'll take your car—"

"No. Don't go, Olivia. Spend the night. You owe me that, at least."

"I don't owe you anything."

"Yes, you do. I opened my heart to you. And you stabbed me right in it."

"Oh, please."

"Well, you certainly didn't treat it with kid gloves. Spend the night, Olivia. I want you to. Don't you want to? We could wake up in the morning together."

I ran my finger along his leg. What he was offering didn't sound bad. "I don't know . . . I should at least call home, make sure everything's okay."

"You'll just wake everyone up."

"Yeah, that's true." And they could always call me on the cell phone, if they really needed me.

"Let them sleep. Spend the night with me, Olivia. I want to see what you look like in the morning. I want to sleep all night with you next to me. We haven't done that. We need to do that. Please."

This was a new Joe, this supplicant.

I curled up tight against him and said, "Okay."

twenty

"**So.**" Dr. Elisa Rubillos tilted her head. "How *are* you, Olivia?"

"Me?" I said. "I'm fine."

She raised her eyebrows. "Are you?"

"I thought I was."

"Until?"

"Until now. Do you have a problem with my being fine?"

She smiled. She had a big nose and the tip of it came forward and hung over her upper lip when she smiled. "Not at all."

When we first got to the office, I had sat with Celia on my lap while she and the doctor talked about things like school and ballet. Nothing heavy. Then I had deposited Celia with Rosivel in the waiting room and come back to talk to Dr. Rubillos alone.

I shifted a little in the big leather armchair. "So what did you think about Celia?"

"What did I think about her?"

"Did she seem okay to you?"

"Okay?"

"Is repeating everything I say the only thing you do?"

"Sometimes I need clarification."

"I want to know how Celia seemed to you," I said. Slowly, like I was talking to an idiot, which maybe I was. "That's why I'm here. To find out if Celia needs some professional help with all the changes in her life."

"Do you think she does?"

"Her teacher does," I said. "And the director of her school. And this guy who's the executor of our father's will."

"And what about you?"

"I think she needs help, but from someone who does more than just ask stupid questions."

Dr. Rubillos leaned back in her chair and crossed her legs at the ankles, smoothing out the fabric of her dress where it fell over her knees. She had a big body—not fat, just big, with man-sized shoulders and no waist to speak of—and her movements seemed to require a lot of effort.

"I'm sorry if you think my questions are stupid," Dr. Rubillos said. "I'm simply trying to find out why you brought Celia here and what you're hoping to gain from it. Then I can tell you whether or not I feel I can be helpful to you."

"Come on," I said. "Would you ever really say we don't need your help?"

A pause. She said, "I think Celia will definitely need the help of a professional through this difficult time. I would very much like to be part of the healing process, but it's up to you to decide whether or not we're a good fit. I would certainly encourage you to meet with other people until you find someone you're comfortable with."

"Dr. Elton thought you were the right person." Dr. Elton was the director of Celia's school. The first day I took Celia back to school after the holiday break, I was sent to the principal's office, which made me vaguely nostalgic for the days when I just went there to get yelled at and wasn't considered responsible for the well-being of a young orphan.

"Dr. Elton and I are old friends," said Elisa Rubillos. "She's an excellent school director, and I respect her judgment. That doesn't mean you have to."

"Look," I said, "I want what's best for Celia. But I need you to give me some real advice, or this isn't going to be helpful. I think she's doing well, all things considered, but maybe I'm missing something."

"Like what?"

"Like maybe she's sadder than I realize."

"She's lost her mother and her father."

"Yes," I said, "I know that. That's why I'm her guardian, and why I'm sitting here right now, when I'd rather be pretty much anywhere else."

"Are you angry that you have to be here?"

I shook my head. "We're not going there. I'll help you with Celia any way I can, but we're not doing *me*."

" 'Doing you'?"

"You know what I mean."

Dr. Rubillos uncrossed her legs and leaned forward again. "Please listen to what I have to say, Olivia. I think I can help Celia, and I'd like to, even if it's just by listening to her. She needs to be able to talk to someone whose feelings won't be hurt if she expresses unhappiness with the changes in her life."

"Okay," I said, "I get that. Go on."

"But I also think we may, in fact, need to 'do you,' as you put it. I can't force you to come in here and talk about yourself, but I want you to think about doing just that. Celia isn't the only one who's lost her father and needs to grieve."

"Oh, wow," I said. "I lost my father, too. I never thought of it that way."

"Sarcasm is a defense," the doctor said.

"It's also good clean fun." I tapped my right foot on the floor. "I don't want to disappoint you or anything, but I'm not grieving. Richard and I weren't close. I'm not happy he's dead, but I'm not crippled by the fact, either."

"Be that as it may—" The eyebrows were up again. "Be that as it may, your life has been greatly affected by his death, and I don't think I'm reading too much into the situation to suspect that you've got to be feeling at least a little overwhelmed by the fact that you're now Celia's guardian and entirely responsible for her." Long sentence, she had to gulp for breath at the end of it.

"Sure. Who wouldn't be? But I'll survive."

"You might find it a relief to talk about it," she said. "There will probably come a time — maybe it's happened already — when you'll feel angry about being stuck at home with a little girl who's crying or whining or sick or something like that. And then, if you're like most people, you'll probably feel guilt over having been angry. It's never easy taking care of a small child, Olivia, and in your case, it isn't even something you signed on to do."

"I'll be fine so long as I know that Celia's doing all right," I said.

"You can't help someone else heal if you're in pain yourself." Man, she was trying hard. Either she really thought I needed to have my head shrunk, or she had a lot of bills to pay. "Your emotional well-being is worth putting time into, Olivia."

"We're officially done talking about me now," I said. "Tell me what I should say to Celia when she starts talking about her parents."

"What do you think you should say?"

"That's it, I'm leaving." I stood up.

"No, wait," she said. She put her hand up. "I'll try to give you the answers you want, but you have to trust me and try not to be hostile."

I stayed on my feet. "Tell me what I should say to her."

"I'll do my best." She recrossed her arms and legs. "Okay. Here's what I think. Let Celia be your guide. If she has questions, answer them honestly, but don't give her any more information than she needs or wants. If she asks where her parents are, tell her the truth, that they're buried in the ground. But don't go on about graves and coffins and worms — she doesn't need that."

"What about heaven? Her nanny told her they're in heaven, but I don't believe in that shit."

"I certainly wouldn't say anything you didn't feel was right. Religious beliefs are a personal choice, so I wouldn't presume to tell you what to say or believe. However, if Celia is finding comfort in what her nanny says, you don't have to completely disavow it, either. You can express your own uncertainty without forcing her to give up an idea that she finds comforting."

I sat down. "I can't tell if she finds comfort in it or not."

"Then just leave it alone. If she asks you any questions, you can say that some people believe there's an afterlife and some don't, and she's free to believe whatever she wants. I think all children — adults, too — need to find their own way when it comes to spiritual beliefs, and they can do that only if they're neither mocked nor rewarded for the beliefs they express."

"What do I do when she gets sad?"

"Does she get sad a lot? What makes her sad?"

"Not a lot. She's actually pretty happy most of the time. And sometimes she's just normal sad, like when she's tired or I say no to her about something. But there was this one time . . ." I told her about New Year's Eve, and the dresses.

When I was done, Dr. Rubillos said, "It sounds like you handled it well. You acknowledged her sadness and let her speak freely."

"What should I do if it happens again?"

"More or less what you did. Ask her questions. Let her tell you what she's feeling and why. Don't impose any meanings on her. In other words, if she says she's sad, ask her why she's sad, don't say, 'Are you sad because your parents are dead?' Don't be angry at her for being sad, but don't feel like you've screwed up in some way when she is. It's a compliment to you and your caregiving if she feels like she can break down in front of you, Olivia. It means she can mourn the parents who are gone without being afraid she'll hurt the feelings of the one who's taken their place."

"She didn't break down in front of me," I said. "She hid in a closet."

"Maybe, but she turned to you once you were there."

"I guess. There's one thing I've been wondering about . . . Is it possible she doesn't really miss her parents all that much? Most of the time she seems pretty happy. And her parents were self-centered jerks who didn't spend all that much time with her. Is it possible she just doesn't care that much?"

"It's possible," Dr. Rubillos said in a tone that implied it wasn't really. "It's possible, but I have to tell you, Olivia, I've never yet met a child or an adult who's lost his parents who hasn't mourned them in some way or another. No matter how dysfunctional your family or your parents, they're still the only ones you've got, and you're going to feel their loss. Sometimes it's even *harder* for the children of bad parents, because

they don't have the emotional resources to process and rebuild. But I
will say this: Celia's doing as well as any child I've ever seen in this
situation. And some of the credit for that has to go to you. You may
not care much for my professional opinion"—and here she gave a tight
smile—"but I think you're doing as good a job as anyone your age
could do under the circumstances."

"I'm always willing to take praise," I said. "My opinion of your professional opinion just went up."

"So you'll bring her back to me?"

"Just tell me when."

"And schedule another time to come alone?"

"No," I said.

We set up Celia's weekly appointment, then I collected her and
Rosivel from the waiting room, and we all went downstairs to the car—
not the Lexus, and not my old Toyota, but what must have been the
"family" car, a Mercedes-Benz station wagon.

The garage charged a sweet five bucks for the hour we'd been there.
Elisa had "regretted" the fact she was unable to validate my parking
ticket and suggested I look for street parking next time.

I realized we'd be going right by Dennis Klein's office on our way
home. I had a couple of financial questions to ask him, but he hadn't
come by the house for a while. He called almost every day, but just
spoke to my mother who always pounced on the phone when it rang.

"Hey, Celia," I said, glancing at her in the rearview mirror. "Want to
go see Dennis's office? Where he works?"

"Okay," she said. She was on the tail end of a cold and her voice was
hoarse.

"Do you mind stopping, Rosivel?"

"No," Rosivel said. She was sitting in back with Celia. I'd offered her
the front passenger seat, but she said she liked to sit with Celia. "Whatever you like. It's just . . . do you know what time is it?"

"Almost four."

"Oh," she said.

"We might be a little late getting back. Is that a problem?" She was supposed to leave at four-thirty, but there was no way we'd be home by then if we made the stop.

"It's fine," she said, but I couldn't tell if she meant it or not. She was a tough person to read.

"I don't want to mess you up," I said.

A pause. Then Rosivel said, "There is a bus stop on Santa Monica, near here. My bus stops there. I could just go home from here. It's a little early, I know—"

"Not a problem," I said. "If you have everything you need, that's great."

She pointed out the bus stop two blocks later. I pulled over, and she kissed Celia good-bye, then hopped out of the car after we exchanged our daily polite thank yous, going back to the life she led that I knew nothing about. I didn't even know where she lived, whether it was a house or an apartment, in a safe neighborhood or a bad one. Just that she always managed to get to the house in Little Holmby at exactly eight-fifteen every single morning. And that, even though I couldn't talk to her without feeling uncomfortable, I was always relieved to hear her key in the door.

I looked in the rearview mirror. Celia was staring out the window, breathing heavily through her open mouth. Her nose was really stuffed. She'd been waking up at night because of it. I wanted to give her some medicine, but I didn't know what kind or how much, and I kept forgetting to ask Rosivel.

"You okay?" I asked. "You sure you're up for this?"

"Yeah," she said. "Why can't Rosivel go with us?"

"She has to go home," I said. "We'll have fun, anyway."

She thought, breathing in and out noisily. "Okay," she said.

Two minutes later, we were at Dennis's building. As I pulled into the garage, Celia said, "It's Daddy's office."

Shit. Why hadn't it occurred to me she'd recognize it as Richard's office? I had never visited him there, but she must have.

I wondered if I should just make up an excuse and back out again, but Celia said, "They have candy here. Can I have a piece of candy?"

"Sure," I said. Maybe it would be okay.

We parked the car and went up to the law offices on the seventh floor. The reception area had huge windows that looked out over Century City.

Celia pointed to a glass jar full of peppermints on the receptionist's desk. "See?" she said. "Candy."

I gave her a mint and sent her over to the sofa to eat it. I told the pretty young receptionist we were there to see Dennis Klein.

"Isn't that Richard Martin's little girl?" she asked in a whisper.

"Yes."

"Poor little thing."

"Yes," I said.

"How's she doing?"

"She's doing okay," I said.

"Poor little girl," she said, shaking her head and watching Celia.

After a moment, I said, "So, is Dennis Klein available?"

"Oh, right," she said. She pressed some buttons then spoke quietly into the mouthpiece of her headset.

I went over to Celia, and she held out her mint. "I can't open it, Livvy. I tried." Her nostrils were caked with dried snot.

"There's a trick to it." I showed her how to tug on the wrapper ends to make them uncurl. She plucked out the mint and put it in her mouth. I pulled a tissue out of my pocket and rubbed at her nose, then balled it up and crammed it back in my pocket.

Celia made a face. "It's spicy."

"Yeah?"

"I don't like it."

"You want to spit it out?"

It was already in her hand. "Here."

I took the tissue back out of my pocket and held it out. She deposited the mint and I folded it up even smaller. Then put it back in my pocket because I didn't see a wastebasket anywhere.

Celia's fingers were all sticky, and she kept reaching out and touching my pants and shirt.

The receptionist called out, "Mr. Klein's assistant will be here in just a sec."

A few moments later, the assistant materialized. The same one I had met when my mother and I had come to talk to Dennis about Richard's will. Holly. She was a tired-looking woman in her thirties, who had told me the previous time that she had three kids and a husband who had recently been injured on the job. He was a carpenter who worked for a big studio and part of a metal gate had fallen on his legs. They didn't know if he'd ever get the full use of them back. Dennis was helping them file a lawsuit against the studio.

Holly said, "Hello, Olivia. Dennis is in a meeting, but he said to tell you he'll be right out. Hey, Celia, remember me? We met once a long time ago."

Hearing her name, Celia ducked and hid her head behind my arm. Not in the mood to be social. Sometimes she was, and sometimes she wasn't. I hauled her to her feet and we followed Holly down the hallway and to her desk, which was separated from other assistants' desks by a maze of walls that went up only to about the height of my shoulders. Holly's was a few feet away from the entrance to Dennis's office. The lawyers got the windows and the views, of course. His door was closed.

"Do you want something to drink?" Holly asked. "Water, coffee, Coke?"

"Coke," Celia said immediately.

"Please," I said.

She just shrugged.

"I'd love a glass of water," I said to Holly, and she left us to get the drinks. "It wouldn't kill you to say please," I said to Celia.

"*You* didn't say 'please.' "

"I didn't? Yeah, I guess you're right. But you don't want to be like me."

"Where's Dennis? You said he'd be here."

"He will be in just a second. He's behind that door over there."

"Is my daddy here?"

"No," I said. "Not anymore, Celia. Do you remember visiting him here?"

"Not really," she said. "I think he was somewhere over there." She pointed vaguely toward the west of the building. "I'm not sure. Do the people here know he died?"

"Yes," I said. "Do you want to walk over to his office and look at it?"

"I'm not sure where it is. Do you know?"

"No. But we could ask someone."

"Who?"

"Someone who works here. Like Dennis. Or Holly."

"There's a piece of candy stuck to my tooth."

"Use your fingernail to scrape it out."

"Rosivel says not to put my fingers in my mouth."

"Well, in general, you probably shouldn't. This is an emergency, though."

"You put your fingers in your mouth all the time."

"No, I don't."

"You were doing it in the car on the way here."

"Oh, you mean when I bite my fingernails. Yeah, I do that. I shouldn't, though. It's a bad habit."

She thought about that for a moment then said, "I need to pee."

"Of course you do."

On our way back from the bathroom, I could see Dennis coming out of his office with a young woman. She was wearing lawyer clothes—a slim pantsuit in dark gray—and glasses. Dennis said something to her that made her laugh.

They stopped by Holly's desk, and Dennis spoke to her. She went over to a nearby file cabinet and started looking through one of the drawers. Dennis and the other woman went back to chatting.

"Come on," Celia said. She was tugging on my arm. "I see Dennis. Come on, Livvy." She pulled me forward, and Dennis looked over and saw us.

"There you are," he said, coming toward us. Celia ran to him, and he scooped her up. She put her arms around his neck. He said, "I thought you guys had pulled a fast one on me and disappeared. Holly didn't know where you were."

"We went to the bathroom," Celia said. "I peed."

"Good job," he said.

"So did Livvy."

"Good job," he said to me.

"I'm gunning for a gold star."

The woman he had been talking to joined us. "Hello," she said to Celia. She looked at Dennis. "Is this Richard's daughter?"

"Yes. Celia Martin, meet Heather Finnergan."

"Hi, Celia," she said very gently and carefully. "How are you?" Up close, I could see she was the kind of woman who wore ugly glasses because she knew they emphasized how pretty she was underneath.

"This is also Richard's daughter," Dennis said, indicating me. "Olivia Martin."

"Hello," I said. We shook hands.

"Oh, wow," she said. "I didn't realize Richard had another daughter."

"He and my mother divorced a long time ago."

"Oh," she said. "I'm so sorry for your loss, Olivia. I was only able to know Richard for a few months, unfortunately, but he was a good man and a brilliant lawyer. It's very sad—" She looked at Celia and then back to me, lowering her voice. "Sad for all of us. A tragedy, really."

"You're a lawyer here?" I said, ready to change the subject.

"Yes," she said. "Only recently."

"Heather graduated from law school last spring," Dennis said. "From *Harvard*."

"Stop with that," she said and pushed his arm a little.

"In a few months, she'll be running the place."

"He gives me a hard time," she said.

"I want my Coke," Celia said.

Dennis brought her over to Holly's desk and put her in the desk chair. Holly was still looking through the file cabinet. Dennis joined her and they spoke for a moment, then he took a turn flipping through the files in the drawer while she watched. Celia drank her Coke. There was a cup on the desk, but Celia was drinking straight from the can. I could see some of it dripping onto her shirt.

That left Heather and me still standing together. "So," she said, "what grade are you?"

"I'm in my third year at UCLA."

"Oh, I'm sorry," she said. "I thought you were—"

"Yeah, I know. I get that a lot."

"It's good to look young," she said. "People always think I'm younger than I am. I didn't like it when I was your age, but now that I'm closing in on thirty, I'm starting to appreciate it."

And here I'd been thinking she was *over* thirty. "I'll remember that," I said.

"You remind me so much of your father. You look a lot like him, but it's something else, too—something about the way you move and your expressions."

"Yeah," I said. "I get that a lot, too."

There was a pause. She looked around, and Dennis saw her and headed back to us. "Sorry," he said. "We're having trouble finding the right file. Holly thinks maybe someone else has it, but she's not sure."

"Dennis," Heather said in a low voice, "we've been through this before. This isn't the first time—"

"I know, I know. She's going through a tough time."

"She's always going through a tough time. And we have too much work right now to be handicapped by incompetence, no matter how well intentioned. Please excuse my tone, Olivia. You're probably thinking I'm incredibly harsh, and maybe I am, but Dennis has the patience of a saint, which is a wonderful thing when you are, actually, a saint, but not so great when you're a busy lawyer."

"The patience of a saint," I repeated, looking at Dennis, who just shook his head.

Heather said, "I get frustrated because he's too nice sometimes, but the truth is I wouldn't even be here if it weren't for Dennis. He's one of the good guys, you know? He proves you can be a lawyer and not sell your soul." Quickly, "Your father was like that too, of course."

"Of course," I said. Wanting to laugh at the thought.

"They must teach you how to flatter people at Harvard," Dennis said. "Heather, I'm sorry about that file. I'll try to hunt it down. Meanwhile, call Walter Stacey and set up a meeting for next week. I need you to review that contract he sent over. If it's as bad as I expect it to be, start marking it up. We may have to rewrite it completely."

"Yes, sir." She snapped him a salute. "He works me like a dog," she said to me. "Kept me late every night this week."

"I thought *you* kept *me* working late," Dennis said. "I would have knocked off early if I hadn't thought you'd be disappointed."

"I can think of worse ways to spend my evenings," she said with a smile that only included him. She turned to me. "It was nice to meet you, Olivia. I really meant that about wanting to help if I can."

"Thanks," I said. "That's very nice of you."

She stopped by Holly's desk to say good-bye to Celia, and then said something to Holly that left Holly looking even more miserable than usual, and then Heather moved on, her narrow high heels silent on the carpeted floor.

"Come on in," Dennis said, turning toward his office door.

"You seem busy," I said. "Maybe we should forget it."

"Don't be silly. You're here, aren't you? Come on, Celia," he called. "We're going in my office."

As Celia jumped down from the desk chair, her elbow knocked over the can of Coke. It spilled all over the papers on the desk. Holly came rushing forward and grabbed the can, but the damage was done. "Oh, shit," she said.

Celia ran over to me. She hid her face in my legs.

"It's okay," Holly said. "I'm sorry I swore. It's okay, Celia. I have kids of my own . . ." She dropped the can into the trash and looked at the mess on her desk. "I better get some paper towels." She left.

Celia burrowed her face deeper into my thigh. I rubbed the nape of her neck. "It's okay, Celia. It was an accident. Everyone has accidents. Come on. Let's go into Dennis's office." I followed Dennis with Celia still attached, leechlike, to my leg.

Dennis closed the door behind us and then squatted down, holding out his arms to Celia. She shook her head and clung to my leg. "You don't need to be sad," he said. "No one's mad at you." Celia's face screwed up like she was going to cry, but instead she sneezed right in his face.

Dennis jumped up and wiped his face with the back of his hand.

"She has a cold," I said.

"You might have warned me."

"Sorry. You got any tissues?"

"Here." He went over to a shelf and brought me back the box.

I swiped at Celia's nose. But it was pointless since she had already rubbed her face against my pants leg.

Dennis was watching me. "You look tired, Olivia."

"I don't get a lot of sleep. Either this one wakes me up—bad dreams or a stuffy nose—or my mother does."

"Why does your mother wake you up?"

"She doesn't like to be alone in the middle of the night. Never has. Makes her nervous."

"So you get up with her?"

"No," I said. "I tell her to go fuck herself, but by that point I'm wide awake, and it's hard to go back to sleep."

"For God's sake, will you watch your language?" he said. "Go sit down, both of you. On the sofa."

We sat down, and he pulled up a chair and sat in front of us. "So what's up? Why are you here?"

"We just thought we'd pass along a virus and spill Coke on all your important papers," I said. "I think it's going well, don't you?"

"You said you had a question about finances?"

I leaned back into the sofa. "Yeah. I need to know how to pay for Celia's expenses—not the household stuff, but things like school and this doctor she's seeing."

"What doctor? Is she okay? Are you okay, Celia?"

"She's fine," I said. "Not a medical doctor. The kind who just talks with you."

"Oh," he said, "that doctor. Was she on the list I sent?"

"You never sent a list. You said you would, but you didn't."

"I did, too," Dennis said. "I faxed it over. I told your mother days ago."

"She didn't tell me. And I never check the fax machine—it's in Richard's office. I thought you just forgot about it, and the director of Celia's school—"

"That's Dr. Linda," said Celia.

"Right. Dr. Linda. She recommended somebody, so we went to see her today."

"And?" said Dennis.

"And it was okay," I said. "Celia seemed to have a good time, didn't you, Celia? With Dr. Elisa?"

"Yeah," Celia said with a yawn. "She gave me a lollipop."

"I didn't forget," Dennis said. "I wouldn't have forgotten."

"Well, you should always tell *me*, not Barbara."

"She answered the phone."

"She always answers the phone. Doesn't mean you can't ask to speak to me." He didn't say anything.

After a moment, I said, "Are you going to set up another account, or should I just pay for Celia's things out of the housekeeping money?"

"I've got an account set up for Celia that I can draw from," he said. "Have them send the bills directly to me."

Celia said, "I'm bored. When are we going home?"

"Soon," I said.

"I want to go in Dennis's car."

"Dennis isn't going home with us."

"Why not?" she said.

"I've got to stay and work, Celia."

"You never come anymore."

"It's been less than a week since I was last there. I don't think that counts as never. It's just I have a lot of work to do now that the holidays are over. But I miss seeing you, Celia."

"You have to come," she said.

"I will. Soon."

"When?"

"I don't know."

"Today?"

"I have to work—"

"Come today," she said.

"Celia—"

"You have to come today," she said. "Please? I want you to."

"And I want to," he said. "I just don't know if I can. Olivia, help me out here."

"It may be difficult for you to come," I said, "but don't you think you *should*?"

He gave me a dirty look.

I said, "Aren't you glad we came to visit?"

twenty-one

I didn't blame Dennis for being pissed off at me. Not only had my mother and I abused his good nature on New Year's Eve—and it's debatable which of us had behaved more badly, her with her "Why don't you join us on New Year's Eve?" approach to getting a baby-sitter, or me with my attempt to drive cross town completely plastered—but we'd managed to make things much worse before the holiday ended.

What happened was this:

I didn't know it until much later, but, at some point on New Year's Eve, my mother got invited to a "breakfast and swimming at dawn" party at the home of another friend, and she went off to enjoy herself without another thought. Which wouldn't have mattered if I'd come home at one or two in the morning like I'd originally intended. But instead I spent the night at Joe's apartment and didn't get home until after nine the next morning. And there was an exhausted Dennis slumped in a kitchen chair, wearing the clothes he'd worn the night before, only now the khakis were badly wrinkled, and his shirt had blue stains on it. Since Celia had blue fingers from eating blueberry waffles, I was guessing she'd used Dennis's shirt as a napkin.

I greeted them, and Celia looked up from her waffle, licked her fingers, and said, "You were wearing that dress last night, Livvy." And then, "I got up but you weren't here. Where were you?"

"At a friend's," I said. "How'd it go last night?"

Dennis told me that Celia had fallen asleep before ten. He had put her to bed and then stayed awake watching TV and waiting for my mother or me to come home. Hours went by. He watched three movies. He dozed a little. Finally, sometime around six that morning, he heard my mother come in, but by the time he'd roused himself enough to go look for her, she had already curled up on her bed and fallen asleep. He could have left then, but he was worried that Celia wouldn't be able to wake my mother if she needed something. So he went back to the sofa.

Forty minutes later, Celia pounced on him, wide awake and ready to start her day.

At seven-thirty, Dennis was so tired he couldn't play with her anymore. He decided to call me on my cell phone. Which worked great. He could hear the phone ringing away on the kitchen counter right where I'd left it.

So then there was nothing for him to do but wait for me to make my way home, which I did a couple of hours later.

"I'm sorry," I said. "I never thought my mother would be out all night."

"It's all right," he said. "I told you not to rush back. And you didn't."

He left as soon as he could find his shoes, which were on the floor in the living room, and hadn't been back to visit us since then.

I guess I couldn't be too critical of my mother's decision to stay out all night without calling home, given the fact I'd done the exact same thing, but the fact I could never count on her for anything was getting to me. Twice now, she'd gone out to smoke a cigarette and locked herself out of the house. One time I was there and threatened not to let her back in. The other time I was out with Celia, and my mother broke a window to get back inside, then cut her arm on the broken glass. When Celia and I got home, she was sitting in the kitchen, nursing both her arm and a glass of wine, convinced she was some sort of martyr. She hadn't even washed or bandaged her arm, just waited for me to come home and take care of it.

She seemed to think all that suffering gave her the right to disobey my rule about only smoking outside. But not openly. I was forever walking into bathrooms that reeked of cigarettes, with butts floating in the toilet bowl.

I was also always finding sticky wineglasses in the sink.

"I wish you'd use a juice glass," I said one day. The wineglasses didn't fit in the dishwasher and, on the days Elena didn't come, I had to wash them by hand. My mother never did dishes. She said it would ruin her hands, which were, admittedly, model-perfect—frequently manicured, slender, and soft. She also said my hands were already ruined, since I bit my fingernails, so it was okay for me to do the dishes.

"That's such a white trash thing to do," she said. "Drinking wine out of a juice glass. People who do that don't appreciate good wine—they just want to get drunk."

"And your motive for downing a bottle every night would be . . . ?"

"I sip a glass or two because I enjoy it. And it relaxes me."

"I thought that's what the Xanax was for."

"You have no idea what it's like," she said, "dealing with anxiety like mine. The only reason I can be calm and rational when I'm with you is because I've learned through the years how to control my pain. You should be grateful I don't impose it on you."

"Uh-huh," I said. "So a juice glass is out of the question?"

"I wouldn't like myself if I used one," she said.

I thought things had gone badly at Dennis's office. At home, they just got worse.

First, Celia tripped and fell getting out of the car and screamed for ten minutes, even though I couldn't find a single mark on her, and she didn't even seem to know *where* it hurt. She stopped screaming when I promised to make her hot chocolate. I mixed up some warm milk and cocoa and gave it to her. For some unknown reason, she decided to get down from her chair holding the cup. A few drops spilled out onto her hand. She cried out that it was hot—it wasn't—and dropped the entire thing on the floor. The cup didn't break, but the cocoa made a mess.

When I asked her to help me clean it up, she shouted, "No!" and went running out of the kitchen. She ran right into my mother who was on her way in.

"Whoa there, little monkey!" my mother said. "Watch out for Barbara's dress, sweetheart." She was dressed to go out.

Celia hid behind her.

"Come on, Celia," I said. "Clean up your spill."

"I don't want to," she said around my mother's legs.

"Careful of the dress!" my mother said and slid away from her. I grabbed Celia's arm and hauled her back to the spill.

"Here's a towel," I said.

She took the towel, dropped it on top of the cocoa on the floor and started to walk away. "I'm done."

"That's not cleaning it. You have to wipe it up."

"You do it." She sneezed and used her shirt to wipe her nose. "I'm sick. I can't clean up. And I'm hungry. I want something to eat."

"I'm not making you anything until you clean up that mess." God, was that me talking? My head ached. "Come on, Celia, just do it."

"I'm hungry!" she screamed.

My mother, who'd been checking out her reflection in the toaster, looked up and said, "Well, I'm off for the evening! How do I look?"

"Breathtaking," I said.

"Oh, you're just saying that."

"You're right. Isn't it kind of early for dinner?"

"Cocktails first, darling."

Celia was opening the refrigerator. "I want something to eat!" she said and pulled at a bowl, which fell to the floor. Tuna salad spilled out. Rosivel had made her some for lunch that day.

"Terrific," I said. "That's another mess you can help clean up if you expect me to make you dinner."

She ran over to the pantry, dashed inside and emerged with a box of cereal. "I'll eat this."

"Not until you've cleaned up."

"Good night, my loves!" my mother sang out. "Have fun!" And she left.

Celia made a snotty face at me and reached in for a fistful of Cheerios. As she pulled her hand out of the box, Cheerios flew out.

"You're starting to piss me off," I said.

"I don't care. I don't like you, anyway. You're mean." She pushed the cereal into her mouth and chewed theatrically, spewing pieces of cereal.

"You're not exactly a joy to be around yourself," I said.

"I'm gonna watch TV." She headed toward the door, still holding the cereal box.

I ran over, blocked her way. "You're not going anywhere until you've cleaned up the cocoa, cleaned up the tuna salad, cleaned up the cereal, and eaten a healthy dinner. Understand?"

She dropped the cereal box on the floor where it fell over and more spilled out—Christ, what a mess she'd made in ten minutes—and tried to push past me.

"Oh, no, you don't," I said, and picked her up. "I mean it." She struggled against me, screaming and crying, but I held her firmly and somehow, bit by bit, forced her to help me clean up all the messes she'd made.

Okay, I was really the one doing the cleaning, but I was holding her the whole time, which made it a lot harder on me, since she was kicking and complaining, and my back was breaking from leaning over without letting go of her, and I could have cleaned it up by myself much more easily without her—in half the time at least—but still somehow I had to figure some message was getting through to her, although when I really thought about it, I couldn't figure out what the hell it could be.

Finally, the kitchen was slightly less of a disaster area, and I dumped her into a chair. I was out of breath and sweating like crazy. "All right," I said. "What do you want for dinner?"

"Nothing!" she shouted. "I'm not hungry! And I hate you!"

"Fine," I said. "Then you can go right to bed."

"I don't want to go to bed! I'm not tired!"

"The hell you're not," I said and carried her to her room. I threw her down on the bed, and I wasn't gentle about it. Later that night, I would remember how rough I'd been and feel guilty, but at that point I didn't much care. "If you don't want to eat a decent dinner, then you can just stay in your bed until you fall asleep."

That turned out to be a really bad idea on my part. Tired as she was, she still wasn't ready to go to sleep—it wasn't even six yet and her bedtime was closer to eight—and so there was this long period of her screaming and trying to get out of her bed and my yelling back at her and shoving her back in her bed . . .

Finally, I was so exhausted and sick of the whole thing that I said, "Oh, fuck this. Go watch TV. Do whatever you want. I don't give a shit. Just don't talk to me again tonight." And I turned my back on her and walked out.

I went to the kitchen and poured myself a glass of water. I was actually shaking. What a little jerk she was. Spoiled, selfish. It wasn't a surprise, given her parents, but now *I* was stuck dealing with the little bitch. Any kid could be a pain at times—I knew that, I wasn't an idiot—but at least if she were my own kid, I'd have had a chance to teach her some sense of right and wrong by now, which her parents obviously never had, and, besides, I had to figure I'd probably feel more attached to her, which would help me not hate her at times like this.

I heard a little noise and looked around.

She stood there, clutching a stuffed animal, tears on her cheeks. She said, "I sorry, Olivia. Don't be mad." Then burst into loud sobs and came running to me, reaching her arms up.

I didn't want to hold her. I was tired and pissed as hell, and I just wanted to be left alone. But I picked her up anyway, because I figured I had to. She pushed her face into my chest and wet my shirt with her tears.

I rested my head on top of hers and wondered how I would ever survive the next few years of my life. Hell, the next few weeks.

She was contrite for the rest of the evening, which was better than her being defiant, I guess, except that it made her more clingy than

usual. She dissolved into tears every time I tried to put her down somewhere, so I had to hold her while I was trying to make us some dinner,
and hold her while we were both eating, and hold her while she
watched TV, which meant I had to watch, too. Then she wouldn't go
to sleep until I lay down with her. She clutched me hard around the
neck.

"Livvy?" she said, after we had lain there for a while.

I kept my eyes closed. "Go to sleep, Celia."

"Can I just say one thing?"

"One thing. That's it."

"Are you mad at me?"

"Yeah," I said, "a little bit."

"I don't want you to be mad at me."

"Then don't drive me crazy."

"I didn't mean to," she said.

"Maybe not. But you weren't exactly being my pal."

"I don't want you to leave," she said.

"I'm here."

"Don't leave. Not even after I'm asleep."

"I may leave the bed," I said, "but I won't leave the house. Not tonight."

"Promise?"

"I said I wouldn't, and I won't."

She was silent for a moment, then she gave a long sigh that turned
into a yawn at the end. "Livvy?"

"You already said one thing."

"I sorry I spilled the cocoa."

"I know, Celia. Go to sleep."

Amazingly, she did, pretty soon after that. Her breathing turned deep
and regular. I waited a few more minutes, then pulled her arms off my
neck. She moved a little, and said something incoherent, and I froze,
but then she turned on her side and was out.

About an hour later, I heard a quiet knock at the front door and met
Dennis in the front hallway.

"Rats," he said when I told him Celia was asleep. "I thought she'd
still be up."

"I'm sorry. I had to put her to bed. She was tired. Actually, she was more than tired—she was wrecked. And I didn't even know if you were definitely coming."

"I said I would."

"Not for sure."

"Yes for sure."

"That's not how I remember it. Anyway, there was no way I could keep her up any later. Not without losing my mind."

"I should have called," he said.

"Yeah." I had been reading in the living room and watching for him, looking up every time a car came down our street, hoping he'd still come even though it was getting later and later. I needed to talk to someone. Who was an adult. And rational. "Can't you come in for a minute?" I said.

He hesitated, looking back toward the door like he wanted to go.

"You used to like hanging around here," I said.

"Used to?" he repeated. "You've been living here for all of two weeks. There's no used to, Olivia."

"You know what I mean."

"I had more free time during the holidays," he said. "That's all."

"No, it's not. You've been pissed off at me ever since New Year's Eve. I don't blame you. I know we screwed up your holiday and I'm sorry for it. But I wish you'd . . . you know. Stop being pissed off."

He sighed. "I'm not angry at you, Olivia."

"Prove it," I said. "Stay and keep me company."

"Where's Barbara?"

"Out. She reconnected with a bunch of old friends on New Year's Eve, and she's been going out every night since."

"And your friend? Joe? Where's he?"

"I don't know. At his place. We're not attached at the hip, you know."

"I was just thinking that if you wanted company—"

"Please come in," I said. "I was just going to have some ice cream."

"Well, for ice cream," he said and followed me down the hallway.

In the kitchen, dishing out the rocky road, I said, "So were you working with Heather from Harvard tonight?"

"Yes," he said. "We work together a lot. She's the junior associate in my department."

"Lucky you."

"I don't know what you mean by that. She's a good worker and very smart. I'm glad to have her on my team."

"Yes, well, if you like them pretty and smart—"

"It's not a question of liking anyone. At least, not in the way you're insinuating."

"You sure?" I said, pushing a bowl of ice cream over to him.

"Olivia, if you invited me in because you needed someone to torment, I'm not going to stay. I've got better things to do with my time."

"I'm not tormenting you. Not intentionally."

"Yes," he said. "I fully believe you're capable of tormenting me without meaning to, because it's the one thing that comes naturally to you."

"I do a few other things, too," I said. I put the ice cream back in the freezer and sat down with my bowl.

"I should go," he said after a moment. He didn't get up, though. He played with his ice cream, not really eating it. Then he looked up. "Oh, wait. There was something I needed to ask you about. I'm so tired I almost forgot."

"What?"

He had to think for a second. "That fax. Did you look at it?"

"Oh, right. No, I forgot."

"It wasn't just the list of therapists. There were some papers I needed you to sign. I'm glad I remembered."

He led the way to Richard's office. I followed a step or two behind, feeling dark and miserable. He hated me.

The fax machine was on a table near Richard's desk. A few pages had printed up. Dennis pulled them out. "Look at the date—Holly sent it four days ago. Don't you ever come in here?"

"Not very often."

He handed me the papers and, as I reached for them, I knocked something off of the desk. Dennis bent down to pick it up for me. "What is this?" he asked, holding up the ceramic paperweight I'd been playing with the night Charlotte and I had fled to Richard's office to escape my mother.

"Oh, that. I don't know. Something Celia made Richard, I think." I was studying the list he'd sent. Elisa Rubillos was one of the five listed therapists. For some reason, I found that reassuring.

I wondered what Dr. Rubillos would have thought about that evening's battle. Had I been too mean to Celia at the end, when she felt bad? How did you stop feeling angry at a kid who went out of her way to make you angry in the first place?

"I hope it didn't get chipped," Dennis said, examining the paperweight. Then, "Hey, Celia didn't make this for Richard."

"Huh?"

"*You* made it," he said. "Look." He drew nearer and turned it upside down, showing me.

There it was on the bottom, an awkwardly carved "LIVVVY."

After a moment, I said, "Couldn't even spell my own name right."

"You don't remember making it?"

"No," I said. "I must have blocked it. It obviously didn't come out very well."

"I wonder how old you were." Dennis turned it slowly in his hand.

It was ugly. A little brown turd of an art project. And Richard had kept it on his desk.

Dennis said, "There's a small chip on the top. But it may have been there before."

"It doesn't matter," I said. "Just toss it."

He carefully placed it back on the desk. "You can't throw it out, Olivia."

"Why not?"

"Richard kept it all these years. You can't throw it out now."

"It's mine, isn't it? Now that Richard's dead? I don't want it." I grabbed it and leaned over the desk to toss it in the wastebasket underneath. The basket was metal and the paperweight made a loud *dong* when it hit the inside.

"Olivia!" Dennis said. "Why would you—" He stopped and blew out a breath between his teeth. "You really don't care much about anything, do you?"

"Not about clay, I don't."

"Richard kept it. For a reason."

"Maybe he just needed a paperweight."

"He's dead now," Dennis said. "Richard is dead and that meant something to him. Jesus, Olivia, can't you even see that that matters?"

"No," I said, "I honestly don't."

A pause. "Okay, forget it," he said finally. "There's no point. Can you just sign these papers before I go?" He flicked the pages in my hand. "You need to read through these. One of them concerns the guardianship, and the other one is for the trust."

I put the papers on the desk, plucked a pen out of Richard's wooden desk organizer, bent over, and started to sign them where the yellow "Sign Here!" flags were stuck.

"Hold on," he said. "Those are legal documents. You should read them first."

"I trust you."

"You shouldn't."

"Why? You trying to put something past me?"

"Of course not. But . . . it's just a good idea to know what you're signing. Plenty of women come into the law firm outraged because all the money is in their husband's name, and now they're getting a divorce. And you ask them how they could have agreed to something so obviously not in their best interest, and they say, 'I just signed whatever he told me to.' "

"But their husbands were assholes. You're not an asshole."

"That's not the point."

"It is to me," I said and finished signing. I stood up.

He was watching me, shaking his head. "Does anything I say get through to you? Anything?"

"Yes," I said and handed him the papers.

"Like what?"

"You'd be surprised."

"Yes," he said. "I would. I have to go now, Olivia."

"Come back soon."

"Sure."

"No," I said. "I don't mean in a 'see you later' kind of way. I mean for real. Come back soon. Like tomorrow. And the day after. And the day after that."

"I'll come when I can."

"When?"

"You sound just like Celia."

"Yeah, well, she needs you, and I need you."

"You're doing fine," he said. "You're taking good care of her."

"I'm not," I said. "I totally lost it with her tonight. I was screaming at her like I was nuts."

"Small children can do that to you. And you've both had a lot to adjust to."

"Yeah, well, it's a lousy feeling. I was scared I'd do worse than scream. You promised me that you'd be around, that you'd help. Remember?"

"Yes, of course, I remember. And I want to. I've just been busy."

"You said you'd help."

"I'll come when I can," he said. "I mean it, Olivia."

"You haven't been. Coming around. Not since New Year's Eve."

"I'm not boycotting you, Olivia. I just haven't had the time."

"You could make the time. I know you could. Tell Heather from Harvard to do a little more work without you."

"I'll see what I can do," he said. "And if you feel like you're losing your temper with Celia again, call me. Anytime, day or night. If you say it's important, I'll find the time to talk or come over. I promise. Now I should go. I can still get some work done tonight. And everything seems pretty quiet around here."

I walked him to the door, my head down, embarrassed by my own neediness. It was Celia's fault, for making everything so hard I didn't feel like I could do it alone.

"You okay?" Dennis said, his hand on the front door lever.

"Of course," I said, raising my chin. "I'm fine."

"All right, then. I'll try to come by some night soon. Earlier. I'll call and let you know."

"Okay."

"Don't look so worried, Olivia. No one's abandoning you. We're in this for the long haul. You, me, Celia . . ."

"It's hard," I said.

"I know. I'm sorry you had a tough night." He opened the door. "Good night, Olivia. I hope they let you sleep."

"Yeah. Good night."

He left, and I stood there for a second, wishing he hadn't.

twenty-two

The second week into the new quarter, I ran into Jacob on campus. It felt like years since I'd seen him last, that night we'd gotten drunk together. Well, I'd lost a father, gained a child, lost my virginity, gained a Lexus convertible . . . Meanwhile, all Jacob had done, apparently, was go home to New York for the holidays and eat too much.

"My mother, the Jewish housewife," he said when I asked about his vacation. "Every day, she'd make me something I liked when I was eight years old and sit over me until I'd eaten every bit of it and then thanked her for being such a great mother. Come get a cup of coffee with me, Olivia, and tell me what you've been up to."

I had a class, but didn't mind skipping. The professor was an idiot.

Once we were sitting together over coffee, Jacob said, "So did you ever find out your grade for English 34?"

Man, was that from another lifetime. "No."

"You're kidding."

"I had other stuff to deal with."

"You must have. Whereas I had nothing to do but eat and obsess about how badly I did last semester. Look." He pulled up his sweater and grabbed a fistful of his stomach. "I put on five pounds in three weeks. Can you believe it? I disgust myself. Fortunately, there's no one else in my life to disgust. Make that unfortunately. Speaking of which, guess who I have as my TA in Shakespearean Drama."

"Who?"

"Our old pal. Joe Lowden."

"Him again," I said.

He rolled his large eyes expressively. "Him again. I was kind of excited at first. I mean, you know how I felt about the man, Olivia. That hair, those eyes . . . but I think I'm ready to give up on him."

"I thought you already had."

"Well, you know, I had, and then I saw him again and thought, oh, God, just give him another chance, maybe he's one of those closet guys who come across all horny to the girls just to hide their true nature, you know? But two seconds into class, it all came back to me. The way he makes eye contact with all the cute girls—that alone tells you all you need to know." He flicked his hand sideways. "Oh, well. Guess I'll have to look elsewhere. Know any cute gay guys?"

"Just you," I said.

I didn't care. I wouldn't have expected Joe to stop flirting with his students any more than I would have expected Celia to stop waking me up at three in the morning just because her blanket fell off or she needed to pee.

I did tell him what Jacob said, that afternoon when I dropped by his apartment.

"He's crazy. No one in that class is cute enough to bother flirting with." He had been writing at his computer when I got there, and his eyes were bloodshot. He kept rubbing at them, which only made it worse. "Are you jealous? 'Cause I'm all in favor of that."

"Sorry, no. I just can't believe I'm hanging out with such a flirt. You're not my type. You couldn't possibly be my type."

"Sure I am," he said. "I'm exactly your type—in fact, I'm the *only* type for you. I was the first guy you ever went out with, right? That's because I had the experience and the—I'm bragging here—the *talent* to break down those incredible defenses of yours. A lesser man would have given up. You should really be grateful to all the women who came before you, who honed my skill. It was all for this one goal, you know, so I could win Olivia Martin's heart. Well, maybe not her heart, because she doesn't have one, but whatever it is in there that keeps ticking."

"Wow," I said, "you're good."

"You have no idea." He raised his eyebrows and grabbed me, burying his face in my neck Dracula-style.

In his bed, I could forget that at the end of the day I'd be taking care of a small child, just like I had at the beginning of the day, starting at six or seven that morning, when she'd jumped on me with some demand and refused to leave me in peace to sleep some more. In Joe's apartment, I had no responsibilities. I could be lazy, rude, selfish, crude, amoral . . . definitely amoral. Wonderfully amoral.

It scared me how much I liked sex. Or sex with Joe, at least—I didn't know it any other way. It seemed like a bad idea, becoming so addicted to something that depended on another person. Maybe that was why I had stayed a virgin as long as I had, some sense I wouldn't be able to stop once I got started.

I liked the life I led at Joe's with its physical pleasures and irresponsibility. It was hard, sometimes, to get back in my car—yes, even into the Lexus convertible, the joy of my life—and head home again after an afternoon spent more in bed than out of it. It helped when Celia greeted me at the door with a hug and an "I'm glad you're home, Livvy." More often, though, I was met with a wail and a complaint—Rosivel hadn't let her watch TV, we didn't have any hot dogs in the house, she didn't want to take a bath . . . whatever.

I was okay, I was getting by, I felt like maybe it would all work. We hadn't had a repeat of that awful night she'd spilled stuff and I'd screamed at her. But still, I needed those hours stolen away from being her guardian. I needed Joe.

Two hours after having coffee with Jacob, I was lying naked in Joe's bed.

And two hours after that, I was sitting on a park bench watching Celia navigate a fairly tricky rope bridge between the two towers of a wooden play structure.

I had gotten home at four-fifteen. At four-thirty, Rosivel had left and, faced with a long stretch of time until dinner and bedtime — a stretch of time that always seemed to bring out the worst in both Celia and me — I decided we needed an outing. Celia chose the park, so we walked over, hand in hand. She dashed over to the play structure as soon as we got there. I picked out a bench within eyesight of her. I curled my legs up to my chest, rested my chin on my knees, and enjoyed the sunset.

Celia successfully made it across the rope bridge. She yelled to me from the new, farther tower, and I waved to her. I thought, "Now, that's a cute girl standing up there with those big eyes, that dark curly hair, those little knees showing . . ." I wondered if I would have thought that a couple of months ago. If I even would have *seen* her.

She started to cross back on the swaying bridge. There were slats of wood to put her feet on, strung together with the same rope that made the handrails. She took each step carefully. She was a cautious kid.

A boy who was a lot taller than Celia headed out on the same bridge, coming from the opposite direction. He stopped right in front of her and deliberately jumped up and down very hard on the wood. Since he weighed a lot more than Celia, each time he jumped she bounced up in the air and would have fallen if she hadn't been holding on tightly to the rope at the sides.

She said something to him — probably "don't do that" — and he laughed in her face and jumped harder. She cried out and looked over to me, distressed.

I got up and headed over. The boy now jumped really high and, when he landed, did a sideways move with his feet that made the rope bridge tilt suddenly. Celia's right foot slipped off one of the pieces of wood and she fell through an opening. She would have fallen all the way to the ground, except her other leg was twisted in the bridge, and she was still holding the rope with one hand. She screamed and thrashed wildly, trapped and falling at the same time.

I was running, already there, reaching my arms out to her. She let go and fell against me, and I untangled her twisted leg. Celia wrapped her arms around my neck and sobbed out, "He was trying to make me fall."

"What the hell's the matter with you, you little shit?" I yelled at the kid who was still standing there, watching us, smirking. "She's littler than you are. You don't go around trying to hurt little kids!"

He made a face at me and ran away, across the bridge and down the tower.

"Excuse me," said a woman's voice. "Did I just hear you swear at my son?"

I turned around. Could have been the kid's grandmother. In her forties, at least, too well dressed for the park, wearing huge sunglasses even though the light was dwindling, well preserved, well tended, well Botoxed, and Pilates-thin but still obviously past her prime despite all the effort and expense.

"Yeah," I said. "He was trying to hurt her."

She rolled her eyes. "He was trying to get *past* her. She was blocking his way."

"Are you kidding? He was jumping up and down. He was trying to make her fall off."

"You must be insane. He was just playing. And your language was completely inappropriate. Disgusting. I should tell your employer. They need to know what kind of girl is taking care of their child. Who do you work for?"

"I don't work for anyone," I said. "This is my sister."

"Then I should tell your parents."

"Good luck. They're dead."

She flung her hand out. "Just tell me who's in charge."

"I am."

She put her hand to her forehead. "That poor little girl. I should call Human Services. It's nothing less than a tragedy. If you're even telling the truth."

"Don't feel sorry for *her*," I said. "She's a lot better off than your kid."
I turned my back on her and walked away.

"They shouldn't allow people like you in the park," she called out.

"They shouldn't allow people like you in LA," I said and kept on
walking, Celia bouncing lightly against my shoulder with each step.

My mother was bustling around the kitchen when we got home.
"Did you have a good time at the park, darlings?" she said as I staggered
in, still carrying Celia who had refused to walk a single step of the way
home, crying that her ankle hurt so much she couldn't even put her
foot down. It looked fine to me. She could be a real drama queen when
she wanted.

I dropped Celia onto one kitchen chair and fell into another. "Great,"
I said. "Some kid tried to make Celia fall, and when I yelled at him,
his mother pitched a fit."

"Really," my mother said. She was looking at a cookbook. "That
sounds unpleasant. I hope you two worked up an appetite."

"Don't tell me you're cooking." That was a first. Except for our Christmas ham, she hadn't made a single meal for us. Neither of us cooked
much, actually. We mostly ordered in or heated up frozen dinners.
Sometimes Rosivel cooked and left food for us. She also did most of
the food shopping.

"I'm making linguine Alfredo," my mother said. "I wanted to make
something special, since we're going to have company."

"Yeah? Who's coming?"

"Your young man. Joe. I invited him to come to dinner."

"You *what?*"

"Joe's your boyfriend," Celia said.

I whipped around to look at her. "Who told you that?"

"Barbara did. Is Joe the guy with the black shirt?"

"Yeah."

"He's funny." Then, "I need the boo-boo bear for my ankle. It hurts."

"Yeah, okay." I went to the freezer and got out the soft teddy bear–
shaped icepack she used when she was hurt.

My mother said, "I invited him to dinner. He called when you were at the park and we had a very nice talk and so I asked him if he'd like to join us for a small supper *chez nous*, nothing fancy."

"Why would you do that?" I said. "Why would you invite a friend of mine without checking with me first?" I put the teddy bear on Celia's ankle.

"Ow! That hurts!" she said. "I don't want it." She kicked her foot and sent it flying. I shot her a look and picked it up. She laughed. "Joe's your boyfriend," she said again. "He gave me a dollar."

"He's not my boyfriend," I said. "If he were, I would be the one to decide whether or not he came to dinner."

"I know you, Livvy," my mother said, looking up from the cookbook. "You and your little secrets. If it were up to you, I would never even talk to Joe, let alone meet him. So I had to take matters into my own hands."

I tossed the boo-boo bear back in the freezer and slammed the door. "Oh, Christ, Barbara, I don't want Joe to come here tonight, and I doubt he wants to come."

"It still hurts," Celia said, examining her ankle. "I need a Band-Aid."

"He was very enthusiastic about the idea. We had such a nice talk. Is he as attractive as he sounds?"

"Yeah," I said. "For a dwarf with a cleft palate. I don't even notice the missing leg anymore. Celia, you don't need a Band-Aid for that— it's not a cut, it's a bruise. And not even that."

"I'll assume you're joking," my mother said. "I'm sure he's not actually a dwarf. Not that there's anything wrong with short men. Richard wasn't even five six, you know. I bought sausage, too. Does he eat sausage?"

"I don't know. He's trying to lose weight. He wants to get down to three fifty by next Christmas."

"You're not helping, Livvy. I'm trying to make a nice dinner for you and your boyfriend—"

"I do too need a Band-Aid!" Celia was twisted almost double in her effort to inspect her ankle. "There's blood."

"There isn't any blood," I said. "That's just dirt."

"Uh-uh," she said. "Look." She pointed to an ancient scratch that had already healed.

"You'll live," I said, but I got a Band-Aid and put it on the nonexistent injury.

"You didn't put it on right," Celia said. She pulled it off and smoothed it down again. "Will Joe give me another dollar?"

"Not if he's not coming," I said, and reached for the phone.

Joe assured me he was looking forward to eating dinner with us. "I've been dying to meet your mother. You make her sound so interesting."

"She's not. Tell her you can't make it. Please."

"I heard that," my mother said. "Tell Joe I'm expecting him at seven. But not to dress up. Unless he wants to. I'll be wearing that little chartreuse dress I bought last Saturday. You know, from that little boutique on Montana that Lindsey told me about?"

"Did you get all that?" I asked Joe. "She's wearing chartreuse."

Celia said, "The Band-Aid won't go smooth." She pulled at it. "Ow! It hurts!"

Joe said, "I'm coming, Olivia."

"Okay, fine," I said. "Celia, don't put the Band-Aid on the kitchen table. That's disgusting. Just don't expect me to be a gracious hostess, Joe."

"Olivia," Joe said, "I can honestly say that I have no expectations whatsoever in that direction."

Joe was late, which my mother said spoke well of him. "I hate people who show up for dinner right on time," she said to me at seven-thirty, when he still hadn't appeared. "You're never ready for them, and you have to pretend you are."

I had just put Celia to bed, but I wasn't convinced it would take. She didn't think she should have to go to sleep when a guest was coming over, but I could tell she was overtired and wanted her out of my hair before Joe got there.

"How do I look?" my mother asked, turning around.

"You're a vision in chartreuse."

"Aren't you going to change?" she said. "You've been wearing the same ratty old T-shirt all day."

"I like this T-shirt," I said.

"Livvy!" The expected call from Celia.

I left the kitchen and went into her room. "Go to sleep, Celia."

"I'm not tired."

"Doesn't matter. It's still bedtime."

"I'm thirsty."

I sighed and went back to the kitchen. When I got back with the cup of water, I said, "Just a sip."

"But I'm thirsty."

"If you drink too much you'll have to pee during the night. That's never a good thing for either of us." She always woke me up when she needed to pee, even though she didn't actually need any help. She just didn't like being alone in the dark.

I sat on the side of the bed and helped her guide the cup to her lips. She drank more than I wanted her to before I could pull the cup away. She lay back against the pillows. "My ankle hurts, Livvy."

"Here. Show me."

She extended her foot out from under the covers and I rubbed it for a minute. "There. That should hold it. It'll be fine in the morning." I covered it back up.

"That boy was mean. At the park."

"Yeah, he was."

"You yelled at him."

"I was mad at him for being mean to you."

"His mommy yelled at you."

"I guess she thought I shouldn't have yelled at him."

"I was glad you yelled at him. I thought I was going to fall, but you got me."

"I wouldn't let you fall," I said.

"I fell off the swing last week."

"You jumped. That's different."

"I hurt my knee. Remember?"

"Yeah, but it was your own fault. You jumped off the swing on purpose. That's different from falling. I can only help you if you're falling by accident—I can't help you if you're going to do things like jump off swings."

"That boy was mean," she said again.

"It's time to go to sleep, Celia."

"Lie down with me."

"I can't. I've got to help Barbara do some stuff. I'll come back to check on you in ten minutes."

"No. Five."

"Okay, five." I got up and was halfway across the room when the doorbell rang. I cursed. Sure enough, Celia immediately sat up.

"Who's that?"

"Go to sleep."

"It's Joe. I want to go see him." She swung her legs over the side of the bed.

"It's bedtime, Celia."

"I just want to see him. Please, Livvy?"

"You promise you'll go right to bed afterward?"

"I promise."

I didn't have a lot of faith in Celia's promises. But I didn't have much of a chance of keeping her in bed now that she'd heard the doorbell. "Okay, I'll let you say hi. Then you have to go to bed."

"Okay." She held out her arms and I carried her to the kitchen.

As we entered, my mother and Joe were raising wineglasses to each other.

"Cheers," my mother said. Joe echoed her and they both drank. He spotted us.

"There she is," he said. "There's my girl."

"I'm not your girl," I said.

"I meant Celia. Hey, buddy. Can I have my dollar back?"

"No," she said.

"Then can I have a hug?"

"No."

"I meant Olivia," he said.

My mother laughed. "I can tell that you and Livvy have a similar sense of humor," she said. "Wait one second, I'm going to get us something to munch on while we're talking." She went toward the refrigerator.

"She calls you Livvy. How cute," Joe said, grinning.

"Try it and you're dead."

"I call you Livvy, too," Celia said.

"That's because you can't pronounce Olivia."

"Yes, I can," she said. "Olivia. So there." She stuck out her tongue at me. I stuck mine out at her.

"Very mature," Joe said to me. "Can we try that tongue thing later, when we're alone?"

"Here we are!" my mother sang out, arriving with a plate of crackers and cheese. The cheese was cut into perfect little squares and the crackers were fanned out evenly. "Eat up, but don't ruin your appetites. Joe, I'm counting on you to be a good eater."

"No problem. I haven't had a home-cooked meal in ages, Mrs. Martin."

"Oh, please!" She rolled her eyes. "Don't you dare 'Mrs. Martin' me. I'm Barbara. To everyone. Even little Celia calls me Barbara. I love the way she says it—like Barbara Walters does, with the lisp, or whatever you call that."

"I'm honored that you've gone to the trouble of cooking for me, Barbara."

"Don't expect too much. Just a simple little pasta, some salad, nothing fancy."

"Just the way I like it."

"Are you Livvy's boyfriend?" Celia asked Joe.

"I was kind of hoping I was yours."

"You're crazy," she said. "I'm too little to have a boyfriend."

"Olivia's kind of little, too," he said. "Have you noticed that? She's not big at all."

Celia pushed away from my chest so she could study me. "She's bigger than me," she said then, nestling back in. "But you're a lot bigger than she is. So's Barbara."

"That's because I ate my vegetables when I was your age," Barbara said, refilling her wineglass.

"Can I have some cheese?" Celia asked.

"Of course," my mother said, just as I said, "No, you can't. It's bedtime."

"I don't want to go to bed," Celia said.

"We had a deal."

"Oh, let her stay up," my mother said. "What difference does it make?"

"It's bedtime," I said. "You made a promise, Celia. You got to see Joe and now you have to go to bed."

"I don't want to."

"I don't care." I carried her out of the kitchen. Celia screamed and struggled to get back down. "Oh, stop it," I said, pinning her tight against me. "We had a deal."

"I want to go back!"

"Would it help if I read you a book?" said a voice from behind. It was Joe. I hadn't even realized he had followed us. "How about if I read to you?" he said to Celia. "Would you go to sleep then?"

Celia said, "You have to read me five books."

"Okay," Joe said. "Five books." He took her from me. "You go on into the kitchen. I'll read to her."

"You sure?"

"Absolutely. Show me which one is your room, buddy." He carried her down the hallway. I followed a little ways behind, and when they went into her room, I sat down outside the door and rested my head back against the wall, closing my eyes. I had had a long day. I listened to Joe reading to her. I think I dozed off at some point because I was startled when he suddenly came back out of her room.

"Hey," he said. "I'm done."

"Is she asleep?"

"Almost. I finished reading, and she turned right over and said good night."

"Well done," I said and yawned. I stood up. "Thank you."

"Can't you do better than that?" He pressed me against the wall.

"All right, all right," I said after we'd been kissing awhile. "Are you satisfied now?"

He rested his forehead against mine. "Actually, I'm feeling deeply unsatisfied at the moment. But we can fix that. Which room is yours?"

"Forget it. My mother's waiting for us."

"Your mother seems like the accepting type. I don't think she'd mind if we slipped away for a few minutes."

"No, she'd probably approve. Which is why I won't do it."

He pulled back. "As someone who has an equally dysfunctional relationship with his own mother, I actually understand the insane thing you just said. But I want some time alone with you later."

"I'm okay with that," I said, and we went back to the kitchen.

My mother outdid herself at dinner with stories about Livvy as the Rebellious yet Adorable Young Girl. Mixed in with the "and then she poked her fingers right into the birthday cake and we didn't even know the people throwing the party" kind of stories were tales of her own years as a fashion model. She never broke into the top ranks or anything, but at dinner that night she was Cheryl fucking Tiegs.

Meanwhile, Joe sat there, drinking his wine, eating his pasta, and charming my mother. She was thrilled with Joe. In every way. Thrilled that he was so good-looking, thrilled that he was my boyfriend, thrilled that he was enjoying her stories, thrilled that he wore a leather jacket and black jeans and looked just a little bit dangerous . . .

My behavior did not thrill her. I just sat there, not saying anything, moving restlessly in my seat, wanting dinner to be over. My mother kept jerking her chin at me, trying to get me to join in the good times. I ignored her.

"I don't know what's gotten into Livvy tonight," my mother said to Joe near the end of the meal. "She's so quiet."

"I'm used to it," Joe said, pouring my mother another glass of wine. He glanced at mine which I hadn't touched, shrugged, and poured some more into his own glass.

"Have you ever heard the saying, 'Still waters run deep'?" my mother asked him.

"Sure. You think that's what's going on here?"

"Oh, yes. I think Livvy is very . . . deep. She's much smarter than I am, you know."

"Yes, well, when Olivia was my student, Barbara—"

"Was she?" my mother said. "I didn't know that. She never told me."

Joe looked at me. "Just couldn't stop talking about me, could you?" I shrugged.

"Anyway, she didn't say much in class, but, Barbara"—he was doing that politician thing of saying her name a lot—"Barbara, if I were to tell you that Olivia's papers were the best in the class, maybe the best I'd ever read . . . well, all I can say is they blew me away."

"My late husband was a brilliant man," she said, "absolutely brilliant. I couldn't understand a word he said. Livvy takes after him, thank goodness."

"I was so sorry to hear of your loss," Joe said.

A sudden moisture in her eyes. She blinked and looked down at her hands. "Thank you. You're very kind."

I muttered "Jesus Christ." Neither of them paid any attention.

My mother lifted her head with a weary smile. "At least I still have my Livvy. I see so much of him in her." Her voice thickened. "And, Celia, too. She's so wonderful. A special addition to our lives just when—" The phone rang and she jumped to her feet. She was like Pavlov's dogs when it came to the telephone. "Excuse me, Joe. You don't mind, do you?"

"Not at all, Barbara."

She went over to the phone and sang out a cheerful "Hello?"

"I am loving hearing all about you," Joe said.

"Shut up," I said. I heard my mother say, "Hello, Dennis. Yes? Oh, no, she's asleep already."

"You think she's got a photo of you naked on a bearskin rug? I'd love to see it. I don't even care what age you are in it. Two, three . . . sixteen . . ."

"Shut up."

My mother, on the phone: "We're having so much fun here tonight—we have Livvy's young man over. Yes, that's right, Joe. You're welcome to stop by and meet him. Livvy would like that. You've been such a father to the girls."

Joe said, "Like you wouldn't kill to see a photo of *me* naked on a bearskin rug."

My mother said, "Oh, well, okay . . . if that's . . . yes, fine. Thank you. We'll see you soon. Won't we? Yes, okay. Good-bye." She hung up the phone and returned to the table. "That was Dennis," she said.

"I know."

"He was going to stop by, but I told him that Celia was asleep—"

"I heard your side of the conversation," I said. "You don't have to repeat it."

"Oh." A pause. She drank some more wine then said, "Livvy will be furious with me, but I've got to have a quick cigarette. Italian wine always makes me crave one. Joe, do you indulge?"

"In cigarettes? No. Sorry."

"I'm trying to quit, but I think I have one last one in my purse. Might as well make use of it." She excused herself and left the room. I wondered if she'd go outside like she was supposed to or just sneak into one of the bathrooms like she normally did.

I shoved my plate away and looked up. Joe was watching me. "What?" I said.

"Why does she bother you so much?"

"Because she's like *that*."

"You should meet my mother. She's a walking suicide note. Barbara is a joy to be around compared to her. Believe me."

"I don't want to play the 'my mother is worse than yours' game," I said.

"Okay," he said. "But mine is. I think yours likes me."

"Are you kidding? If she could call a minister and marry us on the spot, she would. Or marry you herself, if you gave her the chance."

"I'd consider it," he said. "She's gorgeous. Tall and blonde. What happened to you?"

"I don't know," I said. "Probably all the booze and cigarettes she had when she was pregnant with me. Stunted my growth."

"I'm glad," he said. "I like being so much bigger than you." He moved his chair closer to mine and took hold of the top of my head with the palm of his hand, so his fingers dug gently into my skull. "See? I can make you do whatever I want." He tilted my head back and kissed me. He tasted like wine. His breathing sped up. Mine probably did, too.

"Come on," he whispered. "This is our chance. She left us alone for a reason, you know. Let's not disappoint her." Then, after a few more minutes of persuading me with his hands and tongue, he said, "There must be a bearskin rug around here somewhere."

There wasn't. But the Oriental in the guest room worked pretty well.

twenty-three

Joe and I went to a movie afterward. My mother said she was happy to stay home with Celia—there was a TV show she wanted to watch, anyway.

When I got back, the house was quiet. I checked on Celia. She was sound asleep. I touched her sweat-damp little curly head, and she stirred and coughed. I backed away and got out of there before she woke up.

I wasn't feeling that sleepy, so I went into the kitchen, cut up an apple, and munched on the slices while I did some reading for school.

Just a minute or two after I sat down, I heard a strange sound. I went into the hallway. It was coming from the front door—a gentle, scratchy noise centering around the keyhole. Like someone was trying to break in.

I looked out the nearest window. My mother was trying to unlock the door.

I went to the door and opened it. She jumped with surprise. "Livvy!" she said. "You scared me! I thought you'd still be out." She dropped the key back in her purse.

"I got home a little while ago."

"Oh, good. This lock drives me crazy. My key never goes in right. I swear one of these days I'm not going to be able to get in." She entered and shut the door. She smelled like cigarettes.

"Barbara?"

"Yes, my darling?"

"Where were you?"

"Oh, I just ran to the gas station on Wilshire for a pack of cigarettes."

"You went to a store?"

"Just for a minute."

"You went to a *store?*"

"What's wrong, Livvy?"

"What's wrong? Are you out of your fucking mind?"

She blinked. "Excuse me?"

"You left her here," I said. "You left Celia alone here. You were supposed to be baby-sitting. I thought you were upstairs in your room. What the hell's the matter with you?"

"Oh, I see!" she said. "You were worried about Celia. She's fine, isn't she? I knew she'd just sleep the whole time I was gone and I was barely gone . . . not even five minutes, you know. And I knew you'd be home soon. She was probably alone for a couple of minutes, two or three at the most."

"I don't believe this," I said. "I fucking don't believe this."

"Please watch your language. What are you getting so upset about? She's fine, isn't she?"

"No thanks to you."

"Oh, please," she said. "It's not like anything actually *happened*. You're just in your attack-Barbara mode. But I don't feel like being your victim right now, thank you anyway. I'm going to bed." She swept past me.

"How in hell did I survive my childhood?" I said to her retreating back. She didn't answer, just tossed her head and walked away.

I wanted to scream at her some more, but it wouldn't have done any good. The only thing I could do was never let her baby-sit again. Which, when you thought about it, was going to hurt me a hell of a lot more than it would her.

When Alicia was still alive, Rosivel had always dropped Celia off at school and picked her up by pushing her in the stroller. It was a long walk, though, over a mile. Whenever I could, I took over the job.

At first, I ran in and out of there as quickly as possible. I tried not to make eye contact with anyone. The teacher was nice enough, but she spoke in such a soft, slow voice it drove me nuts to talk to her. And I just wasn't comfortable around the real mothers—they were all such a cozy bunch, forever planning play dates and having coffee together, living lives that were completely different from mine. Most of them tried talking to me, but I hated having to explain who I was or listen to their expressions of sympathy, so the conversations never lasted long.

Gradually, though, I started to spend more time in the classroom, especially when I was dropping Celia off. It was kind of relaxing to hang out there in the morning, to read Celia a book in the book corner, to help her put together a puzzle or two, to nibble on the goldfish crackers that were always available, to squish play dough into shapes while sitting in a tiny chair built for tiny asses . . .

No matter how often I hung around, I could never remember the other kids' names. Their faces all looked the same to me. Celia had to remind me constantly, and not always patiently, that *Rebecca* was the one with the blankie and *Rachel* was the one who couldn't eat nuts.

She seemed to get along with everyone but, as far as I could tell, didn't have any special friends. Since some of the other girls were paired off into best friends, I worried that she should be, too. I asked Dr. Rubillos about it, and she said that best friends weren't important in preschool, and the only thing that mattered was if Celia seemed happy at school. Which she did, most of the time.

I had another question for the doctor as we got close to Celia's birthday. I didn't know what, if anything, I should do to celebrate it. She had once asked if she could have a mermaid party, and I'd agreed to it, but I didn't even know what that *meant*. Was I supposed to throw some big affair? Learn how to play pin the tail on the donkey? Search the oceans for a real mermaid?

Dr. Rubillos said the best thing I could do was to keep Celia's birthday low-key—celebrate it, but not make too big a deal out of it. "Be prepared," Dr. Rubillos said. "Celia may not be ready to go through a milestone without her parents. She may fall apart. She may be fine. But prepare yourself for the worst."

As far as the mermaid thing went, Dr. Rubillos had recently seen some Ariel paper plates at Party World. She suggested I go buy them.

Celia's teacher told me that most of the parents brought cupcakes for everyone to share on their kids' birthdays, so I did that. Celia got to pass them out, which she liked, since all the kids crowded around her, begging to be one of the first served. For a few minutes she had all the power in the classroom.

Then everyone sang "Happy Birthday," except for one little girl who was pissed off because all the ballerina cupcakes were gone by the time Celia got to her, so she'd had to take a happy face instead.

Celia showed no signs of breaking down in any way. She beamed at everyone as she licked the frosting off her cupcake and dropped the rest in the trash can.

That night, we had another party for her, what I dubbed her "family party," to distinguish it from her "school party." I was glad she wasn't old enough to figure out that I was the only person at the "family party" who was actually a blood relative, the other guests being Dennis, my mother, and Joe, who had insisted on coming.

Dennis visited fairly regularly those days but always rushed back to work after spending a half hour playing with Celia. He promised to clear his whole evening for her birthday but asked that dinner be a little later than our usual six o'clock.

Celia had picked the dinner menu—sushi and tamales, two of her favorite foods. Talk about your fusion cuisine.

We ate in the kitchen. We always ate in the kitchen. The dining room seemed creepy to me—too big, too fancy, too reminiscent of tense holiday meals.

We ate dinner fast. My mother and Joe did most of the talking. At seven-fifteen we sat down and at seven-thirty-five I pulled out the cake. I had stuck a little mermaid toy of Celia's on top of it. We sang "Happy

Birthday," and Celia blew out the candles and then ate the frosting off
her slice before asking if she could open her presents.

My mother went first. She gave Celia a little girl's makeup kit, complete with fake nails you could paint with glittery pink nail polish. Celia
loved it.

Dennis gave her a board game. She unwrapped it.

"I already have this," she said, dropping it on the table.

"Celia," I said, "say thank you. Dennis didn't know—"

"It's okay," he said. "Sorry about that, Celia. Give it to a friend, and
I'll get you something else. Holly picked it out," he added, not to anyone in particular.

"Sure," I said, "pass the blame."

"You're right," he said. "It's not like I would have done any better.
Lord knows what I would have come up with."

"Something along the lines of a giant Minnie Mouse?"

"Probably."

"She really does like this game," I said. "It would have been the
perfect gift if she didn't already have it."

Joe now pulled a small gift box out of his pocket and presented it to
Celia.

"You got her something," I said, with real surprise. I had assumed he
would just ride in on my gift.

"Of course I did," he said. "Celia deserves something special."

"My God," my mother said. "That's a Tiffany's box! You certainly
know the right place to buy a gift."

"Hey, she hasn't even opened it yet," he said. "She might hate it."

"It's impossible to hate anything from Tiffany's," my mother said seriously.

Celia opened it. Inside was a small folded red handkerchief with little
white hearts scattered all over it. "It's awesome," she said, pulling it out.
Awesome was one of her favorite words.

"You can wear it on your head like this," Joe said, folding it into a
triangle and wrapping it around Celia's little forehead before tying it
in back. "There, that's called a doo-rag and only the coolest people
wear them. And only the coolest of the coolest people wear doo-rags
from Tiffany's."

"How does it look?" Celia turned to me, a huge smile on her face.

"Awesome," I said. She did look pretty cute. "You ready for my present? I can't possibly compete with a doo-rag from Tiffany's, but I got you this, anyway." I handed her my gift: It was a book about a little girl pig who was headstrong and dramatic—totally out there in a great way. The pig was named Olivia, which is why the book had caught my eye in the bookstore, and once I looked at it, she was so much like Celia I had to buy it.

Celia thanked me a little more politely than she had Dennis, but the gifts from Joe and my mother were clearly the leaders of the pack. "I like birthdays," she said, settling back in her chair and sighing with satisfaction. "I like presents the best, but I also like cake."

"You like frosting," I said. "Not cake, frosting. And don't get too comfortable there—you're not done opening presents." There was one more. It came from the stack of gifts that her parents had left under the Christmas tree and that had been hiding out in a closet ever since. Dr. Rubillos thought it was time to give Celia one of them and had carefully coached me on how to do it.

I got the present from the closet and gave it to Celia. Then I said what the doctor had told me to, which was, "Your parents picked this gift out for you before they died. I'm sorry they can't be here to give it to you now, but I know they wanted you to have something special."

It was lame, but I wasn't deviating from the script I'd been given.

Celia said, "From my parents? My mommy and daddy?"

"Yeah."

"Oh." She unwrapped it, oblivious to the tension of the four adults watching her. She got it open and saw what it was: a Barbie cash register, complete with scanner and gifts that had real, scannable bar codes. "Wow," she said, "this is what I wanted! Look, Livvy, look!"

"It's great," I said. "Your Barbie dolls can finally go shopping for real."

"Can I get them? Can we play with it?"

"Sure. Bring them in here."

She jumped down and went running out of the room.

I looked at Dennis. "That was easy."

"Yeah."

"Too easy? Should she have been upset?"

"I don't know. You'd have to ask Dr. Rubillos that."

"I will."

My mother said, "Who'd like a glass of wine?"

"I'll take one," Joe said. Dennis and I shook our heads.

My mother was pouring out the wine when Joe turned to me and said, "Any chance we can take off for a little while? See a movie?"

"I can't. No baby-sitter."

"Won't your mother be home?"

"Yeah, probably. But I won't leave Celia alone with her anymore."

My mother turned around with the full glasses in time to hear that. "Oh, for God's sake, I don't know why you're acting like this, Olivia."

"Yes, you do."

"What's going on?" Dennis asked.

"Nothing. Just that Barbara here thinks that a sleeping child shouldn't keep you from leaving the house if you have something else to do."

"Five minutes," my mother said, appealing to the men. "I slipped out for five minutes to get some cigarettes, and Olivia acts like I tried to murder Celia. Who, I'd like to point out, was absolutely *fine*. She slept like a baby through the whole thing, had no idea anyone was ever gone."

Joe said, "Boy, I bet there isn't a mother out there who hasn't done the same thing, just run out for a minute or two while the kid was asleep."

"Exactly!" my mother said. "And what about people who exercise in their backyard or something like that? Or who work in their garage? Who are out of earshot for hours at a time? What's the difference really?" She'd obviously worked on her defense in her spare time.

"Well," Dennis said, "it's illegal, for one thing. To leave a small child alone. You could go to jail for doing that."

"Are *you* going to send me?" my mother asked coquettishly.

"Not this time," he said. Unsmiling.

She dropped the coy. "Nothing could have happened. I was barely out of the house before I was back."

"Forget it," I said to Dennis. "You won't convince her she was criminally negligent. But I'm convinced. I'm not leaving Celia alone with her anymore."

"It's really your fault," my mother said. "You're always on me about the cigarettes. If I hadn't been trying to give them up, I would have had a carton on me and wouldn't have had to run out for one. I can't help it if nicotine is addictive."

"That would make it the tobacco industry's fault. Not mine."

"So we're not going out tonight?" Joe said. "Or any night ever again?"

"There's always E-mail," I said.

"Great. On the plus side, I guess I'll finally have the time to finish my thesis."

"You're all being silly," my mother said. "I can stay with Celia. I promise I won't go out for cigarettes—even though I still don't think there was anything wrong with doing that in the first place."

"And that's why I can't leave you alone with her," I said. "Because you still don't think you did anything wrong."

Celia came back in, staggering under the load of a large bright pink plastic box filled with Barbie dolls and their paraphernalia. "Help me!" she gasped, and Joe jumped up and went to her aid. He brought the box over to the table, and then she said, "Where's the cash register?"

It was on the floor. "I'll open it for you," Joe said. He crouched down and went to work on the packaging. As he was ripping away at the cardboard and plastic, he said to me, "I guess I could run out and rent us a movie, and we could watch it here. Got any scissors?"

"That's a great idea!" my mother said. "We can make popcorn."

"Popcorn?" Celia said, looking up.

"Forget it," I said. I got a pair of scissors from the phone desk and handed them to Joe. "It'll be bedtime before then."

"I'd better take off," Dennis said, standing up. "Happy birthday, Celia."

She barely acknowledged him. She was standing next to Joe, her hand on his shoulder, watching him slash his way through to the cash register.

I walked Dennis to the front door. "Thanks for coming," I said. "I know how busy you are."

"I wouldn't have missed Celia's birthday," he said. "Although I'm not sure I added anything to it as far as she was concerned."

"Are you kidding? She totally insisted that you be here."

"She was much better entertained by—" He stopped and then said, "Oh, I left that board game. Do something with it, will you? Like burn it or give it away?"

"Yeah. Sorry she was so rude about it."

He waved his hand. "She was just being a kid." He lowered his voice. "Listen, Olivia, I wanted to talk to you. What your mother did, leaving her alone that night—that was pretty bad."

"I know. I was serious about not leaving Celia alone with her. I shouldn't, right?"

"I wouldn't. But I'm sorry for you. It makes your life a lot harder."

"Not that much harder. It's not like I have to be anywhere at night."

"I'm not sure Joe would agree with that. At any rate, you'll need more baby-sitting. Someone reliable."

"Yeah, well if you know any college kids—Oh, wait, *I'm* a college kid. I keep forgetting that."

He smiled. Finally. "Don't forget *that*." He leaned against the door. "Pretty soon you'll have to start thinking about what you'll want to do after college, Olivia."

"I figured I'd just give in and become a soccer mom—drive a minivan and get my nails and hair done every week."

"I don't think so. You weren't cut out to be a soccer mom, Olivia."

"I don't know what I was cut out for. Honestly."

"Something good, I hope."

"Just so long as it involves long hours of sleep. Lots of sleep and good pay."

"If I hear of something like that, I'll let you know. Or maybe take the job myself." He yawned and turned toward the door. "I could use a good night's sleep."

"You work too hard," I said.

"I don't know any other way to do it."

"You could learn."

"Haven't had any reason to, I guess."

"Not even when you were married?"

"In retrospect, that would have been a good time to try." There was a pause and then he said, "Good night, Olivia. Get some sleep."

"You, too."

I ran into Joe on my way back to the kitchen. He said he was heading out to Blockbuster and would be back in half an hour with a movie. "Give me something to go on?" he said, and I gave him a kiss that I was fairly hopeful would qualify.

In the kitchen, my mother was sitting at the table, sipping wine and pretending to clean up by pushing the dirty plates around on the table. Celia was on the floor playing with her new toy.

"Well," my mother said when I entered. "You certainly managed to humiliate me in front of our friends."

"How'd I do that?" I started stacking the dishes on top of each other.

"Trying to make me look bad. Because of the other night. You did it deliberately. You're always trying to make me look bad."

I didn't say anything, just carried the stack of dishes over to the sink and opened up the dishwasher.

She said, "Why don't you just leave that for the maid?"

"She doesn't come on Wednesdays."

"Oh. Well, she'll be here soon enough."

"I don't mind doing them," I said. I started to load the dishes in the dishwasher.

"I'm going to forgive you for treating me so terribly tonight," my mother announced after a moment, "because life is too short for holding grudges. I want to talk about Joe, Olivia. He's delicious. And he's obviously crazy about you. But I wish you'd show a little enthusiasm back. Even the most confident man needs encouragement." I didn't say anything. "You'll see I'm right. Anyway, at first I was thinking that I'd join you for the movie, but then it occurred to me that you might want to be alone. I wouldn't want to cramp your style."

"Watch or don't watch," I said. "It doesn't matter to me." I saw some more dirty glasses farther down the counter and went to get them.

Celia looked up and said, "Can I watch a movie, too?"

"You have to go to bed."

"Livvy! It's my birthday."

"Even birthdays have to end in bedtime."

"Not yet. Please?"

"You have fifteen more minutes to wring every bit of pleasure out of that cash register. Then you're going to bed. If you complain any more, it will be five minutes."

She pouted for a moment then said, "Play with me?"

"Yeah, all right." I got down on the floor with her. "How's it work?"

"You buy things and put the money here. What do you want to buy?"

"That Barbie."

"You can't have her. She's my favorite."

"Then that one, over there."

She considered. "No, not that one, either. You can have this one." She picked one out of the box. I gave her some pretend money, and while she was putting it in the cash register, I examined my new doll. Her hair was hacked off. "What happened to her hair?"

"I cut it," Celia said. "Mommy got mad. She said I ruined it."

"Oh." After a moment I said, "You understand, don't you, that your mommy picked out this cash register for you before she died? That she wanted to give it to you? And your daddy, too?"

"Yeah," she said. "What else do you want to buy?"

I'd have to ask Dr. Rubillos if a complete lack of interest was the response she'd been going for with this gift.

"You were a big hit with the younger crowd," I said to Joe. We were curled up on the sofa, pretty tight against each other, and had been watching the movie he picked out, some modernized version of a Shakespeare play that he thought he should see since he was TA-ing a Shakespeare class that quarter but that had lost our interest pretty quickly. "And with the older crowd, too. My mother was thrilled when you pulled out that box from Tiffany's. She didn't even care what was inside."

"I know. I've learned that the cheapest gift from Tiffany's gets a big reaction—women go apeshit when they see the box."

"Not me."

"Like hell. You were excited, too. Which reminds me . . ." He reached for his jacket, which was lying on the sofa next to him. "I thought we were going out tonight—I was going to make more of a moment out of this, but—" He pulled a light blue box out of one of the pockets. "For you."

"Oh, Joe," I said. "You didn't. A doo-rag for me? I don't deserve it."

"Shut up and open it."

"Wait until I'm done fainting. We girls always faint when we're given a box from Tiffany's."

"One more obnoxious comment and I'm taking it back."

"Let me see what it is first." I took it and pulled at the white ribbon. I opened the box. There was a soft pouch inside. I tugged open the drawstring and found a—actually, I had no idea what I found. It was long and thin like a key, but it had a circle at one end.

I took it out of the pouch. "What is it?"

"Keep looking at it. You'll figure it out."

I laid it flat on my palm and examined it. It looked familiar. Then I laughed. "It's a bubble wand."

He nodded. "A sterling silver bubble wand."

"Does it work?"

"Sure. You want to try it?"

"Later." I traced it with my finger. It was cold and smooth and felt heavy in my hand. I looked up. Joe was watching me.

"Do you like it?"

"Yes. I do."

"It seemed to suit you. All things considered."

"I like it a lot," I said.

I showed it to my mother the next day. She had already spotted the box, which I'd left on the coffee table. She went into raptures and then immediately called Tiffany's to find out how much it had cost, which was something like a hundred and twenty dollars.

"He loves you," she said, overwhelmed. "He really loves you. And this is only his first gift. Oh, Livvy, if he *starts* with Tiffany's . . ."

Lindsey was over, having stopped by on her way back from some fancy spa in Santa Monica, where she'd had, as she put it, "absolutely *everything* waxed." She examined the bubble wand carefully and pronounced it an excellent gift, both original and classic.

My mother said to her, "Isn't it just wonderful? And the boy . . . the boy is everything he should be, handsome and charming and intelligent—"

Lindsey retied the bow around the box. "What was the occasion, Olivia?"

"No occasion."

She raised her silvery-blonde eyebrows. "Really? He got you a gift from Tiffany's for no reason?"

"It's a good sign," my mother said.

"Do you really think so, Barbara?" said Lindsey. "Because I was wondering what he was feeling so goddamned guilty about that he felt he had to get her a gift for no reason."

"Don't pay any attention to Lindsey," my mother said later, after she'd gone. "She's very cynical. It's all the disappointments she's had, you know. With men. But it's a wonderful gift, and Joe is a wonderful boy."

"Life is happiness indeed," I said, blowing bubbles through my sterling silver bubble wand. Celia batted at them and laughed out loud.

twenty-four

The phone rang one day when I was in Joe's apartment. I'd stopped in to visit between classes. Even when we both had to work, it was nicer to hang out there than at a coffee shop or the library. I was sitting curled up in his armchair, reading, a Coke on the side table next to me.

Joe answered the phone and put the caller on hold. He went into the bedroom and talked for a while with the door shut. When he came back, he said, "My mother's really losing it."

"Your mother?" I said, looking up from my book.

"Yeah, she starts getting herself all worked up about nothing—"

"Are you going to see her?"

"Are you kidding? Christmas was enough."

"Oh. I just figured, with her in town and all—"

He sat down on the sofa. "What are you talking about? She's not in town."

"That's strange," I said. "That she would be in LA and not tell you."

"What are you talking about? She's not—"

"The number was a local one."

There was a short pause. Then, "Olivia—"

"Caller ID," I said. "I was sitting right here. I wasn't looking on purpose."

He raised his hands then dropped them, laughing a little. "You caught me. I feel like such an idiot. I'm sorry. It was this old girlfriend of mine. She calls me from time to time. She gets a little . . . depressed. I have to talk her down. I'm sorry I didn't just tell you, but I wasn't sure how you'd feel about it. It just seemed simpler to—" He stopped.

"Lie?"

"Technically a lie, but not in spirit. I'm not trying to hide anything from you, Olivia, I just thought it would be easier not to get into the whole thing. She's such a nut."

"No wonder you confused her with your mother."

"Come on," he said. "Don't be mad. If you don't want me to take calls from other women—"

"I'm not mad," I said. "And you can take calls from anyone you please. Just . . . why lie if you don't have to?"

"You're right. You're right. It just seemed simpler at that moment. I don't know why. It's not a big deal either way. But I won't do it again." He got up and came over to me. "How much longer do you have?"

"My class is at three."

"That only gives us an hour. Let's not spend it arguing."

"We weren't arguing. Were we? And I don't care if I'm late."

"I know you don't. And in this case, I'm all in favor of your being tardy." He took my hand and pulled me to my feet. "I'm starting to like making love in the afternoons. Gives me something to look forward to all morning. And to remember all evening." The phone rang again. We both looked at it. Joe shook his head and pulled me to him. "Fucking phone. Trying to get me in trouble. Come on. Let's go be bad."

"That should be easy for you," I said and let him lead me into the bedroom.

It bothered me, though, that he'd lied. I told Charlotte about it in an instant message when we were both on-line that night.

I had gotten in the habit of using the big computer in Alicia's office. At first, I was kind of uncomfortable hanging out there, but she had a really great setup with DSL and everything, which left my laptop in the dust, so I got over it.

Charlotte i.m.-ed me back. "i know u think lyings a big deal Livvy but for most people its not that huge. i probably lie ten times a day like i like your dress and no its not a cold its allergies u know stuff like that. u need to mellow. are his eyes still incredibly blue and hows the sex?"

"sex is great and eyes are bluer than ever," I wrote back. "maybe he was lying when he said he was lying and it was his mother only hes screwing her—wouldnt that make it all much more interesting?"

"u disgust me," she wrote. "if he is screwing his mother tell me more my life is boring. evan is no longer seeing that girl with the big tits and has moved on to a girl with smaller tits whos very rich. i think im better off without him but i want him to know that which maybe means im not really over him yet. hows Celia and are u still staying home every night?"

"celia screamed last night at 3 in the morning and woke me up just cause she wanted a stuffed animal that was 2 inches away from her hand. otherwise continues to be kind of cute. now wears jeans like me but still likes the color pink and im starting not to hate it so much as a color am i losing my mind? and yes im staying home almost every night with her so i should get a's in all my classes this quarter but i see j. almost every afternoon so its ok i don't really mind or i wouldn't if i didn't have to put up with my mother. she goes out at night more than i do which is good keeps me from having to be alone with her."

"how about her and that dennis guy any interest between them?"

"no way. thank god. i gave up on that idea a long time ago. i like him too much for that. he deserves someone decent."

"so do i livvy but it doesn't do either of us any good now does it."

I was running late for class one day. When I picked up Celia, she wanted to show me the new pet hamster at school, and by the time we'd petted and admired it and I'd brought her back home, I was fifteen minutes later than usual—so then I thought, fuck it, I'll skip the lecture and get to Joe's early. Which gave me time to pick up a coffee at Starbucks.

There was a line, and I was waiting toward the end of it, stretching my neck out to see what kind of cookies were left in the display case, when a voice behind me said, "I'll probably regret asking you, but we've spoken before, haven't we?"

I turned, already recognizing the affected rhythm of her voice. "Professor Greene."

"You have the advantage, I don't recall your name."

"Olivia Martin. I was in your English 34 class."

"Yes, that's right. But we've met since then."

"New Year's Eve," I said. "You were eating pretzels and I . . . I was being bored."

"I may have been eating pretzels, but I was bored, too," she said. "A horrible party. Do you mind if I cut in front of you?"

"Go ahead," I said, and we changed places.

"Thank you," she said. "What do you get here?"

"Coffee."

"I know that. You were looking at the pastries. Which ones do you like?"

"I don't know. Anything but the muffins. Anything with chocolate."

"I usually get a bear claw, but apparently they've run out today, so I'll have to be adventuresome . . . You go out with Joe Lowden."

I hesitated, then shrugged and said, "Yes."

"Now I remember. New Year's Eve, and you also came with him to that English Department thing the other night. Joe is a very charming young man."

"Isn't he, though."

"I also like their lemon scones, but I had one earlier today. I spend an obscene amount of money at Starbucks every day. Joe has the ability to make everyone like him. I sometimes wonder what it would be like to have that talent, how different life would be. Charm was never something I cultivated."

I didn't say anything.

She said, "I considered trying to be charming, but instead I decided to be a big fat lesbian who would say whatever she wanted. I think I made the right decision. I have more fun this way. Charm requires too much energy. It doesn't leave you time for much else, but it's not that valuable an asset in the long run. I don't see you making much of an effort to be charming either, Miss Martin."

"I haven't had my coffee yet," I said. "My charm runs on caffeine."

"I think I'll get a scone, after all," she said as the person in front of her reached the counter. "But not lemon. I'll try the chocolate chip, you've inspired me."

"You're fairly inspirational yourself," I said. "I'm not convinced you don't have any charm, Professor Greene."

"Good-bye," she said and went up to the counter to order her chocolate chip scone.

At home, eating a snack after school the next day, Celia said let's make a party and invite our friends and have a picnic with cupcakes and frozen blueberries. I said sure, we could plan a party for some unspecified date in the future, and which friends did she want to invite?

"I'm *not* inviting Rebecca," Celia said. "She said I wasn't her friend."

"All right," I said. I got a piece of paper and wrote on it, "Celia's Party." Then, underneath, "Rebecca — NOT invited." "Anyone else you don't want to invite?"

I was joking, but she said, "Jacob Wong. He threw sand at me."

"Yeah, Miss Wilcox told me about that. She said you threw sand at him first."

"Because he wouldn't share the shovel."

"Still, you can hardly blame him for wanting a little revenge."

"What's revenge?"

"Getting back at someone who did something you didn't like. Is there anyone you actually want to invite to this party, or will the two of us eat all the cupcakes and rag on everyone who wasn't invited?"

She bit into a slice of American cheese and then examined the bite mark. "Can I invite grown-ups?"

"Sure. Which grown-ups do you want to invite?"

"*Not* Rachel's mommy. She told me not to eat the snack, but we can eat the snack."

"Somehow I think there may be more to the story than that. But you don't have to invite her if you don't want to."

She folded the cheese in half and bit the folded edge. She unfolded it to check out the hole she made in the center. She chewed, swallowed and said, "Can I invite Joe?"

"Sure."

"And Dennis?"

"Yeah." I tapped the pen on the table. "So you like Joe and Dennis, huh?"

"Yeah. Joe's silly."

"He makes you laugh, doesn't he?"

"Yeah. He's silly."

"How about Dennis? Is he silly?"

"No, he's not silly. He's nice."

"Isn't Joe nice, too?"

"He's silly," she said.

"Which is better?" I asked. "Since apparently they're mutually exclusive. Silly or nice?"

She shrugged. "Well . . . silly is more fun."

"So, you'd rather hang out with Joe than with Dennis?"

"Sometimes," she said. "But not if I was scared. Like if I had a bad dream about the Ginch and you weren't home? I'd want Dennis, not Joe."

"Why's that?"

"I don't know," she said, "I just would."

"I guess silly doesn't help so much when you're scared."

A pause while she thought. Then she said, "I don't want to invite Wilson either. He has curly hair."

"So? What's wrong with that? You have curly hair."

"Yeah, but his is yellow."

"Good point," I said and made a note not to invite Wilson to the party.

That afternoon, Joe got another call from his mother. Only this time it really *was* his mother. I knew this, because he called her "Mom" and asked about "Dad," and he stayed on the phone and talked to her for a while with me lying right next to him on the bed where we'd gotten as far as taking off each other's clothes when the phone rang.

After greeting her, he listened for a while, then said, "That's this weekend? This coming weekend? Are you sure?" Another moment, then, "Well, I totally forgot to buy tickets. You should have reminded me when I could still get a decent fare. Now there's just no way I can—" Then, "Oh, thanks. I hate to make you use up your miles just for—" While she was talking, he rolled his eyes at me, but when it was his turn, he sounded pretty sincere. "Oh, yeah, it's important to me, too. I want to be there. It's just . . . I didn't want to get into the whole thing, but you know the girl I'm seeing? Olivia?"

I pointed to myself, and he winked.

"Here's the thing," he said into the phone. "Her father just died. Horrible car crash, up near Big Sur." He listened, nodding. "Yeah, I know, it's unbelievable. Olivia's devastated—it was just so sudden. I'm feeling like I can't leave her alone right now." More listening. "Yeah, I know. Me, too. But if it's important to you, I'll just—right, right. I know. Well, maybe you could call me while you're all at the house and I can at least talk to everyone—" He patted me on the leg, nodding into the phone. "I know. It's bad timing, but it's not like anyone planned any of this, right? Okay, Mom. Call me this weekend. Don't forget. I'll be there in spirit. Tell Grandma I love her. You, too. All right. Bye." He hung up and raised his hands in triumph. "Yes! I escaped!"

"Escaped what?"

"Oh, there's this one-year celebration of my grandfather's death. Well, maybe celebration isn't the right word. Whatever you call it. Anyway, I'd promised my mother I'd come home for it. Hope you didn't mind my making use of you like that, but she was being relentless."

"Why don't you want to go?"

"Are you kidding? Every minute of it would be agony. And look what fun I can have here." He pushed up against me.

"I've got to be with Celia all weekend, you know."

"So? I'll come hang out with you guys at the house. When I'm not working. I'm getting in deep shit with this thesis—people are starting to wonder if I'm actually writing one. I had to tell Professor Greene the other day that it's basically finished, and I'm just 'fine-tuning' it. How long do you think a person can reasonably be believed to be fine-tuning a manuscript?"

"I don't know. What's the difference between fine-tuning and editing?"

"Fine-tuning is what you do after you've already edited, when you're basically just fixing the commas."

"How far along are you, anyway?"

"Nowhere near the fine-tuning stage, I can tell you that. I'm not even up to the editing stage."

"I ran into Professor Greene the other day," I said. "At Starbucks."

"Yeah? How is our sweet young thing? She call you arrogant this time?"

"No, just charmless."

"Did she really?"

I nodded. He put his face against my neck and fluttered his eyelashes against the skin there so they tickled me. He said, "I think you're extremely charming. Especially when you're naked and at my mercy."

"I'm never at your mercy," I said.

"Couldn't you at least pretend to be?"

"No." I pressed his arm lightly. My fingertip left a white impression that faded immediately. "She remembered me."

"Who? Oh, Greene."

"Yeah. She remembered meeting me on New Year's Eve. And also at that English Department thing the other night."

"You're a memorable kind of girl."

"I must be," I said. "I wasn't at the English Department thing, whatever that was."

There was a pause. His head was still buried in my neck. He breathed there for a moment. Then he said, his voice muffled slightly, "Crazy old cow. There must have been someone there who looked like you."

"Yeah," I said. "Someone short and dark-haired who was with Joe Lowden."

He lifted up his head and looked at me. His eyes were very blue and met mine openly. "I wasn't with anyone, Olivia. I mean, she might have seen me *talking* to someone, but I wasn't there *with* anyone. She probably saw me talking to one of the other grad students and assumed it was the girl she knows I'm seeing. Which would be you, only you, and you alone. Would you like me to write that in blood?"

"Sure," I said. "Can I pick where the blood comes from?"

"Only if you make the blood go there in the first place," he said and covered my body with the long hard length of his.

When I went to pick Celia up at school that Friday, I found her crying in the teacher's arms. I thought it was because I was a few minutes late—an accident on Wilshire had backed traffic up for half a mile—but the teacher shook her head when I apologized and said that wasn't it. Then she said carefully, "Celia was feeling a little bit sad, Olivia, because some of her friends were having a play date together, and sometimes it's hard when other people make plans that don't include us."

I was confused, but then Celia sobbed out, "Cheyenne had a party, and she didn't invite me!" and I got the picture. I also knew who wasn't going to be invited to our next picnic.

Another mother who was there tapped me on the shoulder, and while the teacher distracted her daughter and Celia with a book, explained that Cheyenne's mother had arrived with lots of noise and excitement to whisk Cheyenne and a lucky few off for an "afternoon of beauty" at a salon, followed by lunch at Wolfgang Puck's.

"It's bad enough not to invite the whole class when they're this age," the mother said, shaking her head. "But to pick them all up in front of the ones who weren't included, and to make a big deal out of it—I don't know what people are thinking sometimes." She was a pretty woman with thick brown hair cut boyishly short and very light blue eyes. Her oxford shirt had a stain on the collar, and her jeans were holey across the knees.

"Unbelievable," I said.

"Not to mention the whole 'afternoon of beauty' aspect of it . . ." She groaned. "The price we pay for living on the Westside. Lucy was devastated, so I said I'd take her out for ice cream. Do you and Celia want to come with us?"

She seemed nice and I wanted to distract Celia, so I decided we did.

Her name was Caroline, and she drove the girls to Baskin-Robbins in her minivan, while I followed behind in the station wagon.

Lucy and Celia both ordered blue raspberry sherbet cones. We let them sit by themselves at a table. Caroline ordered some kind of frothy coffee drink, and I got a cup of rocky road. We started to sit down at a table right next to the girls, but they protested and said we had to move farther away, so we shifted one table over.

"God," Caroline said once we were settled, looking at my ice cream, "to be your age and eat whatever you want without gaining weight . . ."

"Yeah, right," I said. "There are no fat people under the age of thirty."

"Only at Target. But, seriously, when I was your age, I could eat everything in sight and never gain a pound. Now I can't even look at ice cream."

"Isn't there ice cream in that?" I asked, pointing to her drink.

"Shhh," she said, "I'm in denial." She wasn't actually fat at all, just a little plump in an attractive, cozy kind of way.

The girls laughed loudly over at their table, and Caroline turned around to check on them. "Wipe your face, Lucy," she called, then turned back to me. "A losing battle," she said. "That blue ice cream stains everything. At least they seem to have forgotten the whole Cheyenne birthday party thing. Wish I could get over it so quickly. I could strangle that woman. Slowly. With barbed wire."

"Just tell me when and where."

"I wish Miss Wilcox had let her have it, but she's too nice. Oh, well." She settled back in her chair and started to play with her straw, bending the top of it then letting it spring free. "So, how's it going with Celia, Olivia? If you don't mind my asking."

"It's fine," I said.

"Really? Don't forget you're talking to the mother of three here. I know how hard it is."

"Geez," I said, "three."

"Yeah. And the other two are boys. Active boys." She flicked at the straw. "Don't get me wrong—I love being a mom. I was a lawyer before I had kids, and I don't regret for a second making the switch. But let

me tell you, it was a lot easier being a lawyer. And you're so young. . . .
It's got to be tough."

"Yeah, sometimes," I said. "I was never into kids. But Celia's all right."

"She's a great kid," Caroline said. "Sort of amazing, given her—" She
stopped.

"What?"

"Nothing. I have a tendency to say inappropriate things. You'd think
at my age you'd learn. But I don't."

"You were going to say 'given her mother,' weren't you?"

"I have nothing against Alicia," Caroline said, plucking rapidly at the
straw. Her face was red. "She and I just had different approaches to
mothering." She looked up again. "I like the nanny a lot, though.
What's her name again? Rosivel? We've had a couple of play dates with
her, and she's very sweet. Anyway, I think Celia's really lucky she has
you. You seem like you're doing a great job—she seems happy."

"I'm trying." I looked over at the other table. Celia and Lucy were
giggling about something. Their mouths and chins were all blue. "But
I don't really know what I'm doing. I still can't believe I'm in charge
of a kid, you know? I like Celia, but I keep waiting for things to go
back to normal, only—"

"Only this is normal now," she finished for me.

I nodded and stuck a spoonful of ice cream in my mouth.

Celia shrieked with delight about something, and I called over to her
to be quiet, but Caroline shushed me. "Oh, let her have fun," she said.
"Kids are supposed to be noisy in ice cream parlors." She sucked at the
straw for a moment, then lifted her head and said, "You know, what
you were saying . . . I think everyone feels that way. I mean, I don't
want to trivialize what you're going through—your situation is obviously
unique—but I don't think there's a mom out there who doesn't sometimes look around and say, 'How the hell did I get here?' Like the David
Byrne song, 'This is not my beautiful house.' You know?"

"I was with you up until that last part," I said. "David who?"

She shook her head. "Christ, you really are young, aren't you? David
Byrne? The Talking Heads?"

"I think I've heard of them." I couldn't have named any of their songs,
though.

"Oh, just *bury* me," she said. "Anyway, my point is that I'm thirty-seven years old and I have three kids and I've been married to my husband for thirteen years and we've lived in our house for seven of those years and I still have moments when I can't believe I'm supposed to be responsible for anyone or anything, when I don't feel like a grown-up—or want to be one."

"Still," I said, "it's different for you. At least you made the choice."

"Yeah," she said, "that's true. You got Celia dumped on you."

"It could have been worse," I said.

"Yeah?"

"Yeah," I said. "She could have been named Cheyenne."

"That's my son's name," Caroline said. I froze. Then she grinned, and I realized she was joking.

The girls chose that moment to pounce on us. Caroline pretended to scream at the sight of Lucy's blue mouth, and both girls thought it would be funny to rub their faces on our shirts. We pushed them away, but not before they had done some damage.

"Stop it!" Caroline said. She looked down at herself. "Lucy, that is not okay! You ruined my shirt."

"I didn't mean to," Lucy said. She had her mother's light blue eyes, but her hair was long and reddish blond.

"You rubbed your face all over me!"

"I just wanted to hug you."

Caroline made a strangled sound. "What am I supposed to say to that?" She squeezed the side of Lucy's head against her chest in a rough embrace.

By then Celia had climbed into my lap and was helping herself to my ice cream.

"It's hard," Caroline said then, looking over the top of Lucy's head at me. "It's hard, but it's worth it. You'll see."

I nodded and let Celia finish my ice cream.

When we got home, there was a message on the machine from Joe, asking me to call him as soon as possible. When I reached him, he said, "You're not going to believe this, but I decided I should go home this weekend, after all."

"You're kidding me. After killing off my father again just to get out of it?"

He laughed. "Yeah, I know. But my mother called me, practically hysterical. My brother can't come, my sister's in one of her moods . . . She's already called the airline and set the whole thing up. E-ticket. All I have to do is get over there. I don't want to, but—" He stopped.

"It's probably good you're going," I said.

"Yeah, if anything gets me into heaven, it'll be spending this weekend in hell."

"When do you leave?"

"This afternoon," he said. "My flight's in a couple of hours. I'm heading over to the airport as soon as I hang up. I'll miss you, Olivia. But I'll be back as soon as I can, by Sunday evening at the latest."

"Celia was just saying in the car she wants to go out to dinner with you. Could we plan on it for Sunday night?"

"Absolutely," he said. "I can't wait. Man, I wish I weren't going. This weekend's going to be so god-awful."

"Call me when you get back."

"I will. I love you, Olivia."

"Have a good time. Or at least survive. I'll see you at the other end."

I hung up and looked at Celia, who was hovering, listening. "Joe said he can go out for dinner Sunday night," I said.

"When's that? Now?"

"Today is Friday, tomorrow is Saturday, and then the next day is Sunday."

"How many sleeps?"

"Two."

"But that's too long! I want to go now."

"Joe can't do it tonight."

"I don't get to do anything! I didn't get to go to Cheyenne's party, and I don't get to go out for dinner tonight. I don't get to do anything!" She threw herself onto the floor.

"Hey, we just went out for ice cream," I said.

"But you promised me we could go out for sushi tonight with Joe!"

"I didn't promise. I said maybe. And we can still go out for sushi by ourselves."

"That's no fun. We're always by ourselves." She turned on her side, hands curled into fists. Trying to decide whether to pitch a total fit or not.

I was voting for not and thought fast. "How about we invite Betsy to come along with us? You like Betsy." She had met Betsy several times when I had taken her by my old place to pick up stuff. I had never fully appreciated Betsy's determined energy until I introduced her to Celia. She was like the best kind of baby-sitter, determined to make Celia like her and willing to wear herself out in the attempt.

Celia rolled onto her back, considered the offer, and finally pronounced it decent enough.

Betsy was happy to go out with us. She had a dinner and movie date, but not until nine that night.

I could remember when nine o'clock was a normal dinnertime for me, but I'd been eating dinner with Celia at six o'clock for so many weeks I got hungry if I tried to wait until later.

We picked Betsy up in the station wagon. She hopped into the back next to Celia, so she could play with her on the way to the restaurant. Celia wasn't a lot of fun, though. She kept yawning and whining.

Thanks to Betsy's relentless energy — "Look, Celia, I see a doggy! Do you see the doggy?" — we managed to keep Celia awake in the car, and she brightened up as soon as we got out at the restaurant.

Once we were seated, I said she could get a Coke. I figured she could use a dose of caffeine and sugar. The waitress said they only had Pepsi, and Celia looked at me.

"Am I picky about Pepsi?" she asked.

"No," I said, "you're fine with it."

The food didn't come very fast, and Celia got tired of waiting, so Betsy took her for a walk around the restaurant. I dug into my backpack and found a notebook and pen, and when they got back from their expedition—"I sneezed on someone's food," Celia told me, and Betsy said, "Yes, you did, and I think maybe we should just hide here until they leave"—I told Celia she could draw. She said she wanted to sit in my lap while she drew. The air-conditioning was blasting, and she was always nice and warm, so I didn't mind.

She had recently added fingers and toes to her drawings—just lines, but I liked the way they looked, coming out like spikes from the circles that were the feet and hands.

"You're so lucky," Betsy said to me as we watched her draw.

"Lucky?"

"To have Celia. Look at how cute she is all curled up on your lap. I'm totally jealous."

I didn't answer. Lucky wasn't the word to describe our whole situation, if you asked me. I wasn't unhappy to have Celia sitting there all warm and cozy with me, her hair tickling my nose, but I didn't feel like I'd won a lottery or anything.

"What are you drawing?" Betsy asked, tilting her head to see from across the table.

"It's a picture of Joe," Celia said.

"Oh," Betsy said. "You like Joe, huh?" She tried to catch my eye, but I wasn't interested in an exchange of meaningful looks.

"Yeah," Celia said. "He's silly."

"You're telling us?" I said, looking at the drawing. "He has seven toes on one foot and four on the other."

"I think it's a wonderful drawing," Betsy said. "You'll have to show it to him, Celia."

"Can I, Livvy? Can I show it to him?"

"Of course. We'll give it to him when he gets back."

"I want to give it to him now."

"You can't. He's in Chicago."

"Where's that?"

"Far away."

"I want him to see the picture."

"We'll see him on Sunday. We'll give it to him then."

"I want to give it to him now."

"You could mail it," Betsy said.

"I want to," Celia said. "I want to mail it."

"He won't get it until Monday at the earliest," I said. "Better to just hand it to him on Sunday."

"You could stick it in his mailbox," Betsy said, thinking she was being helpful. "He lives near here, right? It could be a surprise for when he gets back."

"Yeah," Celia said. "Let's do that. Let's stick it in his mailbox."

"Too much work," I said. "Let's just wait until Sunday."

"No!" Celia shouted. She always got loud when she was tired. "I want to put it in his mailbox now!"

"Don't," I said. "Don't scream in the restaurant, or I'll take you out, and you'll eat your sushi in the backseat of the car."

"I can do it," Betsy said. "Just stop by his place on our way back to the apartment, and I'll run it to his mailbox."

"Yeah!" Celia said. "Betsy could do it. Please, Livvy? Please, please?"

"Okay, fine," I said. "If you're a really good girl for the rest of the meal, we'll leave the picture for Joe to find when he gets back. But you have to be good and quiet and not whine for the rest of the meal."

"Okay," she said. And she was, and she didn't.

"Hey, Celia's asleep," Betsy said when we were almost at Joe's building. "You want to skip this?"

"Yeah, right," I said. "She'll wake up in the middle of the night, and the first thing she'll ask is if we dropped the picture off. And if the answer's no, she'll throw a fit, and I'll be making the drive over here at three in the morning." I pulled up in front of the apartment. The curb was red, but I wouldn't be long. "Will you wait with her? I'll run it up."

"You want me to do it?"

"It'll be faster if I go. I know which one's his."

Since Joe wasn't there, I knew I couldn't buzz up. I waited until an old lady came out of his building and grabbed the door from her. She gave me a suspicious look, but I blew by her and didn't give her the chance to say anything.

There are times when it helps to be a small girl. If I'd been a large man with tattoos, she probably would have called the cops.

When I got to the mailboxes, I realized there was no way to get a big piece of paper inside one of them without a key. I figured I'd slip it under his door instead. I ran upstairs.

Joe had left some lights on in his apartment. I could see a glow around the edges of the door as I bent down to slide the paper underneath.

Then I heard voices. I stopped and listened. I couldn't hear words, but I caught the hum and rhythm of two people talking.

Maybe Joe had left the television on.

Maybe not.

I felt funny, kind of excited, kind of sick to my stomach. I stood up, still holding Celia's drawing, and knocked on the door.

"Hold on," Joe's voice called out. I could hear him moving toward the door now, could hear him saying something about how it better be hot since it had taken so long.

I moved to one side so he couldn't see me through the eyehole. When the door opened, I came forward.

He was standing there, with just his jeans on, his wallet in his hands.

"Oh, fuck," he said as soon as he saw me. He put his hand up to his forehead, like he had a headache. "Oh, fuck, Olivia. I just screwed up."

twenty-five

"Yeah, I guess you did," I said. I held out Celia's drawing. "Here, this is for you. Celia drew it. I was going to put it under your door."

"Oh, man." He took it, glanced at it, looked back up at me. "Olivia—"

"It's okay. I'm leaving." I turned around.

"No, don't go. Wait. Let me talk to you. Just hold on—" He tossed the drawing into the apartment then came out all the way and closed the door behind him.

"Careful," I said. "You don't want to get locked out."

"It doesn't mean anything, Olivia. You know that, right?" His hair was slightly messy, his eyes intense. He reached for me, but I stepped back. "This thing—whatever happened here—was stupid and thoughtless and meaningless. It has nothing to do with anything."

I was silent.

"I'll get rid of her. Right now. Christ, I don't care if she lives or dies. Just don't—don't—don't think it means anything. It doesn't. You're the only thing that matters to me."

"Uh-huh," I said.

"It's not a line, Olivia. I know you don't trust me—"

"What makes you think that?"

"My God, Olivia, you're the only girl I've ever said 'I love you' to."

"The only one? Really, Joe?"

"I don't remember ever saying it before." Then, "Why would I say it to anyone else? I've never felt the way I feel about you about anyone else."

I didn't say anything.

He said, "Just wait for me here, and I'll tell her to go."

"I can't," I said. "I have to run. I've got people waiting in the car." I turned.

"Wait," he said. "Just give me one more minute. You have to see why this wasn't about hurting you."

"I never thought it was."

"I mean—I want you to see why I . . ." He took a deep breath, thinking. Thinking fast. "You know, Olivia, we never set any rules. We never said we couldn't see other people. I mean, for all I know, you had something going on all those nights we couldn't go out together. As you'd have every right to. Because we never made any promises to each other. Right?" He was kind of getting into the argument now, rocking forward on his heels, not feeling the cold night air even though he was half naked. "We both liked keeping things kind of casual. But maybe it's time we figure out what this relationship is and where it's going. I mean, I know I'm crazy about you, that you're not like any other girl I've ever met. But does that mean I'm only going to be with you from now on? Maybe it should, but we've never said. We need to sit down together and really think about all this."

"Here's the thing," I said. "I thought some things were obvious. I mean I always assumed—"

"I know," he said. "I'm not surprised. And maybe it's naive of me to think I would have been okay with it if I'd found *you* with—"

"Hold on," I said. "You don't understand. *God*, you don't understand. You think it's about the other girl and it's not. Do whatever the hell you want with whoever you want. You're a free man."

"Oh, come on," he said. "Are you telling me you're not pissed off?"

"Here's the thing," I said again. "I'm not as cynical as you think, Joe. Finding out that someone *lied* throws me for a loop every fucking time."

A pause. Then he said, "I didn't lie to you, Olivia. I know it looks that way, but when I talked to you this afternoon, I really was planning on going home. I was halfway out the door when she just showed up. I had no idea she was coming. And then one thing led to another. It was stupid, unbelievably fucking stupid, but I never lied to you."

"So your mother is still waiting for you at the airport?"

"No, of course not. I called her."

"And told her what? That you weren't coming because a girl showed up on your doorstep?"

"What difference does it make what I told my mother? The only thing that matters is that I didn't lie to you. I wouldn't lie to you. Especially now that I see how much lying would hurt you." He pulled me to him. "I don't ever want to hurt you. I love you." He bent over me.

I let him kiss me, not minding, but thinking my own thoughts.

After a while, Joe whispered, "This is a good thing that you're doing here. Just think how it would break your mother's heart if you broke up with me."

"Yeah. She adores you."

"See? You should always listen to your mother."

"Yeah, I guess." I twisted away. "Except she's the kind of person who gets excited about a Tiffany's box without even knowing what's inside."

"Hey, I gave you a great gift from Tiffany's."

"Yeah, you did. I loved it."

He smiled. "I knew you would. So should I come with you now or meet you back at your place later? I'll do whatever you say. From now on, I'm Olivia's lapdog, her slave."

"Wait," I said. "You'll need a story, won't you? For her?" I gestured toward his apartment door. "She'll be wondering what's taking you so long."

"It doesn't matter," he said. "She doesn't matter. I told you—"

"But you have to tell her something," I said. "How about the one about the suicidal ex-girlfriend? I know you like to keep it close to the truth. I may not be suicidal, but I am pretty moody."

"Hey, I wasn't making all that up, you know. That really was my old girlfriend. I can't help that she still calls me. She has no one else to talk to. I feel sorry for her, that's all."

"There you go. You already have all the back story. And just in time. Look."

Joe turned around. There she was, peeking around the door. I could see how Professor Greene had confused us—she was small and dark-haired like me.

She was trying to figure out what was going on.

"Joe?" she said. She looked young. Then again, so did I.

"I was just leaving," I said. "Sorry. I know I shouldn't have bothered you, what with your being my ex-boyfriend and all, but I'm just so fucking depressed."

"Olivia," he said, grabbing my arm. "Please—"

I pulled away. "No, really, I'll be okay. My shrink says if I take my Prozac I'll be fine, but I think he's just throwing drugs at me so he doesn't actually have to deal with any of my shit, you know what I mean? But don't worry about me. I've got this stuff to help me sleep—"

"Joe?" the girl said again, looking back and forth between us. "What's going on?"

"Nothing," I said. "Good-bye, guys." I started to walk away.

Joe came after me, and pulled me around. "I'm not going to let you go like this, Olivia. Not until—"

"I don't need you to *let* me. Anyway, if I were you, I wouldn't fuck this up. She seems nice."

"Please, Olivia. I'm on my knees here—"

"Only you're *not*," I said, shaking off his hand with a sudden violence. "That's the thing about you, Joe, you don't even know when you're telling the truth or not anymore. I mean, for Christ's sake, you're not *on* your fucking knees."

"Olivia—"

"Good-bye, Joe," I said, and I left.

Betsy wanted to know what had taken so long.

"Well," I said. "He was there."

"Joe was there? I thought you said he was out of town."

"He was supposed to be. Only something better came along, and he stayed. Or maybe he was never really going in the first place. I honestly don't know." I turned on the headlights and pulled out onto the street.

"Something better?"

"Yeah. Or someone better. Someone different, at least."

It took her a moment. Then she said, "Oh. Oh, wow. Oh, Olivia, I'm sorry. I told you about him, though. I warned you. Everyone says—"

"Yeah, I know."

"What happened? Did you yell at him? Did you catch them in the act?" She was getting excited now.

"Oh, yeah," I said. "I caught them fucking and I screamed for a while and then she threw a pillow at me and we got into this huge catfight. The police had to come and break it up. I'm surprised you didn't hear the sirens."

"Wait, are you joking? You are. You're joking. How can you joke about this, Olivia?"

"It was no big deal," I said. "We talked, and I left."

"But you were mad, right? You were angry at him?"

"Yeah," I said. "I was angry at him." But she didn't get why, any more than Joe had.

Betsy offered to come home with me, to help me in my hour of need, but I turned her down and dropped her off at the apartment. I drove home, the adrenaline rush still keeping me more excited than depressed.

It really wasn't until hours later, when I was lying in my bed in the dark, that I started to feel a little less "you-go-girl-ish" about the whole thing.

I wasn't sorry that I had caught Joe. Better not to go on being stupid the way I'd been. Better to know.

And I *had* been unbelievably stupid. Liking it when he said he loved me. Believing it. Not saying it back only because I wasn't sure I did, and I wanted to be absolutely honest when I said those words.

I wasn't like him. I wouldn't say things that weren't true.

God, it had been nice having him around, though. The warmth, the contact, the sex, the fun of being with him, the feeling of not being alone for the first time in my life — I didn't want to give any of that up.

Why'd he have to lie to me?

I turned onto my side, trying to get comfortable. So what did I do now? Find someone else, someone better? Go out searching, with my little lamp held high, for the one honest man out there? Who might not even exist, because, according to Charlotte, it was normal to lie, and *I* was the deviant for objecting to it?

I'd end up alone and crotchety, a crazy old lady hollering about what an evil place the world was.

The phone rang, even though it was past midnight. I wondered if it was Joe.

Of course it was Joe. He'd already left two messages that evening. I'd listened to them while he was leaving them. I stood four feet from the answering machine and listened to Joe's voice telling Olivia he had to talk to her, to please call him or let him come over, to stop listening and pick up the phone goddamn it.

The phone kept ringing until the machine picked up. I couldn't hear it from my bed, but I knew it picked up automatically after four unanswered rings. My mother was out somewhere, which I was grateful for. I didn't have to tell her anything or not tell her anything. Not yet, anyway.

I thought, Joe's awake now. He's awake and wanting me. I could call him. He would be . . . grateful. And repentant. And charming, of course. All I had to do was say, "Come," and he would be here in minutes. In my room, holding me, making me laugh, making me hold my breath with how much I wanted him. And maybe he meant what he said, that he wouldn't lie to me again.

But he had also said he hadn't lied to me in the first place. And that was bullshit.

Joe would say anything to get what he wanted or to get out of trouble. I'd seen him do that, seen him lie like crazy without even blinking to other people — even his own mother — but for some reason I thought it was different with me. I wanted it to be different.

It didn't seem like such a big deal when it was other people he was lying to. But it should have.

On the other hand, now that I knew he'd lie to me whenever it helped him out of a tough spot . . . well, maybe that just made everything easier. Why not hang with him and enjoy the good parts—and, man, there were a lot of good parts to being with Joe—and just never let myself trust him completely? Sleep with him but not believe anything he said?

Nothing wrong with that. What was it Lottie had said? You're not planning on marrying the guy . . .

If the sex was good and hanging out together was fun, wasn't that enough for now? Plenty of people were in relationships like that. The only danger with a guy you couldn't trust was trusting him, but I wouldn't do that.

Celia cried out. I waited, and she was quiet again. But I couldn't sleep anyway, so I got up and went to the kitchen, where I erased the messages on the answering machine without listening to them. I brought a blanket and pillow to Celia's room and lay down on the carpet. She stirred and cried out again but didn't wake up. Pretty soon her breathing grew calm and regular. It was nice listening to it. Made me feel a little less alone.

And I thought, I'd want something better for her, wouldn't I? Something better than a charming, slick guy who said the right things but didn't always do them? I'd want someone who was decent for Celia because it mattered. Decency mattered. Goodness and honesty and decency—those things mattered. And I wouldn't want Celia to go around fucking guys who didn't get that.

I didn't want either of us to.

twenty-six

One day, a week or so later, my mother came into the family room where Celia was watching TV and I was taking notes for a paper, and said to me, "I wanted to invite Joe to dinner—we always have such fun when he comes—but he hasn't called for a while. Or at least not when I've been around. Would it be okay with you if I just went ahead and called *him?*" Her eyes were big and innocent, but I knew the question hadn't come out of nowhere—she had her suspicions.

I said, "Joe's not going to be calling. And you're not going to be calling him. It's over, Barbara."

"You're not serious!"

"Why not?"

"Oh, Livvy!" She sank down onto the sofa. "Oh, you didn't!"

I tightened my grip on the pencil. "Didn't what?"

"Let him get away?"

"Yeah, I guess I did."

"I knew it," she said. "At dinner that night. When you were so unpleasant and wouldn't smile at him or talk. A boy like that—oh, Livvy, he had charm and looks and brains!—a boy like that needs a little something back. He's not going to bang his head against a wall with nothing to show for it."

"No, probably not."

"It's not too late," she said. "You can win him back. Dress up for once, put on some makeup, do your hair, arrange to bump into him somewhere—you must know where he likes to hang out. Maybe you could have a male friend pretend to be interested in you, make Joe jealous enough to see what a catch you are. That's where having gay men as friends can come in so handy. And I'll help you." She thumped her fist on her leg. "You don't have to lose him permanently. This situation can be fixed."

I shook my head. "It's over, Barbara."

Her fist dropped back down. "How could you?" she said. "How could you let this happen? He was perfect, Livvy. You'll never find another one like him. Did he give you a reason?"

"A reason for what?"

"Leaving you, of course."

"Oh," I said. "*He* left *me?*"

"Women like you don't leave men like him," she said. "Not unless they're idiots, and I refuse to believe that my daughter is an idiot." There was a pause. "Unless . . . did something happen? With another girl? Is that what this is about?"

I didn't say anything.

"Because if it is—Oh, Livvy, don't make the mistake I did, of making too big a deal out of a little fling or two. Men are different from women. They need . . ." She searched for the word. And found it. "Variety. They need variety. Women don't need that, so we don't always understand when they—but it doesn't *mean* anything, you know."

She sounded a lot like Joe.

"The problem is you're so narrow-minded," she said. "You're hard on people, Livvy. You expect them to be . . . well, like you. Other people make mistakes. You don't allow for that. You're intolerant. I put up with it because I love you, and I know there's good inside, but others won't be so . . . You know what happens to intolerant people?"

"Let me guess. They end up alone and unloved?"

"I need a glass of wine," she said. "I just can't believe this."

At least it got her out of the room. I tried to go back to work.

But then she came back with her glass of wine. And, after a few sips, she turned nostalgic. "The first boy you ever went out with . . ." she said. "The first one is so special. You'll never forget him, Livvy. The rest of your life you'll wonder where he is, what he's doing. You don't know how lucky you are to have *started* with someone like Joe, someone who's charming and handsome. I'll bet he was good in bed, too. You can tell, just from the way he moves."

"If you think I'm going to talk about that—"

"It can be so awkward with the wrong man. That first time . . . and other times, too. But with a man like Joe, who's put together so well, who moves like a dancer—"

"Stop *now*," I said. I looked over at Celia, but she was oblivious, lost in her cartoons. I usually found it irritating, the way she zoned out in front of the TV set—especially when I asked her a question and she ignored me—but it seemed like a good thing at the moment.

My mother took a good long pull at her wine. "I just wish you'd talked to me more. I could have helped you. I have experience with men. But you never tell me anything. You're my only child and you don't tell me anything about your life. I have to make guesses, suppositions, ask questions that aren't answered—"

"Hello?" said a new voice. I looked up. Dennis was walking into the room. "I hope I'm not interrupting. I knocked, but no one came, so I let myself in."

"We didn't hear you," I said, "but you're not interrupting. Please, *please* come in."

"Hi, Celia," he said, leaning over to drop a kiss on her head. She looked up and smiled.

"Dennis!" she said and held out her arms. He picked her up and sat down, and she cuddled against him. Then went right back to watching her show.

"A warm greeting," he said, "followed by a complete lack of interest." He played with her bare feet a little, running the palm of his hand along the tops of her toes. She didn't react.

"Well, you're competing with *Rugrats*," I said. "What did you expect?"

He looked up. "Your knowledge of children's programming has grown an impressive amount in the last few months, Olivia."

"I know," I said. "So much better than wasting all those brain cells studying for my midterms."

My mother made a snuffling sound and mumbled something about how no one really cared about her.

"Is everything all right, Barbara?" Dennis asked.

"Fine," she said, "just fine. Livvy's lost the only man she's ever had and the best one she'll ever know and won't even discuss it with me. Other than that, we're all just perfect here." She raised her glass to her lips.

"Olivia?" he said.

I shrugged. "A bad case of melodrama."

"Oh, right," my mother said. "*I'm* melodramatic. You're the one who's been moping around ever since she lost her boyfriend, but *I'm* the one who's melodramatic."

"You lost your boyfriend?" Dennis said.

"He wasn't my boyfriend."

"Joe? He did a pretty good impersonation of a boyfriend."

"Yeah," I said. "He did, didn't he? But he wasn't."

"I'm sorry."

"Don't be."

"That's right," my mother said, "don't be sorry for Livvy. She'll never find anyone quite like him again, but don't be sorry for her. We're not *allowed* to be sorry for Olivia. And heaven forbid we try to talk to her about anything that's going on in her life, because that's also not allowed. Nothing's allowed. Nothing. Does anyone else want some wine?"

"No, thank you," Dennis said.

My mother got up and left the room.

"Is there a lock on the door?" I said. "Because if there is . . ."

"No lock," Dennis said. "Sorry." He was gently squeezing each of Celia's toes, one at a time, between his thumb and index finger. She wiggled a little but kept watching the TV. "She seems to be taking the news hard."

"Yeah."

"How about you?"

"Me? Well, according to my mother, I'll never be happy again. But I thought I was doing okay."

"She has a point," he said. "I mean, not about the never being happy again. But about your not liking to talk about things very much."

"In this case, I promise you there's nothing worth talking about. Joe was—" I stopped. "I don't know what he was. Exactly what he seemed to be, I guess. Which makes me something of an idiot for . . . But it's okay. What is it you're supposed to say about these things? We had a good time while it lasted?"

"If that's what you had. If it's any consolation, the guy is obviously a moron."

"That's just what my mother said. Oh, no, wait—she said *I* was the moron. For letting him go."

"I still vote for him."

"Thank you."

"Anything I can do to make you feel better?"

I shook my head. "I'm fine."

I was, wasn't I? It wasn't like I was sitting around sobbing all day or getting drunk or anything.

It was hard, though. Every day I found myself missing the hours I'd spent at Joe's apartment being petted and teased like a spoiled cat. There were mornings when I woke up and realized I had nothing fun to do all day long, just classes, dinner with Celia, homework, bed. . . . None of it was bad, but it didn't give me a lot to look forward to, either. The life that had seemed so unreal and unusual just a few weeks earlier had become routine, and I felt restless again, in that old familiar way, like I was missing out on something. Being with Joe had helped keep the edginess at bay.

The worst was in bed at night, when my skin ached with wanting to be touched.

My mother came back in, breaking the silence that had fallen. She had a fresh glass of wine and as she went past me, I smelled cigarettes on the breeze she created. At least she seemed more cheerful.

She planted herself in front of us. "I've decided we've done enough sitting around and moaning—"

"I can't see!" Celia said.

My mother moved over and tried again. "Enough feeling sorry for ourselves. We need to change the energy in this room, right now! Dennis, what could we do to feel better about everything?"

"Uh . . ." He looked to me.

I said, "I don't know about the rest of you, but a human sacrifice would cheer *me* right up."

"Well, at least you're joking," my mother said. "That's a start."

Celia said, "You're too loud! I can't hear."

Dennis said, "How about I take you all out for ice cream?"

"That's perfect," my mother said. "Who doesn't love ice cream?"

"Don't you have to work?" I asked Dennis.

"Not tonight. I had a business dinner that just got canceled. The client has the flu. Freed me up."

"Are you starving?"

"Nothing ice cream wouldn't fix."

"I'm surprised at you," I said. "Ice cream for dinner? I would have expected Dennis Klein always to eat a square meal. With an emphasis on the leafy greens."

"I eat ice cream for dinner all the time. Proves how little you know me."

"Yeah, maybe it does. All right, let's do it. I'm willing to have a scoop of energy-changing ice cream. Hey, Celia!" She didn't move. "Come on. Look at me, Celia." The TV set held her in a trance. "We're talking ice cream here, Celia."

Her eyes slid sideways, toward me. "Ice cream?" she said. "Can I have some?"

"If you get your shoes on. We're going to go out to get it."

"Why?"

"Barbara says we need to change our energy."

"I want you to bring it here. I want to watch TV *and* eat ice cream."

"Come on," I said, reaching for the remote and turning the TV off. "It'll be fun."

She was furious with me for turning the TV off and cried the whole time I was getting her ready to go out, but I just jammed her shoes on and ignored her wails. It wasn't real crying, anyway, just the annoying whining noise she made when she was overtired.

My mother said she wasn't going to go with us. "Ice cream is just too tempting," she said. "I can't allow myself to be around it. Have a sundae for me, will you, darlings? Take your time and have fun." She seemed a bit too pleased to have us gone. I suspected she was going to be changing her own energy with some more wine and cigarettes.

I was just as happy to have her stay—whatever the reason—and I hustled Celia into the car before my mother could change her mind.

"Who drives?" Dennis said, once Celia was settled in the backseat of the Mercedes.

I handed him the keys. "You." It seemed right. Anyway, if I drove, he'd probably keep telling me to slow down and respect the other drivers.

Once we were out of the garage, I let out an audible breath of relief.

Dennis glanced at me, then looked back at the road. "Glad to be getting away?"

"What do you think?"

"I want Beatles," Celia said.

"The Beatles?" Dennis repeated.

"Yeah. I've been working on improving her musical taste." I shoved in a CD. "I couldn't stand her kiddy music—it all sucked. Have you ever listened to 'The Wiggles'?"

"I don't even know what that is."

"You're lucky. Christ, it's bad. Anyway, I started playing my own stuff. So far, she likes 'Abbey Road' and 'Rubber Soul.' We're going to move on to Dave Matthews next." The music came on.

We listened to "I've Just Seen a Face"—Celia sang along to the chorus—and then, when it ended, Dennis said, "Have you thought about having her move out?"

"Barbara? Yeah, I guess. I never meant for her to stay so long in the first place. I only let her move in with me because I was terrified of being alone with Celia. Now that I'm okay with that—" Hey, that was true. It hadn't sunk in on me till I said it. "I don't think I could get her to leave. She kind of settled in. She's taken over the entire upstairs, you know."

"Do you want her around?"

I shrugged. "She drives me crazy. But I grew up with her, so I'm used to it. And she's so incredibly incompetent. I know she's been living by herself since I went to school, but I swear I don't know how she's survived. She can't even turn on the TV by herself."

Dennis shook his head but didn't say anything. Celia was being unusually quiet in the backseat. I turned to see what she was up to. She was staring out the window, her lips moving inaudibly to the words of the song. She had a glazed look on her face. I sat forward again.

After a minute, Dennis said, "Will you bite my head off and tell me it's none of my business if I ask what happened with Joe?"

"Yeah, probably."

"I'd still like to know."

I said, "It's not an exciting story. Apparently, we forgot to set rules for the relationship. I thought we were operating on the code of basic human decency, but I guess I was wrong about that."

"Meaning?"

"He lied, he cheated."

"I'm sorry."

"Stop saying that, will you? It's no big deal."

"I don't suppose it would help if I told you I never liked him very much?"

"No, not really."

"Then I won't."

"Thank you."

"But I didn't."

"I know. You didn't hide it all that well."

"Sorry. I tried to. Anyone else on the horizon?"

"Not unless someone really cool starts hanging around Celia's pre-school."

"You need to spend more time with people your own age."

I laughed. "Now there's a surprising remark, coming from the guy who told me I should never leave Celia's side, even when Rosivel is there."

"I never said that."

"Maybe it's a slight exaggeration. But you did tell me to spend as much time with her as possible."

He thought for a moment, his hands moving restlessly on the steering wheel. Then he said, "I've made too many demands on you, Olivia. I think I've been so worried about Celia. . . . You need your own life, too."

"Oh, you don't have to worry about that," I said. "I gave up on having one of those a long time ago."

"You must have friends at school. Why don't you go out with them?"

"I see them around campus. I meet people for lunch sometimes. That's enough. It's not worth setting up baby-sitting and all to go out at night. And everyone at school goes out so late. With Celia waking me up at six in the morning, I'm too tired to stay up till two like I used to."

"What about the weekends?" Dennis said. "Alicia and Richard must have had someone baby-sitting on the weekends."

"Yeah, they did. Two people, actually. Didn't I tell you about them?" He shook his head. "They both called after the new year. One was named Denise, or something like that. She sounded really young. She wanted to speak to Alicia, and I told her Alicia and Richard were both dead, and she flipped out. She just kept saying 'Oh, my God, oh, my God.' Then she hung up and never called me back. Totally freaked out, I guess. Then there was Pilar. She came one weekend. *She* didn't seem to have any problem with the whole death thing, took it all very calmly. But Celia had problems with *her*—" I glanced in back to make sure she wasn't listening. "Hey, she's asleep."

Dennis looked in the rearview mirror, arching his neck so he could see her in it. "Is that okay?'

"I guess."

"Should we skip the ice cream?"

"Hell, no. I'll just run in and bring it out to the car, so we don't have to wake her up. Anyway, Celia kept saying she didn't like Pilar, and I didn't like her much, either. She was fat and had a mustache. When she got to the house, Celia started crying and wouldn't go near her. Pilar just kept saying, 'Come on, baby, come to Pilar.' There was something about the way she said it . . . like she was calling her 'baby' because it was easier than remembering her name, you know? And she never really looked at Celia. Not really. So I stayed at home and spied on them. Pilar never got her fat ass off the chair in Celia's room. Just sat there, saying, 'Go play with your dolls, baby. No, don't do that — that will make a mess, baby, and Pilar will have to clean it up. Can baby go into the kitchen and get Pilar a drink of lemonade?' Like that. I swear I'm not exaggerating. I heard Celia ask for me and Pilar said, 'Don't bother your sister, she doesn't want you now.' "

"God, she sounds awful."

"Yeah, and guess how long she'd been working for Alicia?"

"How long?"

"Three years. Most of Celia's life."

"Well," he said, "weekend help is hard to find. Maybe you take what you can get."

"If you're Alicia you do."

"So what happened?"

"After about four or five hours of this, Celia came running to me, and said, 'Make her go away.' So I did. I gave her some money and told her that baby didn't need Pilar anymore."

"Sounds like the right decision. But that leaves you with no weekend help."

"No need for it, either."

"Yes, there is, Olivia. There's a reason even the best parents have baby-sitters. They'd go crazy without one."

"I have Rosivel."

"You need someone at night, so you can go out."

"I promise if I ever get invited out anywhere that's worth going, I'll get a baby-sitter. Rosivel can stay late once in a while, she told me so. She also said she has friends I can use when she's not available. Celia loves Rosivel and I trust her."

Dennis pulled into a minimall and parked in front of the Baskin-Robbins. "You sure we shouldn't wake her up?"

"It's basically her bedtime, anyway. I've found that so long as the car is running, she stays asleep and then I can just throw her into her bed. Although . . ."

"What?"

"I can't remember the last time she peed — I usually make her go right before bed. See the kinds of things I think about now?" I undid my seat belt and opened my door. "Keep the car running. Oh, wait, what do you want? Want to share a sundae?"

"Sure."

"What kind of ice cream?"

"Surprise me."

I returned ten minutes later with a mint chocolate chip hot fudge sundae and two spoons. Dennis expressed his approval, and I sat down, handing the sundae over to him. It was dark out, but the car was pretty bright from the neon lights in the minimall. Dennis had turned the music way down, and I could hear Celia's light snoring from the back-seat.

We both attacked the ice cream like pigs at first, passing it back and forth, taking turns digging deep for the hot fudge on the sides, but after a while I sat back, sucked my spoon clean, and let Dennis finish it. He hadn't had dinner, and I had.

He scraped the last bit of ice cream out, then dropped his spoon inside and stuck the whole thing in a cupholder. "Home?" he said, after wiping his mouth and hands with one of the napkins I'd brought. I nodded and he pulled out of the parking lot. We drove in silence for a little while. Then Dennis said, "Olivia?"

"What?"

"You said you'd get baby-sitting if you had somewhere to go. There's this thing—" He stopped.

" 'This thing'?" I repeated.

"Sorry. I'm just a little embarrassed." He sighed. "Plans were made. I was completely against it, but then they threatened to make it a surprise if I didn't go along."

"Your birthday," I said. "Your fortieth birthday."

"Yeah."

"Who's the 'they' who threatened to surprise you?"

He kept his eyes on the road. "People there. At my law firm."

"Heather," I said.

"And Holly."

"All the 'H' women."

"They're just trying to be nice. I hate the whole idea of it. But I hated the idea of a surprise even more."

"So what are they doing for you?"

"Just a dinner. I said they had to keep it low-key." He braked for a red light and rested his forehead briefly on the steering wheel. "This really is a bad idea, isn't it?"

"What? Having a party or inviting me?"

He sat up again. "Having the party, of course. The only reason I hesitated about inviting you in the first place, Olivia, is because I don't think it's going to be a lot of fun. But I'd like you to come." The light changed to green. We started moving again.

"What night is it?"

"Sunday. It's at the Italian restaurant in the building next door to us. Lorenzo's. It's right there in the lobby. You can park in our building and walk over."

"Will you validate my parking?"

He laughed. "Absolutely. Parking's on us."

"I'll have to ask Rosivel."

"But you'll come? If she says yes?"

"I don't know," I said. "How many times are people going to tell me I remind them of my father?"

"Well," Dennis said, "I think there are going to be about twenty people there. So I'd say roughly twenty times. That's not counting the waiters, who probably knew him pretty well, too."

"Maybe I could dye my hair blonde before then."

"It would cut down on the resemblance."

"I've always wanted to be a blonde."

"Really?"

"No."

There was a sound from the backseat. I turned. Celia was blinking her eyes. "Livvy?" she said.

"Shhh. Go back to sleep, Celia."

"Where are we going?"

"Home."

"Will my mommy be there?"

The ice cream suddenly felt heavy in my stomach. "No, Celia."

"I want her. I want my mommy."

She hadn't asked for Alicia in weeks. Why now? I said, "Your mommy can't be there anymore, Celia. Remember? But I'll be there."

Her face screwed up into a sob. "I want my mommy. And my daddy. I've never seen them for the longest time. I want them."

"I know, I know. I'm sorry, Celia. I'm sorry. They can't be here anymore. They died. But I'm here, Celia. And Dennis is here, too."

She bucked in her seat, arching her back like she wanted to throw herself out. "No, no, no! I don't want you! I want to see my mommy! I want to see my daddy! You don't ever let me see them! I want them!" Her voice rose to a scream.

I knew she was disoriented from the too-short nap she'd just taken. But it didn't make it any easier to know what to say or do.

I just kept telling her I was sorry, and she just kept screaming that she wanted her parents, and Dennis just kept looking worried, and that's how we drove the rest of the way home.

twenty-seven

I called Dr. Rubillos that night. She had said I could, if I ever felt like I needed to. And I felt like I needed to.

Celia eventually calmed down. Wore herself out is more accurate. We got home, and I carried her in—she was still sobbing and screaming—and I lay down with her on her bed, because I thought she needed to go back to sleep. That didn't work so well. Lying there in the dark just made her more hysterical, and pretty soon she was kicking and hitting at me. So I gave up on getting her to sleep and carried her into the family room, where Dennis was pacing, and my mother was still dozing. But even TV didn't work. Celia just kept bucking on the sofa and striking out at me with her arms and legs, crying for her mother and her father and screaming that we weren't letting her see them because we were mean.

I offered her stuff—water, candy, toys. I would have given her anything at that point. She screamed at me that she didn't want anything except her mommy and daddy.

My mother suddenly snapped upright. "What's going on?" she asked, blinking. "What's wrong with Celia?"

"Her energy changed."

"Don't make jokes. Can't you see she's beside herself? Poor baby, what's wrong?" She came over and bent down toward Celia.

"Go away! I hate you!" Celia screamed and kicked out at her, at both of us. She landed a good one on my leg.

"Poor baby," my mother said again, stepping quickly to the side. "Can't you do something, Livvy?"

"Any suggestions?"

"Calm her down," my mother said. "She's scaring herself. She needs you to help her be calm." She headed toward the door. "I'm going to give you two some space." At the doorway, she looked back, shaking her head. "Poor little thing," she said. And disappeared.

I stayed nearby but kept clear of Celia's feet. She kept writhing and yelling, but her screams were starting to sound hoarse. Gradually her movements slowed down. She stopped fighting and let her body go limp. She just lay there for a while, her face pale and wet, her breath coming in short, painful hiccups. I tried to hold her then, but she shoved me away. She didn't have much strength left, but I backed off. After a while, her breathing evened out, and her eyes went blank. She fell asleep less than an hour after she had first woken up screaming in the car. It felt like days.

I carried her to bed, then called Dr. Rubillos's voice mail, following the directions for reaching her in an emergency. The system paged her, and she called back immediately. Dennis came into the kitchen and sat at the table while I talked to her.

"It sank in on her," the doctor said, after I told her what happened. "Tonight, she figured out what being dead means."

"Why tonight?" I asked.

"Who knows? Did her parents take long trips without her?"

"Probably. I don't know. Why?"

"Well, maybe Celia's used to their being away for a while, and it just sank in that they've been gone a lot longer than they usually are. Or maybe it just occurred to her that her birthday came and went, and they didn't show up. Or maybe she had a day when she didn't think about them at all, and on some level it made her realize they were really and truly never coming back, and her situation has changed permanently. Maybe when Celia's twenty, she'll be able to tell us. All I know is, one way or another, she's finally gotten the idea."

"So what do I do?"

"What do you think you should do?"

"I swear if you start that shit again tonight of all nights—"

Dennis raised his head at this. I turned my back on him. I didn't need anyone to tell me to watch my language. I was barely holding it together.

"Olivia," Dr. Rubillos said after a short pause, "you're tired. This has been a tough night for you. I'm not trying to 'start' anything. I've just found that your instincts with Celia are usually good, and I trust you to do the right thing. You know her better than I do."

"You're the professional," I said. My voice was getting ragged. I swallowed hard. "Tell me what to do. What if she wakes up during the night and starts it all again? Or in the morning? I can't take it. I can't deal with her like this. She hates me. I don't know what to do."

"You can't stop her from crying and screaming," Dr. Rubillos said. "Not if that's what she wants to do. And maybe even *needs* to do. Just make sure she doesn't get so wild she hurts herself. And be there to hold her when she wants you. Most of all, don't be hurt or angry if she *doesn't* want you, or even if she seems to hate you, which of course she doesn't really. On some level she probably feels as if you supplanted her parents and that your presence is directly related to their absence. So if she wants them, she can't want you. Something like that. She may have to go through a phase now where she treats you badly—"

"Oh, that'll be fun," I said.

"I promise you it'll just be a phase. She does love you, Olivia. I've seen it for myself. Bear with her. Don't resent her if she's hard on you for a while. She needs to know that you love her, no matter what she says or does. She's figuring out that you're all she's got left, and that's got to be a tough thing for her to accept, even if you're the most wonderful parent in the world."

"I'm not a parent at all," I said.

"Do you have a better name for it?"

———

When I hung up, Dennis asked what the doctor had said.

I came over to the table and dropped into the chair next to him. My head was vibrating with exhaustion. "Oh, a lot of analyst shit. You know, stuff about love and discovery and phases and God knows what else. And at the end she said, 'I'm not worried. I think this is all very healthy.' I'm glad she's not worried, aren't you? And she said Celia may feel like she has to be hateful to me for a while because it's like I took her parents away. Dr. Rubillos isn't worried about that, either." I folded my arms on the table and put my head down on top of them. "Fuck, fuck, fuck."

Okay, maybe it wasn't the most mature thing to do at the moment. But it was a lot better than crying, which is what I was within seconds of doing. I'd grown up with my mother's sniffs and moans as my lullaby virtually every night, and I wasn't about to inflict mine on anyone.

Dennis sat there without saying anything for a minute, and then he said, "Maybe she'll be fine tomorrow. She was tired tonight."

"Yeah. Maybe."

Another silence. Then he said, "I can stay. All night, if you want. In case she wakes up again."

"Thanks." It would be nice to have someone else to call on if she woke up, but I didn't want to make him hang out there all night, especially since there was a good chance she'd just sleep through. "It's a nice offer. But we'll be okay. Anyway, if she's like that again, it's not like anyone can do anything."

"You shouldn't have to deal with it alone, though."

"Why not? I have to deal with everything else alone."

"I know," he said. "There's been too much on your shoulders. I'm sorry, Olivia. I really am." He reached out and touched my shoulder.

"No, *I'm* sorry," I said, sitting up again. "That was self-pity. Which I hate."

"Go easy on yourself. You've earned a little self-pity."

"How can she? Miss them. I mean, we're talking about Richard and Alicia here."

"For what it's worth, I think you're a far better parent to Celia than Alicia ever was."

"Aw, shucks," I said. Then, "A pig would be a better parent than Alicia was. But I know, I know, a dysfunctional parent is still a parent."

"Well put."

"I was quoting Dr. Rubillos. Who isn't as stupid as she looks and acts. And occasionally sounds."

"Are you talking about me?" My mother, walking in.

"No," I said. "You're exactly as stupid as you look and sound."

"Hey, hey," Dennis said.

"Sorry." I shut my eyes and pressed the heels of my palms hard against the sockets. "It's been a long night. Sorry, Barbara. Didn't mean it."

"Oh, yes you did," she said. "But I'm used to it. Is Celia asleep?" I nodded. "Poor baby. That was quite a tantrum she threw. It's the age, you know. You were always throwing tantrums when you were four."

I dropped my hands and opened my eyes. "Yeah, except mine were because my parents *weren't* dead."

"Kids always want what they can't have," she said. Seriously.

"At least now I'm halfway there."

Before she could figure out what that meant, Dennis jumped in. "We're worried about Celia, Barbara. She was so sad tonight. I was telling Olivia that I could spend the night here, on the sofa, if she thinks that would help. Just in case Celia gets upset like that again."

"Oh, I'd be surprised if Celia woke up. That was just a little bit of temper, that's all — here and then gone. It didn't mean anything."

"How do you know?" I said. "What do you know about kids who've lost their parents?"

"I may not know about losing parents, but I know more about children than you do. Don't forget I raised you. You haven't raised anyone."

"I raised myself. You supplied some clothing and food."

"How could you say something so . . . so hurtful?" Her mouth trembled at the corners. "Deliberately hurtful. You know I was always there for you."

"Oh, right. Always there to—"

"Olivia," Dennis said, quietly but loud enough to cut me off. I looked at him, savage with the need to attack something. He just looked back at me. Asking me to stop without saying anything.

I took a deep breath. "Forget it," I said to my mother. "I didn't mean it. There. That's two apologies in five minutes out of me, so I think one of us better leave the room before I make it to three. I'm going to go work on my paper. See, Dennis? I do my homework like a good little girl. That's all I ever fucking do now is homework."

I left the kitchen and went to the family room, but the pages of my book blurred when I tried to read, and I threw it down. I went into the guest room and lay down on my bed and cursed my father for driving his car off a cliff when I wasn't in it.

Celia didn't wake me up in the middle of the night. My mother did.

Somewhere around two or three in the morning, I startle awake, the way you do when someone else comes in your room, and she's sitting down in the chair near my bed, wineglass in her hand, her hair a cloud of light in the dark.

"So you can't sleep, either," she said. "I had a feeling you'd be awake."

"I wasn't awake until you woke me up. What do you want, Barbara?"

A sip of wine. "You never call me Mommy anymore. Why is that?"

"I haven't called you Mommy since I was six. Is that why you woke me up?"

"I've just been thinking. About the two of us. Alone, depressed . . . You know why I was so upset with you for losing that man, Livvy? That beautiful Joe?"

"Why?"

"Because I saw myself in you. You're just like me—you can win a man, but you can't hold on to him. If I had just been able to hold on to Richard, our lives would have been so different. You could have grown up in a real family. But I couldn't and you won't be able to, either. Hold on to a man, I mean."

"Joe wasn't worth holding on to."

"You're just saying that to make me feel better. Don't forget, I met him. He was perfect. And we lost him. We're always going to lose them,

Livvy, and we'll end up together forever, two old maids, unloved and unwanted."

"I can live with the old maid part," I said. "The ending up together part scares the hell out of me."

"You make jokes," she said. She was refilling her glass. In the dark, I hadn't even noticed until then that she'd brought the bottle in with her. "You always make jokes. Like Nero fiddling while Rome burned. I don't blame you. It's either that or fall apart, like me."

"You shouldn't drink so much," I said. "Seriously, Barbara. You've got to stop this. It's not doing you any good."

"I don't drink that much," she said. "But if I do, who can blame me? I was the prettiest of all my friends, and I'm the only one who's alone now. Tell me why. What's wrong with us that we end up alone?"

"There are worse things than being alone," I said.

"How would you know?"

"I've been alone a lot." All my life, it felt like.

"You're too young to know how awful it is yet. How it's worse than anything else. Do you want some wine? You know I hate to drink by myself."

"Then don't. Don't drink."

"Where do you get the right to act so superior? Who was it who got drunk on New Year's Eve and wanted to drive that way?"

"Me," I said. "That would be me. Can I go back to sleep now? Please?"

"What's going to become of us?" she asked. "Where's our happiness?"

"I'd be happy if I could just go to sleep."

"Make your jokes," she said. "Laugh all you want. You're young. But someday you'll be old and alone like I am, and you'll say to yourself, 'She tried to warn me and all I did was laugh.' "

"Good night, Barbara." I lay down and closed my eyes.

"Can I stay here for a little while?" she asked after a moment.

I kept my eyes closed. "Sure. So long as you don't talk anymore."

"I'll just sit here for a few more minutes," she said. "I don't want to be alone."

"Stay as long as you want," I said.

When I woke up the next morning, she was still there, snoring away, wineglass clutched in her hand, drips of wine across her nightgown, empty bottle leaning against the chair leg.

I groped on the side table for my watch and checked it. Seven-thirty already. Usually Celia woke me up before then.

I rested in bed a little while longer, thinking she'd come in any minute, but she didn't. I couldn't go back to sleep, so after a half hour or so I got up. My mother stirred but didn't wake up as I went by her.

I heard Celia's voice as soon as I was in the hallway. She was in her room playing with some of her dolls. She was talking quietly to them, telling them she was going to go shopping, but would be back soon, and they should wait for her and not be afraid. "Mommy always comes back," she said and gave them each a kiss on the cheek.

I wondered what it was like for her to hear the other mothers at her school say that when they said good-bye to their kids.

I came into the room and stood by the door watching her. She noticed me but didn't say anything, just kept rearranging her dolls and speaking quietly to them.

After a while, I came over and knelt down next to her. "Thanks for not waking me up this morning."

She smoothed a blanket over one of the dolls. Didn't look at me.

"I was pretty tired," I said. "The sleep felt good."

She said, "Night-night," to the baby. Then she pulled the blanket off again.

I said, "You were pretty mad at me last night. Remember?"

"Put this on," she said and held out the blanket, still without actually looking at me. "I can't do it right."

"Like this?" I put the blanket over the baby.

"No!" She pulled it off. "The right way!"

I tried again.

"You're doing it all wrong."

"I'm sorry," I said. "I don't know what you want. Can you show me?"

"No, I want you to do it!"

"But you said I was doing it wrong."

"Try again!"

I did and she screamed, "No, no, no!"

"I can't do it, Celia," I said. "I can't do it the way you want. I'm sorry."

"You have to!" she said. "You have to do it right. I can't do it."

Once again, I tried. I smoothed the blanket as carefully as I could over the baby, tucked it in around its arms, made sure its feet were covered. "There. Is that right?"

"No!" She snatched the blanket off of the baby and threw it at me again. "Not like that! Do it right!"

"I can't!" I said, my patience gone. "If you don't like the way I'm doing it, do it yourself."

"No! You!"

I tried one last time.

She screamed that I had messed it up, and I hurled the blanket at her.

"You're driving me crazy! I can't deal with this." I got to my feet and headed toward the door. "I'm leaving."

"No!" She ran after me, grabbed my arm, pulled on it. "Don't go! Don't go, Livvy! I can't do it. I can't do it. You have to do it. Don't go, Livvy!" Her face was tight and pale, too small for her huge eyes and the dark circles under them.

I knelt down again and put my arms around her. I rested my head on her shoulder, like you do with someone bigger than you. "I'm trying, Celia," I whispered. "I'm really trying. I know I'm not doing it right, and I'm sorry. I can't help it. It's all I can do."

"Don't go," she said, and squeezed her face down against my neck. "Don't go."

"I won't," I said and we stayed like that for a while, folded in on each other.

I got a call from Holly that afternoon. She was making the final guest list for Dennis Klein's birthday party and wanted to know if I'd be there. I told her to hold on and went in search of Rosivel. I found her and Celia in the backyard. Celia liked to swing on the play structure. Rosivel would push her for as long as she wanted, but I always made her pump her legs, so I didn't have to stand there the whole time.

Anyway, I ran out and asked Rosivel if she'd be willing to come and baby-sit on Sunday night, and she thought for a moment then said she could do it.

"I'm glad you're going out," she said. "A young girl like you should go out."

Even Rosivel was worried about my social life.

I went back inside and told Holly I'd be there. As soon as I hung up, though, I wondered if I'd made a mistake. Everyone else there would be a lawyer and much older than me. I wouldn't know anyone except for Dennis, unless you counted Holly and Heather, and I didn't count them as people I really knew.

But Dennis had invited me to his birthday party, and I figured I should go.

He came by that night at dinnertime, to check on us. He'd also called several times during the day.

He greeted Celia with a hug and a kiss and sat down at the table, pulling her up onto his knee. Over the top of her head, he looked at me, questioning.

"We're doing okay," I said in answer. "Better."

"Did she sleep?"

"We both did."

"Good. Where's your mother?"

"Out. She was feeling sorry for herself, so I said she should go to one of the spas and get the works—massage, facial, whatever."

"Barbara's going to get her toenails painted purple," Celia said.

"Really?" Dennis raised his eyebrows. "Purple toenails? You can do that?"

"That's what Livvy says."

"Pure speculation," I said. "Celia asked what color they'd be, and I made a guess."

"I think they're going to be green," Dennis said to her. "Green with pink polka dots."

"You can't paint polka dots on fingernails," she said.

"Sure you can. I know one woman at work who paints entire faces on her fingernails. With eyes and noses and everything."

Celia thought about that. "I want polka dots on *my* fingernails."

"Yeah?" I said. "Go get some magic markers and I'll see what I can do."

"Really?"

"Sure."

She jumped down from Dennis's knee and went running out.

He said, "So today's been okay?"

"Yeah. She was a little . . . on edge, I guess, this morning. But the teacher said she was fine at school, and when I picked her up, she seemed basically happy. A little tired, a little withdrawn, but nothing like last night. Thank God."

"And how are you? Recovered?"

"More or less. My mother woke me up at three in the morning, though. To tell me I would never be happy for the rest of my life."

"Oy," he said. "I'm sorry."

"Oh, she's been telling me that since I was a kid. I see it as a good thing. Since I never do anything she tells me, I figure I'll be happy even if it kills me."

Celia came dancing back in with a handful of markers. "I want pink and purple polka dots," she said. "On this hand. And yellow and blue ones on this hand."

"Wow," I said, "you're going to be dazzling." I bent over her hand and started in on the dots. She was so excited she couldn't stop shifting from leg to leg, raising the other leg like a stork. "Try to stand still," I said.

"Okay."

Dennis said, "Holly tells me you're coming."

Celia turned to look at him. "Where? Where is Livvy going?"

"I told you not to move," I said. "Now you've turned a dot into a line."

"I don't want a line. I only want dots."

"It's okay. I fixed it. Dennis invited me to a party, Celia. An adults-only party. For his birthday."

"How old are you?" she asked him.

"You moved again," I said.

"I'll be turning forty."

"Like me?" she said.

"No, you turned four," he said. "I'm turning forty. I'm ten times older than you. Can you count to forty, Celia?"

"No," she said. "That's too big a number."

"That's exactly how I feel about it."

"What do you want for your birthday?" she asked.

"An excellent question," I said, looking up. "What *do* you want for your birthday?" It hadn't occurred to me until then that I should probably bring something.

"Not a thing," he said. "Just your company. I'm glad you're coming, Olivia. I can't promise it'll be a lot of fun—a bunch of lawyers sitting around eating pasta and boring each other—but if you're there, at least there'll be someone interesting to talk to."

"Why can't I come?" Celia said.

"I told you, it's adults only." I let go of the hand I'd been marking. "Give me your other hand."

"There are too many purple dots and not enough pink ones," she said, examining the one I'd just finished.

"If you complain any more, I'm going to stop right now and this hand will never get finished."

"I guess it's okay."

"Why don't you ask Dennis if he wants something to eat or drink? That's called being a good hostess, and it's something I never learned to be."

"Do you want something to eat or drink?" she said to him.

"No, thank you. I've got some dinner waiting for me back at the office. I just wanted to see how my girls were doing, but I've got to head back there soon."

"Can you read me a book before you go?"

"Sure, if it's a quick one."

"You're all done," I said. "How's that?"

She looked at both hands. "You made the blue dots too big."

"It's not my fault. Someone had squished the tip of the blue marker. I wonder who could have done that?"

"Probably Rosivel," she said.

"You think?"

"Come on," Dennis said, standing up and holding his hand out to her. "Let's go pick out a book."

I followed them down the hallway and into Celia's room. Celia picked out a book and brought it to Dennis, and they sat down together in her pink armchair. He read the book to her while I watched from the doorway.

When he finished, she brought him another one and then another one, and then he said, "I really do have to go now, Celia."

She clung to him and begged him to stay. He said, "My dinner's getting cold back at the office. And people are waiting for me."

"Please," she said. "Please, please, please."

He sighed. And then he said, "Yeah, okay, one more book." While she went to get it, he gave me a helpless shrug.

I came over then and sat down on the floor. I curled up against the side of the chair and listened with my eyes closed while he read us one more book.

twenty-eight

I wished Heather from Harvard would stop saying how great it was that I'd come to Dennis's birthday party. The way she kept saying it—like it was the last thing anyone would have expected—was only making me feel like a mistake had been made, that Dennis should never have invited someone—me—without her permission. I don't think that was an accident, either. I think Heather from Harvard knew exactly what she was doing when she said for roughly the tenth time, "I am just so happy you actually came tonight, Olivia. It's such a nice surprise for all of us!"

Well, fuck Heather from Harvard.

Only I wasn't having such a great time, anyway.

What was it with me and the parties I'd been going to lately? Nothing fit right. The party Joe had taken me to was too sloppy, too cheap, too noisy. This one was the exact opposite—too elegant, too dressy, too quiet. The lawyers and their spouses didn't raise their voices above a murmur as they sipped their wine and waved away trays of hors d'oeuvres. A pianist in the corner played jazz so softly you could hardly hear him.

I was wearing the same black dress I'd worn on New Year's Eve, but some impulse to make myself look older had led me to pin my hair up and back in a sloppy bun. My head hurt. And I felt stupid. I thought about going to the ladies' room and pulling it down, but I knew Heather from Harvard would notice the change and probably comment on it, and for some reason I didn't think I could take that.

It would have been okay if at least Dennis had been around to talk to, but he was pinned into the far corner of the room by some old men with huge guts who were clutching glasses of liquor and talking his ear off. He had waved to me when I first came into the room—a private room, separated from the rest of the restaurant by a hallway and a door—but hadn't come over to say hello. So I was stuck there, feeling stupid and headachey, with only Heather from Harvard taking any notice of me at all.

"I am so impressed with the amount of time Dennis spends with little Celia," she was saying to me now. A black-jacketed waiter came by with a plate of bruschetta, and she shook her head so emphatically that he backed away without offering it to me. I wasn't hungry, but they smelled good. "It seems like every night he runs off to see her. I told him the other day he'll probably spend less time with his own kids when he has them than he does with her."

"She likes him a lot," I said.

"That's so sweet." She had removed her glasses for the evening and could definitely have been cast as the heroine of a "Why, Miss Jones, you're beautiful!" moment. Her hair, which had been pulled back when I first met her, fell smooth and shiny over her shoulders. "It's like Dennis to take her under his wing. I think he'd take care of the whole world if he could. He's like that, you know?"

"Yes," I said.

She looked past me, and I knew she was looking at him. She stretched her throat up and smiled in that direction. "You should see him now, the poor guy. This is supposed to be a party—*his* party—but they're going to make him talk business. He's the guy everyone goes to first around here. He doesn't get a minute to himself."

"He told me you're a big help," I said.

That got her attention. "Did he?" She studied me for a moment.

Trying to decide whether that bit of information spoke more to Dennis's relationship with her or with me. "I hope I am. I'd like to be."

Someone came up and greeted her. A thin young man with curly hair and large anxious eyes.

Heather introduced us. "Henry Williams, Olivia Martin."

"Hi." He shook my hand. His was slightly sweaty. "Nice to meet you. Do you work at the firm?"

I was shaking my head when Heather answered for me. "No, Olivia is Richard Martin's daughter."

"Oh. Oh, wow. I'm so sorry about your father. I didn't know him well, but everyone says he was a brilliant lawyer."

"Thank you."

"Excuse me," Heather from Harvard said and glided away, having successfully passed me on to someone else. She made a straight line across the room to Dennis's side.

Henry Williams said, "Do you know many people here?"

"Just the birthday boy."

"I don't know that many myself. I just came on board here. I don't really know anyone, except Heather. She and I were at law school together."

"That would be Harvard," I said.

He nodded. "It would. I'm sorry."

"For what?"

"I don't know. People always look annoyed when they find out you went to Harvard, so I've gotten to the point where I just automatically apologize for having gone there. Anyway, it must have been Heather's idea to invite me. I mean, I know Dennis—I do work for him all the time—but I don't think he would have invited me. It's not that big a party." He leaned forward. "To be honest, I'm terrified. Everyone looks old and scary here. Except you and Heather, of course."

"Hey," I said, "don't complain to *me*. I'm younger than you are. And I don't even work at the firm. The only reason I'm here—" I stopped.

"Why *are* you here? Because of your father?"

"He and Dennis were friends," I said. That *was* why, wasn't it? More or less?

At least I had found someone other than Heather to talk to, so the party was slightly less agonizing than it had been a few minutes earlier. "Did you and Heather hang out together back at law school?"

"No, not really. We've actually gotten closer since being here. Back at school, we were in different circles. She was editor of the Law Review, you know. I was just . . . one of the crowd. On a good day."

"And yet here you are in the exact same place. So none of that mattered."

"You'd think so, wouldn't you? But if you look into a crystal ball and check out our futures, I promise you you'll see Heather right in this room, having *her* fortieth birthday celebrated by getting her name on the letterhead."

"And you?"

"See that guy over there?" He pointed to a waiter who was walking past us with a tray of skewered shrimp. "That'll be me. With any luck, I'll get some good tips that night and will be able to afford that month's rent. Who do you have to know to get a drink around here, anyway?"

"I don't know, but I'm guessing Heather."

"Come with me to the bar. I want to keep talking to you."

We walked across the room together, and when we reached the bar, Henry appealed to me. "What should I get? What are people here drinking? I don't want to get the wrong thing."

I looked around the room. "The women mostly have wine, but the men mostly have—what is that? Scotch?"

He checked around. "Yeah, it's scotch. I should probably get that, huh?"

"Up to you. You could buck the trend."

"Not with this crowd. I'll get the scotch. You want anything?"

"No, thanks." He ordered, and the bartender moved off to make his drink.

Henry said glumly, "I hate scotch."

"Do you? But think of how manly you'll feel when you're holding it in your hand."

"If I were to tell you I actually would have preferred wine, would you question my masculinity?"

"I think I'd have to," I said.

"Then ignore everything I just said."

"Okay."

Another waiter came by with a tray of bruschetta. Henry said, "I'm starving," and stacked three together. The waiter handed him a napkin and walked away. Henry said, "Aren't you going to have one?"

"Are you kidding? I'd spill it all down the front of my dress."

"You're right," he said, frowning down at the three pieces he held balanced on his fingertips. "This is way too risky. I better not."

"But you're starving," I said.

"I know. What do I do?"

"Eat carefully?"

"Okay. But if I spill this, let it be on your head. I don't mean that literally, of course."

"You better not."

But he managed to eat it without making a mess. He took big bites and swallowed quickly. Then he wiped off his hands, wadded up the napkin, and stuck it in the pocket of his jacket. "There. Now at least I'm not starving. But I'm not eating anything else until I'm sitting at the table. Too stressful."

The bartender slid the scotch over to us.

Henry picked it up and turned it around in his hand. "Yuck. Do I have to drink this?"

"No, just carry it around. In a manly way."

He put one hand on his waist and held the drink up as if he were about to take a sip. "There. How do I look?"

"Very *Maxim*."

"That's good, right? Hey," he said, relaxing back to a normal position. "What?"

"I'm actually having fun. How'd that happen?"

"Maybe you just needed to eat."

"The only thing that worries me is that you may not be seated near me at dinner. I mean, look at the size of that table. You've got to sit next to me. You're my only hope."

"Only hope for what?"

"Having a good time."

"I don't think it's going to be up to us where we sit—there are place cards."

"Are you sure?" He took my wrist and pulled me over to the table, which was really two tables pushed together in the shape of the letter T. "Oh, Lord, you're right. We'll have to sit where we're assigned. I should have known. These are *lawyers*, for God's sake — can't have any spontaneity here. Heaven forbid you should sit where you want to."

"Calm down," I said. "Why don't we just change the place cards around?"

"Really? Do people do that?"

"You're not supposed to. Which isn't a bad reason to do it."

He grinned at me. "And here you seemed so proper."

"Did I? It's the hair, isn't it? I knew it would mislead people."

"I like the hair," he said. "You have a nice neck. Do you mind my telling you that?"

"No. Should we change our place cards?"

"I don't know. I'm worried I could be fired for it."

"Then I'll do it. There isn't much anyone here could do to me. Oh, except cut me off from my inheritance."

"How's that?"

"Dennis is the executor of Richard's trust."

"Oh. Uh, I feel kind of stupid asking this now, but you're not under eighteen, are you?"

"No, I'm twenty-one. Richard just didn't trust me."

"That's a relief," Henry said. "I was suddenly thinking that the thoughts I was thinking were vaguely illegal."

"I didn't think statutory laws applied to fantasies," I said.

"They do in some states. Mostly in the Bible Belt."

"How old are *you*? Since we're asking each other."

"Twenty-four," he said.

"Isn't that young to be a lawyer?"

"Yeah. I did everything young — went to college when I was sixteen, law school when I was twenty. Do you have any idea what it's like to always be the youngest person in the room?"

"Well, *yeah*," I said.

"That's why I'm so glad you're here. You're saving me from my usual fate. Plus I get to act all grown-up and patronizing toward you. This could be the beginning of a beautiful relationship, Olympia."

"Olivia."

"Yeah, right. I did say the beginning. We can work on it."

"Look at you two," said Heather from Harvard, coming up to us with Dennis. "Whispering away together over here. Looks like I made a good introduction."

We hadn't been whispering, but it wasn't worth correcting her. And it wasn't like she had gone out of her way to have us meet. Henry had just showed up. But I didn't correct her on that, either.

Dennis said, "I'm glad you're here, Olivia. I'm sorry I got stuck in the corner for so long."

"I extricated him," Heather said. "I said that this was his birthday party, and they weren't allowed to make him talk shop anymore. I was very tough with them, wasn't I, Dennis?"

"Very tough," he said. "Very impressive. They all quailed before you. As they should, since you'll be running this firm one day."

"Stop," she said, smiling.

"Hey," Henry said, "what's the rule on the seating arrangement? Are guests allowed to rearrange it at will? I mean, if they have a really good reason to?"

"Absolutely not," Heather said. "Holly and I spent hours working out where everyone should sit."

"Sounds like a good use of your time," Dennis said. "Who'd we bill for those hours?"

She pushed at his arm. "It was important!"

"Where is Holly, anyway?" he asked, looking around. "I thought she'd be here."

"Oh, there were a couple of things to be taken care of still," Heather said. "She'll be here soon."

"I hope so," he said. "She should get a chance to enjoy herself." He looked at me. "You're being quiet, Olivia."

"Just taking it all in."

Henry took my hand and tucked it under his arm. "Don't worry, Dennis. I'm taking care of her. I've fallen madly in love with Olympia. I mean Olivia."

"You'll have to get in line," Dennis said. "Heather, am I allowed to check out the seating arrangement?"

"It's your party," she said and walked him around the table. They stopped, near the center at the top of the T, and started discussing something. Heather pointed to a place farther away, and Dennis shook his head. They talked some more.

"Oh, God, he's arguing with her," Henry said, as we watched them. "Heaven help him. Heather is not a woman to be crossed. Then again, if anyone could get away with it, it would be Dennis."

"She likes him, doesn't she?"

"Likes isn't the word. If she could eat him up and wear him like an overcoat—wait, that was a mixed metaphor, wasn't it?"

"Doesn't matter. You made your point."

He squeezed my arm. "You know, you're the perfect age for me, Olivia. Three years younger. When I'm eighty, you'll be seventy-seven. How much more perfect than that could you get?"

"No more perfect."

"You don't think I'm coming on too strong, do you? I don't want to scare you off."

"No offense, but you're not really that scary," I said.

"Good. Now, see—it looks like Dennis won. That shows you how crazy she is for him. She's actually letting him change her unchangeable arrangement."

He was right. Dennis had gone over and picked up one of the place cards and brought it back to where Heather was. As we watched, she reluctantly exchanged it with the one in front of her, which he took and put at the farther spot. She pouted a bit, but he smiled and whispered something to her and her face relaxed and they walked off together.

"Well, if he can get away with it, why can't we?" Henry said, turning back to me.

"We can do whatever we want," I said. "But she won't *like* it."

"Let's at least see where we've been put and whether we'll survive."

We found his name as far down the bottom of the T as you could go. "Talk about below the salt," he said. "Nothing like being one of the peons."

"Should I have understood what you just said?"

"Doesn't matter. The point is, you're not sitting near me, and my heart is breaking."

"So where *am* I?" We separated and walked up opposite sides of the long table, checking out the place cards, then circled around the shorter table so we met in the middle of the top, where Dennis and Heather had argued a few minutes earlier.

"Well," Henry said, holding up a place card with my name on it. "This explains the mystery. Right next to the birthday boy, like he wanted. And Heather didn't."

"I don't see why she'd care," I said. "She's right over here, on his other side. It's not like *she* had to move anywhere. Why would she care?"

"Do you really have to ask?"

"It wasn't her idea?"

He shook his head, smiling a little. "Olivia. Heather doesn't want the competition."

A sudden rush of blood to my cheeks. I said, "She doesn't need to worry."

He addressed the ceiling. "She's modest, too. I can't believe my luck. Tell me, Olivia, do you have any flaws? You'd better tell me now, because I plan to propose to you before the evening is out. Although"— he lifted the scotch he was holding—"I might have to actually drink this to get up the courage. I wonder if you're worth the sacrifice. What am I saying? Of course you are."

A voice rose above all the others. Heather's. Telling everyone it was dinnertime, and we had to sit down.

"It's not too late," Henry said. "You could still come with me down to my end of the table. They'll never look for you there—it's like being in another country. A very distant, impoverished Third World country. And if they do get mad, I'll just tell them that we're engaged, and it would be cruel to separate us. And also that it was your idea."

"If this is what you're like sober," I said, "I think you're better off not drinking that scotch."

"Wise beyond her years."

"I'll see you after dessert."

"Don't forget me."

"I don't think I could."

After Henry went to sit down, I spotted Dennis and Heather walking together across the room. Heather whispered something into Dennis's ear, and he made a comical face in response.

It was strange watching him from a distance—like when I was at the park, looking at Celia, and thought, what a cute little girl, as if I hadn't seen her every day for weeks on end, as if she and I were strangers. I watched Dennis laughing with Heather across the room, and I thought, what a nice-looking guy, what a great smile. Like I'd never seen him before.

He was, admittedly, no Joe Lowden. Women wouldn't fall over him wherever he went. But that was in his favor, too—he was no Joe Lowden. He'd probably never told a lie in his life. Not Dennis.

Heather had figured it out. Heather from Harvard had looked at Dennis Klein and seen that he was a good-looking guy with a kind heart, who was smart and funny and—

I blinked. My cheeks felt hot, like they had when Henry had said—what was it he had said?

Oh, yeah. Heather doesn't want the competition.

Dennis saw me watching them and smiled at me, raising his hand in greeting. I looked away like I hadn't seen him, and the burning in my cheeks got worse.

What the hell was going on?

I didn't like it. I cut and ran.

I slid past groups of people all moving toward the table and ducked out the door and into the hallway. I went into the ladies' room there. Some middle-aged woman in a dark purple suit was putting on lipstick. I didn't know if she was from our party or not, so I just went straight into a stall without making eye contact. I closed the door and leaned back against it, closing my eyes, trying to think.

Oh, shit. What was going on?

Since when had Dennis been anything other than, you know, *Dennis?* The guy who doled out money and advice and always looked a little silly when he got down on the floor to play with Celia?

I didn't like Heather from Harvard. But I knew she wasn't an idiot. Was that what made me suddenly look at Dennis in a different way? The fact that someone who was smart and pretty could look at him that way? Or did it go further back? When *didn't* I feel happy just to hear him walk in the door?

Oh, man. Talk about acting like an idiot. This was as low as I'd ever fallen, standing in a bathroom stall wondering . . . what? If I had a *crush* on someone? On someone who thought of me — at best — as a sullen teenager? I'd managed not to have any crushes for my entire school career. Was I really going to start now that I was technically an adult — well, of legal drinking age, anyway, and the guardian of a little kid?

No. No, I couldn't possibly be *that* stupid.

Oh, *shit*.

twenty-nine

At least I knew better than to hang out for a long time in the bathroom staring at the toilet. The last thing I wanted to do was make a grand solo entrance into the dining room with everyone watching.

When I got back to the table, Dennis and Heather were already sitting side by side. I slipped into the chair on his other side, and he said, "There you are. I thought you'd run out on us."

"Never before I've eaten," I said. Forcing myself to sound normal. Surprised at the effort it took.

He nudged at a spoon with the tip of his finger. "You looked like you were having a good time with Henry Williams. He's a nice guy, isn't he?"

"Yeah," I said. "As far as I could tell in ten minutes."

"He's close to your age, too. I should have thought of that before, asked to have you seated with him."

Heather was listening over his shoulder. She said, "It's not too late. Laura Shammas didn't show. There's an empty chair right next to Henry. If you want to move, Olivia—"

"Thanks. I'm okay for now."

Dennis didn't say anything. I thought, he put me here because he felt bad I didn't know anyone, and now he's sorry he did. Because if I were sitting near Henry, he wouldn't have to worry about me at all.

Heather called Dennis's attention to the flower arrangements, and while they were discussing them, the man on my other side introduced himself. His name was Jerome, and he was a lawyer. Big surprise there. He identified me as Richard's daughter and said that Richard had been one of the most brilliant lawyers he'd ever known and that his death was a loss to the law firm and the legal community in general.

Neither of us found this subject very interesting. After we'd both fallen silent, he turned his back to me and joined in the conversation that was going on to the other side of him.

I was sitting above the vertical part of the T so there was no one across from me, just the long stretch of the other table.

Heather kept talking to Dennis in such a low voice I couldn't possibly hear and join in.

I saw Henry way down at his end of the table, with an empty chair on one side of him and an older woman on the other. She was clutching her purse on her lap with one hand and picking through a basket of rolls with the other. Henry waved sadly at me. I saluted him.

A waiter brought around the first course of prosciutto and melon. Right on his heels was another waiter with two bottles of wine.

"Do you want red or white?" he asked me.

"Neither," I said. "Just some water, please."

Dennis saw this. His conversation with Heather was briefly on hold since a waiter was reaching between them. He said, "You're not drinking?"

I shook my head.

"You sure?" he said. "I promise not to lecture you. And, if you want, I can drive you home."

"I haven't had a drink since New Year's Eve."

"Why not?"

"I don't know." Because I had hated being drunk in front of him that day. Because I hated watching my mother burning through drink after drink, bottle after bottle. Because I didn't want to be drunk and have Celia need me for something.

It was easier just to shrug than to try to explain.

Dennis waited a moment, and when I didn't say anything else, he sighed. "Olivia. I know we talked about it, and maybe it's a good thing you're not drinking, but I'm starting to feel like you never get to act like a normal kid anymore. And it's my fault."

"It's okay," I said. "I really don't mind not drinking. I mean, what with the cocaine and heroin and all, I'm so wrecked I hardly notice the difference."

He shook his head, but he was laughing.

Heather's voice cut through. *Now* she was loud. "Dennis, I want you to tell Ruben that story you told me yesterday. About running into Bruce Millford at the Coffee Bean."

Dennis obliged. Being the obliging type. He tried to include me as he told the story by leaning back and looking in my direction every once in a while, but I didn't know any of the people or references, and when the others laughed at the end, I had no idea why. Heather said something I couldn't hear—back in soft voice mode—and Dennis and Ruben laughed again.

Jerome had actually hitched his chair around, so it angled away from me and he could talk with his friends more easily. Which was fine with me.

I looked at my plate of food, and my stomach curled up. I didn't want to eat.

When I lifted my head again, I saw that Henry was watching me. He raised his wineglass, toasting me. I toasted him back with my water glass. I drank and was startled when Dennis spoke to me.

"You sure you don't want to move down there?" he asked.

"After all you did to put me here in the first place?"

"What do you mean?"

"I saw you change the names. Over her objections." I jerked my head to indicate Heather. She was watching us, but I was using her trick of keeping my head down and speaking too quietly for the other person to hear.

"Oh. That doesn't matter. I was just . . . You were stuck in between two of the most boring people at the firm. I didn't want you to have a bad time." He glanced at Jerome's back. "I guess I didn't do you any favors. You would have been better off if I'd put you down by Henry. But I was being selfish."

"Selfish?"

"Keeping you next to me. Hey, can you keep a secret?"

"Yes."

He extended his hand straight out in front of him. Heather saw him do that and leaned forward, curious, but her companion on the other side—Ruben, I guess—was talking rapidly into her ear, so she couldn't listen in. She bobbed her head in an impatient nod at something Ruben said.

"Look," Dennis said to me, "I'm shaking." You could actually see the fingers on his outstretched hand trembling a little bit.

"Why?"

He picked up his wineglass. "I'm supposed to give a speech later. Thanking everyone. Saying something about how turning forty has given new meaning to my life." He drank, then put the glass down but kept his fingers on the stem. "I hate speaking in front of lots of people. That's why I never became a litigator."

"Don't do it."

"I have to. Everyone's expecting it."

"Who cares?"

Heather couldn't stand it any longer. "What are you two talking about?" she asked, shifting suddenly toward us. Ruben looked vaguely annoyed. He had been talking.

Dennis said, "Olivia thinks I shouldn't give a speech if I don't want to."

"Are you kidding? After all the work Holly and I did for this party? You sure as hell better thank the two of us, Dennis. And everyone else here."

"You see?" he said to me. "I have to give a speech."

He did give a speech. After the salad and before dessert.

But first he was given a gift. It was a set of golf clubs, which Holly carried in, stumbling a little under their weight. She looked tired, and her blue dress was wrinkled. A big white bow was tied around the necks of the clubs.

Heather took the clubs from Holly and presented them to Dennis, saying, "This is from all of us here—"

Not true, no one had asked me to contribute to the gift.

"—with love and affection and because we know you'll never use them." Everyone laughed and clapped as Dennis eyed the clubs with a look of comic dismay.

"It's a joke gift," Jerome said to me. He had turned his chair back around to watch the speeches and I guess he noticed I wasn't laughing. "Because Dennis hates the whole idea of golf. He's the only guy here who refuses to play. They're really good clubs, though, cost a fortune." He drank from his water glass and put it back down. "Wish I had a set like that."

I didn't say what I was thinking, that spending a lot of money on a gift that would never be used was one of the stupidest things I'd ever heard.

Dennis got up then and made his speech. Once he was actually talking, he didn't seem especially nervous. He thanked everyone for coming and for the gift, which, he said, "Is really, absolutely . . . the worst present you could have gotten me. I'm touched that you all know me well enough to disappoint me so deeply." Big laugh.

Then he thanked Holly and Heather for all the work they'd done to make the party happen. "If you're going to have a party forced down your throat," he said, "you certainly couldn't have it forced down by a nicer pair."

He went on. Very smoothly. "My father used to say to me, 'Son'—he called me son, but then he also called my sister 'son,' so I'm not really sure what that was about—He would say, 'Son, every decade is better than the one before it.' Well, I'm here to tell you . . . there's no truth to that at all. My twenties were much better than my thirties, and I suspect that my forties are going to completely suck." Everyone laughed again, and he held up his wineglass. "So here's to turning forty. If I could have not done it, I wouldn't have."

"Hear, hear," someone shouted and everyone drank. Dennis sat down in his chair, and dessert was served.

"I liked your speech," I said to him when I had a chance, which wasn't for a little while, since Heather had to tell him all about the golf clubs and how they were her idea and now he had to give them a try and she'd book them time at her club next weekend. It was only because a waiter had come between them to pour coffee that I was able finally to break in. "I especially liked that you used the word *suck.*"

"I did, didn't I?"

"Do I get any credit for that?"

"Absolutely. You brought the word into my life."

"Awesome," I said.

Pretty soon after that, people were saying good-bye. Dennis stood up and shook hands and thanked everyone for coming, while Heather stood at his side and smiled at everyone as if . . .

Well, as if she were his wife. Fucking Heather from Harvard.

I was waiting for my turn to say good-bye, when I felt a tap on my shoulder. It was Henry. I had forgotten about him.

"Was your dinner as deadly as mine?" he asked in a whisper.

"Couldn't you tell? I had no one to talk to."

"Me, neither. One person didn't show—actually, I got along fine with the empty chair—but on my other side was the wife of one of the senior lawyers in my department. I figured I should try to charm her and within five minutes I had charmed her into moving her seat farther away from me. Possibly because I spilled red wine on her skirt."

"Oh, man."

"It left this horrible stain. I couldn't stop looking at it all through dinner. Neither could she." He passed his hand over his forehead. "Maybe I should just fill out a job application now, before we leave the restaurant. My law career is over—I might as well go ahead and become a waiter."

"You might not want to mention spilling the wine in your job interview," I said.

"You're right, I'm not even qualified to be a waiter. So what's the story with the golf clubs? They hit me up for my share, but I didn't get it."

I told him what Jerome had said, and then we made fun of people who play golf, and then I realized that the room was almost empty. "We'd better thank our hosts and leave," I said. I looked at my watch. At least I wouldn't be late getting home—I had told Rosivel I probably wouldn't be home until eleven and it wasn't even ten yet. These people weren't exactly party animals.

"Wait," Henry said, "before you take off . . . I'm not very good at this, but . . . can I have your phone number? I had fun tonight. Seriously. I mean with you, not the rest of it."

"Sure."

"Really?" He rubbed his hands together. "You've made my night. You don't know how happy this makes me." Then he patted at his pockets. "Oh, no. Disaster."

"What?"

"I don't have a pen. What do I do now?"

"Ask a waiter," I said.

"Oh, right. You're brilliant. Don't go anywhere, okay? Wait right here." He started to move away. Then he stopped. "You *will* wait here, right? You're not going to leave?"

"I'll be here," I said, and he went chasing after one of the waiters.

I was watching him when Dennis came up to me. "How's it going?" he said.

I turned. "Great. Thanks for inviting me."

"You had a terrible time."

"Yes, I did. Not your fault, though."

"I'm sorry. I forgot how miserable these things can be."

"Birthdays?"

"Firm parties." He bobbled suddenly and grabbed at the back of a chair.

"Dennis. Are you drunk? How much have you had?"

"I don't know. A few glasses of wine. I lost count because the waiters kept refilling it. I was nervous about having to talk."

"You're not driving like that, are you?"

"Of course not. I'll call a car. The firm has an account."

"I can drive you," I said.

He hesitated, then said, "Thanks, but I don't want to keep you. It's no problem calling a car."

"Oh, come on," I said. "I brought the convertible. The wind will clear your head. And it gives me a chance to rub it in that this time *you* drank too much, not me."

"I just wonder if I'm any safer with a twenty-one-year-old driving sober than I would be with me driving drunk."

"Hey, I've got a perfect driving record," I said. "Do you?"

"Yes."

"Oh. Well, that makes two of us, then."

Henry came up, waving a pen. "Got it! Oh, hi, Dennis. Happy birthday. Great speech. Now"—casting about—"what do I write on?"

"How about a napkin?" I said.

"They're cloth."

"Not the drink ones."

"Oh, right." He tossed through a pile of linens on the table and found a reasonably dry paper coaster. "Got one. Okay, shoot—"

I gave him my number. He wrote it down, then showed me what he'd written. "Double-check it," he said. "I don't want to find out I got it wrong and destroyed my future happiness. This is destiny, Olivia. We're meant to be together. I feel it in my bones. Would later tonight be too soon to call you?"

"Depends. How pathetic do you want to look?"

"Scratch tonight. How's tomorrow morning? Early?"

"Morning still seems kind of desperate—you might want to wait until the afternoon."

"Twelve-oh-one, and that's my final offer."

"Sounds good," I said. Actually, that was when I picked Celia up from school, but I figured he was joking. "Good night, Henry. It was nice to meet you."

We shook hands, and he kissed me on the cheek. "Our first kiss," he said, pulling away with a sigh. "We'll tell our grandchildren about this."

"Good night, Henry," Dennis said.

Heather materialized as Henry left. She must have been in the bathroom. I couldn't imagine any other reason she would have left Dennis's side. "Okay!" she said. "Everyone's gone. Except for Olivia, I mean. You can walk out with us, Olivia. Dennis, we've got to get those golf clubs to your car."

"Olivia's driving me home," he said.

She froze. "Excuse me?"

"Olivia's driving me home. I had too much to drink. I was going to call a car but—"

"I can drive you," she said. "It's no problem at all. I only had one glass of wine. I'll drive you."

"Actually," he said, "I was kind of looking forward to Olivia's convertible. Wind in my hair and all that. And I'm in completely the wrong direction for you."

"Oh." She hesitated, biting at her lips, then said, "Well, okay. Then you two can take care of the clubs, right?"

"Good night," I said.

She held out her hand and we shook. "I'm so glad you made it, Olivia. It was really sweet of you to come." She turned and said over her shoulder, "Good night, Dennis. I hope you enjoyed your party." She walked away.

Dennis and I just stood there for a moment.

Then, "Excuse me," Dennis said.

He caught up with her by the door. He took her by the arm and said something, but I was too far away to hear what it was. Heather pulled her arm away. He said something else and took her hand, then kissed her on the cheek. She hung back for just a second. Then threw her arms around him. They embraced, then he gently extricated himself, patted her on the shoulder, and came back toward me. She watched him for a moment, then realized I was looking at her, and turned around and walked off.

"Hey," I said when he came up to me. "Just one thing—"

"What?"

"No fucking way are we lugging those golf clubs to my car."

The manager of the restaurant promised to send the clubs over to the law firm the next day, and Dennis and I walked to my car in silence.

I was driving out of the garage when it occurred to me that I had no idea where he lived. I said so.

He gave me an address in Santa Monica, and I headed in that direction. After a few minutes of silence, I glanced at him. He was staring at the road.

"What are you thinking about?" I said.

He startled slightly. "I don't know. Turning forty, I guess."

Not a happy thought, to judge from his expression. "What's it like?" I asked. "Being forty? Does it feel any different?"

"I'll tell you tomorrow—that's my actual birthday."

We were both silent again. The night and the wind and Dennis's silence all made me feel strange, more restless even than usual. I wanted to bang hard on the steering wheel or shout or something.

I said suddenly, "Why didn't you go with Heather?"

"Huh?" He looked up.

"She really wanted to drive you home."

"Oh. She was just being nice."

"No, she wasn't. She's in love with you."

"I swear, Olivia, if you're going to start that up again—"

"Are you in love with her?"

"God, no." Then, after a moment, "I should be, though. If I were smart. She's exactly the sort of woman I should be in love with."

"Yeah," I said, "she's got it all."

"You think so?"

"Sure."

"You think I should be in love with her?"

I shrugged. Then I said, "No."

"Why not?"

"I don't want you to be."

There was a pause. He said, "You don't have to worry about it. I'm not."

"Good."

"She's not my type."

"Yeah? You don't like them beautiful and smart? What's your type, Dennis?"

"I don't know," he said. Then, in an angry rush, "I like them snot-nosed, I guess—half my age and half my size and completely uninterested in me."

I suddenly felt really cold. I pulled the car over to the side of the road and hit the button to close the top.

"Olivia," he said.

"Wait a second." I huddled in my seat, hugging my arms across my chest. I was shivering.

The top clicked smoothly into place, but I didn't shift back into gear.

"I'm sorry," Dennis said after we'd sat in silence for a minute. "I'm drunk or I wouldn't have said that. It was . . . inappropriate. Wildly inappropriate. Forget it. Please. Let's just go."

I shook my head. I looked sideways at him, out of the corners of my eyes. He was slumped down in his seat, head sunk on his chest, hands jammed into his pockets. Not looking at me.

"Wait," I said again.

"What?" He sounded angry.

"I want you to mean that."

"Olivia—"

"I do. I want you to mean that."

"Forget it. It was a stupid thing to say. I can't—I shouldn't even be thinking about that. It would be wrong. Christ, I sound like Richard Nixon—"

"Yeah, you do," I said. "Listen to me." My teeth were actually chattering, I was so cold. "Listen to me."

"No," he said. "Let's just go."

"I hated her. When I first met her and again tonight."

"Who are you talking about? Heather?"

"Yeah."

"Why the hell do you keep bringing her up?"

"No, listen. I thought I didn't like her because she was a jerk, or a bitch, or something like that. I had barely met her and I kept thinking, 'She's such a horrible woman, she should die.' And I didn't even stop to think about why I hated her. Until tonight. She's probably not that bad. She's actually been kind of nice to me. But I thought you liked her. I was jealous. I was *jealous*. I didn't know that's what it was about. It didn't even occur to me. Not until I saw you with her tonight and . . . I didn't want you to be in love with her. I wanted you to be in love with me. But I didn't think you could be."

There was a pause. He said, "You're getting it all wrong. You were supposed to tell me to shut up and leave you alone. That I'm a dirty old man even to be thinking about you like that."

"You're not that old."

"Old enough to be too old. And even if I weren't, your father put his trust in me. I'm supposed to look out for you. Not—" He stopped. Started again with an effort. "I want to do the right thing. But when I saw you flirting with Henry tonight—"

"I wasn't flirting. He was."

"—I thought, I can't go to the back of the line again. I can't just stand there like an idiot and watch someone else whisk her away. Like New Year's Eve all over again."

"New Year's Eve? It bothered you then that I—"

"Yes."

"I didn't know." I shook my head. "Jesus, I just thought you were mad because you got stuck baby-sitting. Anyway, it doesn't matter. I want to be with you now. I don't give a fuck about Henry. Just you."

"Please don't say that. I'm trying to do the right thing."

"Ask me what the right thing is," I said. "Ask *me*."

"No. I shouldn't have said anything in the first place. I thought maybe if I made a fool of myself, it would make me see how insane I was to even think about it. But I didn't think you'd—"

"Didn't you even notice?" I said. "How happy I was whenever you came over? How I did everything I could to get your approval?"

"Drive me home," he said. His voice was hoarse. "Please, Livvy, drive me home and leave me there and let me think about this."

"But—"

"Just take me home," he said and put his head in his hands.

thirty

We didn't talk for the rest of the drive. I looked over at him every once in a while, and he was just sitting there, staring through the windshield, his face unreadable in the dark.

I pulled over to the curb in front of his apartment building. "Good night, Olivia," he said, opening his door before the car had even come to a complete stop.

"Thank you for the evening," I said. "I had a lovely time. Let's do it again soon."

He looked at me, then shook his head and got out of the car. "Good night," he said and shut the door. He walked up to the front door of his building. Looking a little unsteady.

I turned the car off and got out. He didn't notice at first, not until I came up behind him. He was getting his key out of his pocket.

He turned and saw me. "Olivia—"

I didn't say anything.

"Go away," he said. "Please."

I backed up a couple of steps. He unlocked the door

and went in. I caught it before it had closed and followed him. He stopped.

"Your car," he said. "That's not a legal space, you know."

I shrugged.

"They'll ticket you. They might even tow you."

I didn't say anything. He shook his head again and headed down the hallway. I followed from a few feet behind. He stopped and unlocked a door. This time he held it open for me, and I walked in ahead of him.

He flicked the lights on. We were in a large living room, nicely furnished, neat. Boring, really. Nothing out of place, nothing unusual. Why were the men I knew so much neater than I was?

Probably because I was a slob.

"Thank you for walking me in," he said. "Now please go."

I sat down on the sofa. He passed his hand over his forehead. "Olivia, let me sober up. And sleep on it."

"Okay," I said, "I'll wait."

"You have to go home. We both need time to think."

"We do?"

"It would be a mistake to—"

"To what?"

"To—" But he couldn't finish his sentence. "Oh, Christ," he said and came toward me. I stood up before he even reached the sofa and fell against him.

Nothing had ever felt so good as his chest. Or so much like home. I just wanted to stay there for a while, listening to his heart beat and feeling his hands moving in my hair and against my back.

But then he pushed me away. "You have to go, Olivia. Really. This isn't right. Please go."

"I have to tell you something first."

"Okay," he said, "talk. Then go."

"Hold on. I need a second." I took a deep breath. Then I said, "Okay. Listen."

"I'm listening."

"You sat there. In your office. And you told me I had to do what was right. Remember that? Just days after my father had died. You said, 'You should take care of Celia because it's the right thing to do.'"

"Of course I remember. It was only a few months ago. Why—"

"Just *listen*. No one's ever told me to do something because it was the right thing to do. My parents never once . . . My mother doesn't even *know* what's right and what isn't. My father probably knew, but I don't think he ever cared."

"All I've ever done is lecture you," he said. "Told you what you should and shouldn't do. Acting all holier than thou—"

"For the first time in my life, someone said, 'This is what you should do.' Not, 'Do what you want to do' or even 'Do what *I* want you to do.' Just 'This is what you should do. This is what's right.'"

"I thought you'd hate me for it."

"I did a little. But I also did what you told me to."

"You fought me hard."

"Only at the beginning. And then I did everything you wanted."

"I know," he said. "Only I didn't realize it at first. I thought it was all a huge disaster. I kept hoping maybe I could break through to you, get past the rudeness, get you to do the right thing. And then—I don't even remember when—it suddenly hit me you *were* doing the right thing. No one could have been kinder to Celia. No one could have been more responsible."

"Because you told me to be," I said. "Did you know that in my whole fucking life, I've never wanted to please anyone except myself? Not anyone. And I think I would have done—would do—anything, just because you told me to. Without even asking why."

"No. I've seen you with Celia. It's more than that. The way you are with her, it's more than just about pleasing me."

"Now it is," I said. "But for a long time it was just because you told me to."

"How could you *like* me for that?" he said. "For forcing things on you, for criticizing you, for making your life harder?"

"Yeah," I said, "how could I? All you ever did was make me feel like what I did mattered. Like I wasn't just . . . some little shit. Like maybe I had a chance at being someone that someone like you could think was a decent human being."

He came closer and touched my face with his hand.

"I know, I know," I said, pushing his hand away. "I'm crying. What a loser."

He shook his head. Then he wiped my cheeks gently with the back of his fingers. This time, I didn't push his hand away. I just closed my eyes and held my face up. He bent down and kissed where he had wiped.

Nothing in my entire life had ever felt so kind. Nothing. I hardly breathed. More kisses, moving to the edge of my mouth, then over my mouth. His mouth stayed there, growing more urgent. Mine did, too. We pushed against each other, wanting more.

Then he stopped. I opened my eyes, and he was moving away.

I caught his arm. "Come back. What are you doing?"

"I'd better stop. I have to stop now, Olivia. I don't . . ."

"But I don't want you to," I said.

"I don't want to, either. But I can't keep going . . . I don't . . . Christ, this is embarrassing. But it's better. To stop. To stop and think."

"No, don't stop. Please."

"I have to. Even if I wanted—I mean, I do want to—but . . . I *can't* . . . We can't—" He couldn't look me in the eyes.

And then I realized. "You're not . . . *prepared*."

"No." The word came out in an embarrassed whisper. He looked like a little boy, his cheeks flushed, his head bowed.

"Guess you weren't expecting to have sex tonight."

"No," he said. Still looking at the carpet. "Or any night, ever. It's not something I've been doing much of in the last decade or so."

Even that gave me pleasure. Maybe it was silly. But Joe . . . Joe kept a condom in his wallet. And a packet in his car. And an economy-sized box in his bedroom.

"But it's a good thing," Dennis said. "Forcing us to stop and . . ." He took a deep breath. "It's better to wait and to make sure, to really think about this. There are so many reasons this might not be a good idea. Being forced to slow down, maybe it's for the best."

"No. It's not."

He swallowed and nodded. "No, it's not."

"This is Santa Monica," I said. "There's got to be a drugstore or a convenience store or *something* nearby."

"Around the corner," he said.

"Go," I said.

"I don't know—"

"Go," I said again. Impatient now. "I have to call home, anyway."

"I forgot about all that. I forgot about Celia. Will she be okay? Is Rosivel still there?"

"Yeah. Don't worry about it. I'll figure it out. Just go, will you? And come back fast?"

"Yeah, okay." He went to the door. Stopped and looked back. "Why do I feel like you're not going to be here when I get back?"

"I'll be here," I said.

"If you do think better of it—"

"Think better of it?"

"I was going to say, even if you do, don't go. Please be here when I come back."

"I will."

He left.

I went to the kitchen. Spotless. Gleaming. Like it had never been used. Then again maybe it hadn't—he probably never ate there. I splashed cold water on my face and rubbed it hard with a dishtowel. I suddenly thought, "What if he's hit by a bus and never comes back?" and felt terrified. Then I laughed at myself. Then I felt terrified again.

The apartment was too quiet. It was all strange and new, and I didn't belong there.

I found a phone in the kitchen and called home. It rang for a while and then the answering machine came on. I said, "This is Olivia," and there was a beep, and Rosivel picked up. She sounded tired.

"I'm sorry," I said. "This is going later than I thought. I don't know how late. Could you go to sleep there for the night and I'll give you the day off tomorrow? Paid?"

She said, "You know your mother is home? I think she's sleeping now."

"Doesn't matter. I'd still like you to stay. I'd feel better."

"Okay," she said. "I can go to sleep in Celia's room."

"Do you mind?"

"No. I can have tomorrow off? Paid?"

"Yes. And I'll pay you for the whole night, too. Obviously."

"All right," she said. "I'll call my husband now. He was going to pick me up."

"I'm sorry if I inconvenienced both of you," I said. "Thank you for staying tonight. Thank you."

"Are you having a good time, missus?"

"Yes," I said. "The best time I've ever had."

"That's nice," she said.

He still wasn't back. I used the bathroom. His towels were thick and dark blue. I went into his bedroom and then into his closet. His suits and shirts were lined up neatly on one side, khakis and jackets on the other. I pressed my face into a bunch of his suits. Celia had done the same thing with her mother's dresses. Now I understood why— something of Dennis lingered in the suits he'd worn. A clean, soapy smell and the scratchy-soft feel of expensive wool, just like I'd felt when my cheek was against his chest earlier that night.

I heard the front door open and ran back into the living room to meet him.

"You're still here," he said. He was holding a small paper bag. "I saw your car when I turned the corner and . . . was glad. Did you call Rosivel?"

"Yes," I said. "She's sleeping over."

"You do this to all the baby-sitters, don't you? But at least you called *her*."

"I'm sorry about New Year's Eve," I said.

"I don't want to talk about it. I don't want to think about it. I've thought about it way too much already. For weeks." Then, "Why him? He was so . . . so exactly like the kind of guys who . . . I mean, they get the girls, they always get the girls, but it's all . . . How could you fall for *that*?"

I liked seeing Dennis incoherent. He was usually so well spoken.

Anyway, I knew what he meant. "I didn't know any better. He was my first."

"First *what*?"

"Everything," I said. "I'd never even kissed a boy before him."

He grimaced. "And here I was hoping you hadn't even kissed him."

"My first and only," I said. "Not *so* bad for a twenty-one-year-old."

"Still. You couldn't have waited a few more months?"

"If I'd known—"

"I tried to stay away after that. Why torture myself. But—"

"But Celia and I always wanted you there."

There was a pause. "The clerk was laughing at me," he said. "And I pictured what I must have looked like, running in at this hour, desperate for condoms . . ."

I walked across the room and took hold of his suit jacket, looking up at him. "Fuck the clerk," I said.

"He wasn't such a bad guy."

"Him? He was an angel. He sold you those. Can we use one now? Please?"

He turned red. "Olivia—"

"I'm not suddenly going to be a nice girl," I said. "I'm still me."

"Thank God," he said, pulling me close. "Thank God."

There was no reason to wait any longer, which was a good thing because I don't think either of us could have.

I already knew I liked sex a lot. What I didn't know was that when you added trust and generosity to something that was already pretty awesome, it got even better.

A while later Dennis said to me, "You're wrong, you know. You are a nice girl."

"Didn't your mother teach you better? Nice girls don't do . . . that. Not until their wedding night and then only with a lot of tears and misery."

We were lying side by side on our backs, our shoulders touching, holding hands.

"No, really," Dennis said, "I mean it. In all the time I've known you, you've never done anything bad."

"Are you kidding? I've made my mother cry. In front of you."

"Your mother . . . Yeah, you say mean things to her. Most of which she deserves. But those are only words. The truth is that you take care of her."

"You're nuts."

"Am I? You house her and feed her—not that I've ever seen her eat anything—and you look after her and keep her company. Even in the middle of the night. You let her think she's helping you, when all she's doing is giving you one more person to take care of. As if you didn't have enough to deal with already."

I moved my leg so it would be right up against his. I kept feeling like I couldn't get close enough to him, like I wanted to glom right onto his body. "Tell me more about what a good person I am. I like this game."

"Sure," he said. "I could go on for a while. It's all I've been thinking about lately, how good Olivia is."

"So . . . ?"

"Well, you never lie."

"That's because I don't care if I hurt people's feelings."

"Maybe, but I still think it's a virtue."

"*You* never lie, but you manage to be much nicer than I am. Why's that?"

"Age," he said. "Experience."

"You like pointing out how much older you are than me, don't you?"

"I hate it," he said. "I hate that I'm so much older than you. If I could trade places with Henry Williams and be twenty-four and still have you lying here—"

"I don't want you at twenty-four," I said. "I want you like this."

He lay there for a moment, thinking. Then he sighed and said, "I wonder what a psychologist would say about this. A girl loses her father and then gets involved with a guy twice her age who's taken on this paternal role in her life—"

"I think it's obvious what a psychologist would say. Don't you?"

"Doesn't it bother you?"

"Not really. You could probably pull apart any relationship and find beetles hiding in all the corners. I mean, I could fall in love with someone exactly my age, and it could be about the fact I never had a brother to love, so it's all really incestuous."

"Okay," he said, "I'm going to pretend I buy that. But only because I don't want to give you up."

"Anyway, you were supposed to be telling me how wonderful I am."

"Well, I was going to say that you're the least vain person I ever met, but I'm starting to change my mind about that one."

"Shit," I said. "It sounded so good."

"You are," he said. "You're the first beautiful woman I've ever known who doesn't seem to know or care that she's beautiful. Who doesn't fuss with her hair or her clothes but still outshines everyone else."

"Heather's a lot prettier than I am."

"No."

"She is. And anyway tonight I fussed with my hair. I pretended I didn't know why I wanted to put my hair up, why I wanted to look older, look nicer . . . See what you've done to me? It's embarrassing. And you didn't even notice."

"Are you kidding? All night long, all I did was notice. I noticed that your hair was pinned up, only some pieces had fallen out and you kept pushing them behind your ears, and your left ear had a little scratch on it."

"Celia got me with a fork a couple of days ago. It was an accident."

"And I noticed that the strap on your dress kept falling off your shoulder, and your shoulder was this shade of white like . . . like nothing I'd ever seen before, and I wanted to touch it, see if it felt as smooth as it looked."

"I wish you had. It would have made the party a lot more interesting. Just seeing the expression on Heather's face alone—"

"I shouldn't have invited you," he said.

"It didn't work out so badly."

"All night long, I kept thinking what an idiot I was to have invited you. I wasn't going to. I knew all along it was a stupid thing to do. But when I was with you the other day, I couldn't help myself. I wanted to, so badly. That's why I was shaking tonight, you know. I only just realized it. Not because of that stupid speech. Because you were sitting next to me and looked so beautiful and I knew I couldn't do anything about it."

I brought his hand up and pressed it to my face. It was warm against my lips and cheeks. "I'm here now," I said, my mouth moving against his fingers.

"I'm glad," he said. "Don't go away."

It was already getting light out when Dennis said, "I'm going to pass it on."

"What?"

"Being executor of your father's trust. There was someone else named as a backup, in case I was dead or didn't want the job. I'll let him take it over."

"You mean someone else will be in charge of the money?"

"Yes."

"Then I wasted all this sex on you for no reason."

"Very funny," he said.

"Now I'll have to start all over again. He better be good-looking."

"He's not. He's sixty and fat and bald and he'll probably take away the convertible and cut your allowance way back. And it's all your fault for making me fall in love with you."

"It's all your fault for being so fucking ethical," I said. "Why can't I have you *and* the convertible?"

"I'm afraid you're going to have to choose one."

"Well then you'd better give me some time to think about it."

He pushed up on his arm and looked at me. "The honeymoon's over already, isn't it? You were nice to me for four hours. That's all I get?"

"Yes, but the abuse is yours for as long as you want it."

"From your mouth to God's ears. As my mother used to say, although never quite in this context."

"What would your mother say if she saw you right now?"

"Probably something like, 'Well, at least she's half Jewish. Even if it's the wrong half.' And, 'You couldn't have chosen someone closer to your own age?' "

"Yes, well, we already know what *my* mother will say."

"What's that?"

" 'You'll never keep him.' "

"She's wrong about that."

"I hope so. I am worried about Heather from Harvard breathing over my shoulder."

"If you only knew how little you have to worry about."

"Tell me," I said. "Tell me."

He did better than that. He showed me.

A couple of hours later—around eight—I went home. I hadn't slept for more than a few minutes all night long, but I wasn't tired. I stopped at a Starbucks and got myself a coffee, and drank it as I drove home, the top down, the morning cold and gray and wildly beautiful. I even smiled at the parking ticket I noticed on my windshield. How could it be bad when leaving my car there had worked out so well?

As soon as I got home, I sent Rosivel to the bus, thanking her over and over again.

"You're okay?" she said. "You stayed with a friend last night?"

It suddenly occurred to me that Rosivel and I had become teammates. We didn't talk much, and we weren't exactly friends, but we were definitely pulling for the same side. "Yes," I said. "Everything is good. Very good. Thank you for helping out. I'm very happy right now."

"Good," she said and left.

Celia was already fed and dressed and ready for school. Trust Rosivel to see to that. My mother wasn't anywhere in sight. She was probably still asleep.

Celia said, "Where were you last night, Livvy?"

"I slept over at Dennis's house."

"Oh. How was his birthday party?"

"It wasn't such a great party, Celia. But I had an awesome time, anyway."

"Were there party favors?"

I shook my head.

She looked disgusted. "No party favors?"

"Well, I got this." I showed her the parking ticket I had carried in with me.

"What's that?"

"A parking ticket."

"What do you do with it?"

"Pay money."

"Can I have one?"

"When you're a grown-up. If you're anything like me, you'll get a ton of them. Hey, Celia, I've got to take a quick shower, and then we need to pack your lunch for school."

A half hour later, we were arguing over whether she liked yogurt—I said yes, she said no—when there was a knock on the front door. I went into the foyer to answer it but before I even got to the door, it opened, and Dennis walked in.

I ran to him and found out I *was* the kind of person who hugged after all. "What are you doing?" I said once I was safely trapped against his chest. "Don't you have to work?"

"I decided to take the day off," he said. He rested his chin gently on the top of my head. "Your hair smells good. I took a cab to the office and was already in the elevator when I thought about how I wouldn't be seeing you again for twelve hours, and I rode the elevator back down to my car and left. It's my birthday present to myself."

"Have you ever just taken a day off before for no reason? In your whole life?"

"Never. Everyone will think I'm having some sort of midlife crisis."

"Yeah," I said. "Doing something stupid like riding around in a convertible."

"Or sleeping with a girl half my age."

"It's good you're not doing that," I said.

Celia came running out, and we quickly separated. "Dennis!" She jumped up at his chest, right at the spot I'd been a second earlier. He caught her up in his arms. "Why are you here in the morning?" she asked, rubbing her cheek against his. "You're never here in the morning."

"It's my birthday today," he said. "It's my birthday and I wanted to spend it with you two." He gave her a kiss and lowered her back to the floor. "What do you think, Celia, what would be fun for us to do on my birthday? What would you want to do if it were your birthday?"

"Go miniature golfing," she said instantly.

I laughed. "Miniature golfing? Where did that come from?"

"That's what Sarah said she's doing for her birthday."

"Sarah is a girl in Celia's classroom," I told Dennis. "She bosses all the girls around, and they all want to be just like her. A budding Heather from Harvard."

"What's a Heather from Harvard?" Celia asked.

"Something I hope you'll never be."

Dennis grinned at me. "You really are jealous of her, aren't you? I love that."

"I was," I said. "I don't feel very jealous of her today."

"What about miniature golfing?" Celia said. "Can we go?"

"Two problems," I said. "You have school and Dennis hates golf."

"Do I have to go to school? It's Dennis's birthday."

"Dennis's birthday isn't a national holiday. Yet."

"Hey," Dennis said, "if I can skip work, she can skip school."

"I don't believe this—Jiminy Cricket's actually in favor of playing hooky? Aren't you worried we'll get turned into donkeys?"

"It's preschool, and attendance isn't required by law. And I like miniature golf—it's nothing like real golf. There are all those windmills and castles and bells. And virtually no lawyers."

Celia clasped her hands. "So can we go? Please, Livvy? Please please please please please?"

"All right, all right," I said. "Go get your shoes on."

"Awesome!" she shouted and went running off.

I looked at Dennis. Already I was moving back toward him, not even meaning to, just not able not to. "It's so strange," I said. "Everything's kind of the same and kind of not. I'm not sure I can get used to this."

"Try," he said, reaching for me. Then—

"Good morning," my mother said, stumbling in, yawning, satin bathrobe tied over satin nightgown. Both stained from wine and cigarette ashes.

Dennis immediately dropped his hands to his sides and stepped back.

"My goodness, Dennis! What a surprise to see you at this hour. Please forgive the bathrobe. I wasn't expecting visitors. It's early, isn't it? I know sometimes I sleep late, but—"

"It's around nine," Dennis said. "It's pretty early."

"Yes, it is. But don't worry about it. I'm sure *Celia* was glad to see you. Where were you last night, Livvy? I got home from dinner and you were gone. Rosivel said you went to a party."

"Yeah, I did."

"I'm glad. You should get out more. How was it?"

"Okay, I guess. By the end I was having a good time."

"Really? Oh, Livvy, guess what?"

"What?"

"You got a phone call last night. From Joe."

"No kidding."

"Since you weren't here, I had a long talk with him. You and your 'It's all over.' You couldn't be more wrong—as far as Joe's concerned, *nothing* is over. He told me he's more in love with you than ever. I was in tears by the end of the conversation. I'm pretty sure he was, too. He misses you so much! I tried to call you, but then I found your cell phone in the kitchen—you really need to remember to take it when you go out, Livvy. What if there had been an emergency? Anyway, I waited up to talk to you last night, but I must have dozed off. What time did you come in, anyway?"

"Very late," I said. "Morning, really."

"It must have been a good party. I think you need to call Joe right away, Livvy. You have him where you want him now, but if you keep acting like this, he's going to move on. Men like Joe are never alone for long."

I turned. "What do you think, Dennis? Should I call Joe?"

He said, "Let *me* call him for you."

"Why would you do that?" my mother asked.

"Just taking an interest. To be honest, Barbara, I don't think Olivia should waste any more time on the guy."

"You just don't understand the situation, Dennis. Men never do. If you met him—"

"I did. Several times."

She raised her hands, palms up. "Then you should be able to see that he's perfect for Olivia."

"I don't see that at all," Dennis said.

"Well, I'm her mother, and I know he is."

"No," he said. "She's too good for him. If he calls again, you should just hang up on him. And if a guy named Henry calls, hang up on him, too. Actually, from now on, just hang up on any man who wants to speak to Olivia."

"What if it's just a woman with a deep voice?" I asked.

"Hang up. Why take the chance?"

"I don't know what you two are talking about," my mother said. "You're not making any sense. Maybe it's because I haven't had my coffee yet. There wasn't any made. Could you make some now, Livvy?"

I shook my head. "Not now. We're going out."

"But you always make the coffee. I don't know how to use their machine."

"Figure it out. Or go to Starbucks."

"I'm not even dressed yet. Please, Livvy—"

"I'm ready," Celia said, running in and jumping up at me. She was always hurling herself at people.

I caught her under the arms and whirled her around. "Let's go."

"Don't forget," my mother called after me. "Joe."

"Forget Joe," Dennis said, when we were all in the station wagon. He was driving. "Are you going to tell her what's going on?"

"Nah. Let her figure it out for herself. Although she may not ever, given the way her mind works. You and I could be married with four kids and she'd still be telling me I'm always going to be alone because I lost the first guy I ever—" I stopped.

"The first guy you ever—?"

"Hey," I called to Celia in the backseat. "What shall we listen to?"

" 'Bang, Bang, Maxwell's Silver Hammer.' "

"You got it." I punched in the CD and the music started up.

Dennis said, "Do you realize what this song is about?"

"Yeah, more or less. Why?"

"Celia."

"Oh, she doesn't get it. She just likes the way it sounds."

"She's a smart girl. If she listens carefully, she's going to figure it out."

"Who cares? It's a good song."

"Sure, if you're sixteen. Not if you're four."

I shrugged. "By the time she understands it, she'll be able to deal with it."

"Kids can understand some pretty horrible things before they have the emotional maturity to process them. That's why they need adults to edit what they see and hear."

"It's the Beatles," I said. "The fucking *Beatles*. I mean, we're not listening to Eminem here."

"That's like saying it's okay to let a kid play with a sharp knife because it's not a gun."

"Oh, for Christ's sake, it's not like that at *all*."

"As an argument, it is. You're saying that something's not bad just because something's worse."

"So?"

"So that's not necessarily true. There are bad things and there are worse things, and you still haven't turned the song off."

"I know."

He glanced over at me, then looked back at the road. "What are you looking so pleased about?"

"Nothing. Just enjoying myself."

"Yeah, I know what you mean. But you're still wrong about the song. Turn it off, Olivia."

"Okay, fine, but you're being a tightass." I leaned forward and skipped the song.

"This is taking forever," Celia said, leaning as far forward as the seat belt of her car seat would let her. "Why'd you change the song, Livvy?"

"Dennis made me."

"Oh. When are we going to get there?"

"Soon," I said.

"Why are you doing that?" she asked, looking back and forth between us.

"What?"

"Smiling like that. You look weird."

"I don't know," I said. "I guess because for once it seems like maybe the future isn't going to suck."

"You shouldn't say *suck*."

"Good girl," Dennis said. "You're right."

"Fine," I said. "I'll pay you a dollar, Celia. But it's starting to feel like you two are ganging up on me."

"Yes," Dennis said. "That's exactly what we're doing. Get used to it."